AUTHOR OF THE SERIES "A WOMAN OF ENTITLEMENT"

MAGGIE'S REDEMPTION

BY **MARY ANN KERR**

THINK
WELL
BOOKS

thinkwellbooks.com

Maggie's Redemption

Published in part by Thinkwell Books, Portland, Oregon.
The views or opinions of the author are not necessarily
those of Thinkwell Books. Learn more at *thinkwellbooks.com.*

Design and cover illustration by Andrew Morgan Kerr
Learn more at andrewmorgankerr.com.
Copyediting by Dori Harrell
doriharrell.wix.com/breakoutediting

Published and printed in the United States of America
ISBN: 978-9984894-2-18
Fiction, Historical, Christian

BOOKS BY MARY ANN KERR

A WOMAN OF ENTITLEMENT SERIES:

Book One
LIBERTY'S INHERITANCE
Book Two
LIBERTY'S LAND
Book Three
LIBERTY'S HERITAGE

CAITLIN'S FIRE

TORY'S FATHER

EDEN'S PORTION

CADY'S LEGACY

ANNE'S WEDDING BARGAIN

MAGGIE'S REDEMPTION

DEDICATION

I dedicate this book to
the King of the Universe, my Lord and my God.

I also dedicate this book to
Peter and Regina Brown
(I love you!)

ACKNOWLEDGMENTS

Maggie's Redemption is a story about Liberty's maid-turned-friend, Margaret Regan O'Neill. Readers who have read the series will know Maggie to be an assertive redhead from my first two books, *Liberty's Inheritance* and *Liberty's Land*.

I decided to go back and do her life story...and what a story! My editor said it was quite a different story from my other books and highly dramatic. She knows more than me, so I'll take her word for it! All I know is (and I know I've said this a lot), God is the author of creativity. All creativity. I am so thankful he's given me the ability to write stories. I never knew I had it in me, and this is my ninth book!

I have a dear friend who paints rocks. They are sweet, cute, or gorgeous. That creativity comes from God. I have a granddaughter who is extremely creative and can do several different things, and does them well. I have a couple of sons who paint and create lovely pictures for people to enjoy. Creativity, all of it, comes from a God who is always creating.

What a joy for me to be able to write stories. I love my characters, who have become as real to me as some live people! I keep thinking I will start a different line of stories, but Liberty has captured my heart. I just love her!

I'd like to thank my readers—so many of you contact me and thank me for the stories.

My eldest daughter-in-law's mother, Lois Dunn, has read all my books and is such a wonderful Christian. I am grateful for her. Reverend Pamela Merillat reads my books and is blessed with the gift of edification—thank you! Peter and Regina Brown, Delva Lantrip, Cathy White, Allan and Karen Thomlinson, Melissa Peart, Dual and Fran Eldridge, Bill and JoAnn Taylor—wow! Just so many people to thank for their encouraging words and kudos—they are always welcome. I have a facebook friend who is a lovely Christian and who is also named Mary Ann Kerr. We have become friends, and she loves my stories. I thank you for your friendship!

Once again I am grateful for Andrew designing and making such beautiful book covers. Thank you!

Of course, I can't forget my children, David and Rosie, Peter and Rebecca, Stephen, and Andrew and Shari. You are an inspiration and a gift to me. I treasure each of you.

I thank Dori Harrell at Breakout Editing, who does such a great job editing my stories.

I thank Phil, my husband, for his patience and love. It takes a lot of time to write a book, and he suffers my mental absences with aplomb!

And of course, I thank God for giving me the stories. He is an awesome, inspiring, compassionate, holy God. May we all worship Him in spirit and in truth!

mak

List of Characters

Margaret (Maggie) Regan O'Neill. . . . . .Protagonist
Shamus Barra O'Neill. . . . . .Maggie's father
Megdn Whelan O'Neill. . . . . Maggie's mother
Taghd McDermish . . . . Doctor who delivered Maggie
Magda Shaunessy . . . . .O'Neill's daily housekeeper
Clodagh . . . . .Maggie's young friend
Mrs. Harriet Sullivan. . . . . Owner of Eglon Bed and Breakfast
Mr. Elmer Dermott. . . . . Boarder at the Eglon Bed and Breakfast
Chancellor Richard Collins. . . . . .Chancellor of Boston University
Mr. Grant Jamison. . . . . Maggie's first employer
Mrs. Eloise Jamison . . . . .Maggie's first employer
Grant, Thomas, James, and Rachel. . . . . .Jamison children
Otto Graf. . . . . .Jamisons' butler
Millie, Dickinson, Nanny Claire, Bonnie . . . . .Jamisons' staff
Liberty Alexandra Corlay Bouvier. . . . . .Maggie's second employer
Armand Francois (Franz-swah) Bouvier. . . . . . Liberty Bouvier's husband
Monsieur Jacques Corlay. . . . . Liberty Alexandra Corlay Bouvier's father
Sigmund Hintz. . . . . .Bouviers' butler
Matilda, Annie, Pierre, Cook, Rufus. . . . . .Bouviers' staff
Elijah Humphries. . . . . Liberty Bouvier's lawyer
Abigail Humphries. . . . . Mr. Humphries' wife
Ethan Brooks. . . . . Business acquaintance of Bouvier and Dermott
Saul Simmons. . . . . .Partner of Ethan Brooks
George Baxter . . . . Chief Inspector, Boston police
Timothy Taylor . . . . Boston Detective, police
Cabot Jones. . . . . .Boston Detective, police
Matthew Bannister. . . . . .Owner, Rancho Bonito
Kirk Bannister. . . . . .Brother of Matthew Bannister
Conchita and Diego Rodriguez. . . . . . . .Employees of Matthew Bannister
Alexander and Phoebe Liberty. . . . . Guests at Rancho Bonito
Samuel Kerns, Dan Mapes. . . . . .Oakland detectives
Jake Daniels and men. . . . . U.S. Marshals
Janne (Yannie) Nyegaard. . . . . .Prisoner from Norway
Harold Sawyers. . . . . Chief, San Francisco Police

PRAYER

Bless the LORD,
Oh my soul.
May You, my Savior,
Be in control.

Lead me this day
To honor You,
To seek your will
In all I do.

I thank You Father
For Your loving hand,
And pray I always
Will take a stand,

To show Your love
In all I do.
Help me LORD
To glorify you.

Mary Ann Kerr

Prologue

Unto the woman he said,
I will greatly multiply thy sorrow and thy conception;
in sorrow thou shalt bring forth children;
and thy desire shall be to thy husband,
and he shall rule over thee.

GENESIS 3:16

"**MEGDN. ME DEAR SWEET MEGDN.** How I do love you, my precious girl. It won't be long now, me darlin'. I know you're in a good deal of pain, but you're strong. Hold fast, my sweetheart, my love. Hold fast. McDermish says I must leave you to it, but you ken I love you, me darlin'" Shamus' hand had been holding her steady.

The labor was intense, and Shamus hoped his voice sounded reassuring to the woman's ears in a room filled with pain. He, in truth, was worried. He wasn't sure how much more of this his dear wife could take. She'd been in labor for hours and hours. Shamus kissed her—shamelessly, in front of the doctor.

He saw the surprised look of disgust that spread over the face of the man of medicine. He grinned inwardly and kissed her again. Kissing in front of any onlooker simply wasn't done. Shamus O'Neill struggled to conform to the standards set by society. He found most of them an absurdity.

Shamus looked at Taghd McDermish, the doctor, wondering if he'd had any schooling.

"I will leave you now, McDermish, but I will brook no departure of my orders. You will be clean or clear out. Your choice." His voice sounded stern, even to his own ears, but his admonition was perspicuous.

Taghd McDermish, angered by O'Neill's stipulation that he must scrub his hands or that anything else that touched his wife must first be boiled, waggled his forefinger at Shamus angrily.

"Yer edgiecation, Shamus, it's gone to yer head, man!"

The doctor seemed incensed by Shamus standing over him, making sure all was clean, but Shamus didn't care.

With a tender squeeze of Megdn's hand and another kiss on her forehead, Shamus made no reply to the doctor as he headed toward the door.

As Megdn groaned with her next pain, the father-to-be left the small room with reluctance.

Descending the steep, narrow stairs, he strode to the kitchen to make sure everything was in readiness for a newborn. He didn't care that McDermish was unhappy with him. If Megdn hadn't wanted the doctor so badly, he would have had the midwife in. He knew and liked the midwife. She was clean, and she'd delivered many babies in the city in which they lived. Shamus cringed inwardly when he thought of McDermish's fingernails. They were filthy.

Shamus Barra O'Neill, professor at Trinity College, Dublin University, specialized in mathematics, but he was interested in all the sciences and had, in the past, talked to Ignaz Semmelweis, a physician from Hungary. The two, meeting at a conference in Vienna, had taken an instant liking to each other. With their shared passion for research, they stimulated each other's minds, enjoying the camaraderie that comes from like-mindedness. Semmelweis told Shamus he'd reduced the death rate of new mothers dying from puerperal fever in half simply by having doctors scrub their hands vigorously with soap before delivering babies.

Shamus winced when he thought of the doctor upstairs. His hygiene left much to be desired. At least McDermish had washed his hands. Shamus had stood there and watched him, handing him the bar of soap. He'd insisted the doctor scrub them well. The father-to-be wasn't a religious man, but he said a quick prayer, asking God to please spare his wife and the new baby.

Because the O'Neill household had enough money, Shamus had hired a live-in maid to help his wife. They lived modestly in a nice section of Dublin, within walking distance to stores and Trinity College, where he taught.

As Shamus entered the kitchen, Magda, their maid, nodded to him.

"She'll be havin' the babe soon, I ken," Magda said sagaciously.

"Yes, and I see you have everything in readiness. Are you cooking that flannel?" Shamus' eyes expressed his surprise seeing the small blanket folded on top of the cooler section of the woodstove.

"Aye, that I am. The wee one'll be needin' the warmth after leavin' the shelter of its mam."

"You're a good woman, Magda Shaunessy, and we are grateful to have you. Megdn sings your praises nearly every day. We are thankful for your unstinting loyalty and help in our home."

Magda's face reddened under the praise, and she turned back to the stove. Shamus could tell she was not used to compliments. Quite young, she worked hard and was wholly capable. Her curly jet-black hair was scraped back into a bun, but curls escaped and softened her face under the mobcap. She picked up another piece of wood and fed the old stove to keep the heat at a temperature to cook the stew, which simmered on its top.

It was unusually warm this day of May 12, 1864. The cold and damp of early spring had given way to a beautiful feeling of summer. Flowers lifted their heads to the warmth of the sun, bursting forth in a riot of color. Lilacs, usually blooming in April, were now in full bloom. Seemingly overnight, trees had clothed themselves in velvet leaves, soft and new.

Shamus opened the back door and left it open to the warmth of the day. He stood on the back porch, glad he'd had it partially enclosed. When it rained, his stack of wood at the end of the porch stayed dry. Wood was expensive, but he thought it burned hotter than the popular peat. He gathered an armful and dumped it into the woodbox near the stove.

"Thank ye, sir. Air ye hungry?"

Before he could answer, a scream ripped through the house.

"Aye, sir. She'll be havin' that babe afore long," Magda said.

Shamus nodded, wondering how anyone could bear such intense agony overlong.

"She's been at it far too long, Magda," he said, his voice strained. "How can she endure it?"

Another scream rent the air, and a lusty cry followed. Without waiting for an answer, Shamus took the stairs two at a time. He threw open the door. The doctor was cutting the cord on the crying baby, but Shamus could see Megdn had lost consciousness.

"You can't be in here!" McDermish said angrily. The anger dropped away, and his shoulders slumped as he added, "She's lost too much blood. Don't know if she'll make it, but for certain she won't be havin' anymore bairns." He looked at Shamus' shocked face. "I'm sorry." He packed up his bag. "I'll collect payment later, sir." He clomped down the stairs and banged the front door shut behind him.

Shamus ran to the top of the stairs and yelled for Magda to come help. Going back to the room, he wet a cloth from an ewer and wrung it out over the basin. Hearing Magda come up the stairs, he watched as she took the baby and wrapped the wee bairn tightly in a warm flannel. Bending over Megdn, he kissed her lips and bathed her face.

Her eyes opened, looking huge in her pallid face. She whispered, "What is it, Shammy? Is it a boy?"

Surprise spread itself over Shamus' face. He didn't know and looked across the bed at Magda for an answer.

"It's a girl," she said softly. "It's a beautiful baby girl."

"What do you want to name her, Megdn me luv?" Shamus asked.

"Oh, Shammy, I want to name her Margaret—Margaret after your mother. I loved your mam so much," Megdn replied. Tears formed at the corners of her eyes.

"Aye, Margaret's a fine name. I think Regan will do for the middle name. I always did like your maiden name," Shamus said.

Megdn smiled weakly. "Margaret Regan O'Neill it is." Tears seeped from her eyes. Emotional and physical exhaustion claimed her. She seemed almost shrunken in the large bed. Closing her lids, sleep overtook her.

Magda tucked the little baby next to her mam and set about cleaning up.

Chapter I

He that hath pity upon the poor lendeth unto the LORD;
and that which he hath given will he pay him again.

PROVERBS 19:17

THE RAIN SEEMED UNENDING. It beat down, unwavering, day
and night. The outlying fields, thick with mud, lay untended as the rain
poured steadily down with no relief. Plantings had been postponed and
postponed again. The damp brought with it fear. Crops would be few, as
the mud allowed neither horse nor man to plow. Dublin's streets ran
rivulets, and the damp stealthily crept into houses. Cold lurked in the
corners of rooms, and sickness was rampant.

"Oh, Mam, I can't wait until the morrow! Twelve years old, why, I'm
practically grown up!" Maggie sat at the kitchen table, her shining red
hair a halo around her head. She was helping her mother and Magda by
peeling carrots for a cabbage stew.

"Yes, you are practically a young lady, but," Mam said drily, "you will have
to wait until the morrow. Did you ask Clodagh if she could stay tonight?"

"Yes, and her mam said it would be perfectly all right. She's coming
at three this afternoon, and she gets to stay until tomorrow after lunch. I
am so happy!" Maggie rose and danced around the room, her gray eyes
sparkling with excitement. She pranced her way back to the table as she
continued to speak. "Clodagh has a rough cough, but she said she doesn't

feel sick at all. She's bringing her very best dress. I'm excited to go to the concert tonight. Da has such wonderful ideas for birthday presents, doesn't he? Do you think he'll get home on time? Do you think he might forget about it?" Maggie was wound up. She didn't bother about her mother answering any of her host of questions.

"Yes, dear. It's a boon Mr. O'Malley gave your father those tickets. We're beginning to scrape the bottom of the barrel, what with prices the way they are. I'll begin teaching soon, and perhaps things around here won't be so scarce. If Magda didn't work for her keep, we'd not be able to have her with us. We have very little set aside."

Magda spoke up. "I'm grateful fer a place to be layin' me head at night. Me mam told me either get meself married or get meself some work where I'm not needin' a bed at home. Too many bairns and not enough room, is what she said. I don't care ta be shackled wi' a man yit."

Megdn laughed. "I'm thankful you feel that way. We are grateful to have you. It's simply that with Shamus' salary being cut and with the price of food climbing, it's hard to make ends meet. We're facing a paucity of food in the near future, I'm afraid. No one's been able to plant. As you know, I have plants on the enclosed part of the porch. Once they begin to produce, we'll garner what we can and dole it out carefully."

Maggie slid off the chair, wiping her hands on a towel. She leaned against the table. "Well, for certain sure, they shouldn't have cut Da's salary. He's probably the best professor Trinity College has."

Walking to the other side of the kitchen, she felt to see if the clothes hanging on a line strung across the room were dry. She took down a few items, folding them neatly. She'd never helped to cook much, but she was adept at helping to clean house, wash clothes, and perform other household duties.

"Everyone had to take a cut, Margaret. We're thankful your father didn't lose his position. Several professors who are newer to the college have lost their employment. 'Tis a sad happenstance, that's certain. Your father has begun to talk about moving to America. I am hoping things turn around for us, or we'll be making a move across the ocean. I'm not sure I want that for our family. It's not as if we have relatives here, but we have our circle of friends, and I'd hate to move to a new place and have to start over. The thing is, if this rain keeps up, we'll have to do something different. People are going to go hungry, and when that happens, people begin stealing just to survive."

Shamus strode home in the pouring rain. It was nearly dinnertime. This evening his little girl would celebrate her twelfth birthday, beginning with the concert. He hawked heavily, spitting blood into the street as he felt the pain in his chest. He tried his best not to cough around other people, but he was ill, and he knew it. He felt tired all the time, and his lungs ached with a pain that wouldn't go away. He had chills often and then sweats. Most times he could wring out his bed linens from night sweats. It was difficult to take a deep breath.

He mulled over the events of the day.

It was a Saturday, and most of the administrative staff were home, but Shamus had gone to the college at noon to get caught up on paperwork. The term would end in a few weeks. Several staff had come to him, wanting him to join them in their protest against added students and paperwork but less pay. He didn't care to join them. Funding was tight this year, and by joining the dissidents, he could lose his position at the university. It simply wasn't worth it.

Yesterday he'd withdrawn all his savings from the bank. He hoped he'd done the right thing, but the future looked bleak in Dublin. He had a plan and needed to sit down with Megdn to see if she would agree to it.

Shamus, trying to stifle his cough, entered through the back door so he could hang his hat and coat to dry and set his boots in front of the open flame of the huge fireplace, which warmed the kitchen. The smell of drying wool mixed with lamb stew was familiar and welcome.

"Hello, I'm home!"

He heard the sound of running feet and saw a streak of red hair flying across the room. He smiled as he felt the air nearly knocked out of his lungs as his little Maggie hurled herself into his arms.

"Oh, Da, I'm so glad you're home! We need to eat and get ready for the concert."

Shamus hugged her and placed a kiss on the top of her head. "I know, muffin. I know. I hired a carriage, and it will be here at forty minutes past six. Where's your guest?"

"Listen to her. She's in the parlor playing on the piano. She's quite good—a lot better than me. Oh, Da, she has the most beautiful dress and will look lovely tonight."

"No one will outshine you, muffin. You could wear rags and still be the most beautiful girl in the room." He smiled down at his precious daughter.

Maggie smiled back, deep dimples dipping into her cheeks. Her gray eyes sparkled with excitement. Her hair was a crown of glorious red. At twelve, her mouth seemed too wide for her face, but it was always smiling.

"I thank you so much for this present you've given me. I love you!" She squeezed his middle and danced away to the parlor, full of the joy of living.

A short time later, the two girls were getting ready for the concert.

"Clodagh, you look stunning. Wherever did you get that dress?" Not waiting for an answer, Maggie continued, "Don't you wish we could have our hair up? Oh, I can't wait until I'm a young lady and can wear my hair up. Where are my shoes? I'm sure I left my shoes in the clothespress. Are you excited, Clodagh? Oh! Don't you think this evening will be simply divine?"

Clodagh giggled. "Your shoes are under the bed, and I can imagine you with your red hair all done up on top of your head. Someday, my friend, you're going ta be a stunning woman."

Maggie blushed under the observation and comment. "Oh pshaw. I'll always just be me! And I plan for us to be friends forever and ever—even when we're old and gray."

"Me too," Clodagh said. "Friends forever."

She linked her arm with Maggie's and twirled around the room. Both girls laughed, falling onto the bed together. Clodagh had hair the color of black ink. Gleaming in the lamplight, it reflected blue highlights with a natural wave. Her eyes were unusual, a sparkling brown, and merriment lurked in their depths. Sweet lips habitually curved up at the corners, as if she were always amused. She angled her head away and coughed heavily, sitting up to gasp for more air.

Maggie frowned. "Are you sure you're all right? That cough sounds awful to me."

"Yes. I'm fine. Me mam says it's the damp air and nothing ta worry about, although me chest seems ta ache and ache. Enough about that. We need ta finish up here."

A silver watch hung from a heavy chain around her neck, and she flipped it around to check the time.

"What a lovely timepiece!" Maggie exclaimed. "Look at the beautiful engraving on the front of it. It's the eternal knot, isn't it?"

"Yes. Me mam lent it to me for this special occasion." Clodagh opened the face cover. "Oh, Maggie, look! It's nearly time to go! Won't this evening be sublime?"

"I'm glad we don't have to wait another day. Yes, it'll be a sensational evening for us!"

Maggie and Clodagh, with much chatter and laughter, finished their toilette. Starting down the stairs, they saw Megdn as she stood at the bottom of the steps. She was dressed in her very best, a creamy confection of satin and lace. At thirty-two, she looked fragile and utterly feminine. The dress enhanced her sweet figure. Pearls ringed with tiny diamonds, inherited from her grandmother, graced her neck and ears, sparkling in the glow of the soft lamplight. She looked up proudly as she watched her daughter descend the stairs.

"Girls," she said, "you look lovely, and my goodness…you look grown up. What a wonderful time we shall have." She kissed Maggie's cheek. "Happy birthday, darling. Are you ready to go?"

Shamus walked into the parlor. "My, my, my, and who do we have here?" He turned to his wife, smiling all the while. "And just who are these two lovely young ladies? Have I the pleasure of your acquaintance?"

"Oh, Da, you know who we are!" Maggie laughed as Clodagh giggled.

He bowed, taking Clodagh's hand as if she were indeed grown up. Clicking his heels together, he bent over his daughter' hand, brushing his lips over the back of it. His mustache tickled, and she pulled her hand away to rub it.

"Are you rubbing off my kiss?" he asked in mock astonishment.

"No, Da, I'm rubbing it in," she responded cheekily.

"Both of you look lovely, and you do me proud," he responded. Taking Megdn in his arms, he planted a kiss on her cheek, hoping she wouldn't notice he'd not been kissing her on the mouth for some time. "And, you, my dear, are beautiful…always beautiful, and I love you forever and a day."

"Shammy, you are and always have been the only love of my life."

Her eyes glowed with love, and in their depths, he could see the truth of her words.

As the girls retrieved their shawls from the coat tree, Shamus said, "Let me help you girls with your wraps."

"You do look beautiful, Mam," Maggie said, thinking she had never seen her mother look lovelier. She closed her eyes and lifted her face heavenward. "I am making a memory and will always remember standing right here on this eleventh day of May 1876, the day before I turn twelve, thinking no one has ever, ever had a more perfect birthday."

Shamus escorted his little group to the waiting hansom cab. He held his umbrella over the two girls and got them into the hansom. Turning back, he ran up the walk to get his beautiful Megdn, but he began to cough. He grabbed his handkerchief to cover his mouth. Taking his kerchief away from his lips, he saw, in the dim light, a smear of blood on it and crumpled it in his hand, lest Megdn see it.

"Careful, my beautiful Megdn," he said with a false gaiety. "We don't want your stunning gown to get wet." He pulled her tightly to his side, and they walked together toward the waiting carriage, his arm around her waist. As he helped Megdn up and inside, he gave directions to the cabby and pulled himself in to sit facing the two girls.

Shamus frowned in the darkness as Maggie and Clodagh chattered happily. He knew tuberculosis was surely a death sentence. *Very few people,* he thought, *ever survive it.* Remembering back to years ago, he thought of the many conversations he'd had with Dr. Semmelweis and now wondered if he'd passed anything on to his wife. He took her hand and gave it a gentle squeeze, focusing on the evening ahead. He pushed his dreadful thoughts into a corner of his mind to be mulled over later, but not tonight.

He squeezed Megdn's hand, and she smiled at him in the dim light of the carriage. As Shamus smiled back, he saw a frown puckering her forehead.

He smoothed her brow with his fingers and asked, "Are you all right? Is something worrying you, my dear?"

"Yes and no, Shammy. I'm fine, and I know we're going to have such a wonderful evening, a memorable evening for our dear daughter." She dropped her voice. "The real question is, I believe, are you all right? I worry about you. Your cough is worse, and you're steadily losing weight.

You're thinner than when I married you. How are you, Shammy? I'm serious, and I want a truthful answer."

Maggie stopped talking midsentence, and Clodagh turned toward her, her face questioning why. She'd not been listening to Maggie's parents' conversation, but Maggie had. She too had been worrying about her da. Clodagh saw Maggie staring at her parents, who at the sudden silence between the girls, stopped their conversation.

"I want to know too, Da. Are you sick?" Worry creased her brow.

"I'm fine," he replied jovially. He clapped his hands as if he were a magician. "We can talk about this tomorrow. I've been thinking of a plan for our family, but tonight we will celebrate. Now, for a change of subject, Margaret Regan O'Neill. You are twelve years old. What a young lady you've become!"

Maggie grinned at her da. "Twelve! Twelve is almost grown up, isn't it?"

"Yes, yes it is. My how the years have flown by. Why before you know it, you'll be havin' a beau come to court you!"

Clodagh laughed. "Handsome and debonair...but he'll have ta be smart too, or Maggie won't give him the time of day."

Everyone laughed. The rain continued to pour down, beating on the roof of the carriage with force. The four sitting in its interior felt the coziness of being safe and dry.

Maggie felt sorry for the hansom cab driver. She looked at her da and was not fooled that he had neatly turned the conversation away from himself with the ease of practice. The dialogue switched to the comic opera they were to watch that evening. Da went over the storyline for the girls so they would better understand. They were to see *Rhampsinitus*, composed by Signer Cellini. It was the first benefit of Mr. Michael Gunn, and Bessie Sudlow was to be the diva for the event.

It seemed no time at all before they arrived at the theater. The rain had tapered off to a light drizzle, and the cobbles gleamed, polished to a high shine. Lamps lined their path to the imposing concert hall and cast a warm glow in the damp air. Gilded doors stood open to the night, and fancily clad people were already pouring into its ornate entryway.

Maggie took Clodagh's arm, and her da took her other as well as Mam's. They entered the great lobby four wide.

The concert was all and more than Maggie could have hoped for. Bessie Sudlow seemed to sing from her heart, and it touched her listeners.

There was an intermission, and their party made their way to the lobby, where Shamus saw a colleague, and the two engaged in a lively conversation about the laying off of professors at the university. Shamus turned to introduce his family and Clodagh, and before they knew it, they could hear the orchestra warming up for the second half of the performance.

Shammy coughed all the way back to his seat, and Megdn felt a dread in her heart.

The concert had been a tremendous success, and the lobby was crowded. They slowly made their way out and waited in a line of people to get a hansom. When it was their turn, Shamus directed the driver to a fancy restaurant where they would enjoy a dessert before going home.

"Oh, Mam, I want to be a diva when I grow up! Wasn't Bessie Sudlow simply divine? She sings just like a bird! I think *Rhampsinitus* was certainly the best concert I've ever been to!"

"As if you've been to so many you can make such an observation." Her mother laughed.

Clodagh was also impressed. "I cannot express my gratitude by saying thank you for such a wondrous experience. I shall never, ever forget it, and the only words I can think ta say are, thank you, Mr. and Mrs. O'Neill. Maggie, thank you for including me in your wonderful evening. Wait until I tell me mam."

She began to cough, and Shamus looked at the girl carefully, a worried frown marring his brow.

Clodagh looked back at him with complete understanding, her eyes shadowed, almost haunted. The two of them were very ill.

Maggie and Megdn missed the look, as they had begun to chat about the dress Bessie Sudlow had been wearing. Maggie was in raptures.

Shamus took Clodagh's hand and tucked it into his arm as they waited for another cabby to take them home.

Maggie had never had such a glorious birthday. It was one she would remember for the rest of her life.

CHAPTER II

To every thing there is a season,
and a time to every purpose under the heaven
A time to be born, and a time to die.

ECCLESIASTES 3:1–2

"**B**UT, SHAMMY, ARE YOU CERTAIN?** You've really had a letter from them? Oh, Shammy, 'tis wonderful. This will be a splendid change for you! My goodness, Boston University! Oh, Shammy 'tis marvelous, to be sure! Why, everyone knows the opportunities in America are boundless. I cannot believe you never said a word to me! I could have been excited and waiting to hear from them right along with you. Oh, Shammy, I *am* so excited!" Megdn looked at her husband with brightly shining eyes.

The two were conversing at the kitchen table.

"I didn't want you to be disappointed, me darlin', if I wasn't accepted. I would simply have swallowed my disappointment and never said anything. Now that they've accepted me, I will proceed with purchasing our tickets. We can start packing. They want me to begin next month, Megdn, me darlin'." Shamus slid into the brogue he'd grown up with. "We shall begin a new life in a young country, and all the world will be an adventure for us. We have no relatives here, and it's high time we make a break and start our new life in America. I can make more money there in half a year than I can here in a whole year, and I understand food is cheaper and plentiful. We will make it work, me darlin'!" Shamus tried to sound cheerful, but he wasn't sure how long he had left. Fever, chills, and his cough had taken a toll on his body, which looked emaciated from lack of appetite.

Magda surreptitiously wiped her eyes on her apron, saddened to hear their discussion. She didn't think she'd ever find employers as nice as the O'Neills had been. She'd be devastated to see them leave—they were like family—closer than family.

Shamus spoke to her. "I am so sorry to have to let you go, Magda. You have been a faithful, hardworking girl for us, and had I the money, I'd pay for your passage. It's simply not possible. I'll be barely squeaking by as it is."

"I know, Mr. O'Neill. I know. I understand, it's just…" Her voice trailed off, and she began to cry, making no sound as she pulled her apron up to cover her face.

Megdn got up and took her by her shoulders, pulling her into her arms. "Oh, Magda, you're like a daughter to me. I am sorry." Tears welled up in her own eyes at the heartbreak the parting would be.

The back door banged shut, and Magda quickly turned toward the stove, wiping her tears on her sleeve.

"Da, Mam, I'm back." Maggie's voice sounded choked as she entered the door, and her feet dragged on the flagstone.

She started to sit at the table, but Megdn saw her daughter's face and pulled her into her arms, where Maggie began to cry wracking sobs.

Holding Maggie away from herself, Megdn searched her face and asked, "What is it, Margaret, me darling? What's wrong?"

Shamus had turned in time to see Maggie's face crumple as tears streamed down. She tried to speak.

"Clo-Clodagh's dying!" Maggie wailed. "The doctor said there's no hope. She has lung fever…consumption, he called it. She is so sick she could barely talk. She just coughed and coughed and coughed, and blood came out of her mouth! Oh, Da, Mam, it was frightening, and I don't think I can bear it! I dropped by there on my way home, because I hadn't seen her for several weeks. Her mam kept telling me she had a bad cold, but now she's in bed. Her mam was bawling, sitting at the kitchen table, telling me it wouldn't be much longer. Oh, I can't bear it! I can't bear it!" Her shoulders shook with her sobs.

Magda put some water on to make a stiff cup of tea, and Megdn stared over the girl's head at Shamus, with fear and knowledge in her eyes as she rubbed Maggie's back.

Shamus stared back, knowing his wife was quite aware of his condition.

Megdn held Maggie tight, and in a voice strangled by the truth she saw in her husband's eyes, she spoke with a heavy heart. "Oh, me darlin' colleen! I'm that sorry fer ye. Oh me darlin,' how Clodagh's mam's heart must be a breakin' fer her. Aoch, 'tis a sorrowful time wid so many folks a perishin' from th' damp. Ah, Margaret, I be that sorry, I am." Tears streamed, knowing her husband faced the same disease claiming Clodagh's life. There was no cure. Tears welled as she hugged her daughter, trying to alleviate some of the pain of loss, but knowing her own loss was knocking at her door.

Shamus got up and took Maggie from his wife's arms, sitting her on his knees. He held her tight in his arms with the knowledge that more heartbreak was coming her way. There was nothing he could do to stop it. He only hoped he could get his little family settled in a land where they'd have a chance to find work and live a decent life without him. There was nothing in Ireland where Megdn could earn enough to keep bread on the table. His head dropped onto Maggie's shoulder. He wanted to weep himself.

The heavy rain finally abated, and the sun smiled upon a day Maggie thought should be pouring with rain. They'd been to the church and were now at the graveside. A casket containing her best friend's body was draped in black cloth. Maggie sobbed, feeling out of control. She'd hated the service in the kirk. It seemed cold, unfeeling, but Clodagh had been full of life.

That minister of the kirk knows nothing about her! Maggie was angry. *He doesn't know how fun she was or how much she loved life. He didn't even say anything about how much her parents loved her and were going to miss her. I think I hate church!*

Maggie was dressed in a black dress that matched her mood. She loved Clodagh third best in the whole world. She'd been like the sister Maggie never had. *The minister said God took her because He needed her more than her family did. If that's true, He's a cruel God, and I want nothing to do with Him!* She grabbed a handful of dirt and hurled it on Clodagh's casket before she stalked off. *Clodagh would throw that dirt right back at me if she could. Oh, my heart aches for me friend…oh, Clodagh!*

The days seemed to run into each other as the family packed. Megdn gave many things to Magda and also to the church, which had a clothing bank for the poor.

"Mam, is it all right if I keep this doll? I've always loved her, but I know I won't be playing with her anymore…" Her voice trailed off.

Megdn looked at her, love filling her eyes.

"Of course, my dear. You've already given away most all you own. This trunk is entirely yours to fill as you wish. Just remember clothing is of utmost importance, and your blankets and pillow must fit in it as well. Your da and I decided one trunk for each of us and one trunk for our household goods. I'm right sorry to be leaving a few of these pieces of me mam's, but Magda will love having them. I just hope she can find a good position before we leave. 'Tis why she's not been here during the day. She's walking the streets, looking for a house in need of a cook."

"I suppose I should learn to cook someday." Maggie sighed.

"In all seriousness, it's past time you learned, young lady," Megdn said. "I don't suppose you'll be marrying some rich toff who can keep you in silks and velvets and out of the kitchen. Magda and I have been remiss in your education. I know you've balked at learning, but I should have put my foot down and made you."

"Oh, Mam, I have plenty of time, and I'll practice on you and Da!" Maggie said cheekily. Her mam turned away abruptly, and she wondered why.

"Is something wrong, Mam?"

"N-no, I am just going to miss Magda and our house and friends. This is not going to be easy on your da and me."

"Well, I'm glad we're moving. I have nothing here anymore except Clodagh's grave. Her mam can't stop crying, and I don't like being alone with her for overlong. She clings to me as if I'm her girl, and I'm not!"

"Aoch, Maggie, 'tis no way for you to be talking. For shame. Her mam misses Clodagh, and now you're the closest thing she has to a daughter. Her mam isn't trying to make you her girl—she's just mourning her only child and knows you loved her mightily too."

Maggie hung her head in remorse. "I am sorry for her, but I still don't like her clinging to me."

Her mother changed the subject. "Are you packed? Is your trunk full? I'm having a terrible time of it. I'll put something in that one trunk from the parlor, and then I'll see something else I might want to take, and I can't seem to make up my mind what to take and what to leave. We only have three more days, and we set sail."

Shamus' little family boarded the ship headed for America. They'd sold their house within a week of putting it on the market. Shamus set the price low, and the people buying it knew they'd gotten a great bargain. The O'Neills were thankful it sold quickly. They could use the money.

It was horrid to say goodbye to Magda. She was family, and even Shamus cried as he hugged her goodbye.

"It's all right," Magda said, wiping her eyes. "I've started saving me money and hope ta come ta America. Please write and let me know where you'll be a stayin'. Mayhap I will join you one day."

She went with them to their ship, and the wind cavorted, now blowing into their faces. They boarded and waved down at her from the deck, thankful it wasn't cold.

The damp seemed to weigh heavy on Shamus' lungs. He coughed and coughed and could never seem to get enough air. He sometimes felt if he could claw his chest open, he'd be able to breathe easier. Hoping to get his family settled before he passed, he was quite aware that his time was short.

Megdn turned him to face her and straightened his cravat. Her eyes looked worriedly into his. "I know ye won't be gettin' any better, me love. I am just that scared about our future. I know you are doing the right thing, Shammy. There's no work for me here, and I'm quite sure they'll be plenty of opportunity in the New World. I wish...oh, how I wish things were different. We've made a good time of it. I love you, me darlin'...with all my heart I love you."

The wind snatched her words and cast them into the air whirling around their heads.

Shammy looked at her with sadness in his heart. He was quite sure he'd not step foot onto the New World. He had garnered all his strength to get everything accomplished and on board the ship. Now he was done. The pain in his chest had spread to his joints, and it was an agony to move. The lack of oxygen had turned his lips blue, and he coughed incessantly. He'd tried to be cheerful when all he wanted was to crawl into bed. Now that they were on board, his plan was to act seasick and take to his bed. It wouldn't be difficult.

Maggie waved down at Magda, her gray eyes sparkling with excitement. She'd gone to Clodagh's funeral two weeks before and mourned deeply for her friend. It would take her a long time to get over losing her. She wasn't sure she'd ever find another friend as close as she'd been to Clodagh. But now, with the excitement of a new adventure, she had high hopes of forging new friendships in a new country. She wanted to leave sorrow and sad memories behind her. America would be the answer to all her problems. She waved at Magda until the ship gave a couple loud blasts and slowly moved away from the pier. When the shoreline was out of sight, she headed to the cabin where she, her mam, and her da would share one small room.

Maggie was surprised to see her father had already taken to his bed. His thin cheeks looked hollow but flushed with fever. His eyes were closed, but Maggie spoke with no hesitance. "You have consumption, don't you,

Da?" She spoke with bated breath, hoping she was wrong, yet knowing in her heart what her head refused to accept.

He opened his eyes and looked at his daughter, sorrow filling his gaze. "Yes, I do." He coughed and coughed, aching in every joint. "I am so sorry, my little muffin. I don't know where I contracted it. I thought to get you settled in a comfortable new place, but you and your mother are going to have to make your own way. I am dreadfully sorry, little one."

Maggie laid her head on his chest and sobbed out her despair. "Oh, Da, you are the best man in the whole world. I don't know what Mam and I will do without you."

They were three days out from Dublin. The sun had not yet risen, and most of the ship's passengers slept. The pale moon hung high in the sky, shining fully, then hidden as a rack of cloud blurred its light. The decks had been swept clean by a raging wind during the day, the ship corkscrewing through mountainous waves. Rigging had been pulled down before the wind slashed them to bits. Many passengers had fallen ill from the ship corkscrewing and tossing about. Some were frightened, as many ships were lost at sea.

As dusk had fallen, the gale had calmed in intensity, but the waves were still enormous as the ship plowed its way through the froth. The rigging had been put back up, and the captain guided them on course once more.

Gusts plucked at Megdn's dress, sometimes lifting her shawl or pasting her dress against her as she stood motionless as a statue, alone at the rail. Strands of hair loosened and whipped around her face, but she didn't bother to tuck them back into her bonnet. Gripping the rail, she stood for nearly an hour as tears trailed down her cheeks. Maggie stayed in the cabin with Shammy, who wasn't going to see the end of this trip to America. Megdn's silent tears escalated into sobs. *I am going to have to be brave and strong, and I know I am not. Whatever shall I do without me sweet love? I have to be strong for Margaret, but I feel I can't go on without me Shammy. He's been me everything since I was just a young lass. Oh, how can I bear this?*

It was pitch dark, except for the fleeting light the moon cast, and no one was about. She lifted the hem of her dress to wipe her tears. Taking a deep quivering breath, she composed herself before going back to the cabin in case Shammy was awake. She was frightened by a future that seemed empty and bleak. She would have nothing except the comfort of her daughter. Megdn returned to their cabin and sat by Shammy's bed for the rest of the night.

Several hours earlier, Maggie had cried herself to sleep. Shammy had said a final goodbye to her. She had sobbed and sobbed after going to bed, trying to cry silently lest she upset her da further.

Megdn tried to comfort her, but there were no words. *There's nothing I can do to console her,* she thought. *I need solace myself. We have no beliefs…what will happen after Shammy dies? Does he just go into the ground? Is that all there is?* She had rocked her daughter back and forth, but peace of mind was not to be found. Maggie had finally gone to sleep with the quiet murmurs of her parents talking and her da's horrible cough.

Now, Megdn and Shammy were talking quietly. He had told her about their finances, about the need for her to get a job, and about reporting his death to the university, but his words came out haltingly. He paused many times in speaking to try to catch his breath from the wracking cough.

"There's enough…to see you through…to find work." A paroxysm of coughing gave him pause. The energy to sit up was gone. After the bout of coughing, he rested while Megdn sat quietly.

She wiped the blood from his lips and sat back, her hand on his chest as if she could ease his pain. It was quiet, but Megdn could hear the rattle of Shammy's lungs. She heard very little sound from the crew, but she could hear the swish of water as the ship's bow cut through it.

"I love you, me Shammy. One look at you, and I niver looked back. I shall miss you, me love…miss you desperately. But you will always be wid me. I will carry you in me heart."

He squeezed her hand. "I love you, Megdn. You must take care…you must make"—he coughed—"make enough to keep Maggie." He took a shallow breath and was gone.

Megdn, never moving from his side, sobbed on his breast for a long time. She sat up the few hours till dawn as silent tears ran unchecked down her cheeks. Before any light appeared on the horizon, she stirred herself, wiping away the tears. She stood slowly, stiff from her vigil, and achingly kissed her Shammy for the last time. She pulled the blanket up and over Shammy's face. With dragging feet, she went to notify one of the ship's crew. He, in turn, found help, and they quietly removed Shamus from the cabin without awakening Maggie. One of the crew alerted the captain, who made his way to the passenger area.

"We will have a sea burial later in the day," the captain said in a quiet voice. He put his hand on Megdn's shoulder, giving it a gentle squeeze. "I am deeply sorry for your loss, madam."

She nodded in response, too choked to talk. Walking slowly back to their cabin, she took a trembling breath, which ended in a cough. She spoke aloud to herself. "I must be strong. I have to be strong. I must be strong for Margaret." Tears streamed down her face, and her shoulders shook with sobs. She crawled into bed and cried herself to sleep.

CHAPTER III

Hear my prayer, O LORD, and give ear unto my cry;
hold not Thy peace at my tears: for I am a stranger with Thee,
and a sojourner, as all my fathers were.

PSALM 39:12

MEGDN TOOK A DEEP BREATH AND straightened her shoulders as she sighted land. The sun shone brightly, and she put her hand up to shade her eyes, almost in wonder at the vast change in weather. This sunshine was amazing! It'd been raining steadily since Shammy died. *The weather matched my sorrowing heart. Wonder if I'll ever lose the memory of seeing me Shammy's body roped into a sheet of canvas and tossed overboard.* She bowed her head and vowed to make life better for Margaret. *The poor bairn is having nightmares.*

Maggie, who had been quite subdued since her father's death, stared at the land as their ship entered the Massachusetts Bay. Her carefree, joyful countenance was gone, and she wondered if she'd ever be happy again. Losing her best friend had been horrible, but losing her da only weeks later was a devastation from which she thought she might never recover. She stood, her feet planted solidly on the deck, as she waited for the ship to dock. She realized with a jolt that normally she'd be jumping up and down. It was the middle of July, and the breeze that blew on her face was warmer than any she'd felt in over a year.

The ship slipped into its moorings next to the long pier of Boston harbor. The wind blew hard across the waterfront. Whitecaps whipped up in the breeze, and terns rode the rolling waves with aplomb. Seagulls swooped and screamed their welcome, diving into the waves and coming up with fish in their beaks. The gusts, though warm, snatched at women's bonnets and men's hats. A whistle blew, announcing it was time to disembark, and Maggie and her mam left the rail to collect their things. Both were quiet. There was no thrill or sparkle in their eyes at having arrived safely to this new land.

"I know we've packed," Megdn said, "but be sure to open every cubby and make sure we've not left anything, me dear. I'm sure we haven't, but wouldn't it be awful if we did?"

"Yes, Mam," Maggie replied. "I wouldn't want to leave anything either." She opened the numerous cubbies in a systematic manner, and in one found a shawl. "Oh, Mam, I'm glad I looked." She pulled out a soft gray woolen shawl.

Megdn looked horrified. "Oh, Margaret, thank you! Your da gave that to me, and I tucked it away so it wouldn't get damaged. I would be sorry to lose it. Are you finished, lovey? There goes another whistle. We need to get off this ship."

Earlier, they had thought to leave Shammy's clothes and items of his they wouldn't need, but Megdn rethought that idea.

"We might be able to sell some of these things. I won't keep all Shammy's clothes, just the best ones, and we'll leave the items that we can't use, but anything we can sell will help to tide us over until I can find work."

Maggie simply sighed and nodded her head. She picked up her da's frock coat and smelled it. "It still smells like Da," she said and cried as she slipped it on.

Maggie and her mother gathered up their things. They were ready. Loaded down, they left the cabin, Megdn with a kiss to her fingertips and a caress on the bed that had been Shammy's. She picked up a weighty satchel and left the cabin with misted eyes. Maggie trailed behind her, shoulders sagging, not only with the burden of personal items, but with the burden of a heavy heart.

Mother and daughter walked on trembling legs down the long ramp to solid ground. Both felt strange. The passengers headed toward the immigration and customs shed, where their trunks would be waiting for them. Megdn, her face white with fatigue, put the heavy satchels down, as did Maggie. Megdn was short of breath and coughed.

It took two hours of waiting in line to arrive at the desk, where they signed their names and several forms. When they were finally finished, Megdn had a chit for their luggage and handed it to a waiting porter.

"Can I exchange money before I collect our things?"

"Yes, ma'am, you sure can. Follow me." The porter led them to another short line of people, but there were three windows of exchangers, and they didn't have a long wait. He hovered, ready to help them with their belongings.

Megdn turned and gave the man a slight smile. Her face felt stiff, as if it had been frozen for the past few days.

"Thank you for waiting, sir." She handed him some bills, having no idea what a tip was worth. He peeled off one bill and handed the rest back to her.

"You need to know one of these"—he waved a greenback—"is more than I make in a day." He spoke to the exchanger and asked for coins, which he handed back to Megdn. He took her over to her pile of luggage and proceeded to show her and Maggie what each of the denominations of bills were worth compared with Irish pounds sterling. He had a feeling they had endured a tragedy, and he wished he could be of more help to them. Both females listened carefully to his little lesson and thanked him profusely. After piling their luggage onto a steel handcart, he led them out of the customs shed and over to a main street. He flagged down a hansom cab and told the driver his passengers would be staying at the Eglon Bed and Breakfast.

"It's a clean and modest bed and breakfast. I think it'll be suitable for your needs," he said. "It will be a perfect place for you to stay. I just hope they have a room open. Let me see your money." He took two coins and said, "Good luck and God's blessings on you both." He smiled and gave them a salute as the carriage pulled away from the curb.

They couldn't hear the prayer he lifted up for them. "Lord, I pray Your hand to be upon those two. They desperately need Your help."

As the hansom cab maneuvered the streets of Boston, Megdn and Maggie looked with wide eyes at the busyness and newness of the buildings. Dublin dated back to the Viking raids of the eighth and ninth century. Boston was little more than two hundred years old. Even the shape of the buildings seemed different from what they were used to.

It seemed no time at all before they pulled up in front of a two-storied building with a shingle hanging perpendicular to the edifice with the name *Eglon Bed and Breakfast* scribed on it.

The cab driver hopped down to help his passengers out.

"Thank you, kind sir," Megdn said. "Please wait while I make sure there is room for us." She left him unloading the three trunks onto the cobbles behind his cab. Maggie stayed with him, as Megdn went into the cool dimness of the bed and breakfast and over to the reception desk.

"Good afternoon. My name is Megdn O'Neill, and I was wondering if you have a room available for my daughter and me?"

The lady behind the counter was unusually tall for a woman and quite thin. With her thick gray hair pulled back into a fat bun and an angular face, she looked severe. She gazed solemnly at Megdn. It was intimidating, but when she smiled, her features lit up bright as a lantern.

"I'm Mrs. Sullivan, and I own this place. Yes, I am happy to say, we do have a room. You are fortunate to have arrived at this time. We were full this morning, but one couple staying here found a house and unexpectedly moved."

She gave her rates, which were fairly incomprehensible to Megdn, who pulled out some bills and handed them to the lady.

Mrs. Sullivan thumbed through the bills, counting them rapidly. "This will cover about three months."

"I plan to find a teaching position and will, depending on the board and room here, be willing to pay more as I am able." Megdn stood with her back straight and her head held high.

"Well, madam, you are welcome to stay, and I'm quite sure you will be pleased with our accommodations. Please let me show you around."

"I need to get my luggage indoors first, as our cabby is waiting."

"Of course." The proprietress rang a bell. "I'll get Sully to help you."

"Is Sully for Sullivan?"

"No. My husband passed away a few months back. Sully is from some eastern country. He has been a wonderful employee, a true all-around help."

Sully entered the room. He was tall, slender, and wore a turban around his head. He nodded respectfully at Megdn and Mrs. Sullivan.

"You want I should bring in her trunks?" He spoke with an accent, and his command of English was halting.

"Yes, please. This is Mrs. O'Neill, and she will be our new boarder."

He nodded again and went outside.

Maggie watched to make sure all was transported inside before she left the boarded walk to enter the massive foyer.

"Oh my, young lady, you have such beautiful red hair! What is your name?" Mrs. Sullivan asked.

Maggie gave a small curtsy. "My name is Margaret Regan O'Neill, but most everyone calls me Maggie, 'cept me mam."

"Well, Maggie, I am just about to take you on a tour of our facilities. I think you will enjoy staying here. Come. Let's show you the lounge and dining area first."

She led them across a long hall and waved expansively at a huge room that harbored settees, wingbacks, coffee tables, and end tables with lamps on the side of each, for evening reading.

Megdn could tell Mrs. Sullivan was proud of the room. "'Tis a lovely room, madam," Megdn said. "I can see you've taken much time in coordinating colors and making everything seem homey. It looks comfortable, and that fireplace…my goodness, why, it would be at home in a mansion."

Mrs. Sullivan beamed at the words and proceeded through the end of the lounge area and into the dining room. The table was immense and seated twenty-four comfortably.

"I have eight rooms upstairs, four on a side, with a ladies' room on one end and a men's on the other. I've never been one for shared bathing rooms." She then led them up a wide staircase with elegant spindles and railing to the second floor. She opened a room halfway down the hall with a key and ushered Megdn and Maggie inside.

"Oh my!" Megdn exclaimed. "I never thought the rooms would be so large or accommodating." The room looked huge after the cramped quarters of their ship cabin. "Look, Maggie, you'll have your own little section over here. Why, we'll do quite nicely here, Mrs. Sullivan. Thank you for showing us around."

Sully entered with the first of their trunks and placed them under the windows, where they'd be out of the way.

Maggie looked around and opened cupboards and a wide armoire. It was more than sufficient for their clothing. She sat on the bed, which had clean linens and a beautiful quilt made of red, white, and blue. She smoothed it with her hand and spoke to their new landlady.

"This is lovely. It's like stars bursting all over it."

"Yes, I made it special for this year. It's our centennial. Our country is one hundred years old this year. I know that sounds a bit fantastic given the fact that Ireland is so ancient. We are proud, though, of our independence from England, and the Fourth of July is a memorable celebration. You just missed it. Our country didn't really celebrate much until about 1783, but the Declaration of Independence was signed on July 4, 1776. It took a bit longer to win that independence." Her eyes sparkled her enthusiasm.

"Frankly, we know very little about this new country we've come to," Megdn said. "The decision to come was made the first part of June. My husband was to take a teaching position at Boston University. He died just a few day ago at sea. I've not even had time to find clothes for mourning."

"Oh, my, I am sorry. What a difficult time for you! Please let me know if there is anything I can do to help. Oh Lord above, have mercy on these two."

Megdn glanced at Mrs. Sullivan with surprise in her expression, but didn't say anything.

"Well, I'll leave you now. It looks as if Sully's brought up all your things. Dinner is served from six to six forty-five. Breakfast is served from six till eight, and lunch from eleven thirty to twelve thirty. It's all written down there on the desk, but I need to get downstairs and oversee things. The women's bathing room is out your door and on your right, at the end of the hall. If I have single men boarders, I always put them on the opposite side of the stairs nearer the men's room. You can freshen up and join us in the dining room." She opened a watch hanging on a chain from her neck. "Goodness, I must go!" Mrs. Sullivan smiled sweetly and left their room, but immediately she tapped on the door and reentered. "I nearly forgot. Here are two keys, but you mustn't lose them. There. I think that about covers it. See you in a bit." She left again.

The room held a feeling of peace that invaded Megdn's and Maggie's souls.

"Well, Maggie, do you care to clean up a bit first, or shall I?"

"You can, Mam. I just want to sit here a bit and soak up this feeling."

Megdn nodded, and taking a washcloth and hand towel off a rack, she left the room and made her way to the ladies' room.

Maggie sat very still. She was grateful for the ease of moving from the ship to a room that seemed a safe harbor from the storm she'd been feeling. "I don't know who to thank for this balm I feel," she said aloud. "I suppose it'd be that kind porter who directed the cabby to this bed and breakfast. I am grateful for it. I think Mam and I will be able to stay here and make a go of it. I've just felt so numb. I don't think I'll ever forget the way Da was thrown overboard. I can tell Mam doesn't want to talk about it. I wish I'd get over the nightmares of fish eating him."

Megdn took care of her business and cleaned up in a clean bathing room, for which she was thankful. She dried her face, straightened her hair, and hurried back to the room.

"You're next, Margaret." She smiled, albeit a bit hollowly. She felt incredibly tired.

Maggie returned shortly, feeling hungry for the first time in days. Her gray eyes sparkled as she spoke to Megdn.

"I'm hungry. We have such a nice place to stay, and it's clean. I was worried we'd live in a place that might have bugs. I do hope the food is good, but there's nothing like your cooking, Mam. Come on. Let's go eat."

Megdn, wanting to go to bed rather than eat, carefully locked their door. They made their way down the wide stairs and into the dining room.

Several people nodded their welcome as the two sat down. Mrs. Sullivan sat at the head of the table and introduced Megdn and Margaret to the group.

"These are our new boarders, Mrs. O'Neill and Miss Margaret O'Neill. They will be a welcome addition to our bed and breakfast, and I do hope you will make them welcome. Please introduce yourselves around the table after I say the blessing. Now, join with me as we give thanks to the Lord."

Everyone bowed their heads except Megdn. She sat stoically looking out the window as Mrs. Sullivan prayed.

"Lord, how grateful we are for Thy beneficent hand. You provide for us, and we humbly thank Thee. May our lives reflect Thy love to those who do not know Thee. Now we ask Thee to bless this food. May it nourish us so that we can apply ourselves to do the work Thou hast laid out for us to do. We ask this in the precious name of Jesus. Amen."

As she prayed, Megdn stifled a cough as she stared bitterly out the window. *I don't believe in a God who would take me Shammy from me at such a young age. I love me Margaret, but Shammy was everything to me.* Tears filled her eyes, and she quickly took a handkerchief out of her sleeve and dabbed at them before the prayer was over. She took the handkerchief from her eyes and stared in horrified wonder at it. Blood stained it, and she realized when she'd coughed earlier into it that her sputum was bloody. A ripple of shock spread through her as she stared at the stained piece of cloth. *Oh, Shammy, I suspect I'll be joining you soon, me love.* She crumpled the handkerchief and stuffed it back into her sleeve as the prayer ended, sitting, numbed by the revelation.

Someone was speaking to her, but it seemed as if through a tunnel. She was stupefied. Lifting her head, she stared at the man who was introducing himself. She tried to smile and nod, but her ears seemed stopped, and she couldn't hear him. *I'm going to die, oh, me Margaret, such pain in store for you. I must find a teaching position and save all I can. What will become of me Margaret?*

She stuffed her thoughts down, trying to focus on the man speaking to her. He'd asked a question, but she couldn't process it. Emotionally drained and physically ill, she could only think about her daughter.

CHAPTER IV

A talebearer revealeth secrets:
but he that is of a faithful spirit concealeth the matter.

PROVERBS 11:13

WITH A GLANCE AT HER MOTHER'S whitened face, Maggie spoke up for the first time, trying to cover her mother's lack of attention to the conversation.

"My mother and I arrived late this afternoon from Dublin, Ireland." She spoke in a quiet voice as she surreptitiously patted her mother's leg under the cover of the table to jolt her into awareness.

The pat jerked Megdn's thoughts back to the present, and the man came sharply into focus. She spoke up. "Yes, it took seven days because we hit some rough seas." Trying to divert the man and avoid conversation, she asked, "Are you native to these United States?"

The man, mesmerized by Megdn's gray eyes darkened by sadness, gave a lengthy response, and Megdn was glad to have him speak as she thought about what needed to be done. *I must prepare her. I must make some money until she finds work.*

The woman next to him spoke in English with a heavy German accent. "Mr. Baum, please halt! That's enough! We also would like to welcome Mrs. O'Neill." She nodded her head in a friendly manner and continued. "I am Mr. Baum's wife, Inga. We welcome you, and we can show you around Boston if you like." She smiled and tapped the shoulder of the lady on her left. With a wave of her hand, she nodded for the woman to introduce herself.

Midmorning the next day, Megdn visited the chancellor of Boston University. She walked to the school of higher education and pondered what she would say to him. She coughed, as the effort of walking pumped her weakened lungs. She slowed her steps, realizing she was extremely tired.

The day was already warm and promised to be hot. The sky was seamless, not one cloud marring its surface.

Megdn walked along the boulevard lined with trees and heard birds chirping. A squirrel sensed her approach and scurried up a tree trunk. *Shammy would have loved this,* she thought as she stepped onto the long brick walk leading to the administration building. It was an imposing edifice, but she was used to the campus at Dublin, and it did not intimidate her.

She entered the building and approached the office marked *Administration* in bold letters on the door. She gave it a little tap and opened the door herself.

A secretary, his head bent in concentration over a stack of papers, looked up in surprise.

"Can I help you?" he asked.

"Yes, my name is Megdn O'Neill, and I would like to speak to Chancellor Collins, if I may."

He nodded. "Please follow me." He led her to an anteroom of the administration office and said, "Please be seated. I'll tell the chancellor you're here."

She sat, but rose to her feet after the secretary left the room. She felt nervous as she walked around looking at a wall covered with pen-and-ink drawings of the building's beginnings. She heard the door open and turned to see the chancellor enter.

He was a tall, spare man with bushy side chops and a full head of snow-white hair.

"Good morning, Mrs. O'Neill. I am Chancellor Richard Collins. It is a pleasure to meet you, but I was expecting your husband."

Megdn proffered her hand, and he took it in both of his. His hands were cool to the touch. She looked up into warm hazel eyes looking concerned, which was her undoing.

"Yes." She took a deep breath and coughed into a handkerchief she had ready in her left hand. Tears welled up in her eyes, and her throat was clogged with sorrow. "M-my husband died aboard ship on our way here. You will have to find someone else to fill that p-position. I'm sorry, but I'm having trouble keeping my emotions under control." She dabbed at her eyes and took a deep breath that ended in a cough.

The chancellor took a couple steps back, realizing she had lung fever. "I am sorry for your loss, madam. I know it is great. Professor O'Neill's résumé was impeccable, and we have greatly anticipated his arrival at our fair institution." He frowned, as if he had some sort of responsibility toward this poor woman.

"What will you do now?"

"I am well educated and will try to find a teaching position."

"You'll not get one if it's discovered you have lung fever." He spoke without hesitation, coming to the crux of her problem. "I am not a talebearer, nor will I reveal your secret."

"Thank you, kind sir, and yes, I know if it is found, I will not be able to obtain work." Her face was calm in the face of the huge obstacle. Her cheeks were flushed with fever, and she ached all over. A fleeting thought of what Shammy had endured, hoping to keep her innocent of his illness, crossed her mind.

The chancellor waved her to a chair and continued to talk, pacing around the room with his hands clasped behind his back.

"I know of a primary school in need of a teacher. It is difficult for females to get a position in our Boston schools unless it is private, you understand. The Puritan influence is still quite strong here."

"I believe Dublin is a bit ahead of you there," she replied calmly. "It's not difficult to get a good teaching position even if one is female. I don't know how much time I have left on this earth, but I have a twelve-year-old daughter who doesn't yet suspect I'm ill. I will need to provide for her as much as I can for the next few months."

The chancellor grimaced in sorrow for this lady who stood calmly before him stating the fact of her own demise.

"The primary school is the Mayflower School of Public Learning and is found on Abraham Street. I'll contact the head there and see if we can't get you employed for the duration. Please give me a few days, and I'll secure the position for you. I am deeply sorry for your loss and dilemma. You must be beside yourself with anxiety for your daughter." He rang a bellpull, and the heavy door was opened by the same secretary who'd ushered Megdn into the anteroom.

"Thank you...thank you very much. I am most grateful." Megdn stifled a cough as she was shown out.

The days passed swiftly. Megdn began teaching and was soon feeling comfortable in her new position.

Maggie stayed with Mrs. Sullivan when Megdn left every morning to go to work. They did not have enough money for Maggie to attend school, so evenings, Megdn, stretched beyond normal endurance, prepared lessons for Maggie to do during the day.

Several weeks passed, and Maggie settled in and seemed happier than she'd been in quite some time.

One afternoon when her lessons were finished, Mrs. Sullivan sat down to teach Maggie to knit. She was a good teacher.

"You will feel clumsy at first, but once you find your own tension on the wool and your own rhythm, you'll see it will become so natural you won't ever have to look at it while you knit."

"I seem to be all thumbs," Maggie said with a little laugh.

"Well, you'll get the knack of it in no time." Mrs. Sullivan looked closely at Maggie and continued to talk. "Your mother is very ill, isn't she?"

Maggie, startled, looked up into Mrs. Sullivan's gentle, deeply sympathetic eyes.

"I…I…" She stood up, threw down the tangled mess, and ran from the room. An almost total stranger voiced something she should have recognized herself. Her mother had lung fever. All that coughing! She was going to lose her mother too!

Maggie ran up the stairs, taking them two at a time, and opening the door to her room, she flung herself onto the bed and began crying. The horror of it ripped through her, and she felt she couldn't bear another loss. Her da had died only a few weeks after Clodagh. He'd been gone now less than two months, and to find out her mother would die was more than she could bear.

Mrs. Sullivan hurried up the steps, sorry she'd spilled the beans to the girl. Striding down the hall on long legs, she berated herself. *What did you go and open your big trap for, Harriet? You know Mrs. O'Neill is ill…why'd you have to go tell her daughter like that? Lord help me…help me to help the girl. How ill is that woman anyway?*

The door was open to the O'Neill's room, and with no hesitation, she entered without knocking. She sat on the bed and took the sobbing girl into her arms.

"I'm sorry, my dear. I suppose I thought you knew your mother was ill. It was idle talk, and I'm right sorry for it."

Maggie, with a flash of insight beyond her years, said nothing. She suddenly realized if she told anyone the true source of her mother's illness, they'd most likely be put out on the street.

She pulled a clean handkerchief from her sleeve, blew her nose, wiped her eyes, and gave a tremulous smile to Mrs. Sullivan.

"It's all right. I do know my mother is ill. Usually she just gets a bad headache, but this time she has a bad cold. Most likely she got it on board the ship. As you know, she is teaching, and it's wearing her out, but she'll be just fine, you'll see. Sorry for the drama. I tend to overreact when I'm frustrated, and that knitting is frustrating. I do wish to learn, so let's go back downstairs, and I'll try harder."

Mrs. Sullivan, mollified by her words, took Maggie by the hand, and the two went down to do some more knitting.

Maggie tried to block all thoughts except her concentration on learning to knit. By the time Megdn made it home, Maggie had perfectly knitted two long rows on the beginning of a scarf, and there were no tear stains on her cheeks.

The days sped by. Megdn enjoyed teaching at the Mayflower School of Public Learning, but she came back to the Eglon every day dragging her feet and thoroughly exhausted. She wondered how Shammy had been able to work at the university, keep a cheerful countenance, and hide his disease for so long. Somehow, having the same illness brought him closer to her, as she felt she shared some alive part of him in her misery. She thought she'd done a good job hiding her illness from Margaret. It came as a shock to discover Maggie knew.

"Mam, I have been making friends with Mr. Elmer Dermott. He seems very kind."

"The new boarder? When have you talked to him?"

"I see him every day. We sit in the lounge after lunch and talk and talk. Actually, I knit, and he does most of the talking. Mrs. Sullivan doesn't like it, but I love talking to him."

"How old is he?"

"He's thirty-six. He's been telling me about the age of consent."

"What does that mean? What is the age of consent?"

Maggie grinned. "I never thought I'd know more about something than you, Mam. The age of consent is the age when a girl can legally get married. Here in America, it's ten years old, except for Delaware. In that state, it's seven."

"Why, I've never heard of such a thing! Whyever are you even talking about a subject like that?"

"I've been doing a lot of thinking, Mam, while you've been at the school. I'm going to need to find work or get married. I know Da only had a bit of money saved, and it's not enough to live on for very long. I don't know how long you will be able to teach, and I'm going to need to take care of you. I think I may just marry this man and not have to worry about how I'm going to care for you when you become too sick to work. I know what I'm saying sounds preposterous, but Mr. Dermott has been talking about us getting married. I told him you were sick, but I didn't tell him you have lung fever. He promised to keep it a secret. We have several secrets."

Megdn looked at her daughter, so shocked by her words that she couldn't form any kind of response. Tears of fear, remorse, and incredulity filled her eyes and trailed down her cheeks.

"Mam, you don't have to worry about me. I am perfectly capable of taking care of myself...except for cooking," she said with a grin. "Please don't fash yourself. I've had my cries over your being sick. I told Mrs. Sullivan you had a heavy cold, but we both know better, don't we? I don't want her to know the truth and put us out on the street. I know you've tried to hide the signs, but with Clodagh and then Da having it, I know you have it too. You do not have to try to be strong for me. I can see you are fair drooping with trying to hold up your end, but don't you see? Mr. Elmer Dermott could be the end of our troubles."

"You are too young to get married. I want you to start looking for a job as a maid first thing tomorrow. You can find some big house that would take you in the way we did Magda. Married! Goodness girl, you don't know the first thing about marriage."

"I know I really like Mr. Dermott. He told me I could call him by his first name, but that's not proper until you're married, is it? I have called him Elmer a couple times. It's another secret between us. He lived in another boarding house, but some friend of his told him he should move. I don't know why. He hasn't shared that part yet. I love you, Mam, but I also know I don't need your permission to get married. I think this is the best plan for us. I don't want to be someone's old maid, emptying out chamber pots and scrubbing floors and making beds. Maybe I am spoiled, but being married sounds a whole lot better than being a drudge."

Megdn started coughing and had a difficult time catching her breath. Her chest ached, and she was bewildered by this new Margaret who thought she'd like to marry an older man she'd met scarcely two weeks before. She plopped down onto the bed as if the wind had been knocked out of her, which in a way, it had. When the paroxysm was over, she lay sideways on her bed, wondering what in the world she could do to convince Margaret she was making a tremendous mistake.

Megdn felt horrible. Her appetite was gone, and she merely stirred the contents of her plate around, not really eating much. She tried to think back to when she began to cough. It was months ago. She ached in every joint, and the effort of trying to suppress her cough was more difficult than coughing.

She was quiet at dinner, listening to Mr. Dermott talk about horse racing. Maggie was all ears and lapped up every word that came out of the man's mouth. Megdn was sure she didn't like him…not at all. He was impeccably dressed, his hair sleeked back with heavy pomade, but to Megdn, he gave off the air of a lecher and popinjay. She didn't know exactly what a lecher looked like, but she was certain this man had ulterior motives. He was what Shammy had called a "fancy skirt man." She sat listening with half an ear, trying to figure out a way to draw Margaret back to her.

As soon as dinner was over, Megdn rose from the table. "Please excuse me," she said softly. Without acknowledging Mr. Dermott, she spoke to Maggie. "Margaret, please come with me." Brooking no opposition, she left the room abruptly. Maggie rose, smiled, and mouthed *I'm sorry* to Mr. Dermott and hurried after her mother.

"Whatever is the matter with you, Mam?" Maggie followed her mother up the stairs. "That was the rudest thing I've ever seen you do!" she said in a loud whisper.

Megdn's lips were blue, and chills rippled up and down her spine. "I n-need your help, Maggie." She coughed heavily and leaned against the wall once she'd gained the stairs, to catch her breath.

"Oh, Mam, I'm sorry! I know you are ill. Let me help you." She slipped under her mother's arm and realized she was as tall as her mother. Helping Megdn out of her clothes, Maggie got her into bed. She poured water out of a jug and set a glass on the nightstand.

Megdn pulled the covers up to her chin and closed her eyes. Chills, starting at the base of her spine, clawed their way up her back, and she shook with cold.

Maggie took the ceramic hot water bottle and left the room, hurrying down the stairs to the kitchen. She ran into Mr. Dermott, who grabbed her and kissed her on the lips.

The blood flooded into her cheeks. She wanted to slap him. She didn't like the way his mustache had touched her, nor his full, wet lips. She tried to keep a shudder to herself and simply said, "Please don't do that again." The kiss had been repulsive, and she tried pulling away from hands that held her fast. His grasp was tight on her shoulders, but he released her. She straightened her skirt and added, "I know enough, Mr. Dermott, to know you don't kiss a girl unless you're married to her!"

"Well, I can't be sorry," he said. "You are lovely, my little girl."

Maggie turned abruptly toward to kitchen in time to see Mrs. Sullivan pull herself back out of sight of Mr. Dermott, who headed up the stairs.

CHAPTER V

The LORD killeth, and maketh alive:
he bringeth down to the grave, and bringeth up.

I SAMUEL 2:6

MAGGIE ENTERED THE KITCHEN, heading for the fireplace, where a pot of water always sat on the hob. She glanced up to see Mrs. Sullivan with lips pressed together in a thin line, a sure sign she was holding in what she'd like to say.

"I am sorry you witnessed that," Maggie said, her voice low, catching on a sob. She turned away so Mrs. Sullivan wouldn't see the tears slipping down her cheeks. "I suppose it's my own fault for spending so much time with him. He's never done that before. I don't know what came over him."

"A gentleman never does what he just did, young lady. To take advantage of a girl your age who's lost her father and her mother lying ill…it's inexcusable, in my book." Mrs. Sullivan nodded her head sagely. "I'll not say more, as you seem to like him well enough, but I'd say you need to steer clear of him, my dear."

With the tears standing in her eyes, Maggie looked at Mrs. Sullivan. "I don't know what to do," she whispered. "My mother has lung fever, as I suppose you've guessed by now. I can't make enough as a maid for our keep. I know you are generous, but I also know you have to make money to keep your bed and breakfast going. I've seen how frugal you are. I've lived long enough to know we cannot stay here and be a burden on you if we can't pay. I feel my only recourse is to marry. Mother thinks I want to marry Mr. Dermott. I'm trying my best to make her feel that way. I don't want her to think I'm sacrificing my freedom for her. She'd feel she is a burden, and she will never be that. Frankly, I'm scared…I'm so scared. I don't like the way Mr. Dermott smells, I don't like the way he looks at me, and I certainly didn't like him kissing me! He makes my skin crawl when he looks at me the way he does."

Mrs. Sullivan, with shock in her eyes but also a bit of approval, nodded her head. "I see. Well, you won't be the first girl to marry someone who is like a stranger to you. I wish there was something I could do to help, but you're right. I am barely keeping my head above water. Once I get Herbert's debts paid off, this enterprise will make money for me, but it's going to take all I have for the next two years to keep myself out of the poorhouse. Oh, my dear girl, I am so sorry for you." She walked over to Maggie and enfolded her in a big hug. "I do wish there was something I could do to help. Your poor mother is so ill. I'll keep my eyes open for some type of employment for you, but I understand your dilemma."

"Thank you, Mrs. Sullivan. You're a good woman, and I'll never forget your kindness in letting us stay here. Now, I need to get this up to my mother. She is suffering mightily, and I will do everything in my power to ease her pain. She has been the best mother any girl could wish for."

Mrs. Sullivan nodded her head again, saddened by this turn of events. She wished she could help the O'Neills but knew in her heart she could not.

Maggie went back up the stairs, wiping her cheeks free of tears. She entered their room and realized her mother did not need the hot water bottle anymore, for she was now sweating profusely. She was asleep, but it wasn't restful. Maggie did not think her mother would be able to teach anymore. With shoulders sagging, she picked up her toothbrush and washcloth and made her way down the hall to the bathing room. When she finished, she retired to her bed, crying herself silently to sleep.

The next morning found Megdn unable to rise, as Maggie had predicted. She threw a shawl around her shoulders before breakfast and made her way to the Mayflower School of Public Learning. The day was warm, but Maggie snugged her shawl closer. She felt burdened thinking about her mother, who seemed bewildered by Maggie's cavalier attitude and determination to marry Mr. Dermott. She'd talked cheerfully to her mam that morning, pretending marriage was exactly what she wanted. As for Maggie, just contemplating it made her cold with fear. She wished she could go back in time. *Clodagh, me da, me mam…could I be next? Perhaps that would be a good thing. Old Mr. Dermott wouldn't want me if I were ill. Why doesn't he go after a woman his own age? Why me? Something about him doesn't seem honest.*

She walked with hurried steps, not wanting to miss breakfast, but needing to notify the school that her mother would not be teaching there anymore.

Once Maggie had left the Eglon, Mrs. Sullivan hurried up the stairs. She tapped on the door, and hearing no reply, she let herself into Megdn's room. She was shocked by what she saw. Megdn was very ill. *She most likely pushed herself to the extreme, trying to keep up appearances that she is all right, poor soul.*

"I know I shouldn't tell you this, Mrs. O'Neill, but I know you are a strong woman. Your daughter, Maggie, does not want to marry Mr. Dermott, but she feels she has no recourse. I am telling you this because she feels weighed down by the fact that you are so disapproving."

Megdn stared at Mrs. Sullivan and swallowed before speaking. "Are you telling me she is doing this for me?" A paroxysm of coughing left her breathless.

"Yes, that is what I am saying. She feels there is no other way to keep the two of you going, and I tend to agree. I've spent a long night mulling over what can be done, and praying. I'm afraid what Maggie has determined is the only answer."

Tears of frustration, weakness, and sorrow filled Megdn's eyes. Gasping for breath, she said, "Thank you for speaking to me about the matter. It eases my heart to know she's not wanting this. The thought of it is abhorrent to me."

"Yes, I feel the same. There is something about that man that doesn't ring true." Mrs. Sullivan's brows puckered in thought. "Well, I need to get back downstairs, but I wanted you to know this is not something your sweet daughter is wanting. I'll leave you now, but please don't tell her I said anything."

"No, of course not."

Megdn looked worn and frail in the bed.

Mrs. Sullivan pulled the covers up around Megdn's shoulders, patted her arm, and left the room, her heart heavy with sorrow for the widow and her daughter.

Elmer Dermott hurried down the steps of the Eglon Bed and Breakfast. He had an appointment with his friend, Armand Bouvier, an émigré from France. He whistled as he walked.

Armand Francois Bouvier had a reputation as a ladies' man, although he was married. His wife was the granddaughter of Breckenridge and Charity Browning, a surname that opened all kinds of doors in polite society. Although the Brownings were deceased, memories were long in Boston, and Armand was able, due to his marriage, to enter the most prestigious of homes. Elmer had many business contacts, and he and Bouvier had collaborated on several deals. Elmer knew of some shady affairs Bouvier, along with his business partner and father-in-law, Monsieur Jacques Corlay, had done. Elmer thought the information he'd garnered might come in handy and bring him a few extra greenbacks if he decided to cash in on what he knew. A little squeeze on those who squeezed others might not be a bad thing. *Think I've about got that little Maggie in my future too. I want that little petticoat. I may need some extra money put aside for setting up the wedding. I'll talk to Ethan Brooks about that.* Elmer smiled to himself as he strolled jauntily down the street.

His feet led him to a beautiful, stately manse. He walked with alacrity up the front stairs and using the brass knocker, rapped it sharply on the door. He was ushered in by the servant with a heavy German accent, whom he'd met previously.

"Please come in, Mr. Dermott." Sigmund took Elmer's hat and frock coat. "Monsieur is in the library." He led the way, but Elmer stopped dead in his tracks when he saw the most beautiful woman he'd ever laid eyes on descending the stairs. He smoothed his hair and paused, hoping to be introduced to her, but Sigmund opened the library door and announced, "Mr. Elmer Dermott, sir."

As he walked toward the doorway, his eyes stayed glued on the woman, who said, "Good morning, sir," and glanced away. She was breathtaking, and he drew a deep breath as she disappeared from his sight.

Sigmund closed the door behind Elmer.

The library was dark, the only light coming from a lamp on Bouvier's desk, casting an eerie aura of shadows looming large as Dermott approached. Books filled the shelves on three walls, and the fourth wall was of heavy drapes, which were closed. Elmer felt as if he'd entered a tomb, and it gave him a creeping feeling along his spine. Evil emanated from the man sitting in front of him.

Armand rose from his desk. "Good morning, Mr. Dermott. You asked for this meeting, and I'd like to know how I can help you."

Elmer's eyes shifted around the room and came back to rest on the inimical dark eyes of Armand Bouvier. They almost made Elmer shudder.

He swallowed down his fear and spoke softly. "I know why Mayfield died." His fingers nervously fidgeted with his jabot. "I'd like a little recompense to keep my mouth shut. I can be very discreet, and I don't need much. Perhaps one hundred dollars would suffice."

Armand's head jerked around to face Elmer's fully. "You are blackmailing me? You, whom I have helped in numerous and sundry ways, think to blackmail me?"

"Well, I wouldn't necessarily call it blackmail. I'm short of cash is all, and I'd like a few dollars to keep my trap shut. I could do you a bit of harm if I was to blab what I know about some of your business dealings." He swallowed when he saw the look that blazed in Armand's eyes.

Armand reached into his desk and pulled out several bills. "I trust this to be enough, but I'm finished with you, Dermott. I'll not be doing business with you in the future. You dare to approach me again, and you will be a close companion of Mayfield's. Do you understand?"

Elmer didn't even bother to count the money. "Yes. Thank you, sir. I'll not trouble you, not ever again." He backed toward the library door as if he didn't want his backside exposed to Armand. Once he gained the door, he spun around and exited without any assistance.

Armand strode to the library door and told Sigmund, who hovered close, "Get Pierre. I have an errand for him."

Returning to his desk, he took his quill, dipped it in the inkwell, and quickly scribbled out a note of directions for one of his servants to carry to an important henchman.

Elmer Dermott walked down the street, whistling a ditty through his teeth. *Now I have enough to set up the wedding and find another place to live for a while. I'll have that little girlie in just a few more days for my very own little toy. She's gonna be a real looker, too. Right now she has a bit of that gangly look, but with those deep dimples, red hair, and gray eyes…uhm-uhm!*

Elmer arrived at Ethan Brooks' place and walked up the two flights to his flat. He knocked on the door. It was a small apartment, but adequate for Ethan's needs. No one answered, so Elmer walked back to the Eglon.

Maggie saw him coming up the walk through the window and ran to the stairs to avoid talking to him. She was halfway up when he entered the bed and breakfast. He saw her immediately.

"Hello there, sweet pea. Come on down and talk to me. I have something I want to say to you."

Maggie faced him, trying to hide the foreboding she felt, schooling her face to a noncommittal look. "It's nearly time to eat, and I need to get some soup for me mam."

"Mother...we don't say *mam* in this country. She's your mother. I think I've told you this before."

"Yes, you have, but I am Irish, and if I want to call her *mam*, I'll call her *mam*. You, sir, are not my boss. I love my mother, and in Ireland the familiar form of endearment is *mam*." Maggie was on familiar ground, quite sure of her English. Her mother had drilled her in correct speech and manners.

Elmer felt a flash of anger course through his veins and looked at the girl, trying to hide his desire to slap her face. "All right, sweet pea, but come on down here. I have a question I want to ask you."

Maggie walked slowly down the stairs, feet nearly dragging for the dread she felt.

"Maggie, my dear, sweet pea. I would like you to marry me. Soon, if possible."

Maggie looked at him with tears in her eyes. She was able to stifle the shudder that started to run through her body.

"Why the tears, sweet pea?"

"Oh...tears of happiness, I'm sure, sir." She wiped her tears on a handkerchief tucked in her sleeve. "Let me go share the news with me mam." She started to leave, but he grabbed her upper arm, his grasp tight. He caressed her cheek with his forefinger.

"Wait a minute. I am setting the date for Monday. That gives you several days to prepare." He pulled her to him, seeing her heartbeat race in her throat.

Maggie knew nothing of romance or of the relationship between a man and a woman. She'd loved what she'd seen between her parents and knew she did not feel that way about Mr. Dermott. She didn't think he felt that way about her either. She looked into his eyes and shrank from what she saw there.

He pulled her closer and said, "Just a few more days, my love...just a few more days." He patted her back but let her go.

She turned and ran up the stairs and down the hall as fast as her legs could carry her.

She halted once she was outside her door, blinking away tears that coursed down her cheeks. Not wanting her mother to see, she strode blindly down the hall to the bathing room. Locking the door, she stood next to it, her hands pressing against the rough wood behind her. She dropped to her knees, and with the bathtub's rim like an altar rail, she sobbed out her sorrow.

Megdn lay tired and worn from coughing and the pain of every breath. Death was near, and she knew it. *I don't know how to do this. All my life I've known what I wanted and what to do, but not now. I don't know how to die. I never put much credence in believing in God, but...*

A fit of coughing hindered completion of her thoughts, but when it ceased, her thoughts went back to contemplation. Megdn's thoughts entered the soul of her being.

You are there, aren't You? She thought back to a time when she'd gone to church with her grandmother. She'd been about seven years old, and the kindly minister of the kirk had laid his hand on her head and had spoken a prayer. It had frightened her and comforted her at the same time. She'd thought, many times, about that prayer in the next few months, but it had been pushed down and forgotten by the busyness of life.

Dear God, I'm sorry for not acknowledging You. I'm sorry for the disappointment I must have been for You. That minister prayed for my heart to belong to You. I want to belong to You. I know nothing of what I must do. I beg Your forgiveness for not recognizing You in all the good things that happened in my life, and I ask You to be with Margaret. She drew as deep a breath as she could, and the pain seared her lungs. She coughed and realized that Maggie had come into the room.

Maggie knelt by her bed, holding her hand.

Tears seeped out the corners of Megdn's eyes. She whispered, "Margaret...God loves you." She drew one more breath, exhaled and the labored breathing stopped.

Maggie's head jerked up in shock. "No, Mam! You mustn't leave me! You mustn't! I cannot bear it!" Her shoulders shook with the weight of sorrow and fear of the future. She lay her head on her mother's breast and wept bitterly.

CHAPTER VI

There is an evil which I have seen under the sun,
and it is common among men.

ECCLESIASTES 6:1

MAGGIE DIDN'T KNOW WHAT TO DO. The undertakers had carried her mam's body to the morgue, and a funeral would take place the next day. Megdn would be buried in the cemetery behind the little church on Rice Street, which was a relief to Maggie, who didn't want her buried in some potter's field with no marker. Mrs. Sullivan had spoken with the minister, and he'd agreed on a cheap plot mostly paid for by Maggie and a little by Mrs. Sullivan.

The minister, a Mr. Tucker, had tried to talk to Maggie, but she was having none of it. She didn't tell him that she felt God was only a crutch people used when they needed Him. She didn't believe in God and had never been taught a thing about Him. She had and would get by just fine without Him.

Maggie's wardrobe was already black due to her da's death. She owned little, and marrying Mr. Dermott was her only option. She felt so forlorn, and without Mrs. Sullivan's help, she didn't know what she'd have done.

Maggie knocked on Mrs. Sullivan's bedroom door, and it opened immediately. She drew Maggie inside and closed it behind her. Maggie had never been in the room before and glanced around at the homey decor. The bedspread was a masterpiece, but Maggie's thoughts were elsewhere.

"I can't begin to thank you for all you've done for me, Mrs. Sullivan. I am grateful to you from the bottom of my heart for letting me stay here until Monday. I would like to ask you to stand with me at my wedding, if you would."

"When is it taking place?"

"Mr. Dermott said one o'clock. He said everything was in readiness. His only stipulation is that I'm not to wear black. I think me mam and da would understand that, but I will be putting my black on right after the wedding. I have a white dress I wore to a concert not two months ago. It's seems a lifetime ago when I was so happy. Me da took me mam, me best friend, and me to a lovely concert in Dublin. Now, I'm the only one left of the four of us. Perhaps I could get that lung fever and be done with it!" Her voice, starting out on a happy note, ended bitterly.

"Hush, Maggie! You mustn't speak like that!" Mrs. Sullivan chided, her voice sounding harsh to her own ears. She took Maggie's chin in her hand and looked deeply into her eyes. "Oh, child, I'd love to be with you on Monday, but I am seeing a solicitor about drawing up a will. Your mam's death has put me in a frame of mind that I shouldn't wait. Oh, my dear, dear girl." She patted Maggie's arm tenderly and said, "You be sure to come visit me."

"What do you mean, come visit you?" Maggie's voice sounded alarmed.

"Mr. Dermott has found a new place of residence and will not be living here anymore. He told me he'd found the right place for the two of you. I suppose I shouldn't have said anything. It is to be a surprise present for you."

"But I don't want to live somewhere else." Maggie's voice was pleading. "I want to be close to you, Mrs. Sullivan. You're my only friend now."

Mrs. Sullivan took Maggie into her arms and hugged her long and hard. "Well, my girl, you're the closest thing I have to a daughter. You will come visit me, won't you?"

"Of course, and often, I hope." Maggie's eyes filled with tears as they were wont to do the past month and more. "Do you mind if I store a couple trunks here for the time being? I don't know anything about the arrangements at the new boarding house. I had reckoned we'd be staying on here. Mr. Dermott won't like that I have so much stuff. I'll leave this and come back some day and sort them out. Me mam and I couldn't bear to part with all Da's things, and now I can't part with some of hers." Tears slipped down Maggie's cheeks. "I hope Mr. Dermott doesn't expect a lot from me. I don't have an idea of how to cook. I hope he's found another place that includes our meals."

Elmer Dermott, back at Ethan's apartment, realized he didn't know Ethan's real last name. Posted on the apartment's list of names was *Ethan Brooks*, but Elmer knew it was Ethan Williams or Williamson or something like that.

Elmer knocked softly on the rough surface, and it was as if Ethan had been waiting for him. The door swung opened abruptly, and Ethan stood there grinning.

"G'die, mate!" Ethan said. He affected an Australian accent, always trying something different.

He grinned widely at Elmer. Ethan's hair was carrot red, and his baby-blue eyes, with lashes that seemed nonexistent, held no guile unless the observer had discernment. Astute observation would render his eyes without any moral fiber. There was no goodness to be found in them. They were devoid of light.

"Hello, Ethan. I came by to finalize everything. You're sure no one is in that church on Mondays? It'd really shoot a hole in my plans if Maggie were to catch on. She'd bolt like an untamed colt if she knew it wasn't a real honest-to-goodness marriage."

"You are a caution, Dermott, an' no mistake," Ethan replied, grinning. He always looked unkempt, his hair greasy, his face needing a shave, and his coat rumpled. "Nope, there's nary a soul about on a Monday. Seems funny to have a huge church an' all and no one there."

"Well, I'm glad no one will disturb us. My wife is in Alabama for the summer and due back the middle of September. I've got a few weeks to tame my little girl, Maggie," he boasted.

Ethan lost his Australian accent and, stroking his unruly red beard, uttered his affirmation in a normal voice. "No, no one will disturb us. So, you're going to hole up in that cheap hotel, huh? Better be on the lookout for bedbugs. You get those, and you'll never get rid of them. I plan to come by a little after dinner on Tuesday night and offer you a solution to all your money problems. I need to fix it with another man, but no doubt you will be totally surprised."

"What is it? Some easy money?"

"I'm not telling you, sir, not another word until I'm sure everything is set. Then I'll spring it on you." He chuckled. "You'll be right surprised, that's certain."

"All right, reckon I'll have to wait till Tuesday." Disappointment was clearly stamped on his face. He was more than curious as to what Ethan might have planned. "Now, do you have a robe an' all for the wedding?"

Ethan jerked his thumb back toward the bed. "Sure thing. Look here." He strode over to the bed and held up a black robe. "I've even got a stole…see!"

"That looks like the real deal, all right. Maggie will definitely think you're a man of the cloth. That stole is beautiful with the gold threads in it." Elmer opened a flat satchel and took out a piece of parchment. "I bought this and want you to fill it out in your best handwriting. Good thing she doesn't know we should have a marriage license or post banns."

"If you were Catholic, you'd have to post them, I should think."

"Well, this ain't as if it was legal in the first place." Elmer grinned. "I'll go now, but I'll see you at the church on Monday. Remember, one o'clock sharp."

He started to leave, but Ethan said, "Aren't you forgetting something? I'll take half now and half after the deed is done."

"Oh, sorry." Elmer reached into his pocket and pulled out the wad of money Armand Bouvier had given him. He peeled off several greenbacks and handed them to Ethan, who eyed the wad. "Here is half of what we agreed upon. I'll pay the other half later."

"Yes, and don't forget about Tuesday night. I'll come around about eight. You can pay me the other half then."

Elmer looked at him smugly. "Don't make it too late. I'll be wanting to bed down early." He guffawed.

Ethan laughed. "It won't take long. See you on Monday then, at your wedding." He spoke in a sarcastic voice and then laughed.

Elmer laughed with him.

Elmer took his leave, pleased with the care Ethan had taken to get a cassock and stole. *He'll look like the real thing, that's sure, if he combs his hair.* With hands in his pockets, he whistled through his teeth as he walked down the boardwalk. He fondled the money in his right pocket. *Wonder if I should buy me some new duds. Maybe not. I'll hang on to this in case the idea Ethan has doesn't pan out.*

It was Monday, midmorning. The month of August was proving to be hot this year, and already the air was warming in Harriet Sullivan's bedroom. She went over to close the window against the warmth flooding the room. She stood fingering the lace curtain as she stared unseeingly out the window. *What can I do for that poor little girl?* she wondered. She felt disgust with herself that she couldn't figure a way out for Maggie.

Walking with slow steps to her clothespress, still in contemplation, she lifted her bonnet off a hook. Back at her chiffonier and standing before her mirror, she stared at herself as her fingers tied her bonnet in place. "All right, Harriet, my girl, is there anything else you can do for Maggie? Lord, help me find a solution…help me to help that girl. I know many girls are married young and unhappily, but Lord, I don't want that for Maggie." She stood staring at herself, tweaking the bows to perfection, when a thought came to her. "Thank You, Lord. I'll go there right now, before my appointment with the solicitor. Perhaps that will be the solution."

She stepped onto the street and walked with hurried steps to her friend Alice's house. She recalled several weeks ago talking to Alice at a church function about Mrs. Jamison. Alice had told her that Mrs. Jamison was looking for a maid who spoke good English.

"Hopefully she hasn't hired anyone yet." Harriet strode with determined steps to Alice's.

Maggie checked the floor of the clothespress to make sure she had everything. She crouched to her knees, looking under both beds. She found nothing, and as she smoothed her mother's bed skirt back into place, she bit her lip softly to keep from crying. *That's all I seem to do anymore is cry. Well, I need to stop. I'll be a married woman before this day is over. I'm scared. I can't stand Elmer Dermott, but I have nowhere to go…nothing else I can do. I'll do what Da used to tell me—"Chin up, me girl. Chin up."*

Maggie stood up and dusted off her white dress. It was wrinkled, but she didn't care. She'd taken a bath that morning and had braided her red hair. She had pinned it up for the first time in her life. She thought back to the day of the concert when she'd told Clodagh she couldn't wait to grow up and be allowed to wear her hair up. Now, she wished she could go back and be the young girl in Dublin where life was so fair and every day a delight with her mam and da.

She sighed and looked around the room one more time. She hadn't eaten lunch. She'd gone down, dressed in unrelieved black, but had only toyed with her food. Conversation had flowed around her, but she was excused from conversation, the guests thinking she was upset about her mother. Of course she was, but it was Mr. Dermott and the idea of putting herself under his control that scared the appetite right out of her. She'd eaten two bites of the apple pie and excused herself, hurrying up to her room to dress for the wedding.

Mr. Dermott had already moved out and would be coming to collect her shortly. She drew a trembling breath as she picked up her satchel. Her future husband had already taken her trunk and large satchel to the hotel they'd be living in. She glanced one more time around the room and slowly made her way downstairs.

Maggie had wanted to say goodbye to Mrs. Sullivan, but she'd gone out earlier, and Maggie had missed her. She saw Mr. Dermott coming up the walk and wanted to burst into tears.

"Hello, sweet pea, are you ready?" He took her arm and tucked it into the crook of his arm, and together they went out the door and down the steps to the boardwalk.

Mrs. Sullivan, even though it was quite warm, had hurried to her friend's house, a small brick edifice set well back from the street. Flowers of all kinds lined the walk and across its front on both sides. Their blooms dripped scent in the still air. The porch was only one step up but spread itself across the entire right front of the house, curving outward to display wicker chairs, love seat, swing, and table. It looked inviting.

Mrs. Sullivan hoped her friend was home. She knocked on the door and breathed a sigh of relief that Alice opened the door.

"Good morning, Alice. Have you a minute? I'm on an errand."

"Of course. Come on in out of the hot air."

Harriet stepped into a small front entry and breathed in the coolness of the room.

"Glad you could drop by. Have you time for tea?" Alice was nothing if not a polite hostess. She had a busy morning planned, but would always take time for her friends.

"No, not really. I'll get right to the point of my visit. I was wondering if you know the address of Mrs. Jamison and if you know whether she's found a lady's maid or not."

"Why, I do have the address, but as to whether she's found someone or not, I don't rightly know." She looked curiously at Harriet, but seeing there was no forthcoming explanation from her friend, she added, "Wait here a moment, and I'll get that address for you." Alice hurried off to a desk in her small sitting room. She pulled open the front, which made into a writing table, grabbed a pair of glasses, and perching them on her nose, reached into a cubbyhole containing her small address book. As she strode back to the front entry, she was opening the book to J.

"Here it is, right here, my dear." She ran her forefinger down the page, stopping at Jamison, Grant and Eloise. "Four thirty-five Baker Lane. Nice area. Quite a large and lovely house. Her husband owns the Jamison Textiles Company, you know. It's quite a prosperous business. I've heard he's planning to expand in the near future. Yes, four thirty-five Baker Lane. Is there anything else I can help you with, Harriet?"

"N-no, thank you. You've been quite helpful. Sorry to have interrupted your morning."

"Not at all, my friend. Perhaps we can take a day next week, and you could come over and have lunch. I know how busy you are, but you really must take some time for yourself."

Harriet, usually reticent, hugged Alice, who hugged her right back. "You are a dear friend, Alice. How I do enjoy being with you. I'll let you know about next week after I have a look-see at my calendar. I have several appointments coming up, and I need to get myself sorted out before I make a commitment. Bye, now."

"Goodbye, Harriet. I'm hopeful about Mrs. Jamison."

"Me too, Alice. Me too."

Alice closed the door after watching her friend hurry down the street. "It's too hot to walk like that," she muttered to herself.

Harriet slowed to a regular walk when she began to pant from the heat. Sweat ran down from her hairline. She wished she didn't have on a bonnet. It only made her hotter.

It was about three miles to Baker Lane from Alice's house and another half mile down the road to the address she was looking for. The homes in this area were not what she would consider houses. They were stately mansions, and she was in awe of the imposing structures.

She felt hungry, hot, and anxious by the time she reached the proper manse, a beautiful edifice with several gables. Stark-white, the shutters, door, and trim were painted black. Lacy white fretwork hung from the eaves. As she started up the walk, she reached up to her breast to check the little clock she wore around her neck.

"Drat!" she exclaimed. "I've forgotten to wear my timepiece. Wonder what time it is?"

She mounted the steps to the double front doors, hoping she was at the right place. Tentatively clanging the brass knocker, nothing happened. She rapped it hard, and the right door opened immediately by a man in black and white livery.

"Yes, madam, may I help you?" The man spoke with a slight accent, but Harriet couldn't place his country of origin.

"I believe you may. My name is Harriet Sullivan. I don't have an appointment with Mrs. Jamison, but I believe you can answer my question as well." She paused and drew a deep breath as she started to speak, but the butler beckoned her to come inside so he could close the door against the heat.

"Please, come inside, Mrs. Sullivan."

She stepped over the threshold into a world she'd only read about in the papers and magazines. The heavy double front doors opened into an enormous foyer, and she swallowed down her nervousness as she looked around. The floor was marble slabs cut in squares of black and white. A huge mirror showed her face to be beet red, and she stopped her exploration and spoke quickly.

"I don't wish to take up your time, but have you hired a lady's maid for Mrs. Jamison?"

He looked surprised by her question and answered with one himself. "Are you looking to put in an application for it?"

"Why, yes, I am—not for me, you understand. I own the Eglon, a bed and breakfast in the middle of downtown. I have a young girl, just twelve, who has been staying at my place. Her mother passed away a couple days ago, and she's now looking for employment. She is Irish, but you'd hardly know it. Her mother was an English teacher, and there's little accent unless the girl is upset or excited. She's been educated, and if the position is open, I am hoping you'd consider her for it."

The butler smiled and replied. "No. The position has not been filled, and it's my place to fill it. If you could please bring the girl around, say, the day after tomorrow, I'll have a look at her, talk to her, and see if she'd be the right person for the job."

"Oh, thank you, sir, for your consideration. I'll be on my way, but what time would you like me to bring her by?"

"I think nine o'clock Wednesday morning would suit perfectly."

"Well, I must be on my way, but I'll be bringing her at nine. Talking about time, could you please tell me, sir, what time it is now?"

"Certainly, it's…" Just then a grandfather clock started to chime. He smiled at Harriet. "It's noon, madam. Twelve o'clock noon."

"Thank you, sir. Thank you. I'll be on my way then. Bye."

He opened the door for her, and she thanked him again as she started down the walk to the road. She rushed a bit, thinking to skip the solicitor and get to the church before the wedding took place. She could rescue Maggie from Mr. Dermott. She hadn't walked a quarter of a mile when she realized she didn't know what church Maggie was supposed to get married in. Tears stung her eyes, and she took out her handkerchief to dab at her face.

CHAPTER VII

Fret not thyself because of evildoers,
neither be thou envious against the workers of iniquity.
For they shall soon be cut down like the grass,
and wither as the green herb.

PSALM 37:1–2

ELMER DERMOTT COULD FEEL MAGGIE'S nervousness, and it excited him. He walked faster.

But Maggie shook off his arm. "It's too hot to walk so fast. We've plenty of time to get there by one o'clock. I don't wish to be all sweaty and feel grimy when I get married. Why the hurry?"

"Sorry, sweet pea. Reckon I'm excited to call you my wife. Can you cook?"

"No, but I suppose I'll have to learn, won't I?" She had slowed their pace, and Elmer slowed his to keep pace with her. "Can you cook?" she asked.

"Of course not. Men don't cook!" He looked down at Maggie, who was tall for her age, but not fully grown.

"Yes, in all honesty, some men do cook. Me da could cook if he had to. One time when our maid was really ill and me mam was teaching, he cooked a decent meal. It sure surprised me mam when she got home.

Chefs in finer restaurants are men." Maggie spoke a bit smugly, knowing more about the subject than Elmer did.

"Well, la-tee-da, Miss O'Neill. Aren't you the princess then?" He spoke in a stinging manner, but it didn't fash Maggie.

"I was…I think I truly was…but not anymore. I'll never be a princess again." She turned her head away so he wouldn't notice the tears.

"Well, don't worry about it. From now on, I'll be taking care of you. You can be my princess."

He leered at her, but she shrank back from his hard gaze.

"We'll be at the church shortly," he said. "Sorry Mrs. Sullivan couldn't come too. I know how much you like her."

He spoke the lie in a solicitous tone, and Maggie eyed him, wondering how much of what he said was true. Instinctively, she didn't trust him.

"Ah…here we are."

The cathedral was impressive. A spire soared upward, and Maggie craned her neck to see the top of it. The outer walls were of hewn stone but nearly as smooth as marble. The massive oak double doors were stained a dark honey color, showing the wood's beautiful grains. Elmer pulled a door open and bowed, sweeping his arm in a grand gesture to usher Maggie inside.

Maggie swept in with her head held high, although her knees were nearly knocking. She gazed about in awe of the splendor of the interior. It made her forget for a moment the reason she was there. She stared with pleasure at the stained glass windows and the ornately carved wooden columns. Row upon row of pews lined either side of the marble aisle. In some small way it reminded her of Trinity College at Dublin University. The tears of remembrance stung her eyelids, and she blinked them back, determined not to show any emotion.

Elmer Dermott took Maggie's arm and led her, with measured steps, up to the apse, where a man in a long black robe stood waiting with an open Bible in his hands. His fingers, grasping the cover of the good book, looked strong but were fat as sausages.

She stared at him and swallowed down the fear she had just determined not to show. The minister's hair looked as if he'd tried to comb it, but it was greasy, and he had an unkempt stubble of hair on his face. He was a big man, and the cossack didn't really fit him well, which added to the unkempt appearance.

"Good afternoon, mistress. Mistress Margaret, are you not?"

Maggie curtsied. "Yes, sir, I am."

"What a sweet little morsel you are! I am Bishop Brooks." He cleared his throat, which sounded a bit like a chuckle. "Well then, let's get started, shall we?"

Maggie stared, wondering if that was how a minister should talk. She knew in Ireland, what he'd just said was improper, but she wasn't sure of what was acceptable in America.

The bishop read from a small book inside the Bible and enunciated his words in sonorous tones. "Dearly beloved, we are gathered here this day in the sight of God…"

Maggie's attention wandered as she stared at the figures painted on the wall ahead of her. The phrase "in the sight of God" echoed in her head, and she heard nothing more until the minister of the kirk cleared his throat and repeated his question.

"Miss Margaret, are you listening, girl? Please repeat after me. I, Margaret Regan O'Neill, take Elmer Dermott to be my husband, to live together after God's ordinance in the holy estate of matrimony. I will love him, comfort him, honor and keep him, in sickness and in health, for richer, for poorer, for better, for worse, in sadness and in joy, to cherish and continually bestow upon him my heart's deepest devotion. Forsaking all others, I will keep myself only unto him and obey him in his every desire as long as I shall live."

Maggie looked at Elmer and repeated the words in a whisper.

Ethan continued with the ceremony, glad he had the little book. He'd have botched it for sure without it. "May you always share with each other the gifts of love—be one in heart and in mind. May you always create a home together that inspires your hearts to love, generosity, and kindness. And so, by the power vested in me by the State of Massachusetts and Almighty God, I now pronounce you man and wife— and may your days be good and long upon the earth."

Ethan smiled at Elmer, and with a wink of his left eye said, "You may now kiss your bride."

Elmer took Maggie by the shoulders, but she shrank from his embrace. He grabbed her and held her close as his mouth came down on hers.

Ethan grinned but quickly wiped his face clean of expression when Elmer released Maggie.

She was shaken to the core of her being.

Ethan whipped the parchment paper off the altar rail.

"I need you both to sign this, Mr. and Mrs. Dermott."

Maggie, embarrassed at being addressed as Mrs. Dermott, took the quill and wrote her name on the parchment, as did Elmer.

"Thank you," Ethan said. "Now I'll leave you to it." He left, going out a small side door.

Maggie looked piteously up at Elmer. "What shall we do now?"

"I am taking you to our new quarters," Elmer replied. "I already have your trunk and things there."

"I...I think I'd like to have something to eat first. I feel a bit shaky. I didn't eat lunch. I was so nervous, but now I'm really hungry."

"All right, sweet pea. We'll get a bite to eat first. I didn't eat much either." He took her by the arm and led her back down the aisle and out of the church, thankful no one had come in. *Ethan is right. There's nary a soul around on Monday afternoons. Wonder if it's that way every day?*

Elmer and Maggie ate a leisurely lunch, and Maggie was beginning to feel a bit more comfortable with him.

Elmer went out of his way to help Maggie to enjoy herself. She was his, and he would enjoy introducing her to real life.

"Shall we take a stroll in Boston Common?"

"What's Boston Common?"

"Oh, sweet pea, Boston Common is the oldest park in the United States. It's huge. Fifty acres or more."

"I'd like to see it," she replied. "Can we walk around it?"

"Yes, right after we eat."

They continued with an unhurried lunch. The waiter was solicitous, and Elmer ordered Maggie a drink, but after one sip she pushed the glass away.

"Ugh, how can you drink that?" She wiped at her mouth with the cloth napkin, as if she could wipe the taste from her mouth.

"I'll drink it for you. I was hoping it would help you relax, sweet pea. You seem wound up tight as a tick."

They finished their meal, and after Elmer paid with a flourish, making Maggie think he had a lot of money, they strolled to Boston Common. The day was warm, but they strolled slowly and enjoyed the fountain that shot ninety feet into the air.

"It's hard to believe that this lovely park used to be a cow pasture. The city outlawed the cows about forty years ago or so. They built the fountain about thirty years ago. Pretty nice, isn't it? Now, I think it's time to head toward my...our new flat." He felt Maggie stiffen, but he'd delayed and coddled her enough.

They walked for over a mile and entered a hotel that, to Maggie's eyes, looked shabby. Elmer took off his top hat as they entered, and they mounted the stairs to his room. He took a large key from his pocket and opened the door, pushing it inward in a grand gesture that was out of place.

He put his hand on Maggie's back and pushed her into the room. She stood looking around. Wallpaper was peeling and the bed mattress sagged. Thin muslin curtains hung at the windows and were tattered and dirty.

"Welcome home, sweet pea," Elmer said.

Ethan Brooks sat comfortably in the darkened room of Armand Bouvier's library. One sconce was lit by the door, and a small lamp burned steadily on his desk, but neither put out much light.

It was difficult to see the expressions on Bouvier's face or any expression in his eyes. Ethan wondered how the man could stand such a dimly lit room.

Armand stood, leaned over the desk, and offered Ethan a cigar from a case on his desk. He opened the drawer and pulled out another one for himself. Armand never gave his better cigars to his minions. They both cut the ends with a clean slice. Ethan lit up, drawing heavily to get his stogie to burn.

"So, you are ready for tomorrow night? You have made arrangements to visit Elmer?" Armand asked.

He tapped his ash into a tray on his desk and quickly shoved another tray over so Ethan could use it. The room, always smelling of stale cigar, was soon full of the pungent smell of fresh smoke, which hung heavy in the drapes.

Ethan flicked the end of his ash expertly into the tray. "Yes, I told Dermott I needed to finalize things with another man afore I let him know the solution to all his money problems."

Armand sat back and thought for a moment.

"What are you going to do about the girl?"

Ethan looked at Armand in surprise. "I hadn't thought about it. I'll just get rid of her. She'd be extra baggage, and we don't need that."

Armand nodded in approval. "On second thought, don't do that. You can bring her to me. I'll ship her out to San Francisco. I've got a warehouse full of girls ready for shipment to Hong Kong and Chile."

Ethan's eyes gleamed in admiration. "You do have your fingers in a lot of pies. Yes, I'll bring her here."

"No, not here. I have a flat in downtown Boston. You can take her there. Stay there tomorrow night until I get there. I'll pay you well for your trouble."

"Right, I'll do that."

Armand wrote down the address, handing the paper to Ethan, who tucked it into his vest. The men chatted until their cigars were gone, and Ethan took his leave, making his way back to his apartment.

Mrs. Sullivan wished she'd had the forethought to find out where Mr. Dermott had his new living quarters. She knew she couldn't help Maggie by having her stay at the inn, but Mrs. Sullivan wanted the girl to know if she cared to try for a job, an interview had been set up.

Mrs. Sullivan barely scraped by. Mr. Sullivan had run them into serious debt. There were several businesses dunning her on a regular basis. She lost sleep over the worry.

"I need to stop worrying and trust You, Almighty God, to take care of me. Lord, help me remember Thy provision and Thy word where it says Thou wilt supply all my needs according to Thy riches in glory. Seems I pray about it afore I go to sleep, and when morning comes, I take up the burden again, forgetting to keep it at Thy feet. Lord, I pray for that little Maggie girl. What a burden for a little twelve-year-old to bear, to lose her parents in such a short time. Lord, I know Thou art a gracious God, slow to anger and abounding in loving-kindness. Please open the door for me to help her. I pray she comes here soon so's I can send her to the Jamisons'."

Tuesday morning couldn't come soon enough for Maggie. She lay in a huddled mass as close to the edge of the bed as she could, feeling bruised and broken. Silent tears ran down her cheeks.

Elmer got up, dressed, and slammed out the door.

Maggie, hopeful, sat up, but she heard his key click loudly in the lock, and she lay back down. She tried to hold back her tears, but she couldn't.

Elmer didn't return for the entire day. Maggie was glad. She wasn't hungry, and her eyes were nearly swollen shut from weeping.

When Elmer finally did come back, she heard the key slide into the lock and cringed when he opened the door.

He stood over the bed, looking at her with eyes full of disgust. He didn't say a word, but his body weaved sideways, and he reeked of whiskey. He simply grabbed Maggie tightly by the arm and led her down the hall, waiting outside the bathing room door to make sure she didn't bolt.

"Wash your face and quit your bawling. I'm sick of it. Do you hear me? I mean it! I got a friend coming by in just a short while, and I want you presentable." Elmer, through the dimness of his clouded mind, suddenly had a moment of clarity. He couldn't let Maggie see Ethan. She'd know he was no minister able to marry them.

"What's taking you so long? Hurry up, girl. I don't have all night!"

Maggie took her time. When she entered the bathing room, she hoped for a window to crawl out. She didn't care that they were on the second floor—she'd risk breaking a leg to get away from Elmer. She took care of her business, but there was no window. She splashed water on her face, which was stiff from the salt of her tears.

I'll get away from here. I'll find some way, and I'm going to get out of here. I could break the window in our room the next time he leaves me locked up in there. That's what I'll do. I thought being married would be the best thing for me, that Elmer would take care of me, but I was wrong. I would rather empty chamber pots than spend another night with him.

She came out of the bathing room with her head held high.

Elmer had had hopes her demeanor would be different. He didn't want a frightened rabbit. He liked a little spunk.

He held her arm, and Maggie tried to pull away from his grasp. She looked into his eyes and saw them glitter with excitement. Forgoing her struggle, she acquiesced meekly, not wanting to excite him further.

He locked the door, dropping the key into his pocket, and spoke to her, his voice harsh. "I have a friend coming over here in"—he pulled his watch from his fob pocket and peered at it in the dimness of the room —"about five more minutes or so. When he knocks, I want you in that there clothespress. You hear me? I don't want no one seeing your eyes nearly shut from crying on our honeymoon."

Maggie eyed the clothespress. It had a few holes in it from knotholes dropping out. *At least I don't have to worry about suffocating in that thing. Wonder if there's any spiders in there—everything is so dirty.*

There was a knock on the door, and Elmer pointed to the clothespress. Maggie went in and Elmer shut it, but it wouldn't close all the way. The knock sounded again.

"I'm coming…I'm coming," he said in a cheerful voice. He anticipated a job that would reap major benefits. He'd wondered several times what it could be. Ethan had said it would solve all his money problems. He opened the door with a flourish.

"Good evening, Elmer." Ethan spoke in a genial tone. "Where's the little girl?"

"Good evening, Ethan Brooks. I didn't want the girl around for our meeting, so I sent her back to the boarding house I was staying in."

"What boarding house is that?"

"Why…that's strange. I don't rightly remember the name…that's odd, isn't it?" Elmer fondled his cravat as he lied to Ethan, sensing something, but not knowing exactly what discomposed him. "So, now down to business. What is this idea you have planned to solve all my money problems?"

Maggie thought, for some reason, she'd heard the visitor's voice before. She quietly bent to her knees and peeked out of a knothole. *It's the minister who married us!* She blinked to clear her vision, which blurred because of her swollen eyes. *Why, he's no more a minister than I am! Why does he want to know where I am?*

"Well, seems Monsieur Armand Bouvier and you have had some business dealings. Is that correct?"

"Yes. He's hired me to do a few jobs for him."

"Well, little man, this is what he has in store for you!"

Maggie almost retched when she saw the man she'd thought was a minister grab Elmer and give his head a snap sideways. Instinctively she knew Elmer was dead. The other man's muscles bulged out of his back as he lifted Elmer up and laid him on the bed.

"That's the solution to your money problems, Elmer," he said grimly. "It's not a good idea to blackmail a man like Armand Bouvier."

Maggie saw Ethan reach into Elmer's pocket and withdraw the large room key and a handkerchief, both of which he dropped onto the floor. He reached into his other pocket and pulled out a wad of money. He also took the fob watch Elmer had on him. He stood and looked around. Maggie shrank back but realized immediately that she might make a noise. She watched through the knothole as the man walked over to the shabby bureau and fingered several items, obviously looking for any other valuables, but he saw nothing of any worth. With a last glance around the room he left, closing the door with a decided click.

CHAPTER VIII

O taste and see that the LORD is good:
blessed is the man that trusteth in him.

PSALM 34:8

MAGGIE WAS CRAMPED FROM CROUCHING on her knees. She waited long minutes to see if the man might return. Standing up, she felt woozy, but she'd never fainted in her life. Part of the problem was she'd had nothing to eat or drink all day. Taking a deep breath, she heard the rapid beating of her heart. Listening with bated breath for any sound, she felt as if her ears were stopped up. It was so quiet.

With great care and trepidation, she opened the clothespress door. The hinge creaked loudly setting off an alarm within her. She flinched from the sound, catching her sleeve on a nail in the clothespress. The room was silent as a tomb as she tried to loosen it, but she was stuck fast. She pulled hard, and the material ripped, but she didn't care. Her one focus was to collect her things and dash out of there.

Keeping her eyes averted from the bed and the body that lay there, she looked for her satchels. They were empty, and she quietly rummaged through her trunk, glad the other two were at the Eglon with Mrs. Sullivan. She wondered if the man who'd been here already knew of the Eglon Bed and Breakfast and had only asked Elmer to confirm the information.

Maggie was scared. She reached under the bed with shaking hands and pulled out Mr. Dermott's satchel. She dumped the contents onto the floor. Leafing through the papers, she took the marriage certificate out, crumpled it, and stuffed it into her satchel. She hurriedly looked through the other papers but saw nothing else pertaining to her. There was an opened letter, and she glanced at it. It was to Elmer and signed *Your loving wife, Elsie.*

I knew it! I knew in my heart of hearts he was wicked! Married! You louse! She looked over at the bed for the first time and spoke to the body there. "I'm glad you're dead, Elmer Dermott! Glad, glad, glad!"

I suppose the best thing I can do now is to go to Mrs. Sullivan's for the night, and in the morning figure out what can be done.

She sifted through the trunk's contents once more. It was mostly clothes, and she stuffed what she could into her and Elmer's satchels.

"Now I know for sure I've never been married," she muttered. "That man is no more a minister than I am a princess, and worse…he's a murderer. I'm not sorry for you, Elmer Dermott! I shall never have to see you again! You were such a liar and so nasty!"

She took a deep breath and then held it as she heard footsteps outside the door, but they continued down the hall. Her breath came out in a whoosh. She tried to calm herself as she went through the contents of the room one more time to make sure she had everything she'd need of her belongings and that nothing was left to identify her.

Maggie went over to the door, loaded down with three heavy satchels. She paused for a few seconds before going back for the key lying on the floor. She opened the door quietly and peeked out into the hallway. No one was about. She locked the door and slipped the key back into the room through the crack at the bottom. She descended the stairs and didn't even look to see if anyone was at the desk. She didn't want to look anyone in the eye or catch anyone's attention. With head held high, she went out through the open door of the decrepit hotel.

It surprised her that it was still light outside. The dimness of the room and all that had transpired had made it seem later than it was. She took a deep breath and headed for the Eglon.

Maggie's shoulders ached with the weight of the satchels. It was hot, but she plodded on, finally arriving at her destination. She breathed a sigh of relief when the building came into sight. She stepped around to the back, which opened to the kitchen, not wanting to run into any boarders.

Mrs. Sullivan stood at the sink with her back to the door, but she turned when she heard it open.

"Oh, child, you gave me a start!" She put her hand over her heart, taking in the swollen eyes and the heavy satchels.

"Goodness, girl, did you have to walk far with that load?" She helped Maggie take the straps off her shoulders and led her to a chair.

Maggie sat with a plop and burst into tears. Harriet Sullivan scooped the girl into her arms and sat with the twelve-year-old on her lap, as if she were a very little girl. She rocked Maggie and crooned love words to her.

"It'll be all right, Maggie dear. It'll be all right. You'll see, sweetheart. Everything will work its way out. Oh, I'm so sorry you've had such a difficult time of it."

When Maggie's crying subsided, Mrs. Sullivan stood and gently pushed Maggie back into the chair. "Let me get you a cuppa. I always believe a body feels better with a cup of tea in them." She bustled over to the huge fireplace, and taking a towel, she lifted the hot teapot and poured two cups of tea.

"Are you better, dearie?" She handed Maggie her cup.

"Yes, thank you. Oh, Mrs. Sullivan, he…he was awful…like a monster. And…and now he's dead! I thought I was married, but I never was. It was all a fake, and the man who married us came to our room, and he snapped Elmer's neck like he was a wishbone from a chicken. It…it was awful."

"Oh my sweet Lord!" Mrs. Sullivan again put her hand over her heart in shock. "He's dead? Elmer Dermott is dead? How did you ever get away? The murderer must have had plans for you!"

Maggie, wide eyed, stared up at Mrs. Sullivan and took a big gulp of the hot tea, the cup rattling against her teeth in shock as she digested what Mrs. Sullivan said.

"He…he knows who I am, Mrs. Sullivan. He was the fake minister who supposedly married us, and he knows who I am!" she wailed.

"Well, we'll get you out of here early tomorrow morning. I want you to take a nice hot bath. I'll heat up some water for you. You can sleep with me tonight. I've set up an interview for you at a very wealthy estate. It's for tomorrow morning with the butler. You won't be emptying chamber pots either. You'll be a proper lady's maid, speaking proper English. If the murderer figures out you were staying here, why—if he comes looking, you won't be here."

"What if I don't get the position? What if they think I'm too young?"

"I have a feeling they'll be amenable to you, my dear. The butler seemed very nice and was interested. I think the job has been open for some time, and they can't find a suitable maid with proper English."

As she spoke, she filled the hob teapot with water and traipsed outside to pump more water into a large pot.

"Let me do that, Mrs. Sullivan. I'm grateful to you for all your help."

It was still light, with that soft buoyancy of air that was like a lover's kiss on the cheeks.

Ethan, after his final encounter with Elmer, made his way to Bouvier's flat in the middle of the city. He whistled softly into the evening air, feeling no guilt for the evil deed. He was reprobate, thinking evil, good and good, evil.

Wonder if I should cut my ties with Bouvier? I don't care to wind up like ole Dermott. I'll see how the land lies, but I have a feeling of unease meeting Bouvier. He's not going to like it that the girl wasn't there. She could have fetched him a goodly sum. I'm thinking Dermott told me he had stayed at the Eglon afore moving to that bug-infested hotel. I'll tell Bouvier and see if he wants me to go there and check on the girl. I should think he'd just let sleeping dogs lie. I'm certainly not going to look for her.

Dusk had crept in by the time he arrived at Bouvier's apartment building in the middle of the city. Glancing up to the second floor, he saw a dim light in one window, curtains drawn tight. He thought of Bouvier and all the man owned, of his huge manse, and was glad he didn't have to worry about wages for employees and all that came with owning a large establishment such as Bouvier's. He liked living by himself. He threw the toothpick, with which he'd been picking his teeth, into the bushes and made his way up the steps.

He noticed several nameplates listing the building's occupants, but he didn't see Bouvier's. *Must be using an alias, like me. At least I have his address. He's one smart man.*

The stairs to the second floor were narrow, and the door opened immediately at his knock.

Armand drew Ethan into the room and firmly closed the door. Smoke streamed from his nostrils, and he said sharply, "Where's the girl?"

With evil standing before him, Ethan did not recognize it, because his heart was as wicked, or more so.

"She wasn't there." Ethan tried to keep a tremor out of his voice. "Dermott said she went back to the bed and breakfast they were both staying at afore I married them. She was visiting the woman who runs the place. He said he couldn't rightly remember the name of the place, and I didn't press him. I just wanted to get the deed done and be gone." He reached into his vest pocket for the wad of money. "This was what was left in his pocket. I couldn't find anything else of value."

Ethan walked over to Armand and looked him in the eyes when he handed him the money. "It's all there…I took none of it." Ethan didn't mention that Elmer had paid him a handsome bit of the money to perform the wedding.

Armand smoothed the greenbacks out and counted them. "It's a fair amount left. He hadn't spent all that much, which surprises me."

"So…" He scooped up the greenbacks and handed the pile to Ethan. "I'll pay you that amount again if you can find the girl. If you don't want the money, don't worry about it. I have a plan, and I need to work out some details first, but I'd like you to come back at the end of the week. I think I have a proposal to make to you."

He tapped his ash into the tray and gestured Ethan to sit down. Reaching over, he took a case of his best cigars off the table and offered one to Ethan.

Maggie slept fitfully on half of Mrs. Sullivan's double bed. She dreamed the man who murdered Elmer was walking to the clothespress in which she was hiding. She was there in the clothespress but lying in a casket when he opened the door. She started to scream but saw her mother and father standing over her casket, crying. She yelled, "I'm not dead! Mam, Da, I'm not dead!"

She awoke in Mrs. Sullivan's arms, sweat streaming down her face, and she felt distraught and damp all over.

"Do I have night sweats? Am I going to die of lung fever? Oh, Mrs. Sullivan, I'm so scared."

"Hush, child," Mrs. Sullivan said in a soothing voice. She rocked Maggie, who continued to sob. "Hush, baby, you've had a bad dream, is all. You'll be fine, you'll see, sweetheart. You've had so much to bear in the last couple months. I'd have bad dreams too if I had all the things happen to me that you've had. You're a strong girl, Margaret, and you'll make it through this. God will see you through this."

"I don't believe in God!" Maggie was angry with Mrs. Sullivan's words. "I don't believe in Him at all!"

"Hush, child, my hush. It'll be all right. God believes in you, and I will pray someday you come to the place where you will rely on Him. He loves you, Maggie—He loves you more than you will ever be able to comprehend."

"How can you even say that? He…if there is a God…took my best friend, me da, and me mam away from me. How can you say He loves me when He's taken those who love me best in this world away from me?"

"Well, Maggie, to tell you the truth, I don't understand why we have to go through the things we do. My husband was not a kind man, and he never had any time for me. He spent money he didn't have and left me with a huge debt to pay off. I'll do it. I'll pay off his debt, and when I do I know I'll finally be free financially. I've forgiven him, but I forgave him not because I felt like it, but because I was commanded in God's Word to do so. I know God has been with me through everything good or bad that's happened to me. I don't understand it all, but God gave His only son to die on a cross. Jesus bore all the sins of the world. His heart was so pure I cannot imagine the agony He suffered—not only physically, which must have been excruciating, but being pure and holy, no sin in Him. It must have been unbearable to have all our sin heaped on Him. God allowed that because He desired us to have a relationship with Him, and we couldn't before because we are wicked to the core. Those of us who accept Jesus as Savior are able to enjoy a personal relationship with God. I have that, and I'll tell you girl, I wouldn't give it up for anything this world has to offer. His Word tells us to 'taste and see that the Lord is good: blessed is the man who trusteth in him.' I trust Him with every fiber of my being. Now, let's try to get a bit more sleep before we start a new day."

Maggie lay for a long time thinking about Mrs. Sullivan's attitude and words. *I don't have anyone, but I don't need anyone either. After what I've been through, I am quite sure I can make it on my own.* It was a long time before Maggie went back to sleep.

The next morning, right after breakfast, Mrs. Sullivan took her flatiron and placed it on the woodstove to heat. She pressed wrinkles out of Maggie's best black dress as she thought about their conversation during the night. She said a prayer for Maggie to come to a saving knowledge of Jesus Christ. She shook the dress out and hung it on a padded hanger. She went back to her bedroom, wondering if she should say anything to Maggie about the possibility of having a child. She decided she shouldn't. *It simply isn't the thing to do, discussing such personal matters. Better to let sleeping dogs lie.*

Maggie was sitting on Mrs. Sullivan's bed, combing out her thick red hair.

"Here you are, dear. I ironed out your dress. I want you to look your best." She looked at Maggie's face to see if her words had made any impression, but she could tell Maggie wasn't having any of it. The girl looked tired.

"Let me help you, sweetheart. We'll get you all beautiful and pray he will hire you."

"Thank you, Mrs. Sullivan. I know I think I can make it on my own, but I realized that if you hadn't been here to help me last night, I don't know what I would have done. You've helped me, and I hope someday I can repay your kindness to me."

"Thank you, Maggie, but I've only done what most people would do in this instance."

"No, you've been so good. Not everyone is like that. Believe me—I know. I've done a lot of growing up in the past three months, and I don't take what you've done for me for granted."

"Shush, child. I care about you. I care what happens to you, and if you do get this position as lady's maid, I expect you to come visit me on your day off. Now, let's get going. Your appointment is at nine o'clock."

The two left the bed and breakfast via the door to Mrs. Sullivan's private sitting room. No one at the Eglon Bed and Breakfast had seen Maggie since she'd left to marry Mr. Dermott, and Mrs. Sullivan wanted to keep it that way.

It was midmorning before Ethan Brooks made his way to the Eglon. He stood across the street from the bed and breakfast, watching to see if he might catch a glimpse of Maggie. *I wished I'd kept a copy of that fake marriage certificate. For the life of me I can't remember that girl's name, except for Margaret.* He ran through the alphabet trying to see if he could remember her surname, but it was no use. He stood there most of the day but saw nothing that caught his interest. Several people went in and out, but he didn't think to even ask them if they knew Margaret.

This is a waste of my time. I've got other things I want to do, and it doesn't include watching for a little girl to come out of that building. Wonder if I should just break with Bouvier or meet with him and see what his plan is. I don't trust him, that's one sure thing. I don't trust him at all. That bit about there being honor among thieves is not true. There's no honor in me, that's certain, nor Bouvier either, for that matter.

He laughed at his thoughts as he started back to his apartment. *Nope, no honor at all,* and he laughed again.

CHAPTER IX

Remember ye not the former things, neither consider the things of old.
Behold, I will do a new thing; now it shall spring forth;
shall ye not know it? I will even make a way in the wilderness,
and rivers in the desert..

ISAIAH 43:18–19

THE DAY WAS ALREADY WARM. The sun, hidden by an overcast sky, cast its unseen rays onto the cobbles, beating heat into them. It radiated up from their surface, adding to the feeling of mugginess. The air was heavy, not a leaf trembled on the trees, and the sky was cloudless with the portent of even more heat to come.

"Here we are," Mrs. Sullivan said cheerfully. She could feel Maggie's reluctance and hoped to calm her fears.

Maggie, her chin down for most of the trek to the Jamisons', lifted her head to gasp at the lovely home before her. It was a mansion, and in her short twelve years, Maggie had never been inside one. Although quite familiar with the grandeur of the marble-floored halls of Trinity College at Dublin's prestigious university, a private home was quite another matter.

Maggie swallowed hard. She was tired in the extreme. Some of it was from the stress she'd endured for the past few months, some from being frightened out of her wits for the past few days, and some was just a lack of sleep two nights in a row. Striving for some sort of composure, she swallowed.

Maggie and Mrs. Sullivan started up the walk to the imposing mansion. Maggie's mouth went dry, and she wriggled her tongue and sucked on her cheeks, trying for some moisture.

Maggie took a deep breath as Mrs. Sullivan knocked on the door. It opened immediately, as if the butler had been waiting for them, which indeed he had.

"Welcome," he said genially, taking in Maggie's appearance at a glance. He approved her black dress and tight crown of braided red hair.

"My name is Otto. My parents had a sense of humor, as my full name is Otto Graf." He smiled and chuckled, trying to put Maggie at her ease.

She smiled back at him, and her cheeks dipped inward as the dimples surfaced. "My name is Margaret O'Neill, but most folks call me Maggie. A good maid's name, don't you think?" she added cheekily.

Otto needed to interview the girl, but his instincts told him she would be a permanent fixture in the Jamison household. He beckoned them with a gesture and said, "Please follow me." He led them into a magnificent parlor off the foyer, opening one of a set of double doors. "Sit," he commanded as he pulled a fancy rope pull.

Harriet and Maggie sat in ornately carved French armchairs with plush purple cushioning for the backs and seats. He sat facing them in one of two Queen Anne chairs that flanked the fireplace. They were done in a purple damask, the design weaving purple and gray together in an intricate pattern. A large square coffee table separated them, its top the exact shade of gray as the Queen Annes and the drapes at the windows, whose tiebacks were purple velvet.

A petite young woman, not much older than Maggie, replied to his summons by scurrying into the parlor. She was dressed in the same type of livery as Otto, black and white with a pocket emblem of red and silver on the breast pocket, the Jamison crest.

She glanced curiously at Maggie, but asked her boss in a pleasant voice, "Yes, Otto, what would you like?"

"Tea for the three of us, please. And, Millie, some of those scones Bonnie made this morning. There's a good girl."

Millie hurried out to do his bidding. Maggie, observing the interchange, was impressed by the respect she saw between the two. She looked around the room, trying not to show how awed she was. The walls were a creamy off white, and everything looked beautiful and expensive.

Her eyes swung back to Otto, who was waiting patiently for her to finish her perusal, his blue eyes twinkling with good humor.

He smiled. "Now, let's get down to business. How old are you, and what kind of education have you had?"

Maggie sat on the edge of her chair, back ramrod straight, knees together, and one hand in her lap, the other placed over her wrist, careful not to wring them, with the way she felt. Inconspicuously, she drew a deep breath, and in her mind, thanked her mother for proper training. Thinking about her mam, an overwhelming sense of self-composure came over her, and with a quick glance at Harriet, she answered Otto's questions in a manner that would have done her mother proud.

George Baxter was chief inspector for Boston's estimable police force, detective branch. He'd had a busy day and sat back in his desk chair, which could lean back, swivel, and best of all was extremely comfortable. He stretched, clasping his hands behind his head, and thought it was about time to head home.

George was married, but his wife, Adeline, was very ill. He felt helpless in his devastation. He was devoted to Adeline. She was the light of his life. They had no children, and although it was a common sorrow between them, they had a contentment in each other that few couples seemed able to achieve and maintain. He knew if the Lord did not intervene, Adeline was going to die. He faced it with a depth of sorrow nearly unbearable. "Lord," he whispered. He sat up and clasped his hands together on his desk. "Thou knowest what is best, but I still ask for Thy healing hand to touch Adeline. Thou art a God of love and compassion. I ask for that merciful compassion to be with me. I cannot bear the thought of life without my sweet Adeline. I thank Thee, Father."

A knock sounded on the door, and at his bidding, it opened.

"What is it, Taylor?" he asked as the younger man entered.

"Looks to be a murder, sir. Downtown in a cheap hotel. Left it for you, Boss. Nothing's been touched by us. Looks as if his pockets were emptied. The proprietor's not saying a word."

George got up from his desk. "Thanks, Taylor. I'll go and see if there are any clues." He'd taken off his frock coat because of the heat. He donned it, and turned to join Timothy Taylor, who looked at his boss with admiration.

"You always look so well turned-out, Boss. Looks as if you've just walked out of your clothier, sir, if you don't mind me saying so."

"Thank you, Taylor." George didn't elaborate. He'd always had an eye for nice clothes and had saved his money until he could afford the best. After he'd married into money, he no longer had to worry about the cost. He had married for love though. A love more precious than he'd ever dreamed. What had been a great bonus was his adorable wife had been a Cunningham before she married him. She was an only child of one of the wealthiest families in Boston, but he hadn't known it when he fell head over heels in love with her. Money opened many doors for him that would otherwise have been closed. Before Addie became ill, the two of them had attended numerous dinner parties, soirees, and concerts. Socially, they were a sought-after couple, and the hostess who could boast of their attendance had the ear of the society column writer for the *Boston Globe*. George and Adeline had hosted numerous dinner parties themselves. He sighed, picked up his top hat, and left his office, locking the door behind him.

The hotel was a sty. The owner nodded at George and silently led him and Taylor up the narrow stairs. He picked a key from a large ring full of marked ones and unlocked the door. Gesturing them to enter, he stood at the door, burying his nose in the crook of his arm. A wretched stench filled the room.

George pulled a pristine handkerchief out of his breast pocket and held it to his nose. The room was closed up, the window sealed shut from old paint. He picked his way to the bed, careful not to disturb a jumble of papers on the floor. He stood over the body, looking the man up and down. He reached out and pinched the skin on the dead man's wrist.

"He hasn't been dead all that long," he said to Timothy. "The stench is from his bodily fluids."

Taylor nodded. "I know, sir. Happens every time."

He leaned over and moved the man's head. "Broken neck." He looked for any bruising. "No sign of a struggle. This man knew his attacker, I'd say."

He stood and looked around the room. Beside the mess of papers on the floor, there was little to see. He went to the clothespress. The wood was old, and there was a new gash in the wood on the bottom. He opened the door and saw a bit of black material on a nail. He gently lifted it and tucked it into his pocket.

George spoke to the proprietor and asked, "Who was the woman with him?"

"Weren't no woman, but a girl. She couldn't a been much older'n twelve or thirteen at the most. He"—the proprietor jerked his thumb at Elmer—"signed 'em in as Mr. and Mrs. Elmer Dermott." Spitting a stream of tobacco chew into a spittoon in the corner of the hall, he continued to speak, his voice sounding loud in the quiet room.

"Dermott moved in a few days ago, and late yestiday afternoon, he brung the girl with 'im. She looked scared as a rabbit caught by a mountain cat, she did." He chewed, shifted it, and spit again at the spittoon. "I think the girl done it. I talked to Josey, who watches the desk fer me afta dinner. He said a big fella with red hair comed in, asking what room Dermott was in, but Josey said he weren't here more'n five minutes. Josey said the girl walked outta here last evenin', shortly after the red-haired man, loaded down with satchels and nary a word nor a by your leave outta 'er." He nodded his head and said, "Yep, shore as I'm standin' here, that there girl done it."

Timothy Taylor and George Baxter looked at the man, surprised he could talk so much when he hadn't vouchsafed a word until then.

George stared at the body. "No, the girl did not do it." George spoke in a soft tone of voice. "It'd take a big man or someone very strong to snap a neck. Women usually kill by strangulation or suffocation—they don't have the strength to snap a neck like this, and especially if, as you say, she was just a girl. No, it wasn't the girl, but I'd bet my bottom dollar she witnessed the crime." His hand felt in his pocket for the bit of material he'd found.

He spoke to Timothy. "I'd like you to gather up these things." He gestured to the mess of papers. "Please put them on your desk, and I'll collect them in the morning." He addressed the proprietor, "You need to get the mortician over here to collect the body forthwith. If you wait till morning, your entire establishment will smell to high heaven. Any questions?" He folded his handkerchief when he exited the room. His mind was already onto figuring out how he could find the girl who most likely witnessed the murder.

Maggie was hired on the spot.

"I'd like you to start immediately. For a few days, you'll accustom yourself with the house and the way we do things here. I'll set you to work on a few tasks, such as cleaning madam's shoes, airing her dresses and the like. Madam and Mr. Jamison are on a trip and not expected back for another week, but that could change at a moment's notice. We will also have a tailor in to size you and get you a correctly fitting service uniform. You will have three sets and will keep your own clothing for your day off. At this time, your day off will be Tuesday."

He said to Harriet, "I thank you from the bottom of my heart, for you coming here and setting up this appointment. We've had a most difficult time finding someone madam would approve and who has a good command of English."

Eying Maggie, he said. "I'll have Millie show you around. We have quite a large staff, but you will be answerable, staff-wise, only to me. Sorry you cannot have your own room. Millie will share her room with you. Now, let's enjoy our scones, shall we?"

Harriet Sullivan was satisfied with the arrangements and could only hope Maggie would be found suitable by Mrs. Jamison.

After talking about the upcoming elections, Harriet kissed Maggie on the cheek. "I'll expect a visit on Tuesdays from you, young lady." She gave the girl a hug and made her goodbyes.

Maggie saw her to the door, feeling forlorn as she watched her best friend in the world walk down the cobbles.

Otto had come up behind her and squeezed her shoulder to give comfort, but Maggie shrank from his touch, and he wondered what had happened to this young girl.

"Come with me, Maggie. Perhaps you prefer to be called Margaret?"

"No, the only person in the world to ever call me Margaret was my mother, and Mrs. Sullivan a couple times." She'd dropped saying *mam* because she desired, above all things, for this job to work out. She sensed a tranquility in this house she hadn't known since Dublin, and pleasing the butler who was in charge of the staff was of utmost importance.

Otto led Maggie to the kitchen. He gestured to a chair, and she sat down. A woman was backing out of a pantry closet, and he tapped her on the shoulder.

"Bonnie."

She started and nearly dropped the jar of peaches she had in her hand. "Oh, Otto...you gave me a fright, that's certain!"

"I'm sorry. It was not my intention. I want you to meet madam's new lady's maid."

Bonnie carefully placed the jar of peaches on the counter and swiveled around to look at Maggie for the first time.

"Bonnie, head cook, meet Maggie, our newest addition to the Jamison household."

Maggie quickly stood and curtsied to Bonnie. "I am pleased to make your acquaintance, Bonnie."

That one gesture of respect won Bonnie's heart. "I'm happy to meet you, young lady, to be sure."

They smiled at each other, and Otto breathed an inward sigh of relief. Bonnie could be a curmudgeon if she took a dislike to someone. Usually, she simply ignored people she'd taken a dislike to, even when they spoke to her. Otto was pleased that somehow Maggie was "in," so to speak.

"Where's Millie? I'd like her to show Maggie around."

"I sent her out back ta tell Harry ta pull a few carrots fer dinner. She should be back by now."

They heard the back door to the hall open and close, followed by footsteps.

Millie entered the kitchen with a few large carrots in her hands. She glanced over at Otto and Maggie and smiled warmly.

Otto introduced the two of them, and Millie, after rinsing her hands, said, "Come with me, Maggie." She led her out of the kitchen. "I'll take you on the grand tour. What's yer full name?"

"Margaret Regan O'Neill. I have only been in this country a couple months. My father died on board the ship, and my mother just last week. It seems like ages ago that I lived in Dublin, Ireland. How about you? What's your full name?"

"My name's Matilda Leah Parker. I comed from a large family, and on my days off…well, that's where I kin be found. I go home an' help my ma. My pa runned off when my little brother was borned. There's eight of us kids, an' I'm the oldest. I tries ta help my ma all I kin. I'm fifteen, an' I'd love to learn proper English. I want ta be a lady's maid someday. There's good money in it.

"You mean I get paid to live here?"

"You didn't knowed that?"

"No, I didn't. It's a nice bonus to me. I supposed I never thought about it before. We had a maid when I lived in Ireland, and I guess my parents paid her, too, although she lived with us. I always thought of her as family."

Millie showed Maggie the downstairs. Maggie's favorite room was the library.

"Oh, look at all these wonderful books!" she exclaimed.

"You kin read?" Millie asked in astonishment.

"I certainly can! I understand we'll be sharing a room. I can teach you proper English and how to read and write. That's going to be my mission in life for the time being. I'm going to make a proper speaking, educated maid out of you, Millie!"

They grinned at each other.

"I'll make you a maid what knows all the tricks ta get by here."

"*Who knows*, Millie, not *what knows*."

"I'll make you a maid who knows all the tricks ta get by here."

Maggie let the "ta" slide. If she corrected Millie too much, she might become frustrated or angry, and Maggie was hoping they could be friends.

Millie led Maggie up the stairs to the second floor. They peeked into each of the rooms, and there were many.

"These are always kept in readiness in case there's a party or people who jest comed to visit. When there's a party, most people stay here for one or more nights, an' then we's so busy running here and there. Being as how yer a lady's maid, you'll mostly take care of Madam Eloise, but you might jest end up doing some of the other women's hairs if they don't bring their maids. You, Maggie, will end up a going on trips with madam an' doing her hair an' keepin' her clothes an' shoes clean an' wearable. Yer gonna be right busy, I kin tell you that."

She led Maggie up a flight of stairs at the back of the hall that joined with another flight that went down.

"These are the back stairs, an' most times it's the ones we servants use. When the Jamisons is out of town, we kin use the main stairs."

They went up to the third floor. "These is our rooms. It's not in many houses that we gets our own bathin' rooms, but madam, she don't want no stinkin' servants, so's they have bathin' rooms between our bedrooms, an' there's a stove at the end of the hall so's we kin heat our own water and not have to bring it up two flights. An' here's our room. S'not fancy, but it does me jest fine."

"I think I'm going to like it here. I've always helped my mother make my clothes, and I've a good hand when it comes to knitting or crocheting. I didn't want to be a maid at first, but I am pretty sure I'm going to like it here just fine."

CHAPTER X

Cast thy burden upon the LORD, and he shall sustain thee:
he shall never suffer the righteous to be moved.

PSALM 55:22

MAGGIE THRIVED IN HER NEW ENVIRONMENT. The next few days were an introduction into a life of service. She was grateful to Mrs. Sullivan for finding this position for her. Remembering back to Magda, she knew she was fortunate to have landed such a position. She wondered, now, at all the work Magda did for Maggie's family. She'd been a part of it. Maggie knew she'd never be a family member here, but she was well on her way to having Millie for a confidante and friend.

Otto taught Maggie special tricks to take care of Madam Eloise's things, such as cleaning madam's leather shoes with champagne.

"I don't want you drinking this"—he laughed—"but it is a wonder for polishing leather. I heard that at the turn of the century, Beau Brummell shared this tip at his club in London."

"Who was Beau Brummell?"

"Oh goodness. He was an arbiter of fashion for the upper class in England. He was a close friend and companion of the prince regent who would later become King George the Fourth. He himself did not come from the upper class, but he admired their lifestyle and became quite popular. He did away with the more ornate fashion and was a trendsetter for anyone who desired to be someone." Otto smiled. "I understand we even heard of him in Germany and followed his fashions. At any rate, he said champagne was the best polish for leather shoes. It does seem to work well. Beau Brummell died back in the late thirties or maybe early forties, but his name has carried on as a person who understood fashion."

Otto had worked himself up from stableboy to butler in a prestigious household. His knowledge surpassed his formal education, as he borrowed books from the Jamisons' library and read about all kinds of subjects. His desire to improve his mind was insatiable, and a real joy was that in Maggie, he found a willing pupil to impart his learning.

Maggie felt some trepidation for when the Jamisons would return, hoping she would please Madam Eloise. She was thrilled to help Millie with learning to read.

Millie, because it was a deep desire, was an apt pupil.

The two girls loved talking together, sharing snippets from their backgrounds. Because being with Elmer had been so traumatic, Maggie buried the hurt and betrayal deep in her heart. She hoped never ever see the man called Ethan Brooks again, and she never spoke of that time with Millie.

Liberty Alexandra Corlay Bouvier took a deep breath as her maid, Annie, slipped the last diamond-tipped pin into the braids crowning her head. It was a new hairstyle for her, and she looked into the mirror to see if she liked it.

"Oh, Annie, 'tis a work of art! I adore it. Thank you!"

"You're almost ready, ma'am. I fail to understand why you become so nervous before these dinner parties when you are the hostess and certainly the most beautiful woman there."

Liberty had no idea of her beauty. She knew, looking into her mirror, she was certainly passable, but because of her husband's indifference to her, she didn't think she was a showstopper. Winged eyebrows arching over wide green eyes stared back at her. She wrinkled her nose at herself, and Annie laughed.

"I get nervous because I never know what Armand will do at these functions. If he's in a bad temper, he can be—well, Annie, you know how he can be. And because I am undermining his attempts at company takeovers…why, if he knew, he'd…" Her voice trailed off.

She had dressed to please Armand and wore a stylish black brocade with taffeta insets around the hem. The sleeves, slashed every few inches from her shoulder to elbow, revealed bare skin. Her décolletage was cut low, as ordered by Armand, but a wisp of black covered the deep vee and made the dress daring yet modest. Diamonds glittered at her throat, and onyx and diamond-studded earrings completed her attire.

"Yes, ma'am, I know how he can be. I pray tonight is one of those special evenings you enjoy so much."

"So do I, Annie. So do I." She redid the screw on her earring, loosening it. Diamonds glittered in the lamplight. "Say a prayer, Annie," she said, taking a deep breath. "Here I go."

"I'll pray, madam." Annie watched as her mistress descended the stairs as if she were a queen. Her head held high and her back straight, Annie thought she looked gorgeous.

Liberty entered the parlor, and talk hushed at her appearance. Armand, his back to her, stiffened when he sensed she'd entered the room. He kissed the hand of his next victim's wife and turned to greet his own. He strode to the doorway, knowing he was the envy of many a man there.

"My dear." He spoke softly so no one could hear. "We've been waiting an abominably long time for you to show yourself. You ever come down this late again, and I'll make sure you will regret it. Do you understand me?"

Liberty nodded her head. "Of course, Armand. I'm sorry if I kept you waiting."

He kissed her hand for show and straightening up, he spoke to his guests. "Madam Bouvier and I welcome each of you to this evening's festivities. Please make yourselves at home and enjoy an evening planned for your entertainment."

Sigmund stretched to his full height in the doorway and made his announcement. "Dinner is served."

Couples filed into the dining room, looking for their names on porcelain nameplates at the table settings. Elegant candelabras graced the tabletop, interspersed with camellias, their lovely scent permeating the room. Three chandeliers hung over the lengthy table, casting a glow of elegance over the scene.

Too many camellias. Their scent is too heady for so many guests.

Liberty had little to do with hostessing. Armand took care of all the arrangements, and his guests were nearly all his sycophants—friends who stood to profit if they found favor with Armand. As she moved away from the man who'd escorted her into the dining room, she stood behind her chair, waiting for her guests to find their places. She glanced to her right and was delighted to see Lars Jensen, the journalist who wrote a popular society column for the *Globe*.

"Good evening, Mr. Jensen!"

"Madam Bouvier." His face lit up. "It's a delight to see you again."

Lars Jensen had wavy blond hair combed straight back from a high brow. His deep-blue eyes smiled into hers, friendly but not overbearingly so. He was dressed very much for the evening, his cravat perfect.

"Once again, I must say I feel privileged to sit next to you. Of all the dinner parties, concerts, and soirees I attend for the job, I enjoy a scintillating conversation with you as the best way to spend an evening."

They chatted about inconsequential matters for a few minutes while the soup starter was being served. Liberty turned to the man on her left, but he was engaged in conversation with the pretty blonde on his left.

Once they began to spoon the soup, Lars launched into his political views on the upcoming elections.

"I have listened to both Tilden and Hayes. I am finding it difficult deciding for whom to vote."

"I understand your dilemma. Samuel J. Tilden is quite popular, but I like some of the ideas postulated by Rutherford B. Hayes, and I think he'd be true to his promise to loosen the Reconstruction's restrictions on the Southern states. It's time, don't you think?"

Liberty sparkled with enthusiasm, and she nearly forgot she wanted to warn Mr. Smithson that her husband had designs on his business.

The Jamison house had been cleaned from top to bottom. Bonnie had been cooking since early morning, and the kitchen smelled so heavenly that Maggie's mouth would not stop watering. There was a feeling of excitement within the household. Mr. and Mrs. Jamison were returning sometime in the afternoon, and everyone had jobs to finish.

Otto had taken Maggie under his wing, showing her how to clean madam's hairbrushes, combs, and hairpins. Although Maggie knew how to iron, he gave her tips on what materials could stand the hot flatiron and which ones she'd need to have a cooler one for. He demonstrated how to iron ruffles and how to air madam's clothes and what chemicals to use to sponge off spots. He had her practice on Millie's hair, styles he knew Mrs. Jamison liked. Otto had taken a shine to Maggie, knowing she was a willing pupil and proving herself to be a hard worker.

Maggie's days had been full, and to her surprise, she found she was enjoying herself. She hoped she could make herself indispensable to Mrs. Jamison and that the woman would like her work and keep her on.

Otto had said if there was any problem with Mrs. Jamison, he'd find another spot for her in the household, but Maggie knew she'd end up like Millie, constantly cleaning and emptying chamber pots.

Although Maggie felt the Jamison household a place she could call home, she missed her mam and da. Several nights she'd cried herself to sleep. She'd also had nightmares about the man whom she called the bishop in her mind, and also the physical attack on her person from Elmer Dermott. Once she'd awakened to find Millie holding her, trying to wake her up.

This did not go unreported to Otto. Millie told him about the nightmares.

He sent her to get Maggie.

Maggie, expecting to be instructed in yet another task, was surprised when she entered the kitchen and Bonnie told her to meet Otto in the parlor.

He had a tea trolley there with all the trappings, as if she were a Jamison instead of a lady's maid. She stood in the doorway, wondering if he was expecting someone else.

Otto bade her come in, gesturing to a chair directly across from him, where the light from the bay window would illuminate her face. He noticed the faint smudges under her eyes and wondered what was bothering her.

"Good morning, Maggie. Would you care for a cup of tea?"

Maggie gave a sweet curtsy before sitting. "Yes, sir, I'd like that just fine." She sat on the edge of the chair with her back straight, wondering what she might have done. *Is he going to tell me I'm to go? Have I done something I shouldn't have?*

Otto busied himself pouring tea. "Sugar? Milk?"

"Two sugars and a little milk, thank you." Maggie's gray eyes were enormous, and it took all her self-control to keep from wringing her hands. She swallowed, waiting for whatever was to come.

Otto handed her the saucer and saw her hand shake a bit as she placed it on the coffee table in front of her.

"Maggie, are you happy here?"

"Yes—yes I am. I am quite happy here. Am I doing all right? Have I made a mistake or something?"

"No, child. You have been doing a wonderful job. You're a hard worker and a quick learner. I have a feeling Mrs. Jamison is going to be very pleased with you. No, I wanted to talk with you because I understand you are having a difficult time sleeping through the night."

He voiced the statement as a query, his eyebrows raised.

Maggie, flustered, felt the blood creep up her neck and suffuse her cheeks. Her eyes, which had been questioning his, dropped to her lap. She had no idea what she could say. Certainly not the truth. She took her time to respond, as Otto waited patiently.

"I...ah...I miss my mother." Her eyes filled with tears, and she tried her best to hold them back, but they slipped down her cheeks. "I lost my father coming to America just a couple months ago. I h-have nightmares remembering some of the crew wrapping his body in canvas, tying it up, and dropping it over the side of the ship. It was horrible, and I-I have dreams of fish eating h-him." She swallowed, knowing what she'd said was true, but it certainly wasn't the entire story.

"Would you mind if I prayed for you?"

Maggie looked up into his face, and surprise filled her eyes. "Do you really think it'd help? I don't put much credence in a God who took my best friend and my parents in less than six months, leaving me an orphan with no one."

Otto responded to Maggie's look, his face gentle and caring. "Maggie, you have no idea how much God loves you. I don't have an answer for all that's happened to you, but I do know that God takes special care of the widows and the orphans. You can be sure He is now your father. He led you to us via Mrs. Sullivan."

"Yes, sir. If you say so, sir."

"You don't believe it, do you, Maggie?" Otto leaned back against the chair and took a long draught of his tea. Taking a napkin, he wiped his lips and spoke softly to her. "I am sorry you have had to endure so much. You are young, and I know you are bright. You will see all I have said is true. God is your father, and He will watch over you. And now I will pray." He took one of her hands in both of his and patted the back. "Our gracious Father, how blessed I am to know Your great love. I pray that one day Maggie will know the fullness of life that comes only with a personal relationship with You. You are the author and finisher of our faith. May Maggie feel the comfort only You can supply. I pray You take away her nightmares, and may she feel this is home and we are her family. May Maggie know You are gracious and tender and care about her every need, and may You grant healing from the pain she has suffered in the loss of her friend and parents. We know You suffered much for us. Thank You for Your sacrifice. May we learn each day to love You more. Thank You, Father. Amen."

Maggie looked a bit awed. Otto talked as if God were right there in the room with them. It gave her the shivers, and she sat quiet under Otto's stare.

"Maggie, I won't belabor the point, but if you take nothing away from our time together today, I'd like you to remember that God loves you. You are never entirely alone. Even when life seems darkest, or bad things happen, God is still there. He doesn't want you to have to endure bad things, but we're not puppets for Him to manipulate. He gives us freedom. Because of that freedom, it's abused by many people, and thus bad things happen even to good people."

Maggie nodded her head but decided if there was a God, He didn't like her much.

Otto looked at this girl whose mouth was set into a thin line and knew she was not open to what he'd said. He sighed inwardly and spoke again.

"Well, that's that, then. The Jamisons will be home this afternoon. I have a feeling Mrs. Jamison is going to take a liking to you, Maggie. She's a wonderfully kind lady. If you need any extra help or advice, I'm here for you. Now, let's take our mess into the kitchen and get on with our chores." He smiled and patted Maggie on the head.

Ethan Brooks sat across from Armand in an upstairs, secluded booth of Donatelli's. Lighting in the booth was dim, as the glow of only one glass-covered candle lit the table. Heavy drapes enclosed the two in their own little world.

Their talk was low and secretive as Armand sat watching his henchman picking at his teeth with a toothpick.

"So you're saying you couldn't find the girl? If that's true, I think it best if you move to a new location."

"Why's that?" Brooks had removed the toothpick and rolled a little goo off the end of it between his thumb and forefinger.

"Well," Armand replied, thinking quickly, "I'm thinking if the girl should ever happen to run across you, say on the street or in a store, she might know you had posed falsely as a bishop. I would imagine your face is imprinted on her brain. She won't be thinking highly of you. I don't imagine Dermott was good to her in the twenty-four-plus hours she thinks she was married to him. No, I think it best if you disappeared."

Ethan didn't know if Bouvier meant permanently disappeared, as in dead, or moved to a different location. He was on his guard, and his right hand slipped under the table to finger his gun. Surreptitiously, he loosened his gun, sliding it up from its bed in his holster.

"I have a sweet little position I'd like you to fill in San Francisco, if you're interested," Armand said.

"I'm listening."

"I own a company in San Francisco. It's a salmon company, all on the up and up. I have a man who oversees things and keeps them running. The thing is, I've expanded that company to cover for an operation I call les filles seulement. In English it means girls only." Armand smiled as he continued his explanation. "I run a trafficking ring. I get girls from European ports and have a warehouse in San Francisco where I keep them for shipment. They go out to buyers, mostly in Hong Kong and Chile, but sometimes it's other ports—several in the Far East. I need someone who can keep a tight rein on the men who hold the girls. I'm losing a bit of money because my buyers don't want damaged goods, so to speak. In other words, I need someone I can trust to head up this part of my salmon company."

Ethan grinned as he pushed his gun back into his holster. "I do believe you've found your man. I've been looking to make a change. I have several people searching for me, and not because they're friends." He stuck the toothpick back into his mouth and listened to Armand Bouvier clarify his plans.

CHAPTER XI

Lo, children are an heritage of the LORD:
and the fruit of the womb is his reward..

PSALM 127:3

THE DAY WAS A PERFECT AUTUMN DAY, the air crisp, tinged with the smell of burning leaves. Frost from the night before had melted into diamond beads clinging to stems of grass, creating prisms of light glowing from the earth. The skies overhead had cleared, and the sun shone brightly, as if to welcome everyone within its rays with the last warmth of the year. It was a true Indian summer day.

The Jamison family arrived home in late afternoon, amid much noise. Otto had every servant of the Jamisons, from the lowliest scullery maid to himself, lined up at the door to greet them.

As she lined up next to Millie, Maggie realized she had no idea there were so many personnel. She'd only met a few of the house staff and now realized there were many she'd never seen. The gardener seemed to have his own crew. There was much banter and laughter until the coach-and-four pulled up to the front the mansion. Everyone stood at attention, and all talking ceased.

The head stableman, Dickinson, ran toward the horses and grabbed the bridle of the lead horse. The coach-and-four came to a full stop, and a liveried coachman opened the door. Three boys bounded out. The coachmen held the door wide open with his body and reached a hand toward the nanny—Claire, according to Millie's whisper to Maggie—who held a baby girl in her arms. After helping her down the step of the carriage, he assisted Mr. and Mrs. Grant Jamison out. The older children ran up the walk, passing the line of servants with a loud "Hello, everybody!" They took the wide stairs as fast as they could, clearly excited to see if their rooms were as they had left them. Nanny Claire strode quickly up the walk behind the children, followed by the Jamisons, who ambled arm and arm up to the door.

"Welcome home, Mr. Jamison, Mrs. Jamison." Otto bowed and spoke warmly. "It's a pleasure to have you back again."

Mr. Jamison nodded. "Thank you, Otto. It's nice to get away to have a break from the regular routine, but for me, it's always a pleasure to come home."

Mrs. Jamison went down the line of servants, shaking hands, speaking pleasantly to each. When she got to Maggie, she asked, "And you are new to our employ. What is your name, my dear?"

Maggie dropped a beautiful, full curtsy and replied, "Maggie, madam. My full name is Margaret Regan O'Neill, but you may simply call me Maggie." She grinned and added, "It's a good name for a maid, don't you think?"

Eloise Jamison chuckled. "I do. I do indeed. Otto sent me a telegram telling me he'd hired you. I have a feeling we're going to get along just fine." She smiled at Otto, who, watching the interchange, breathed a sigh of relief.

It'd been quiet in the mansion since Maggie had arrived, but with a baby and three little Jamisons running around, the stately house echoed with laughter and the sound of children's voices. Maggie had not heard that sound since the last time she'd stayed overnight with Clodagh. It warmed her heart.

Mrs. Jamison, as soon as she was in her suite of rooms, rang for Maggie, who hurried up the wide staircase, whispering under her breath, "This is it, Margaret Regan O'Neill. Make a good impression. Oh, I do hope I can remember everything Otto has taught me."

She tapped on the door, and Mrs. Jamison bade her enter.

Maggie entered, closing the door, but she didn't curtsy again. She stood wide eyed, waiting for instructions.

"Come here, Maggie...there's a dear." Eloise Jamison reached out a hand, taking Maggie's cold one into both of hers. "Now, please tell me all about yourself as you help me undress. I feel quite weary from my travels and wish to take a nap. I'll tell you a secret too. I'm pretty sure I'm expecting my fifth baby, and I'm so delighted. I was told years ago that I'd never have children. How wrong that doctor was!" She smiled at Maggie.

"Oh, Mrs. Jamison, how wonderful for you. My mother was only able to have me. I'm sure I was pampered, but I have lovely memories that I can hug to myself and will never lose. My father and mother were so in love with each other, yet I never felt excluded from their love."

"What happened to your parents? I noticed you speak in past tense. You poor dear."

Maggie explained about her father and coming over on the ship to America. The two chatted together as if they were friends.

Maggie was surprised at how comfortable she felt with Mrs. Jamison. She told Mrs. Jamison about losing Clodagh, followed by both her parents, but she omitted everything that had happened to her since leaving Mrs. Sullivan's.

"Oh, child," Mrs. Jamison said. "I have no words to comfort you other than to say I'll pray to God you find peace in your soul. What tragedies you have had to bear."

Maggie could hear the sympathy in her voice, and it was all she could do to hold back the tears filling her eyes. It was with a sense of shock that she realized it hadn't been long since her mam had died. So much had happened in the past couple weeks that she'd lost track of time.

After removing the woman's clothing, she helped slip a nightdress over her head and tucked Mrs. Jamison in as if she were tucking her ill mother in, and said, "You have a good rest now, Mrs. Jamison, and I'll go meet your children." She patted Mrs. Jamison's hand, wondering at how easily the two had bonded.

Maggie gently pulled the door closed and walked slowly down the hall, thinking how well she fit into the household. *Did God really have anything to do with it? I think not. Mrs. Sullivan is the one I need to thank, and Otto…Otto has definitely smoothed the way for me.*

She stood in the open doorway of the children's sitting room, quietly observing the scene before her. A smile spread over her face.

Nanny Claire was sitting on a settee. She looked, to Maggie, to be quite grown up, but she was only eighteen. Her bun was a bit askew and her bodice wrinkled. With two children on one side, another on the other side, and the baby lying on her lap, she sat snuggled in, reading a story to them. She glanced up and stopped the story, and the children looked at her questioningly until they saw Maggie.

"I'm Maggie O'Neill, the new lady's maid. Please, don't let me interrupt. I simply wanted to meet the children, but I can do that some other time."

"No, please do come in, and excuse me for not standing." Claire spoke softly, as she realized Rachel, the little girl on her lap, was sound asleep. "I'm Nanny Claire, and this is Rachel, who is nearly a year old." She waved to a chair. "So you're the new lady's maid. You're young— may I ask how old you are?"

"I'm twelve," Maggie replied as she took a seat on a plush, slightly stained wingback.

"My goodness. Do you come from a large family? Are you helping to support them?"

"No. No, I'm not. In truth, I was an only child. My parents have recently passed away, and finding a position was necessary. Now, who is this?" She smiled at the children, diverting attention from herself.

"Introduce yourselves, children," Claire said.

The eldest, a sturdy boy, slid off the sofa and sketched a little bow. "My name is Grant Leon Jamison the Second, and I'm six years old." He prodded his younger brother, who sat close to Claire and had buried his face into her side.

"C'mon, Tommy. Your s'posed to stand and introduce yourself. If you don't, I'm gonna call you a baby. Babies don't have good manners. They don't know anything, and you do. You're smart, so get up right now!"

Tommy, clearly shy, took his time getting off the settee. He swallowed before he spoke. "I'm Thomas Gene Jamison, and I'm four years old." He motioned to the youngest of the boys. "C'mon, JJ. It's your turn to introduce yourself."

JJ, who'd been sitting wide eyed beside Claire, pulled his thumb out of his mouth, and slid off the sofa on his tummy. He stood with his shoulders held back as far as he could get them, his tummy sticking out. "My name is James Jude Jamison, an' I yam tree years old." He held up three fingers and then made a little bow, grinning at Maggie, knowing he was a darling when he chose to be. "An' my fambly call me JJ. You can call me JJ if you live here."

Maggie grinned right back, her dimples dipping deeply into her cheeks and her gray eyes sparkling with amusement. "I do live here, and I am very pleased to meet all of you. I like your mama, and I am sure you each do her credit. I am amazed at such good manners. I think your nanny, Claire, is doing a wonderful job teaching you how to behave. Now, I need to go, but if your nanny ever needs a break, I'd be happy to read to you or play with you." She backed toward the door and said, "Bye for now." She waved her hand in a farewell, and the boys waved back.

"See you later," Claire said. "And thank you. I just may take you up on your offer." She shifted a bit on the sofa, careful not to awaken Rachel.

Maggie went down to the kitchen and found Otto having a spot of tea. "Is there anything else you'd like me to do? Mrs. Jamison is having a toes-up."

"Sit," he commanded. He rose and poured her a cup of tea.

"Thank you, Otto." She sat down gratefully, wondering why she felt so tired. "I'm beginning to feel as if I'm a family member rather than a maid. It's a nice feeling. I just met Claire and the children. They seem sweet."

"You are a family member here. All staff are family. We can share our talents with one another as well as share our woes, if we wish. And yes, the children are actually a pleasure to be around. They mind and are not spoiled. Now then, we need to talk." He glanced over at Bonnie, who seemed to be engrossed in her cake making.

Otto lowered his voice. "I want to know if you'd like Mondays or Tuesdays for your day off."

"I thought you said Tuesday, but it doesn't matter."

He smiled before answering. "Lady's maids have a more difficult time taking a day off if their employer is a socialite. You are expected to go to overnight dinner parties where you will take care of Mrs. Jamison's needs. You will rub shoulders with maids from extremely wealthy homes where a lady's maid has her own sitting room. That, as you well know, is not the case here. Sometimes Mrs. Jamison will travel, perhaps even to Europe, and you are expected to go with her. You will also be paid for your services. Cooks, nannies, lady's maids, and butler's make a bit more than the average servant. There is a starting pay for each position, and it increases at a prescribed rate. I will pay you every two weeks on a Friday. Do you have any questions?"

"No. At least I don't think so. I had no idea this position would be so enjoyable. I believe I will enjoy serving Mrs. Jamison. She has an amenable demeanor and seems to be as sweet as her children." She took a sip of her tea.

Otto nodded. "Frankly, I don't know of another household in Boston that has such a pleasant atmosphere. I'm sure there must be some, but if there is, I don't know about it. The servants have each other as a source of information. News travels fast among servants, either by their own tongues or from the vendors who come to the back doors."

"Well, I just hope my services will satisfy Mrs. Jamison."

"If you have any questions, you can come to me at any time."

"Thank you, Otto. I appreciate your instructions and guidance, more than you know."

Liberty sat tatting in her sitting room. She'd been up late the night before, hostessing a large dinner party. All the guests had been invited by Armand. Liberty had never been allowed to choose guests for any dinner party. Her father, Jacques Corlay, who was Armand's business partner, had been there with a new woman on his arm. She was beautiful and not much older than Liberty. Sparkling with jewels, she'd hung on Jacques' arm in the parlor before going into the dining room. Liberty had been grateful the woman was dressed appropriately. Not all Jacques' or Armand's guests were modestly attired. Liberty had no doubt the woman her father had brought to dinner was a wealthy widow.

Armand had placed Mrs. Burgess on his right, a place of distinction and honor. Mr. Burgess had been placed on Liberty's right. He seemed a thoughtful sort of man, and the two of them had engaged in an interesting conversation about the upcoming election and the candidates.

After the starter and before the soup, Liberty made her move. She spoke in soft tones about her husband taking over various businesses when those business owners had taken loans from him for expansion. She warned him of a possible takeover of his own business. Once she related the facts to him, he didn't have much to say to her, except to thank her for the information and say that his wife looked to be having the best time of her life. After that, he'd sat in quiet contemplation, observing his wife, who laughed more than he'd seen in years.

After the dinner party, when all the guests had departed, Armand, in a rage, had ranted on about Liberty's lack of hospitality toward Mr. Burgess.

Liberty, now ensconced on a chair of Armand's choosing in her sitting room, had endured a poor night's sleep, tossing and turning. She wondered if Mr. Burgess would expose her warning to Armand. She prayed not, knowing a couple of businessmen had committed suicide rather than face the ruination of their businesses and thus their family's livelihoods.

Liberty sighed as she tatted lace, the shuttle in her hand stilling as she thought about her husband. Armand was out, and she wondered where.

She wove the shuttle over and under the thin threads as she spoke softly into the empty room. "Is he out plotting with my father? I hope Mr. Burgess takes my warning to heart." She slipped into prayer, which she did often. "Lord, could You please soften Armand's heart? I am afraid of him, and I know Your word says to trust You. I do trust You and know Your ways are higher than my ways, and Your thoughts are higher than my thoughts. Still, I look down the years and see only a life of stifled hopes and dreams, living with Armand, unless You save him from his sins. I know, Lord. He must have a willing heart. But don't You even make our hearts willing?" She sighed again and continued to tat, weaving the shuttle back and forth.

Armand had an important meeting with the owner of a large textile manufacturer. He nearly licked his lips, thinking about the increase in his income once he took over the man's business. This was going to take careful planning a—long-term plan. He didn't aim to share this one with Jacques. It was too big.

He rode his horse along the cobblestone walk on his way to a popular establishment, the French Hotel and Restaurant. The French element of Boston could be seen dining there, as the food was haute cuisine. The owner, Luis Levernet, always had special seating for Monsieur Armand Bouvier when he dined there.

He met his future victim with a jovial, spirited welcome.

Maggie thoroughly enjoyed her new place of employment. The Jamisons were wonderful Christian people who lived out their faith in all their relationships. Even the children were well disciplined and a joy to be around. There were many dinner parties, and the Jamisons seemed to be constantly on the go.

Maggie had a calendar her mother had given her, and she marked off the days, surprised to realize two months had gone by. She was so engrossed in her job that she hadn't really paid attention. She sat on the side of her bed, thinking over the past two months.

She helped Mrs. Jamison to dress, sometimes up to five times a day. Mrs. Jamison was a socialite and attended breakfasts, lunches, soirees, teas, and elaborate dinners. Maggie worked hard at sponging off stains, brushing shoes, and keeping Mrs. Jamison looking fresh and better than she'd ever looked. She made sure her mistress rested between events, and when the Jamisons hosted a dinner, the entire staff willingly strove to make sure it was a success.

As she sat staring at her calendar, she realized she hadn't marked off her monthly for the last one. She stared at the dates, knowing she was due for another, and flipped back a page. Her heart thumped heavily in her chest as a sudden realization came over her. I'm expecting a baby. She knew it from things she'd overheard spoken between her mother and Magda. She knew she'd been extremely tired and had blamed it on her new position. Because Mrs. Jamison rested and had told her women who carried babies took naps, Maggie figured now that was why she'd been so tired.

Tears formed in her eyes, and she spoke bitterly into the empty room. "If there is a God, He sure doesn't like me. Why, oh why me? What am I going to do now?" She lay down and sobbed into her pillow.

Chapter XII

And she said, Behold my maid Bilhah, go in unto her;
and she shall bear upon my knees, that I may also have children by her.

GENESIS 30:3

A COUPLE MONTHS PASSED. WINTER was well on its way. A cold wind blew into Boston from the harbor, and the dampness of it cut through heavy scarves and coats. People wrapped up warmly before venturing outside.

Thanksgiving was just around the corner, and the Jamisons were planning an extravagant dinner party for the date.

Grant Jamison tallied up expenditures in his office and was gratified to see his business was doing so well. Cold weather brought more customers for heavy textiles. He was seriously considering expanding the mill and branching out, perhaps setting up another mill in Cambridge, across the Charles River. Cambridge seemed to be exploding with new companies, and businesses were popping up at an ever-increasing rate. He'd talked several times with Armand Bouvier, a prominent Boston lawyer and also a private lender. He thought he just might take out a loan from him.

Maggie could see her tummy beginning to round. She wasn't sleeping well, for worry, stress, and fear had taken hold of her. It was as if a knife was twisting in her gut. She had no idea what she was going to do.

Mrs. Jamison was struggling with her beginning pregnancy and would soon come to her three-month date. She tried her best to not tax herself, taking naps and limiting her night activities. She'd been told after her last baby not to have any more children.

She awoke during the night to find herself cramping. She lay in misery for hours and finally rang for Maggie.

"Maggie dear," Mrs. Jamison gasped. "I want you to get Dr. Anderson…please…don't wake Grant. Wake Otto and have him go with you, or send him. I need the doctor right away, girl! Uhoooo…I think I'm losing this baby. Go!"

Maggie ran to the suite of rooms Otto occupied. She knocked on the door, and Otto appeared, tying a robe around himself.

Maggie related the message, and Otto said, "Go back and stay with Mrs. Jamison. I'll be back as soon as possible. Wake Bonnie and tell her to heat water." He closed the door on her face.

Maggie went up a flight of steps and knocked on another door on the third floor.

Bonnie's door swung open with unusual force. "What is it child? What's wrong?"

"It's Mrs. Jamison! She says she might be losing the baby! Otto is going for Dr. Anderson, and we're going to need hot water." Maggie's eyes filled with tears of sorrow for Mrs. Jamison and also for herself. Her emotions seemed to run high, and she swallowed, struggling for self-control.

"I'll go down immediately. You go back and be with the missus, poor dear."

Maggie didn't even reply. She simply ran back to Mrs. Jamison's room, where she saw the older woman sobbing.

"It's too late…it's too late. I've lost it, Maggie, dear. I've lost it."

Maggie looked in the chamber pot and wanted to retch.

"I wanted another baby. Dr. Anderson said there'd be no more after Rachel. Oh, I so want another baby!" She wailed.

"Mrs. Jamison…you can have mine."

Mrs. Jamison's eyes snapped open. "What did you say, child?"

Maggie swallowed, knowing this could be the end of her employment with the Jamisons. Bravely, she took Mrs. Jamison's hand in her own. "I have quite a story to tell you, when you're ready to hear it, but I am quite sure I am expecting a baby."

Mrs. Jamison's eyebrows rose in astonishment, but she believed the girl. "Take that chamber pot and wrap my baby in newsprint. Don't let anyone see you."

Maggie stared at Mrs. Jamison, transfixed as if glued to the floor.

"Hurry, girl! Maggie! Listen to me! Take that chamber pot, and… and look there in the clothespress. I have a hatbox. Take my little baby and put it in there. We'll bury it later. Hurry, girl!"

Maggie hurried to comply, wondering what Mrs. Jamison was thinking.

"Rinse out the chamber pot and dump it into the sink." Mrs. Jamison felt weak with the loss of blood, but stood. She removed her nightdress.

"Here. Hand me a clean one." She spoke hurriedly as she donned the nightie. "Now, take these sheets and ball them up in the press. Get clean linens at the end of the hall. Hurry. I don't want the doctor to suspect anything. Run, girl!"

Maggie ran and grabbed clean linens. She raced back and remade the bed, tucking the sheets in tightly at the bottom.

Mrs. Jamison crawled into it, thankful for Maggie's competence.

"Now, give me the covers."

Maggie snugged the covers around Mrs. Jamison's shoulders.

"I'm nearly done in Maggie, but tell me your story. All of it, girl!"

Maggie related all that had transpired since her father's death. She left nothing out except the deeper details of the night of her supposed marriage to Elmer.

"I didn't know when Mrs. Sullivan found work for me here that I was expecting a baby. I wouldn't know now if it wasn't for things I wasn't supposed to overhear back in Ireland. My mother and Magda, our maid, would talk sometimes when they thought I couldn't hear. I'm in my third month, Mrs. Jamison. How many months does it take?"

"Nine. Nine months, but sometimes…ohh…shh, shh, here comes the doctor. Hold my hand, child."

Otto tapped on the door for the doctor.

"Enter," Mrs. Jamison said, but her voice quavered, sounding weak. She squeezed Maggie's hand, and before letting it go, took a deep breath.

Dr. Anderson was ushered into the room by Otto, who barely peeked in before he closed the door. Seeing Maggie standing close to the bed seemed to reassure him.

Mrs. Jamison spoke in a softened voice. "I am sorry to get you out of bed at such an hour, Dr. Anderson. False alarm. I am feeling better now."

"Well, I must say, this is a surprise, Eloise. I didn't even know you were expecting another baby. I am quite sure I told you and Grant, no more babies." His bushy eyebrows were raised as he admonished his patient. "And who are you, little girl?"

"This is my personal maid, Maggie, who will watch over me. Thank you for coming, Dr. Anderson, but I want to go to sleep now. I'm extremely tired from all the excitement."

"Not until I examine you, my dear."

"I told you, I'm fine, sir."

Taking out his stethoscope, he tried to divert Mrs. Jamison's attention. "Did you know, Eloise, that doctors used to put their ear to the chest of their patients to listen to their heart? And this"—he waggled his stethoscope—"changed all that. Yes, a doctor way back in 1816 by the name of René Laennec was uncomfortable putting his ear to a young woman's chest, so he rolled some thick paper into a tube shape and was surprised he could hear her heart just fine. Later, he made an instrument that looked a bit like a trumpet and used it, calling it a stethoscope."

"Interesting," Mrs. Jamison said dryly. "But there is nothing wrong with my heart."

"No, but I can also hear your baby's heartbeat."

Eloise Jamison closed her eyes against his knowing ones and thought quickly. "I am fine, Dr. Amos Anderson. I had some cramping earlier, and my maid, Maggie, thought I should send for you. Although young, she is careful of my health." Trying to divert his attention, she asked, "If the stethoscope looked like a trumpet, why does it have two earpieces instead of one, like a trumpet?"

Dr. Anderson smiled widely. "So you were listening to me. Yes, it's quite an achievement. I've studied much about the way some things in the medical profession have progressed. The stethoscope is one of them. In 1851 an Irishman named Arthur Leared made the improvement to a binaural device. And a year later it was refined by George Cammann."

Surreptitiously, Eloise took a deep breath and sat up, swinging her legs over the side of the bed. She stood resolute, trying not to show a sign of weakness.

"Would you care to join me in a hot toddy? I need to get to sleep, and I find a hot toddy the best way to relax and go to sleep."

Dr. Anderson realized his examination had been terminated and wondered why, but he was tired, having delivered two babies on the opposite sides of Boston since noon and having treated a little boy needing numerous stitches in his arm.

"Thank you for the invitation, but I must needs get myself home and to bed. I never know what the morrow may bring, and I am exhausted."

"Again, I'm sorry for the false alarm, Dr. Anderson. I know you give much to so many. Grant will happen by your office to make your time worthwhile, but truly, I am fine." She sat down when her legs began to shake.

Dr. Anderson folded his stethoscope and placed it in his medical bag.

"If you have any more problems, please let me know. You don't want to lose that little one. I am surprised you are not having more problems and pray all goes well for you."

He took his leave, and Eloise slid back into bed. Maggie pulled her covers up over her shoulders, wondering what Mrs. Jamison was thinking.

"Go to the kitchen and tell Bonnie to go back to bed."

As Maggie headed for the door, Mrs. Jamison added, "And tell her I'll have a late breakfast, so she can sleep in if she wants." Tears of emotional stress and physical weakness trailed down Mrs. Jamison's cheeks. She was grateful she'd been able to hold up and fool the doctor, but the trauma of losing her baby was more than she felt she could bear.

Maggie went to the bathing room, wetted a cloth, and went back to wipe the older woman's cheeks. "I meant what I said," she told Mrs. Jamison. "You can have my baby."

"We will make a plan," Mrs. Jamison said. "I don't know what just yet. I am exhausted, but we'll think of something." She patted Maggie's hand. "I am blessed to have you, girl. Truly blessed."

Liberty heard Armand in the foyer but couldn't hear what he said, although his voice sounded curt with irritation. Soft steps padded outside her sitting room door. She took a deep breath and let it out in an effort to calm her nerves. Trepidation climbed up her spine when she heard a tap on the door, but it wasn't Armand. He pushed unopened doors unannounced. Before she could respond to the knock, she heard the door to the library slam shut.

"Please enter." Liberty spoke the words after swallowing down her fear and saying a quick prayer.

Sigmund opened the door on silent hinges, and spoke softly. "Monsieur wishes to see you in the library, madam." His voice and demeanor never gave away his feelings. Liberty had no idea what Sigmund thought of his employer, or her for that matter. He was discreet and silent, one of the reasons Armand kept him. Liberty knew too that Armand, being from France, loved to lord it over Sigmund, who was German.

"Thank you, Sigmund." She rose sedately and leisurely strolled to the library door across the hall from her sitting room. She felt Sigmund's eyes on her and wondered what he was thinking. As her hand reached for the doorknob, she breathed another quick prayer for wisdom in dealing with Armand.

She was startled to see Sigmund take the knob before her stretched-out hand and open the door for her.

"Thank you, Sigmund," she said again.

He nodded and stood aside for her to enter. She started toward Armand's desk and heard the door close gently but firmly behind her.

Liberty stood at Armand's desk, but her husband acted as if she hadn't entered the room. A small flame of anger curled in her stomach at his lack of manners and rude attitude.

"What do you want, sir?" Although she spoke softly, her voice sounded loud in the quiet of the library.

"Sit!" Armand spoke without looking up. He never liked anyone standing over him. He continued to peruse a paper he was looking at, making his wife sit and wonder what he would say. He flipped the paper over, but he really had no idea what it said. He glanced at Liberty, but her head was averted as she looked at the heavy drapes that blocked all light or any prying eyes.

"So, my dear." Armand sat with his elbows on his desk. He templed his hands together and rested his chin on them. "Mr. Burgess had no time for me today. Why is that? What did you say to him? I noticed the two of you talking quite pleasantly, and then suddenly, nothing. If I didn't know better, I would think you'd snubbed him or offended him in some way."

"We had a nice conversation, Armand. We discussed the upcoming election and the candidates. Mr. Burgess has actually met Mr. Rutherford Hayes."

"What say you about his silence before the entrée? The two of you were having such a nice chat during the soup." He sneered. "Then all the sudden, he seemed to have nothing to say."

Liberty veiled her moss-green eyes with her lashes to hide her thoughts. She looked up abruptly and smiled into his cold, inimical face. She spoke boldly. "Do you really care to hear why he stopped talking to me?"

Armand stood unexpectedly, reaching out for the arm of his chair when it began to wheel away from his violent movement.

"I told you, I want to know!" His voice was raised in rage. He seemed to lose control when it came to Liberty. With anyone else, he always felt in command, but with his wife, his emotions were unpredictable. There was some part of her that she kept aloof from him. He couldn't break her, hard as he'd tried.

"All right, Armand, I'll tell you. Mr. Burgess' last words during dinner were, 'It looks as if my wife is having the best time of her life.' I don't think he liked it."

Armand picked up his brass paperweight and threw it, missing a Ming vase by inches. The brass piece crashed to the floor, marring the wood's surface.

"You are not attending dinners to think! Your job is to entertain! That will be all! Get out of my sight!"

Liberty rose, the pulse beating rapidly in her throat—the only evidence of her feelings. She moved toward the library door, her shoulders well back, head held high, and her step measured. To Armand she looked the epitome of self-composure, and it angered him. "Get out!" he screamed.

Liberty's step hastened, and as she opened the door, she glanced back at Armand.

He was ripping in two the paper containing his plans for Mr. Burgess' company.

Pulling up her skirts, Liberty hurried up the stairs, and thinking no one was about, she took them two at a time. She didn't see Sigmund watching her. She ran down the hall to her rooms and closed the door silently. She took a deep breath as she walked over to the calendar she used as a diary. She made a little round dot in the left corner each day a company escaped Armand's clutches. She looked back to see the last time Armand had screamed at her, signified by a tiny x. It was over a month before, but there were many black dots on the calendar.

Maggie had a difficult time getting to sleep. After everything had settled down, she'd returned to Mrs. Jamison's room to find her sobbing into her pillow.

Maggie went to the bathing room and filled a glass from the water jug next to the sink. She took the woman into her arms and rocked her as she were the child and Maggie her mother.

"I'm so sorry for your loss, madam—so, so sorry." She rubbed the older woman's back.

Eloise pulled away, dabbing at her eyes, and blowing her nose. She sniffed.

"Thank you, Maggie. Your words are a comfort to my heart. I am thankful to have you as my personal maid. I don't know what I'd do without you. I have decided we shall sail to Europe. Just you and me, Maggie girl. We shall stay until your baby is born, and I...I shall take your baby if you feel the same way then as you do now."

"I will, Mrs. Jamison. Believe me—I will. I wish it was me who lost her baby tonight, not you." Maggie's lips were set in a determined line. "Do you know when we'd leave? I know I'm not showing much yet, not that anyone else would notice, but I need to let Mrs. Sullivan know. I visit her on my day off. She knows all about my story, as much as you do, except she doesn't know I'm expecting a baby. You are the first and only person I will ever tell about it. It's a good plan you have. I can have my baby in Europe, and no one will be the wiser. Thank you, madam. I thank you from the bottom of my heart."

Maggie started to get up to leave, but Mrs. Jamison forestalled her.

"Maggie, I want you to take that hatbox and bury it, or better yet, take it to the churchyard and leave it on the step. The minister will see to it that it's buried. Perhaps in an obscure place, but at least buried."

"Madam, I'll do it right now. Everyone is abed, and I'll just slip out the door with no one the wiser. What about the bed linens?" As she spoke, Maggie went to the clothespress and retrieved the box. Her hand shook, and she spun around so Mrs. Jamison wouldn't see. She loathed the contents and wished not to do the deed, but out of respect for her mistress, she hastened to do her bidding.

"Take them too. You can leave them with the hatbox. There's no monogram on them."

"Rest now, madam. I'll see you later this morning or this afternoon, whenever you ring for me. Please get some sleep, and drink some of that water. You'll need liquid after what you've been through tonight." Opening the heavy door, she whispered, "Good night, madam."

CHAPTER XIII

The LORD gave, and the LORD hath taken away;
blessed be the name of the LORD.

JOB 1:21b

"**B**UT, GRANT, DARLING, I NEED THIS TIME alone. I want to go, and Maggie will attend to all my needs. Please reconsider."

"I hear what you're saying, Eloise, but Maggie is just a girl. She could be your daughter. With you expecting a baby Dr. Anderson said you should never have in the first place…no and no. I'm simply not comfortable with having you gallivanting around Europe."

"Grant, please understand. I've another two months before my confinement. I must return invitations in kind, and I'm tired. I'm tired of all the parties and entertaining. I need to get away, and I'm not going to travel all over Europe. I think I'll go to Denmark and stay there. If I feel like it, I'll look up your relatives. If I don't feel like it, I won't. I'll bury myself near Amalienborg Palace and confine myself when I begin to show. I've always enjoyed Copenhagen, and you know they are an advanced nation with up-to-date medical doctors, should I have any problems. Please, Grant. I'm begging you. Please let me go."

Grant looked at his wife with surprise clearly evident in his eyes. He'd never heard his wife beg for anything. She was a proud woman. As he perused her face, he realized she looked tired. There were dark smudges under blue eyes misted with tears. Her eyes usually sparkled with life, and his heart smote him for being unchivalrous.

He sighed heavily. "I'll not say yay or nay just yet. Let me sleep on it, and I'll give you my answer on the morrow."

Eloise stood and looked down at her husband. How she loved him! She hated deceiving him this way. She was tired and felt the loss of her baby deeply. It was the first time she'd kept anything of real import from him. She'd always shared all her deeply felt ideas or emotions with him, and it pained her to keep such a loss to herself. The only one she could talk to was Maggie, who was a boon to her heart. The young girl had also experienced deep loss.

"I'll say good night then, my dear."

Grant rose at her words and hugged her to himself. He felt something was different couldn't put his finger on it.

"Good night, Eloise. I promise I'll give you an answer in the morning. I love you and miss you when you travel without me. Frankly, I don't wish for you to go, but I can't get away just now. I am in the midst of figuring if an expansion is the way our business should go. I would be out on a limb with the loan, but I know a lawyer who is also a creditor. I need to do an in-depth study of our company to see if it is feasible."

Eloise, a wry grin on her face, said, "Grant, you know I support you in whatever you decide, but I wouldn't want us to upset the applecart, so to speak. It seems to me we are doing quite well with the way things are now."

"Yes, in truth, we are."

Maggie, who had been dreading the trip, stood at the rail of the Cunard ocean liner and thought how completely different this journey was from the one she'd endured with her parents only a few short months before. She was now in the lap of luxury. She had her own cabin, and the accoutrements were beautiful. There were several other people traveling with servants, but those servants were ensconced belowdecks, sharing cramped quarters. She felt fortunate Mrs. Jamison treated her as if she were family.

She thought back to her life in Ireland and growing up there, how her days had seemed endlessly the same for twelve years. So much had happened to her since leaving that fair isle, she felt as if she were a different person. She looked back with longing to the little girl she had been.

Mrs. Jamison was lying down, as she'd experienced extreme depression and was exhausted from keeping up a pose of good health and happiness in front of her husband. She knew Grant had sensed something, but she had done her best to keep things normal until the ship departed. After the ship left harbor, she had nearly collapsed. Maggie assisted her to her cabin and disrobed her, helping her into a nightdress. Maggie felt distressed at Mrs. Jamison's wracking sobs.

"Are you sure you are all right? Can I get you something? I could go to the lounge and get a drink for you if you wish."

"N-no. I'll be fine, but it's as you said to me. 'Time is a healer of the pain, but the loss is never healed.' I just need more time to get over this horrible feeling of knowing I'll never carry a baby to full term again. I was so happy carrying that baby, and now I am bereft."

"I think I know how you feel, but a body can never know the depth of another's pain. I'll leave you for now, hoping you will rest, and I'll come back to check on you every so often."

"That's fine, dear. You are a boon to my heart, and no mistake!" She closed her eyes, but then they flew open. "How are you feeling? You look tired. Why don't you lie down for a bit too?"

"I may, but first I'm going to explore and see what is available to us." Maggie left after tucking Mrs. Jamison in as if she were quite ill or a child herself.

Maggie stood at the rail. She had explored the ship, and there was a large game room as well as the lounge. Mrs. Jamison said the captain had invited them to dine at his table that evening. Maggie was surprised that she was included in the invitation.

She stared out at the seemingly endless ocean trying to analyze her feelings. She had felt some butterfly movement in her tummy and wondered if it was the baby or just her digestion.

I don't hate this baby, but I don't love it, that's for sure. I hate Elmer for what he did to me. Such wickedness. I'm glad, glad, glad he's dead! I hate that other man, Ethan Brooks, too. Evil, that's what he is, posing as a bishop and acting as if he had the authority to marry us. I wish he were dead too. He's a murderer! What a farce it all was. Now, here I am, damaged goods. If truth be told about me, I'll never be married. I suppose I should realize I'll never have a husband or family. I'm worth nothing to anyone except Mrs. Jamison. She is my lifeline to survival, and I will survive. I'll make myself so indispensable to her, she'll never want anyone else as her personal servant.

Liberty sat in a most uncomfortable chair in her private sitting room. Because no one was around, her legs were curled up underneath her, and she leaned her head back against the hard padding of the wingback, letting her tatting drop to her lap. It was a dark, depressing room. The wall color looked like split pea soup. Armand had had a decorator come in and do all the interior of the manse. The rooms looked dark, stiff, and uncomfortable. The paintings on the sitting room walls were dull and unremarkable. She'd been tatting a doily as a house gift for a dinner invitation Armand had told her they were to attend. She didn't care for Armand's friends and dreaded the dinner party. Conversation usually centered around someone not present. Liberty wasn't a person who liked small talk or gossip.

But a redeeming factor was that many times she was able to warn the next victim of Armand's and her father's perfidious plan to take over the man's company. It was a dangerous venture for Liberty, and she knew if any of the men spoke to Armand or Jacques about it, she could end up locked in her room for the rest of her life.

As she sat there, her thoughts swung to Annie, her personal maid. She wasn't well, but Liberty could not get her to go to the doctor. Annie was afraid of doctors. To her, they spelled a death sentence because her mother had died after seeing a doctor. Liberty had tried to explain to Annie that her mother had already been very ill before seeing the doctor, but it made no difference. Annie was adamant—she would not go.

Liberty sighed, and because she felt oppressed by her circumstances, she began to pray. She knew God was in control of her life. She felt His grace and goodness. Sometimes she didn't, but she knew He was always there, leading and guiding her. She didn't go by her feelings but by her knowledge of Him through the Scriptures and prayer. If she went by her feelings, she would hate Armand and her father. Instead, she felt a sense of mourning for them, that their only goals were self-serving. There could be no joy in swindling other people just to accumulate more money, and people who thought money brought joy were to be pitied. People who despised money were also foolish. Money made things easier and opened doors that those in poverty could never enjoy. People who scoffed about money were just expressing their sour-grape attitude. The real problem for Jacques and Armand was their love of money. Liberty's Bible spoke about it in First Timothy, saying that "the love of money is the root of all evil."

"Lord," she whispered, "I lift Armand and Jacques up to You. I pray You would soften their hearts and help them to accept You into their lives, that their goal would be to do good and not evil. To follow Your will and way is the path to true joy. Nothing else can satisfy our souls the way You are able. You have created within us the desire to worship, but to worship You, not anything else but You." She sighed again and began to pray for Annie.

Ethan Brooks arrived into San Francisco on a blustery day. Overcast skies, with no hint of blue, promised rain in the offing.

Hailing a hansom cab, he stopped to look up at the cabbie before stepping in.

"Would you please be so kind as to direct me to a reputable boarding house? I am new here in town and plan to stay for some time." As he spoke, he was loading his trunk into the back catchall of the cab.

"I just happen to know of one not far from here."

The cabby seemed an affable type, and Ethan grinned at him. "Thanks. I'll rely on your excellent taste, my good man." He climbed into the hansom, sat back, and leaned his head against the headrest, closing his eyes in exhaustion. It had been a long trip west. The train ride hadn't been too bad, but there was a woman on the train who wouldn't stop talking. Every time he went to eat or stroll to stretch his legs, there she was right at his heels, blathering about things he didn't care to hear. He'd snubbed her, been rude, and finally at his wits end, told her to leave him alone, all to no avail. It had ruined the trip for him.

Ethan decided to take a couple days and acquaint himself with the city before he showed up at the salmon cannery as the new president. *I have my work cut out for me, that's for sure. Armand has assured me the monetary benefits will exceed my expectations.*

Ethan hardly had time to think before the hansom was pulling up to a two-storied building with clapboard siding. *Looks decent, and that's exactly what I need, a decent cover for indecent business.* He smiled to himself as he reached for a greenback to pay and tip the cabbie.

A frightful storm had taken control of the ship. Rain beat heavily on the deck, and all hands were working to lower the masts and lay tarpaulin over the hatches and batten them down with strips of wood. The ship was corkscrewing in the treacherous waters.

Maggie was thankful she didn't have problems with seasickness. She sat in her cabin wondering how Mrs. Jamison was faring. She donned a shawl and let herself out of her cabin to tend to Mrs. Jamison, who seemed to be in better spirits. The wind tore at the door, and it was difficult to close, but the wind cavorted, and the door slammed shut.

Maggie started toward Mrs. Jamison's cabin. Suddenly, her ankle twisted as her foot tripped over a thick piece of hemp. She fell heavily as the ship listed. Sliding on the wet decking, her body slammed into the side of the ship, bounced off, and slid again, only to slam into the wall once more. She slid again, her head connected with an iron capstan, and she knew no more.

Eloise Jamison was feeling much better. She'd prayed and prayed for another baby, and when she'd realized she was enceinte, she'd been ecstatic. Not so, Grant Jamison.

Grant hadn't been happy at all. He'd been worried sick.

I know Dr. Anderson said no more babies, but I wanted one so badly. Although I feel guilty about deceiving Grant, he'd never approve of me taking Maggie's baby for my own. I am grateful to Maggie for this chance to hold another baby in my arms.

Eloise sat in an easy chair in her stateroom, feeling a bit queasy, but not really seasick. The tossing and corkscrewing of the ship made for uneasy walking, and she stayed seated. *I do hope Maggie won't try to check on me. Knowing that sweet girl, she most likely will. I'll be glad for her company. She's really beginning to show if you look at her closely. She's a good girl, and I am right sorry for what has happened to her in her young life. What tragedy she has suffered!*

She sat, her hands busy with knitting a bunting for the new baby. *Wonder…will she have a boy or a girl? I don't know why I am so obsessed with having another baby, but I am.*

There was a loud bang on the door, and it startled Mrs. Jamison out of her reverie. A ship's officer kicked the door open with his Wellington-booted foot. In his arms, he carried a bundle.

"Sorry, madam, but our sickroom is full and this being your niece, we thought you could perhaps keep her in here. She's had a terrible accident, but the doctor hasn't seen her yet." He laid Maggie, drenched and dirty, on the bed. "She fell and slid down the deck, hitting the side several times. I'm quite sure she's full of slivers, broken her ankle, and as you can see, she's been knocked unconscious. The doctor has been notified." He grabbed for the rail on a sidewall as the ship listed heavily. "As I was saying, the doctor's busy, but he knows your cabin number and will see to her as soon as he can. I'm sorry, madam, to leave you like this, but all hands are needed on deck." With that statement he left abruptly, without so much as a by your leave.

Eloise's face was ashen as she made her way to where Maggie lay.

Maggie, wet and disheveled, opened her eyes slowly, but shut them immediately as the hammers in her head began a staccato beat on her brain. She started to speak but made no sound. She licked her lips and tried again.

"Wha...what happened?" Putting her hand to her brow, she added, "Oh, my head is pounding. Oh, Mrs. Jamison, I'm so sorry! I was coming to che—ahhh! Oh my goodness! Oh...the pain. Make it stop, Mrs. Jamison!" She curled up in a fetal position.

Eloise knew what was coming. "Oh my poor, poor girl." Eloise went to a trunk and took out a soft linen nightdress, tears dripping off her face. She pawed through her dresses, looking for the one she liked least, and shook it out. Helping Maggie up, she helped her out of her clothes and into the nightie. It was voluminous. She spread the gown she'd found over the bed linens, and as she had Maggie lean back onto the pillows, she pulled the back of the nightdress up and over her pillow.

Maggie began to cry as she realized what was happening. The pain in her head and ankle was nothing compared to the cramping pain as she lost the life growing within her.

Eloise was glad her stateroom was equipped with several jugs of water. She folded up the dress, cleaned everything up as best as she could, sobbing for the loss of life.

The storm was beginning to abate. Eloise took the balled-up dress, opened the door to her stateroom, and hurried to the rail. Throwing the dress out as far as she was able, she watched as it swirled and swirled, puffed up with air, and finally sank to the bottom of the ocean.

Ethan Brooks stood near his desk in Armand Bouvier's San Francisco Salmon Company. He was going to need a new bookkeeper, and quite soon to his way of reckoning.

That weasel who's been doing the books has just signed his death warrant, I'll wager. He reached over and picked up a paperweight, throwing it across the room, anger emanating from every line of his body, which was stiff with rage. *Coming in here and presenting me with his plan to blackmail me. Yep, think he's due for a long walk down a short dock.*

There was a knock on the door, and Ethan yelled, "Enter!" He was not in the mood to talk to anyone.

It was his partner, albeit lesser partner, Saul Simmons, who was nearly illiterate but clothed himself like the best dressed in San Francisco. He looked a stark contrast to Ethan, who was greasy and rumpled but had an extensive vocabulary and educated manner of speech.

If he kept his trap shut, a body would think he's a real dandy, Ethan thought.

"What are you doing here?" Ethan's voice was almost a hiss. "I thought I told you to meet that ship!"

Simmons' voice was whiny. "I bin waitin' an' waitin', but it ain't never showed up."

"Is the warehouse ready for those girls?"

"Yep, bin ready now fer 'bout two days, I reckon."

Ethan, his voice clipped said, "You get your body back down there and wait!"

CHAPTER XIV

But he that is greatest among you
shall be your servant.

MATTHEW 23:11

IT WAS THE END OF MAY 1878. Maggie had turned fourteen on the twelfth. She was becoming a fetching young lady. She'd never been gangly, but now with her blaze of red hair done up and her figure filling out, she was quite pretty.

The trauma she and Mrs. Jamison had suffered two years previously had bonded them like nothing else could have. Maggie would do anything for Mrs. Jamison, who treated her as if she were a beloved daughter.

She'd been with the Jamisons for two years. Time seemed to fly as she was kept busy caring for Mrs. Jamison. There seemed an endless supply of clothes needing repair—a rip here, a button there, shoes to be brushed, underwear needing a new hook.

Sighing deeply, her gray eyes were shadowed by her concern for the Jamison household. She was down on her knees, brushing mud off a narrow leather boot.

Mrs. Jamison seems perpetually worried about Mr. Jamison. This loan he's taking out from some lawyer sounds like it's on the up and up, but Mr. Jamison seems a bit nervous about it. Mrs. Jamison said he's losing sleep over it. She's told him she doesn't want him to upset the applecart, that they have plenty of money, but

Mr. Jamison seems bent on expanding his company. Mrs. Jamison said he has five years to pay it back. He is a good man, and I hope everything works out well for him.

She balled up the paper with the dried mud in it and threw it into the fireplace. Brushing off her skirts, she checked one more time to make sure she was finished with Mrs. Jamison's wardrobe. Opening the clothespress, she examined a few more dresses.

Done. Think I'll go down and see what Otto is doing. Mayhap I can help him.

Liberty Alexandra Bouvier, helped by a frail Annie, dressed for her twenty-fifth birthday party. She wondered about Armand throwing such a gala affair for her and yet knew it wasn't for her. He'd invited all his friends. As she thought about this, she realized she had no real friends here in Boston. *A body can only have friends if they share time together—bonding. Annie is my closest friend and confidante. I worry about her. She insists she's fine, but I know full well she's not. I will have a doctor come look at her.*

"You look stunning, madam," Annie said, her voice expressing the pride she felt in her mistress.

"Thank you! I am not looking forward to this evening. Armand has been acting a bit strange lately." She laughed with no joy in it. "Stranger than normal, I suppose I should say. He's up to something, but I haven't figured out what it is. Today, he returned from going into the city, looking as if he was the cat that ate the canary." She observed her profile in the mirror. "Oh, Annie, I like what you've done with my hair! Those pearl-headed pins are beautiful. You shouldn't spend your hard-earned money on me, but I thank you! They are a lovely birthday present, and I shall treasure them."

"You are welcome, madam. I love your hair all up like that. In truth, I like it down too. You have such beautiful hair—the copper color is gorgeous."

Liberty's dress was midnight blue velvet. Slashes in the sleeves and hem revealed creamy satin. The ribbon tied at her waist accentuated her gorgeous figure. A wisp of the creamy satin covered her décolletage, giving her the more modest appearance she desired, yet seemingly satisfying Armand's command to wear more revealing attire. Her mother's three-strand pearl necklace and earrings were her only adornment besides the pearl pins inserted into the intricate French braid of her hair.

She took a deep breath and said, "I suppose I'm ready. Wish me luck, Annie!"

Annie's pinched face looked gray in the lamplight, but her eyes glowed with admiration for her mistress. "You are so beautiful, madam, and I wish you a happy birthday and the best of luck."

"Thank you." Liberty closed the door behind her, straightened her back, and taking a deep breath, descended the stairs to join Armand's guest and celebrate her birthday.

After she left, Annie picked up the invitation and read it again. Softly she said, "This party is not for madam. It's to show off, as if he cared about her. I saw the painting he bought, and I know how evil he is. There is some kind of motive behind this party."

In honor of Liberty Alexandra Bouvier's
twenty-fifth birthday, you are invited to a gala affair.
Please come. Help us celebrate this special day
with dinner and dancing the night away.
August 8, 1878.
(No gifts!)
Répondez S'il Vous Plaît.

She placed the card back on Liberty's dressing table and sighed deeply. *Poor madam. Wonder who she will get to replace me? The pain is unbearable, and I don't know how long I can keep up the facade of well-being.* Annie knew she was dying.

Liberty awoke, stretched, and lay thinking about the night before. The painting was sitting on a chair next to her bed. She rolled over onto her side and stared at it. She loved it. Armand had given it to her. He did it as an extravagant exhibition for all his friends who were there, but it could not diminish the fact that the picture was perfect.

It had been a grand affair, the painting covered with a sheet in the foyer. Cook had outdone herself, concocting food that was *crème de la crème*. Although the guests had been handpicked by Armand, he'd included Lars Jensen, which in itself had been a gift to her.

Liberty loved it when he was present at a dinner party they hosted. He was such a knowledgeable man. Armand had not been pleased the first time he'd invited him. Lars had written an article for the social column the next day, but it had featured Liberty instead of Armand. Armand had made a horrible scene during that dinner, but since then, he'd been on his best behavior when entertaining Lars Jensen.

She stretched again and smiled at her painting. She remembered what her mother had told her about Jacob Ruisdael. The painter had been taught by his own father and uncle. Both had been landscape artists and taught Jacob all they knew. *Poor man. He'd died in the Netherlands, with very little to his name.*

Mother taught me much about paintings and painters, and also I learned a lot from attending Swiss boarding school. Since mother studied art, she taught me about texture, line, shape, form, color, space—oh so many things. Liberty smiled. *This windmill picture by Jacob Ruisdael,* Tower Mill at Wijk bij Duurstede, *is so beautiful.*

The painting contained muted colors but wasn't as dark as many older paintings. It was painted in 1670. *It's amazing 'tis so old. The windmill is beautiful with the lighting upon it. It's perfectly perfect!*

Annie came in bearing a tray of food.

"Annie! You should let someone else carry the heavy trays."

"I...I can do this for you, madam." Annie was steadily losing weight. Today, it was even more pronounced. Her maid uniform hung on her.

"Thank you, Annie." The tray she brought in was a breakfast replete with a fluffy omelet, croissants, a bowl of mixed fresh fruit, and coffee that smelled delicious. A rose had been placed on the napkin, and Liberty knew Cook had been out to the garden. She picked it up and smelled it. "Mmm...God certainly makes better-smelling perfume than man does."

Annie smiled wanly. "He certainly does. What are your plans for today, madam? Is there any particular dress you'd like to wear?"

"I'd like the gray watered silk, please. I'm going to the bank. My grandfather had a great deal of money held in trust for me until my twenty-fifth birthday. I am going to withdraw some of it and invest. I know nothing about money, but I've talked to an acquaintance who was a friend of my mother's—a lawyer. He said he'd help me."

Liberty smiled, her eyes sparkling. She was going to have some money of her own for the first time in her life. Armand had accounts everywhere, and it was not as if she lacked for anything. Any purchases she made were put on a Bouvier account. But now she would be able to invest on her own, with her very own money.

"Annie, I want you to know I'm also calling on the doctor. I want him to come take a look at you, dear girl. You've said you're all right, and I wanted to believe it, but you're not, are you?"

Annie replied, "Oh, miss, I am fine. Please, you don't need do that."

"Yes, yes I do, but you don't have to go to the hospital or anything. He will come here."

Annie left the bedroom and closed the door gently behind her. She was afraid of doctors. Both her parents had died after seeing a doctor. She prayed for God to calm her fears. She knew she was very ill, but she didn't know what it was and didn't care to find out.

Liberty ate the breakfast set before her with relish. She read the newspaper while she ate, but was excited and found it difficult to concentrate on any one article. She flipped to the column by Lars Jensen and read about her own birthday party in the society section. He'd written a good description of the event. She had enjoyed the evening immensely. Having him there had made all the difference.

Annie returned to help her dress. The gray watered silk was one of Liberty's favorites. Chattering to Annie as she laced up her corset, she told her maid all about the events of the night before. Liberty was eager to go to the bank.

Armand had not cared about the price of Liberty's birthday present. It had impressed his friends, and Liberty had been delighted. *Two birds with one stone,* he thought. *Today she is planning to go to the bank to withdraw some of her inheritance money. The picture, although expensive, cost me nothing since I used her funds for it. There is plenty, an immense amount more for me to use as I see fit.*

She's in for a shock. I don't care for her to have much money. Might make her think she could move out on me and live on her own. It wasn't difficult to remove all her funds and transfer them into my account. Ah well, such is life. I'm richer and will invest her money into that mining company I took over. I will now have Jamison's business too. He borrowed the money two months ago. I'll have Holbein draw up the due date for the end of next month. He's a good forger and will sign Grant Jamison's name on the contract, and voila! His company shall be mine.

Liberty came home in a state of shock. She walked slowly up the stairs. At the top, Armand stood staring down at her. She barely glanced at him. It seemed an effort to put one foot in front of the other, but she kept her back straight and her head held high as she walked down the hall to her rooms. Once inside, she collapsed into a heap on the floor in tears. *Nothing is left. Nothing. Oh Lord, help me to bear it! All these years I've waited to claim my grandfather's trust fund for me, and now there's nothing.*

There was a gentle tap on the door, and Liberty, thinking it was Annie, said, "Enter."

It was Matilda, a housemaid. "Madam! Oh goodness! Can I help you?" She pulled Liberty to her feet and led her to a chair.

"I'm all right, Matilda. Truly. Just had a bit of a shock is all."

"Oh, someone else told you?"

"Told me what?"

"Told you 'bout Annie."

"Wha...what? What about Annie?"

"She's very ill, madam. She collapsed today coming up the stairs. Sigmund had Pierre get the doctor. He's come and gone now, but he...he said...Annie is...is going to die!" Matilda was in tears.

Everyone loved Annie.

Liberty, in shock herself, felt the full weight of guilt for not going with her instincts and getting the doctor months ago. Annie had insisted on no doctor, but Liberty knew she should have overridden Annie and fetched the doctor. Tears slipped down her cheeks as she pulled herself together.

"Thank you, Matilda. Would you please send Pierre and Sigmund here? I have a task for them."

"Yes, madam." She left, nearly slamming the door behind her in her haste.

Liberty went to her bathing room and splashed water on her face. She patted it dry and took a breath. "Lord, you know how much I love Annie. I don't believe I can handle the devastation of losing her. I pray You would see fit to heal her. Nevertheless, not my will, but Thine be done."

Liberty had to wait only a couple minutes before a tap sounded on her door. She opened it to see Sigmund, along with young Pierre, the Bouviers' all-around help.

"I would like you two to go up to the attic and get Annie. I have no doubt you'll have to carry her, but I want her brought to my room and put into my bed. I shall nurse her myself."

Sigmund bowed slightly. "We will do it now."

Pierre swallowed but said nothing. It scared him to think what Monsieur Bouvier would do when he found out a maid occupied his wife's bed.

The two went straightaway up the second flight of stairs to fetch Annie. She wasn't able to walk on her own, so Sigmund carried her, and Pierre opened doors.

Liberty ran down to the kitchen using the back stairs and asked Cook for some broth and hot tea. She took the stairs two at a time and reached the top, only to find Armand watching her.

"What do you think you're doing, Liberty?"

"I am going to nurse Annie. She will be in my rooms, and you will not be inconvenienced in any way. Please excuse me." She started to pass him.

He grabbed her arm and sneered at her. "*You* are going to nurse her?"

"Yes. I am going to nurse her. I love her as if she were a friend, Armand. I know you wouldn't understand that, but it's true."

He flung her arm down, and she slipped by as he shouted, "She bothers me one time, one inconvenience, and she goes to the poorhouse, you hear?"

"Yes, Armand, I hear you," Liberty replied. She spoke respectfully, albeit curtly.

Sigmund was beside Liberty's door, holding Annie, and Pierre stood next to him. Pierre's eyes were rounded, and he looked frightened.

Liberty directed them to put Annie on the right side of the bed. "Thank you, Sigmund. Thank you, Pierre. I will tend to her now."

Sigmund sketched a bow in respect to a mistress who cared about her servants, but Liberty didn't see it. She was all eyes for Annie.

"I knew I should have had you seen by a doctor months ago. I feel bad that I didn't insist."

Annie opened her eyes. "Please don't! You couldn't have changed this outcome. Doctor said had I come in a year ago, he still couldn't have cured me. I don't have long, but please, please don't blame yourself."

"Oh, Annie, I love you very much. I was just thinking last night that you are my only real friend. I'm going to nurse you, and you will sleep here with me."

Sigmund and Pierre took their leave quietly, but Liberty and Annie didn't notice.

"Oh, miss. I have loved you ever since you saved me from old Hank back when you were only twelve years old. I did all I could to learn proper English so I could become your personal maid. I was so afraid when you married monsieur—I thought you'd not be allowed to keep me as your personal attendant. It's about the only thing I thank monsieur for." She smiled wanly. "I'm grateful to you, Miss Liberty." She swallowed and closed her eyes.

Liberty did all she could for her faithful servant—friend. For over a month, she rarely left Annie's side.

Annie knew she was there, and it was a comfort. They talked about many things, but mostly about their walk with God. Liberty had led

Annie to the Lord shortly after returning home from boarding school. Besides doing her chores, Annie had worked and worked learning to read and write. She'd practiced and practiced to rid herself of poor English. The butler at the Corlay house, Percy, had been an immense help.

Annie grew worse and worse, and Liberty felt helpless. She prayed and fasted and prayed some more, but to no avail that she could see.

Annie died one afternoon with a smile on her face.

CHAPTER XV

And he cast down the pieces of silver in the temple,
and departed, and went and hanged himself.

MATTHEW 27:5

GRANT JAMISON, HIS FACE ASHEN, SAID, "You can't do this!
You know the loan is good for five years, not three months! I wrote out a
copy of the contract, and I, sir, have five years to make good on that loan!"

Armand, the contract on his immense desk, rotated the forged paper
around for Jamison to view.

Grant looked down at the contract, identical to the one he'd copied
except for the due date. The signature looked identical to his own.

Grant spoke, his voice harsh. "My lawyer has a copy of the original
contract. You don't have a leg to stand on, Bouvier."

Armand, his dark eyes ever inimical, replied sardonically,
"Your lawyer is going to find that little bit of paper missing from
his files. I had my man remove it without leaving any evidence of
him having been there."

Grant didn't say a word, didn't look another time at Armand
Bouvier, but did an about-face and walked blindly to the door.

Bouvier waited until he knew I'd invested the loan money into the construction of
the new building. How in the world did I get taken in by

a loan shark? Eloise told me to leave things as they were, but no, I needed to expand. Money has been tight, and I've sunk all I own into the construction of that building. Everything, lost. I hocked the house for extra cash for that expansion. I'm worse than poor! What will Eloise say…

Before entering his carriage, he spoke to Dickinson, his driver, who stood with the door open. "Take me to the police station, please." His scarf blew loose, but he didn't bother to tighten it, although it was freezing. He climbed in and leaned back against the cushioned seat. With shoulders slumped, he put his head in his hands. "What am I going to do? Oh God, what am I going to do? Perhaps I should have asked You that before I made my own plans. Lost…everything I've worked for, lost. I can't bear it. I simply cannot bear it."

Dickinson got him to his destination in short order, jumping down to open the door. He
sensed something was wrong and wondered why his boss would go to the police. He stood respectfully as Mr. Jamison alighted, stepping heavily onto the cobbled street. He watched as his employer walked slowly up the steps to the heavy doors. He noticed that Mr. Jamison, who usually had a jaunty step, walked as if he were an old man.

Grant entered the edifice and walked up to the front desk.

"Yes, may I help you?" A young man, with reddish hair, seemed eager to offer his services.

Without the normal smile creasing his face, Grant's expression was somber. "Yes, I believe you can. I'd like to see the chief of detectives please."

"Do you have an appointment, sir?" the young man asked.

"N-no, I don't. Do I need one?" Jamison's shoulders slumped.

"Not always, but it is customary. What is your name, sir?"

"It's Grant Jamison."

"Please wait, Mr. Jamison, and I'll see if the chief's available." The clerk left the desk in a decided manner and took the stairs two at a time. He tapped on Chief Inspector George Baxter's door.

"Enter," George Baxter said.

The clerk peeked around the door. "Do you have time to see someone, sir?"

"Yes, I do. Who is it?"

"Says his name is Grant Jamison, sir."

"Send him up."

"Yes, sir, right away, sir." The young clerk dashed down the stairs.

"He'll see you right now, sir. Please follow me."

Grant nodded, following the young man up the steps. The name Christopher Belden was still on the opaque glassed part of the door, but Grant knew from the *Globe*, which he read daily, that Chief Belden had retired.

When he opened the door, Grant hesitated before stepping over the threshold.

"Thank you, Tommy," George Baxter said as he stood to greet his visitor. "Welcome, Mr. Jamison." Baxter came around his desk to shake Grant's hand. "Please, have a seat." With a wave of his hand, he indicated a chair across from his desk as he walked back around it and seated himself.

"What can I do for you, Mr. Jamison?" George leaned forward. His hands, clasped lightly together, rested on his desk.

Grant sat staring for a moment at George Baxter, wondering if the man could help him. "I've come from Monsieur Armand Bouvier's residence straight here."

As he said the name, George sat up straight and spoke. "I don't know you or your circumstances, but he's taken over your company, hasn't he?"

Grant's eyes were etched with surprise and a bit of hope. "Yes, but how would you know that? I cannot understand how he could do it. I made a copy of the original contract. I had five years to fulfill the terms for the payback. It's been scarcely three months. I saw the false contract not twenty minutes ago. It looks genuine, all of it, even the signature looks like my handwriting."

George sighed and leaned back in his chair. "I am sorry, Mr. Jamison. We've been doing all we can, but our hands are tied. The original contracts must have been destroyed, and we can't find the forger. We know Bouvier to be a swindler. He's growing richer by the day, but we haven't been able to prove his perfidy. You are the ninth victim that we know about, and how many more who haven't come to us, I have no idea. I am sorry. We can look into it, of course, but I have a man on the case full time, and I myself have investigated it, but we haven't found any proof."

Grant felt his limbs leaden. "Thank you. I thought I'd see if anything can be done, but I've played the fool and will reap the consequence." He stood, his shoulders slumped in despair.

George started for the door, but Grant had already reached it.

"Good day, Inspector. I do hope and pray you break open this case, for I am ruined."

There was nothing George could say to help.

Grant went home, down to the basement, and hanged himself.

Maggie had finished polishing the silver on Mrs. Jamison's jewelry. She'd polished the shoes the woman had worn the day before, and she was now checking the dress Eloise had worn to make sure there were no stains or rips. Once she was satisfied all was in order, she left the room, deciding to see the children.

She traipsed down the hall to the nursery but found the children were out for a walk with Nanny Claire. She went downstairs and entered the kitchen, saying to the room at large, "I've finished my regular chores. Is there anything I can do?"

"No, I think I've got everything under control," Bonnie said.

Otto looked up from the table where he was having a cup of tea. "Certainly, young lady. There are masses of things to be done...always!" He took a sip of tea and added, "Why don't you join me for a cup of tea first, and then we'll sort it all out."

"All right. Thank you, Otto. Mrs. Jamison's friend, Mrs. Tucker, picked her up, and she is out for an afternoon tea at Mrs. Conway's house. I'm not needed until she returns."

"*Verrücktes Mädchen! Sie werden immer gebraucht.*"

"What did you say to me, Otto?" Maggie's dimples dipped deeply into her cheeks, and her gray eyes sparkled. She always thought it great fun when he spoke German.

Laughing, Otto said, "I said, 'Crazy girl, you are always needed.'"

"It's good to be needed, isn't it? I feel sorry for people who have no one. I thought I was going to have no one, and here I am feeling as if I'm in a family and cared for by everyone."

"Yes, I am thinking we all crave that feeling of being needed. Now, sit while I pour you some tea." He rose from the kitchen table and helped himself to a cup, tea ball, tea leaves, and hot water.

"Maggie, while I make this for you, could you scoot down to the basement and see if the coal bin is at least half-full? I think snow may be on its way, and we need to be sure we have plenty of coal."

"Yes, and thank you for making me a cuppa!" She strode to the door of the basement. She opened it and felt a draft of cold air. She didn't like the basement. It gave her a feeling of being closed in and was always cold, even in the summer. She hurried down the stairs, rounding the upright pillar, and saw Mr. Jamison hanging from a crossbeam.

Maggie screamed, covering her eyes with her hands. She stumbled backward only to be caught in Otto's arms. The young German looked up to see the horror of Mr. Jamison hanging from the main beam.

He spun Maggie around toward the stairs. "Come, Maggie. Come with me." He led her up the stairs, her weight leaning heavily on his arm. She stumbled several times, but he caught her and urged her up the stairs.

When they reached the top, he closed the door firmly behind them.

"Bonnie! Where's Millie?"

"She's in the scullery. What's wrong? What's happened?"

"Maggie, sit here. Bonnie, give her that cup of tea I made."

His voice was urgent and curt, and Bonnie looked up from peeling potatoes to see his face was ashen.

"Yes, sir."

Otto slammed the door of the scullery behind him and saw Millie washing dishes. "Millie, run tell Dickinson to come in here—as fast as you can!"

"Yes, sir!" She ran out the back door and over to the stable to see Dickinson forking hay into a stall.

"Otto needs you as soon as possible. He's in the scullery."

Dickinson, astonishment at her request, ran across the cobbles. Entering the scullery, he saw Otto throwing up in a bucket.

"Sir, what can I do?"

Otto wiped his face with a towel. "Dickinson, I need you to go to the head of the police department. Have him come here as soon as possible."

Millie entered the scullery, and Otto whispered into Dickinson's ear. "The boss has hanged himself in the basement. Hurry!"

Dickinson, stunned, stared at Otto. "I just took him to the police station at his request. I thought something was wrong, but this…why, it's unbelievable! I'll get my coat and hat and use the boss's horse." He left, clattering down the back steps.

Otto, seeing the curiosity on Millie's face, said. "Thanks for your help. You can finish washing up." He went back into the kitchen to sit next to Maggie, who'd not spoken a word.

She was holding the teacup to her lips, but it rattled against her teeth as both hands shook with shock. The gray of her eyes was nearly obliterated by her pupils, and Otto wetted a clean cloth with hot water. He brought it back, shaking a little of the heat out of it.

"Put your cup down and hold still, Maggie." He laid the warm cloth over her face, covering her eyes down to her chin. "Breathe deeply, Maggie. Breathe deep."

Bonnie turned from peeling potatoes. "Was there a mouse in the basement, Maggie?"

"Bonnie." Otto left Maggie's side and put his arms around Bonnie, who adored Grant Jamison. "Bonnie, Mr. Jamison has hung himself in the basement."

"No!" She dropped to her knees in shock. "Oh my dear Lord, no…it can't be true!"

Otto helped her up and to a kitchen chair, where she broke down and sobbed into her apron. He removed the cloth from Maggie's face. "Is that better?"

She nodded but knew she would never get over seeing Mr. Jamison hanging there. It would be forever etched in her brain.

"What shall I say to Mrs. Jamison?" she whispered. Her throat felt closed off. "How can I tell her? She will be back soon. What's going to happen? What will happen to us?"

Bonnie, still sobbing, replied, "We'll carry on just as we have, my dear. Oh my! My heart is breaking for those poor children. Oh, dear Lord…poor Mrs. Jamison. Oh, how can we all bear it?"

The front knocker sounded, and Otto went to answer it.

"Chief Inspector Baxter." George lifted his top hat in a gesture of respect. "This is Inspector Taylor."

Otto gave a slight bow and said, "Please enter." He swallowed and added, "I would suppose our Mr. Dickinson has related to you what has occurred here?"

"Yes, but we need to be sure there has been no foul play."

"I-I understand. Please follow me." He led the way to the kitchen but heard the front door open.

Mrs. Jamison was home. She saw Otto leading the men to the kitchen and followed, concern and curiosity marking her brow. She removed her hat and scarf.

She watched as Otto led the two men to the basement door, opened it, and gestured for them to proceed. He followed them down. As she rounded the doorway, Mrs. Jamison saw Maggie looking terrified and Bonnie sobbing into her apron.

"What's the matter? Who are those men? What's going on here?" Eloise's face held bewilderment.

As she was speaking, Dickinson, who rarely entered the house, came through the scullery door, stopping dead in his tracks at the sight of his mistress.

Bonnie gave an anguished look at her employer, and the sobs tore out of her throat.

Maggie jumped up and led Mrs. Jamison out of the kitchen. "Come with me, Mrs. Jamison. Come with me, and I will tell you." She led her up the stairs and to her rooms, making her sit on the bed.

"Maggie! Tell me! I want to know this instant! Now tell me—what is going on?"

Mrs. Jamison…oh, Mrs. Jamison…M-Mr. Jamison has hung himself in the basement!"

Mrs. Jamison's face blanched. She put her hand over her heart and fainted.

Maggie went to the bureau drawer containing medicines for megrims and various oils and balms. She grabbed the smelling salts, wondering if it wouldn't be better for Mrs. Jamison to come to by herself. It seemed a mercy to Maggie that she'd fainted.

She undid the stopper, waved it a few times under Mrs. Jamison's nose, and watched as she slowly opened her eyes. Maggie replaced the stopper when she saw recognition come into Mrs. Jamison's eyes.

"Why?" she whispered. "Why? Oh my sweet Jesus, please help me to understand why my Grant would do such a thing."

Maggie looked at Mrs. Jamison and said flatly, "I have found in my short life that there is no God who cares about us."

Eloise stared at Maggie, shocked to the core. "Oh, Maggie, God does care. It's our choices that bring the heartache. He wants what is best for us."

"No, Mrs. Jamison, He doesn't. I know what is best for me. And that was to have my parents alive and well and enjoying life, and me being a girl growing up happily in my own family. I love you, Mrs. Jamison, but you're not my mother. I miss my mam and my da abominably."

Mrs. Jamison began crying at the realization that Grant was forever gone from her. Huge wracking sobs shook her body as she thought about her beloved Grant.

Maggie sat next to her on the bed and held her in her strong arms, rocking her back and forth as she would a baby. She had no words of comfort to give her.

George Baxter looked at Grant Jamison's body with sorrow and with a deep anger directed at Bouvier. He wondered if there hadn't been something else he could have told Jamison to give him a bit of hope, but he knew nothing he said could have brought back Jamison's company to him.

He spoke to Timothy Taylor. "This is the third suicide due to Monsieur Bouvier's perfidy."

Otto, who was standing behind Taylor, with eyes averted, asked, "What do you mean, sir? What does this Monsieur Bouvier have to do with Mr. Jamison's death?"

"Bouvier took over his company just this morning."

"Took over his company?" Otto's lips tightened and, he felt his heart sink. "Poor Mrs. Jamison. Poor, fatherless children. Oh, what sorrow!"

The three men climbed the stairs together.

George spoke to Otto. "I'll send for the coroner. He will legally confirm the death and will see the body transferred to the morgue. You need not go down there again. I am sorry for this circumstance. Will you notify the Jamisons' lawyer?"

"Of course. I can do that. Thank you, sir. I feel in shock. At least now I can understand why he did it."

"I cannot, Mr. Graf. Yes, he would have faced some real hardship, but now he's left that to his wife and children to face. My heart aches for his family and staff. I will certainly keep this household in my prayers. Good day, young man. Should you need anything, please don't hesitate to call me. I am at your service."

George Baxter, along with Timothy Taylor, left the Jamison manse with a heavy heart.

"When we get to the station, I want you to fetch the coroner, Timmy."

"Yes, sir. I wish there was some way to get Bouvier."

"I do too," George said heavily. "I'd like nothing better than to string up him and his partner in crime, Monsieur Jacques Corlay. Both are reprobates. Do you know what a reprobate is, Timmy?"

"Yes. In the church I attend, it's a person destined for hell...they are not in the elect."

"I am not of your persuasion, Timmy. I believe we all have the choice to accept Christ or not. No, to me a reprobate is someone who sees evil as good and good as evil. I know our struggle is not against flesh and blood, but it's difficult to remember when something like this happens because of another's wickedness." He sighed and continued. "I can never seem to get over the wretchedness of mankind, and yet I see it every day."

"Armand, the choosing of a personal maid should be my choice, not yours. You won't have to put up with the vagaries of a maid. For once, I need to make the choice, not you."

"You would take a beggar off the street if they knew the position is open." He sneered.

"Thank you for the compliment, Armand." Liberty smiled.

He was taken aback by her smile and her comment. She was beautiful, and he craved above all things to dominate her. He'd tried his best to break her spirit, but he could not.

He didn't realize her self-esteem, her entire *raison d'être* was bound up in her Savior. He knew there was a part of her that would never be his, that she would never love him.

Liberty had interviewed two women for the position of personal maid, but Armand had vetoed both. She sat in her sitting room, thinking about the conversation she'd had with him. He didn't know how badly she missed Annie. He didn't know she prayed and prayed God would give her someone she could trust.

CHAPTER XVI

For I know the thoughts that I think toward you, saith the LORD,
thoughts of peace, and not of evil, to give you an expected end.

JEREMIAH 29:11

SEVERAL DAYS PASSED. ALL THE Jamison household attended the funeral, but not a word was spoken about Grant committing suicide. It was given out that he'd died of a heart attack. The solicitor had come and gone after the funeral, and the entire household was in a state of shock, Mrs. Jamison more than them all. She knew she'd be welcomed into her sister's house. It would be difficult with the children, but none of her staff, not even Maggie, would be going with her.

Eloise drew a deep breath and looked at all her staff standing around in the library. "I am so sorry for this. All of you must look for new positions. I will most likely move to my sister's in Hartford. As you know, even this house will go to the robber who took my husband's company from him. I am sorry, but we are left with the clothes on our backs. I will give each of you a letter describing your excellent credentials, should you wish it." She took a handkerchief from her sleeve and dabbed at her eyes, leaving the room before she broke down entirely.

Maggie was wide-eyed, wondering what in the world she would do.

Bonnie, who was up to date on news shared by the servants' grapevine, said to her, "Maggie, dear, I don't know if you can stomach it, knowing what we do about Monsieur Bouvier, but Madam Bouvier is looking for a personal maid. I think you need to scoot yourself right on over there and see if you can get the position. I don't imagine you'd have to be around the monsieur much. Here's the address. It's not far from here, only a few blocks. Your position may be one that's sought after, but once a lady's maid is hired, it's very seldom they're let go. Those positions are not open often."

Maggie swallowed and took the slip of paper, looking around at the rest of the staff. *Wonder if that's the same Bouvier who had Ethan Brooks kill Elmer? Bet it is. The name is not common, and if he caused Mr. Jamison's death… well, I can believe it's the same man.*

"Yes, Maggie, I agree with Bonnie," Otto said. "You should get yourself over there as soon as you can. Jobs like yours are scarce, and when you know there is an opening, you need to take advantage of it." He drew her to him and gave her a hug. "This is difficult for all of us. I have looked on you as a little sister and will miss you." His blue eyes misted, but he blinked back the tears. "Go on now. Get yourself over there."

Maggie, with a backward look at everyone in the library, ran up the two flights to her room to get her coat and scarf.

She walked the distance, following Dickinson's directions. It was a beautiful manse, but somehow seemed stiff and disapproving of her. She shook off the feeling of eyes watching her and made her way around to the back entrance. She knocked on the door, her teeth chattering with the cold and with nerves.

Cook heard the knock and answered the door. "Come in, missy. Come in. Come in. It iss too cold to be out there for long. Now, vhat can I do for you?"

Maggie curtsied, which convinced Cook that this was a good girl.

"Thank you, ma'am. I walked from the Jamisons', and I'm freezing! I've come to see if Madam Bouvier would have me as a personal maid. I suppose you know about the Jamison household?"

"Ja! It iss no surprise when monsewer taked hiss business. Ja, it iss sad day." She turned and gestured Maggie to follow her into the kitchen. "You be young, girl, ja. I make you some tea. Ve vill varm your insides." She spoke to a maid. "Tilly, you go see if madam vill see dis girl."

Cook had already been employed there for quite some time and was firmly entrenched. Knowing a good thing when she saw it, she smiled warmly and bade Maggie sit at the kitchen table.

"I yam Mrs. Jensen, but everyone here, they call me Cook. Vhat is your name?"

"My name is Margaret Regan O'Neill, but people just call me Maggie." She smiled hesitantly and was rewarded with a sweet smile from the cook. Maggie was surprised by the warmth of this older woman. It did her good, as she was feeling like a fish out of water what with having to leave Mrs. Jamison and having to find a new job. Her stomach curdled with nerves.

Matilda went first to madam's sitting room and tapped on the door.

"Enter," Liberty said.

"Madam, Cook has a girl in the kitchen, from the Jamison household, who is wanting to interview as your personal maid."

"Get her, please. I'll interview her right now."

Tilly went back to the kitchen, where she found Maggie enjoying a cup of tea with Cook. "Madam will see you now. Please follow me."

Maggie swallowed, hoping madam would like her. *If she doesn't want me, what am I going to do?* She arose as she spoke to Cook. "Thank you for the tea."

Cook nodded, hoping Liberty would like the girl.

Matilda tapped and opened the sitting room door. Maggie entered and Matilda left, pulling the door closed behind her.

Maggie took in several things at once. The room was painted a dark-green color and looked dark, stiff, and uncomfortable. The paintings on the walls were unremarkable and dull, but the room was much warmer than the hall…a fire burned cheerfully in the grate. Her eyes swung to behold the most beautiful woman she'd ever seen. She was much younger than Maggie had expected.

Maggie was only fourteen, but somehow she knew this woman was good. Madam sat in the darkly painted room with her shiny coppery curls swept up from a neck that was perfect. Her face was gorgeous, with green, almond-shaped eyes fringed by dark curling lashes and arched by brows that winged upward. Her full lips were made for smiling. Maggie would have died to have a figure like hers. Her bosom was high and full, her waist tiny. Not many women could boast such perfection.

Maggie curtsied and Liberty smiled.

"You are quite young. Do you have the skills to be a personal maid?"

"Yes, ma'am, I do." Maggie spoke with easy honesty and confidence.

"Can you tell me how you are proficient?"

"Yes, ma'am. I am able to repair dresses and gowns so that the stitches don't show. I can clean shoes, iron, dress you, undress you, and do your hair. Now, to be honest, I've never done someone with such a mass of hair as you, but I am willing to learn."

Maggie smiled, and Liberty saw the deep dimples in her cheeks for the first time. It made her smile back.

"Maggie, my husband has vetoed the last two women I interviewed, but I am going to hire you. When can you begin?"

"Straightaway, ma'am. The entire Jamison household is breaking up." Maggie saw tears spring to Liberty's eyes, which made her suppose Liberty had nothing to do with her husband's business.

"I am sorry to hear that. Can you come first thing tomorrow?"

"Yes, I'm sure I can. I do have one request. Would it be all right for me to check on Mrs. Jamison and help her to pack when she's ready? She is planning to move in with her sister. They have lost everything."

"I know," Liberty said. "Believe me—I know."

She stood, and Maggie once again admired this woman who had such a perfect figure. She wondered how she could be married to such an evil man as Monsieur Bouvier.

"Come with me, and I'll show you where your room is. I...I lost my personal maid last month. She became very ill and passed away."

"I am sorry," Maggie said.

Liberty led her up a flight of stairs and then up another flight to the servants' quarters.

"This will be your room. It's not fancy, but it is serviceable and has heat, a fireplace for winter and two windows for cross air in summer. It has a clothespress. You may put your own clothes and things in here, but we have a uniform—black dress, mobcap, and shoes, and there's a white apron that my husband insists you wear. You will have two sets." She sighed and smiled. "I think we shall get along well, don't you?"

"I do hope so, ma'am. I hope to make myself indispensable."

She grinned, but Liberty could see that her eyes were shadowed.

"I love Mrs. Jamison, and it will be difficult to leave her."

"Do you have family here in Boston?"

"No, ma'am. I have no one."

Maggie did not elaborate, and Liberty did not press her.

Liberty took Maggie down one flight of stairs. "My rooms are there, those double doors." She waved her hand. "These are monsieur's rooms right at the top of the main stairs." She led Maggie down the long hall. "These are the back stairs. When monsieur is in the house, you will use these stairs. He does not like servants using the main stairs. If he is out, you are welcome to use the main stairs to cut down on extra work."

Maggie was getting the definite impression that madam and monsieur didn't agree on quite a few things. *Good! I already despise monsieur for what he's done to the Jamisons, but I must be careful to keep my opinions to myself.*

Liberty next led her down the back stairs to the kitchen. "Cook, thank you for allowing Maggie to meet me. I think both of us are satisfied, and Maggie will be my new personal maid."

"Ja! I am thinking she iss the goot girl. I am habby you haf hired her, Miss Liberty. Ja!"

Sigmund entered the kitchen, whistling, with a silver tray in his hand. He stopped dead. It was a rarity for the mistress to be in the kitchen. He sketched a quick bow as his eye caught the movement of the girl standing behind her.

"Sigmund, please meet Maggie, my new personal maid. Maggie, this is Sigmund your boss and our butler. His word is law in this house."

"I'm pleased to meet you, sir." Maggie bent her leg and executed a deep curtsy of respect.

"The pleasure is mine, I'm sure."

Sigmund was German, and because of Otto, Maggie gave him her best smile.

She charmed him.

"I suppose I'd better be getting back to the Jamisons', but I can't thank you enough, ma'am. I will come back first thing in the morning." She nodded to Cook and Sigmund and left, feeling a deep sense of relief. *I have a job. Making the change won't be as difficult as I thought, but to leave Mrs. Jamison and Otto…oh my, that's going to be difficult. They have become my family.*

Armand wished he had a good confidant. He'd like to be able to discuss his achievements with another man and feel the laudatory praise for his accomplishments. Jacques Corlay was his father-in-law and his business partner, but he couldn't be counted as a friend. *Jacques would probably stab me in the back if he could. I don't trust him as far as I could throw him. I got him out of near bankruptcy by marrying Liberty. I'm not sorry about that. She's a stunning showpiece, and she seems to get more beautiful every day. I love having heads turn and men envying me when I enter a room with her on my arm. I hate that she's a Christian. All that nonsensical folderol. I don't believe in an afterlife. It's all a myth. When you die, you just get buried six feet under, and that's the end of it. It would be nice to be able to brag to someone how I took over Jamison's company. I am excited about acquiring it. It has increased my holdings here in Boston. Holbein does a good job forging papers. I need to be sure to pay him well. I also need to contact Brooks and see how the money for the females is doing. Seems the best place to sell them is Hong Kong and Chile. Brooks is the perfect person for that job. I am so good at getting the right people for the right job. Made a mistake in Elmer Dermott though. Brooks did a good job getting rid of him. Wonder if I should try to find that girl he pretended to marry. That's a loose end, to be sure. Ah well. It's been nigh unto two years. I suppose I'm entirely safe in thinking I don't have to worry.*

Maggie, although tearful, left the Jamison household the next morning. She moved her things, which fit into a large satchel, into her new quarters. Mrs. Jamison had cried and cried the night before. The two of them had spent the entire evening together. Mrs. Jamison told her not to worry about anything. Millie would be packing up her things, and Maggie need not return. They said their goodbyes, and both went to bed, knowing that most likely they'd never see each other again.

Mrs. Jamison wasn't up when Maggie left the next morning. Maggie gave Bonnie a hug and said goodbye to the children, but the most difficult that morning was to say goodbye to Otto. She clung to him, and he hugged her as if he didn't want to let her go.

"I hope Madam Bouvier finds how special you are, Maggie. I would caution you one thing. Stay out of monsieur's way. I've heard he's a philanderer. I tell you right now, I know Sigmund—he's a close friend and a good man. He will protect you as much as he is able. You need only to ask him, and you need to be sure to do that. The fact that Bouvier brought down this house should be enough of a concern that you watch your step." He gave her a final hug. "Now, may God bless you, child."

Maggie, with surprise marking her eyes, thought, *I won't tell him that I don't believe in God. I don't believe in a loving God who allows all the badness that happens—especially to me. And as far as the monsieur being wicked, well, I already knew that. He has Ethan Brooks in his employ.*

She grinned up at Otto through the tears that kissed her cheeks. "I'll miss you…I'll miss you tremendously. If you're such a good friend of Sigmund, please don't make yourself scarce. I'd like to see you again." Her eyes sparkled as she continued. "I'll be sure to let Sigmund know you trained me. If I'm lacking in some knowledge, I'll be able to blame it on you."

Otto gave her another squeeze. "You are an impudent girl! I'll try to visit on my days off. I'll be looking for a new job, but I'll remain here, helping out until Mrs. Jamison leaves. My understanding is that she'll be away from here by the end of the week. Bye now, sweet Maggie. Take care."

"Goodbye, Otto Graf." She smiled, her dimples dipping deeply into her cheeks as her eyes filled in sorrow. She picked up her satchel and headed for the door, but Otto made it there first and opened it, sketching a bow.

Maggie went down the steps, tightening her scarf as the wind plucked at her hair. She walked the few blocks but was freezing cold by the time she arrived at the service entrance to the Bouviers' manse.

She knocked, and Mrs. Jensen let her in. "Ja, you don't haf to knock anymore, girl. You now part of the Bouvier house, an' you let yourself in from now on."

"Thank you, Cook. It is so cold, and it's beginning to snow."

"Ja, I haf heard it vill snow real goot. You go up an' put your things away. I fix you a cup of tea to warm your insides."

Maggie skipped up the back stairs and ran up the second flight. She was used to two flights, having lived at the Jamisons' house. She looked into the clothespress and unpacked her satchel. She had a Bible that had been her mother's, and she put it on a wide shelf that stretched across the width of the closet just above the dowel for hanging clothes. There was no dresser, but a large nightstand with a drawer and a cupboard below it would be ample room to store her few meager things. She looked around the room, glad for two windows. *At least it's not a dark hidey-hole. The walls look like old white stucco.*

Maggie made her way back downstairs, and when she reached the second floor, she saw Monsieur Bouvier come out of his room. He'd not seen her, and she hurried down the backstairs, hoping he'd not spied her once she'd turned her back. Maggie was afraid of Armand Bouvier.

Maggie met Monsieur Bouvier a week after she'd begun working for madam. She was in the kitchen, helping to polish silver. The Bouviers entertained often.

Matilda, also called Tilly, was a sweet, dark-eyed maid. She was polishing a teapot. Maggie, knowing Madam Bouvier was taking a nap, volunteered to help. She had already endeared herself to the staff, taking on chores that were not hers just to be of service.

Matilda, laughing at something Cook said, jumped as the double doors to the kitchen swung open with a violence that nearly ripped the heavy doors off their hinges.

"What kind of soup was that we had last night?" Armand spoke in a denigrating tone. "It was terrible. You know, Mrs. Jensen, I don't usually complain, but you ever serve anything close to that again, you'll get the sack. Do I make myself clear?"

Cook, looking thoroughly surprised, replied. "Ja, you iss clear. Me, I find good job anywhere. Maybe I go looking, ja?"

Armand was taken aback. He had an excellent cook, and they were scarce as hen's teeth to come by. "Perhaps," he ground out, "but you needn't be too hasty. Last night was the first time I found it difficult to swallow." He started to leave but spied Maggie. "Who are you?"

Maggie, wide eyed from the exchange, dropped him a brief curtsy. "I am Maggie, madam's personal maid."

He smiled charmingly at her. She was quite nice looking. "I didn't realize she'd hired anyone. Welcome to our household." He stared at her for a minute, pivoted on his heel, and strode out.

Maggie looked over at Cook and then at Matilda, who swallowed two times.

Matilda was scared out of her wits whenever monsieur was around.

"You stay out of hiss way, Maggie," Cook said. "He iss liking zie women. Ja…he bringed some here. He a terrible man."

"I ate some of that starter soup last night, and it was delicious," Matilda said. "Please don't look for another position, Cook. We couldn't bear it if you left."

"Ja, I yam here for madam, not him. She iss zie sweetest woman I know. She put up with much. Monsewer, he iss zie bully. He not bully me, him!" Cook took umbrage at monsieur's remarks. She muttered to herself. "Me, I take zie rolling pin to hiss head! Maybe fry pan iss better for dat lout!"

Everyone knew Cook was a valuable asset to his dinner parties. The only reason she stayed was because she adored Liberty.

Liberty was lying in bed, but she wasn't napping as Maggie supposed. She'd felt cold and was low in spirit. The dinner party the evening before had impressed Armand's friends but left her needing to pray about her attitude.

I need to keep ever before me that my struggle is against the spiritual forces of evil, not Armand…but, oh Lord, I am weary of all his wicked ways. I know he kept that female guest overnight. Help me to love as You love, because You know my heart and how I despise Armand, and yet I feel such pity for him. He thinks satisfaction comes from his money and the adulation of those around him, but these things can't bring peace to his heart. I know I should not look to tomorrow, but take one day at a time. Please forgive me and help me to respect him as Your word says to do. I suppose my heart feels weary, because I can only see years ahead of unending evil. Thank you for giving me grace daily. Lord, how I do miss my Annie. I can imagine her worshiping you. I could talk to her about anything, since I'd known her since I was ten. I do thank You for Maggie. She is young, and I don't know how loyal, but she cheers my heart.

CHAPTER XVII

These six things doth the LORD hate: yea, seven are an abomination unto him:
A proud look, a lying tongue, and hands that shed innocent blood,
An heart that deviseth wicked imaginations, feet that be swift in running to mischief,
A false witness that speaketh lies, and he that soweth discord among brethren.

PROVERBS 6:16–19

IT WAS THE FIRST WEEK OF DECEMBER 1882. The chilled wind blew continually, snow piling in drifts where gusts had driven it. Temperatures were frigid, and icicles hung from the eaves of every building. Cobbles were slick with ice, and people who ventured out were careful to watch where they stepped.

Maggie had been at the Bouvier household for four years. She'd become a lovely young woman. Her red hair gleamed, her skin glowed with good health, and her sparkling gray eyes and deep dimples gave off an air of goodwill.

Maggie had grown to love Liberty and served her well, attending to her every need. Loyalty ran deep within her veins, and she felt Liberty deserved every bit of it. On mornings when Liberty didn't come downstairs to breakfast, Maggie would carry the heavy tray up to madam's room. She'd learned Liberty's preferences in food, drink, and clothing. There was nothing she wouldn't do for her mistress. Very seldom was Maggie angry, but when she was, no one wanted to be the object of her wrath.

Rufus Bertoli was eating lunch in the kitchen. He was coachman for the Bouviers, and everyone on staff knew he was one of monsieur's minions. They knew, too, he was paid well for any information he imparted to Armand about comments made by servants. They took care in what was spoken when he was in the house.

Maggie entered the kitchen in time to hear him make a disparaging comment about madam. She responded with a blistering tirade. His eyes glittered with hate toward her as she spoke, but he would be careful in the future to not cross her.

Maggie despised Rufus, but more, Armand. She'd witnessed enough of his despicable, denigrating behavior toward Liberty, and she hated him for it, in addition to what he'd done to the Jamisons. She knew him to be a murderer.

It was cold in Boston, the thermometer stagnant—below freezing for over a week. Overcast skies with clouds near to bursting were ready to spill their icy contents.

The forecast was for more frigid temperatures to come. A cold winter storm was blowing its way south from arctic temperatures, and people were preparing for the onslaught. Bundled up with layered clothing and heavy coats and scarves, workmen delivered coal and chopped wood to the wealthier homes. The cold seeped into every nook and cranny, chilling even the most stalwart, who lived in the fine houses.

Armand shivered as he stepped down from his coach. He looked up at Rufus. "You can go around to the kitchen—see if they'll give you something to warm you up. No one should be out in this for any length of time." His breath made wisps of smoke as he talked, and he pulled his scarf up higher to cover his ears.

Walking carefully up the slippery brick path, Armand rapped the brass knocker, grabbing at his top hat to keep the wind from sending it down the street. He shivered again.

Percy, Corlay's butler, opened the door and ushered Armand in without a word of greeting. Snubbed several times by Armand, he didn't open himself up to additional abuse. Percy, who'd watched Liberty grow up, adored her and could not stomach her husband. He showed Armand to the library door without asking permission from Corlay. Tapping on the heavy double door, he opened it, and Armand entered.

Armand and Corlay had been business partners for thirteen years. The library was nearly a twin to Armand's. It was dark with only a lamp to lighten it; the drapes were never opened.

(Liberty, growing up, had all her punishments executed in this room and had always hated it.)

"Welcome, Armand, welcome." Corlay's tone was affable. "Here, let me help you with your coat. Don't know what Percy was thinking." He took Armand's hat, coat, and scarf and threw them over a wooden side chair. "Come close to the fire. You look frozen."

"I didn't give your man time to take off my coat. I'm frozen to the bone." Shivering, he continued, "It's nasty out there." Armand stood before the fire, first facing it with hands outstretched to warm them as he spoke. He spun slowly around to warm his backside. When he felt toasty, he joined his father-in-law, who was sitting in a deep leather chair before the open fire, away from any drafts.

"I came by to tell you I changed my will today," Armand said. "I saw my lawyer, Elijah Humphries, and filled out the final copy. I am bestowing all my worldly goods to you should I predecease you. Liberty would then have to depend upon your mercy to live in our manse. You would have full control. I decided I never want her to enjoy life without me."

Jacques looked at his son-in-law with surprise. *If I had done that, I would never let another person know it.* His eyes gleamed with pleasure. "Thank you. I consider that a compliment to my business acumen. You have taught me most all I know of business dealing. You are still a relatively young man. We don't have to worry about any of that for a long time to come."

Armand smiled his agreement but thought, *I wonder if I should have told him of my intentions, but I have no one else I can claim as a friend. Not even my wife is as close.*

Armand had actually paid Corlay for the privilege of marrying his daughter. Liberty brought a respectable name as a dowry to their marriage. It was the prestige and social class he craved. Armand had no illusions as to the people who attended his dinner parties. They were social climbers, but Liberty's mother had been a Browning, a Boston Brahmin, a member of Boston's traditional upper class on a par with the aristocracy of Britain. Armand, in return for the prestige, had helped Jacques out of financial ruin. He and Jacques had formed an unholy alliance, cheating many men out of their businesses.

"I don't plan on leaving this earth for a long time to come, but against the unforeseeable accident, I want Liberty under your control."

"Here, Armand, have a cigar." Jacques opened his desk drawer, pulling out the box of his best for his son-in-law. He pulled the rope that hung close to his desk, and within seconds, Percy entered the library.

"You rang, sir?"

"Yes, get us a couple shots of whiskey. Armand and I have some celebrating to do."

Percy left, wondering what the two men were up to now. Returning in quick order, he tapped on the door and entered to serve the men their drinks. He left immediately.

"To more money," Jacques said as he raised his glass.

"To much more money," Armand responded, clinking his glass against Jacques'.

After chatting for a lengthy time, Armand departed. Jacques sat down at his wide desk to write a note, having a servant carry the missive to Hans Holbein, the man who did an excellent job of forging contracts, but he had other duties as well.

Maggie was helping Madam Liberty Bouvier to dress.

"Oh, ma'am, you look beautiful!"

"Beauty is in the eye of the beholder," Liberty quoted.

Maggie's eyes sparkled with delight. "How did you ever hear of The Duchess?"

"That's her pen name, Maggie. Her real name is Margaret Hamilton, at least that was her maiden name. She's quite a popular writer among Europeans, and I read a couple of her books while at boarding school. My favorite is *Molly Bawn*. The Duchess was married less than six years to her first husband, who died. I understand she married again this year. I suppose you know of her because she's Irish?"

"That's right. My da…uh, my father knew her and would relate amusing anecdotes about her. My mother loved her books."

Maggie didn't talk much about her past. She'd let Liberty know only snippets.

Maggie stuck a few more pearl pins, from Annie, in Liberty's hair.

"You always look beautiful, ma'am, but that dress is gorgeous!"

Liberty's dress was midnight blue velvet. The blue sleeves had cuts from shoulder to cuff, Spanish style, inset with creamy satin. The bodice was heart shaped and snugged tightly at her tiny waist. She wore a choker of pearls and pearl-drop earrings as well as the pearl drops in the braid Maggie had pinned around her head like a crown. Liberty had never worn her hair thus, and it surprised her how much she liked it.

"Thank you, Maggie. You always make me look my best."

"I don't have to do anything. You would look beautiful in rags, ma'am."

"Thank you. I suppose it's time I go. Company is already gathering in the parlor, so I'd better make my appearance before I'm late. Thanks again for helping me, Maggie."

"You're welcome. You look poised and elegant, ma'am."

"Wish me luck!" Liberty closed the door quietly. She stood at the head of the stairs and took a deep breath, as deep as her stays would allow, and descended the steps, her head up and shoulders well back.

She entered the parlor, seeing that at least half the guests had already arrived.

It seemed time was suspended for a minute as people took in the lovely vision of their hostess.

Liberty caught Armand's eyes on her, but he didn't smile and neither did she.

Mrs. Graydon Gardner, a beautiful brunette, was hanging on Armand's arm. She gave it a tug, laughing up into his face.

Liberty's eyes swung to see Mr. Graydon Gardner watching his wife with a quizzical twist to his lips. His gaze shifted to Liberty, who nodded at him, but she turned to greet a couple who stood by the parlor door, looking lost.

"Good evening. I'm Liberty Bouvier. I don't believe I've had the pleasure of meeting you."

The young man replied, "I'm Thomas Hill, and this is my lovely wife, Rosalie."

"I am delighted you could come. You know my husband, I presume."

"Yes. He visited my company, Hill Textiles. It's small, but we're doing wonderfully. I have been toying with the idea of expansion, and your husband said he specializes in funding companies' expansions."

"Ye-es, he does. Ah, I understand Manning Brighton, owner of Brighton Banking, also offers loans at a very low interest rate. He encourages expansions and is a more secure place to take out loans." She smiled sweetly as his eyes registered surprise at her disclosure. Liberty took a deep breath, knowing he could easily tell Armand of her revelation. "I don't imagine my husband would appreciate me giving you this tip, but just the same, it's true."

"Mum's the word, Madam Bouvier, and I thank you."

"You are welcome." She took another breath, glad that she'd saved the young man from ruination.

Out of the corner of her eye, she saw Mr. Gardner making his way easily toward her, chatting with several people as he slowly but surely gravitated her way. He was to be her dinner partner while his wife would be seated on Armand's right.

"Madam Bouvier." He bent over her hand, and although he didn't kiss it, she felt his breath on the back of her hand. It was all she could do to not snatch it away from him. He was devastatingly good looking, and she felt an attraction to him.

Graydon Gardner was quite wealthy. He owned a large carriage company. Armand had told her the evening before that he was looking to become owner of a lucrative company, and Liberty was quite sure this man was the one he had talked about.

"Mr. Gardner, isn't it?" Liberty smiled warmly, and he seemed bowled over by her charm. "I am pleased to make your acquaintance."

"And I, yours."

He started to say something else, but Sigmund was standing at the parlor door. He drew up to his full height and said to the room at large, "Dinner is served."

"Shall we?" Graydon Gardner smiled down into a pair of beautiful green eyes as he took Liberty's arm.

Others in the room paired up to stroll to the dining room.

Several days passed. The Bouvier staff had finished eating. Dishes awaited them, but Maggie, Matilda, Cook, and Sigmund lingered at the scrubbed-oak table in the kitchen. They were relaxing after a delicious meal, conversing, as Rufus had left.

Maggie chattered a mile a minute.

"Madam was so beautiful, Siggy. I don't know how she gets more beautiful every day, but she does. That blue velvet dress she had on last week, why, she looked like a queen. You should have seen her!"

"I did see her," Sigmund responded drolly. "You forget, I attend to all the guests as they arrive, and the mistress of this house is always present."

"Oh, I did forget. You—"

Her response was interrupted by the knocker on the front door.

Sigmund rose and hurried to answer it. He opened the door to see two men bundled up against the weather.

"Please come in out of the cold," he said. Both looked respectable but serious.

"We're with the police department." They stepped into the foyer, and Sigmund hurriedly closed the door behind them against the cold. "I'm Sergeant Billings, and this is Constable Hayes. Is Madam Bouvier in residence?"

"Yes, she is. Please come this way." He led them to the front parlor and added, "Have a chair. I'm sure she will be with you posthaste." Sigmund left the room, closing the door to the parlor, and ran down the hall to madam's sitting room. He tapped on the door.

"Enter." Liberty hurriedly uncurled her legs from underneath her, but not before Sigmund opened the door.

"Two policemen here to see you, madam."

"The police? Why would they wish to see me?" Her first thought was that Armand and Corlay had been caught in their perfidy. *Perhaps Armand is in jail.* "Can you get Cook to rustle up some tea? I imagine the two men are frozen. The parlor is drafty too. Would you mind showing them down here? It's much warmer."

"Yes, madam." Sigmund left and ran to the kitchen to inform Cook. He winked at Matilda, who had turned toward him while washing dishes with Maggie.

He ran back to the parlor and took a deep breath to still his heart before entering the room.

"Madam Bouvier has asked that you come to her sitting room, which is much warmer. You must be frozen. Please follow me."

Sigmund led them farther down the hall and tapped on the door, opening it for the two men.

Liberty stood and proffered her hand. "I am Madam Bouvier." A question marked her eyes.

"I am Sergeant Billings, and this is Constable Hayes." Billings took her hand and shook it, while Constable Hayes looked at the gorgeous woman with suspicion in his eyes.

"Please be seated. I have ordered tea to warm you, but can you please tell me the reason for this visit?" She waited until they were seated before sitting herself.

Sergeant Billings cleared his throat. "Can you tell me your whereabouts this evening?"

"Certainly. I have been here at home. I've just finished eating, and I haven't been out all day. It's far too cold. Why do you care? Why are you here?"

"Madam, I have some very bad news for you. Your husband was murdered this evening."

"Murdered! Armand, murdered?" Liberty stood abruptly, the blood draining from her face. "My husband was murdered? Where? Who did it?"

"We don't know, madam, but I'm glad you have a solid alibi. We will do everything we can to find out who did this evil deed."

Matilda tapped on the door and entered with a tea trolley. She glanced at Liberty, whose face was white as a sheet. Matilda said nothing, but Sigmund had told her the two men were from the police.

Entering the kitchen, she ran to Sigmund's side. "Oh, Siggy! Madam is white as a sheet. No one spoke while I was in there, but it frightened me."

"It's all right, *mein liebling.* It'll be all right." He gave her a quick kiss, since Cook had turned to make more tea for them. "Sit. We'll find out soon enough why they are here. Perhaps Monsieur has finally been caught stealing someone's company."

Maggie entered the kitchen in time to hear Sigmund's comment. "Did they put him in jail? Oh, I do hope he's been put into jail for the evil things he's done!"

"Hush, Maggie! Sometimes these walls have ears!" Sigmund, although he agreed with Maggie, didn't know if Rufus might be skulking somewhere in the back entry off the kitchen.

Maggie realized Sigmund's intent. She could lose her position if Rufus should hear her comment. "Sorry. I apologize."

Sigmund nodded. Putting his finger to his lips, he tiptoed to the swinging doors to the back entry. He went through with an abruptness that startled those watching.

"No one here," he said, grinning as he came back through the double doors. "You must be more careful, Maggie. You know Rufus hates you. He has only to make up a story about you, and pfft! You'd be gone so fast it would make your head spin. He would do it too, if he had the brains to think of it, but he doesn't."

"You're right, Sigmund. I have trouble with my mouth, as you all well know."

Sigmund laughed and started to speak, but the bell from madam's sitting room rang, and Sigmund hurried to answer it.

"Thank you, Sigmund. Show these gentlemen out, and please come back here immediately."

Sigmund nodded. "Please follow me." He pivoted on his heel and walked the men to the front door, ushering them out with more aplomb than he felt. He hurried back to the sitting room.

"Close the door, Sigmund...please." Liberty indicated a chair and said, "Please sit. I know you have been a most noncommittal employee. I have no idea where your loyalties lie, but I must share with you the news those policemen brought. I have no doubt you'll hear it soon enough over the servants' grapevine. Monsieur Bouvier has been murdered."

Sigmund's eyebrows rose in shock. "Madam! I am so sorry for you! Do they know who has done this deed?"

"N-no, they don't. Evidently I was suspect, but I told them I have been indoors this entire day. I would imagine they will want to talk to all of the staff. I don't even know what to say. I suppose I should make some kind of announcement to everyone employed here. Can I leave that to you?"

"Of course, madam. I will do all in my power to support you. Simply tell me what needs done, and I will see to it."

"I know my father and the lawyer must be informed. It's late, and we can carry out those tasks tomorrow. Oh my…murdered. Armand… murdered!"

CHAPTER XVIII

God is our refuge and strength,
a very present help in trouble.

PSALM 46:1

MAGGIE HAD NO IDEA WHAT WAS GOING to happen to the Bouvier staff. It was déjà vu, but with a difference. Grant Jamison had been a good man, and his death had been devastating. Monsieur Bouvier was not loved by any of the staff except, perhaps, Rufus.

Maggie tossed and turned, but sleep was elusive as she recalled the events of the late afternoon.

After talking with Madam Bouvier, Sigmund had called the staff together, including Rufus, who had stared at her with ugly eyes. Sigmund announced that Monsieur Bouvier had been murdered in his office downtown. The shock, nearly tangible, reverberated throughout the kitchen.

Rufus had stood abruptly, knocking over his chair.

Upset would be considered an understatement, Maggie had thought.

He'd slammed out the door, and everyone knew he was headed to Jacques Corlay's mansion.

Besides being paid by Bouvier for having ears in the Bouviers' manse, he was also in the pay of Jacques Corlay, who wanted detailed information of all that happened in the Bouvier residence. Armand had no clue that Rufus was in Jacques' pay, but Sigmund knew. Jacques Corlay's butler, Percy, was a good friend.

The staff started asking questions, but Sigmund could tell them little else other than the police would probably be questioning all of them in the near future.

Maggie lay in the tangled bed linens, wondering if Madam Bouvier was going to want her to continue. She got up, lit a taper, and put it to the wick of the lamp next to her bed. She straightened the bottom sheet, tucking it in tightly.

What will madam do? Will she remain in this house? I don't think she's been happy here, but what will she do? At least she's not like Mrs. Jamison and left penniless. Finally, Maggie fell into an uneasy slumber.

Three days passed, and the only effect of monsieur's death so far had been an announcement by Madam Bouvier that things would continue on as they'd been until the reading of the will after the funeral.

Maggie had helped Madam Bouvier to dress and undress each day, but little conversation had ensued. Maggie saw no tears, but that was no surprise either. Monsieur had been mean and evil, and Maggie doubted many would mourn him.

As for herself, she was glad he was dead. He'd caused Mr. Jamison's death and untold unhappiness. Everything seemed in a state of suspension waiting for the funeral, which was to occur on the morrow.

Maggie was helping madam to dress. It was the first time she confided how she felt to Maggie. As Maggie finished buttoning up the back of madam's black dress, Liberty spun around and put her hands on Maggie's shoulders.

"Maggie, I feel so wicked."

"You are not wicked, ma'am. Why would you feel wicked?"

"I can't mourn him, Maggie. I only feel this overwhelming sense of release. I'm free at last, and yet I know I'm not. I am quite sure Jacques will come and try to take over the running of this estate. He married me off to Armand for monetary gain."

"I knew it! I knew you wouldn't marry that man as your choice for a husband. Thank you for sharing that with me. As far as mourning, monsieur, I doubt if he'll have many mourners," Maggie replied. "He didn't treat you well, or anyone else that he knew. I know you believe in God, but I don't think even God would have you mourn such wickedness. And as far as the estate, if it belongs to you, you'll just have to be strong and not let Monsieur Corlay make the decisions for it. You are owner, now, not him."

"Thank you, Maggie," Liberty whispered. "I'll think on your words and see if there is some way to thwart Jacques."

Liberty left the room, and Maggie straightened the bed linens. She smiled ruefully. *Madam must be sleeping as badly as I am. All her bedding is a twisted mess.* She remade the bed went through Liberty's black dresses, making sure all was in ready-to-wear order. It took her quite some time before she was finished. She picked up the half-filled coffee cup next to the bed, glancing around to make sure she had everything back on the breakfast tray before taking it down to the kitchen.

The staff had been using the main stairs since monsieur's death. Maggie started down with the heavy pewter tray but stopped when she saw Monsieur Corlay pushing passed Sigmund to enter the parlor.

Her eyes narrowed at his rudeness. Madam had told her Monsieur Corlay had been business partners with Monsieur Bouvier. *They're both crooks. Mr. Jamison would still be alive if it wasn't for them. Wonder if he's going to try to take over. I hope madam sticks to her guns. I think she's afraid of him. I know she was afraid of Monsieur Bouvier. Wicked, so wicked.*

Using her back, Maggie pushed through to the kitchen. She heard Sigmund talking to Cook and Matilda.

"Madam's lawyer is in there talking to madam, and her father arrived. He didn't allow me to announce him, but pushed his way past me right into the room."

"I saw him." Maggie set the heavy tray by the sink and put dirty dishes into the big enamel pan. "He nearly shoved you over, Sigmund, in his haste to get into the parlor. Such a rude man. He's much like Monsieur Bouvier, isn't he?"

"Ja," Cook responded. "He yust like monsewer. They vas the pair, dose two!"

"Wonder what's going on in there? My understanding is that Monsieur Corlay wasn't invited, but then neither was the lawyer, was he?" Maggie asked.

"No, both were surprise visits to madam."

The parlor door slammed shut. Sigmund hurried out the kitchen in time to see Monsieur Corlay slamming out the front door. He heard the bell in the kitchen, and returning, saw it was Matilda's.

"I'd better get in there," Matilda said. She hurried to the parlor door and entered without knocking, since she'd been summoned.

"Matilda, could you please get us some tea and scones?"

"Yes, ma'am."

Sigmund was waiting for her and grabbed her by the arm. "Do you know what's happening? Have you overheard anything at all, Tilly?"

Matilda looked up at this big blond man, and her heart beat faster from the warmth she saw in his eyes.

"No, Sigmund, I've heard nothing. Have you?" She laid her hand on top of his and gave it a caress.

His eyes blazed, their blueness rivaling the skies on a clear day. "No, I've heard nothing, but I don't like the feel of it. Madam's had a bad time of it, that's certain. I fear worse is to come, with her evil father always panting after money." Matilda started to move away. "I must get the tea and scones for her and her guest. Who is he, anyway?"

"He was Monsieur Bouvier's lawyer, Mr. Humphries, but I believe him to be a good man. Hurry now. I'll help you." He swatted Matilda on her bottom.

She pretended to glare at him but ended up giggling. They both headed toward the kitchen.

Maggie heard the bell from madam's rooms and hurried to answer it. When she entered the room, she saw Madam Bouvier undoing the buttons on her bodice.

"I'd like to borrow your maid's clothes," Liberty said.

Maggie was stunned, totally taken aback.

"Ma'am, I have only my maid uniforms and a set of street clothes I wear when going to visit the children at the orphanage."

"Maggie, I know you have two sets of maids' clothing. Is the other set clean?"

"Yes, ma'am, it is."

"Get it, and please hurry." Liberty said as she stepped out of her dress.

"Yes, ma'am. Right away, ma'am." Maggie hurried up the second flight of stairs and grabbed the set of clothes. *Why in the world would she want my maid's outfit?*

Maggie returned to see madam's hair done in a tight bun. As she dumped the clothing on the bed, she glanced at Liberty.

"Oh, ma'am," she said, "you're so beautiful!"

Liberty was scantily clad with only her corset and chemise, but she unconsciously straightened, smiling at Maggie's compliment.

"Oh, Maggie, what'll I do without you?"

Maggie stared in amazement. "What are you talking about, ma'am?" She waited for a reply as madam seemed to be making up her mind about something.

"Maggie, I've always trusted you. I'm going to trust you now as a friend and confidante rather than my maid. My father will be taking over the estate. Indeed, he's taking over everything. That's why the lawyer came this morning, to tell me Armand cut me out of the entire estate except for a property in California. I, at Mr. Humphries' suggestion, am going to California." She hurriedly began to dress in Maggie's clothing.

Maggie halted a moment in assisting Liberty. Making a snap decision, she looked into her employer's eyes.

"I've nothing to keep me here, ma'am. I've no family, no man, and you're the only person on this earth I care about. May I come with you? I've a bit of money saved up for a rainy day. Oh, please say yes!" Tears stood out in her dark-gray eyes.

They fell into each other's arms, hugging.

"Oh, Maggie, I don't know what I'd ever do without you! Yes, yes, and yes! You may come with me, and I'll pay your passage, at least I think I will." She smiled as she spoke, hoping she would have enough funds.

Maggie helped Liberty with the buttons on her maid's dress. The length was fine, covering the tops of her shoes, but the waist was loose.

Maggie looked at Liberty and giggled. "You look the part, ma'am. With my mobcap and apron, you'll be perfect. Where are we going?"

"Into the city. I need to buy some things, lots of things for living in the West."

The two women slipped quietly down the back stairs. Maggie had a heavy shawl wrapped around her sturdy shoulders and lifted its twin off the hooks by the service entrance, handing it to Liberty.

The sharp, bitterly cold air sucked at their lungs. Trees, newly decked out in dresses of white, stretched laden fingers toward the sky. It was midmorning, but no one seemed to have ventured out. Snow crunched beneath their feet as they set off the few blocks into the city proper.

Amazement sparkled in Maggie's eyes at the types, colors, and textures as they strolled through the shop, ordering bolts of rich and varied materials. They added to their purchases anything they could think of that might be needed in an area that had little to offer by way of textiles: large bobbins of thread, needles, scissors, ribbons and laces, trims and more trims.

Once outside, they began to giggle, careful not to let the passersby have reason to stare. It was difficult not to burst into a full-bellied laugh. Maggie had not had so much fun since living in Ireland.

"It is strange that when you dress as a servant, no one seems to think differently. Can they really believe you're ordering all these things for your employer? What next, madam?"

"Well, let's see. We have no need to go to the milliner. I've a large number of hats, gloves, and dresses, as you well know, enough to last us a long time. I think the next stop will be the luggage shop. We'll need a vast amount of trunks to hold all our belongings."

"Ma'am, I don't need a trunk. My things will fit into a satchel," Maggie replied.

"That may be true at this moment, but you're going to need a wardrobe." She faced Maggie "We'll not be going to California as employer and employee. We'll be going as equals, as friends. You're my best friend, Maggie. Once we're on the train, you will no longer be my servant."

Maggie stared at Liberty as her words sank into her heart. "I haven't had a best friend since I was a girl in Ireland." Maggie's eyes sparkled as a wide smile spread across her lips. "I'll be the best, most loyal friend you've ever had, madam!" she exclaimed.

They hugged each other, smiling into each other's eyes.

"I suppose we have much more shopping to do, ma'am, but I don't want you to overtax yourself. You must be getting hungry. I know I am."

The two women stopped at several more shops, Maggie watched as Liberty ordered large amounts of staples: flour; cornmeal; sugar; salt; spices; dried fruits of lemon, lime, orange, prunes, dates, figs, and apricots. She added pounds of nuts and beans, and sacks of rice.

"Ma'am, we'll need molds, plus string and tallow for making candles and soap," Maggie whispered.

"What else, Maggie?" Liberty asked. She seemed humbled that Maggie had more knowledge about their needs than she.

"Well," Maggie continued, "we'll also need lye for making soap, and flint for fires, and a butter churn. I think we should revisit the leather shop and order lengths of leather for replacing worn harnesses and buckles and the like."

"That's a good idea. I will send a note to Mr. Humphries this afternoon, informing him of our purchases and let him take care of the details. Liberty charged everything to Armand's account—nails, hammers, crowbars, saws, much rope, several shovels, pitchforks, and anything else the clerk helping them thought fit for living in California.

"Won't Monsieur Corlay be angry when he sees these bills?" Maggie asked.

"Apoplectic I'm sure, Maggie, but we'll not be here to witness it. Mr. Humphries plans to have us gone the day after tomorrow."

Maggie's eyebrows rose. "The day after tomorrow!"

"Yes. He doesn't know what shape the California house is in that a man built for Armand, but it's all I own. Mr. Humphries thinks the move away from Boston will be the best move I've ever made. I have to agree with him. Now, I have one more important purchase." She spoke to the clerk. "Madam also wants me to order two handguns and two rifles with a lot of bullets because where she's sending this stuff is wild with outlaws."

The clerk recommended two rifles, two handguns, and an enormous amount of bullets, which Liberty charged to the Bouvier account.

By the time they returned to the manse, both women were famished. They entered the back door, and Sigmund's eyes registered shock at madam's attire, but he spoke with aplomb.

"A detective to see you, madam."

Without wasting time on decorum, Liberty took the back stairs two at a time, speaking to Maggie as she climbed. "Maggie, please hurry. I need your help!"

Maggie, close on her heels, grabbed a dress from the clothespress. It was unrelieved black. She did Liberty's hair, while Liberty buttoned up the front of the dress. She left the room, and Maggie watched as Liberty took a deep breath and descended the stairs with decorum.

Maggie took the back stairs and was able to eat lunch, feeling sorry for Madam Bouvier, who was hungry too. When she finished her meal, she climbed the stairs and began sorting through an enormous amount of items, putting them into piles to have Liberty check them later.

Trunks had arrived from one of the shops, and Maggie packed necessary things.

Liberty after talking to the inspector, scribbled a quick note to Mr. Humphries about her purchases. Liberty felt blessed by all that man was doing for her. Since her father would be virtually left with everything, she decided to tell Mr. Baxter he was free to peruse anything in the desk he might find interesting. She felt no sense of ownership. As far as she was concerned, it was not hers and might give the detective some knowledge of Armand's dealings and with whomever he was in contact. Liberty went into the kitchen and delivered her message to Cook to give Mr. Baxter when it was her turn to be interviewed. Finally, Liberty made her way upstairs.

Maggie had emptied some of the drawers in the chiffonier. Liberty started in on the clothespress. She reached in and pulled out her favorite gray watered silk dress. She handed it to Maggie. "This is for you. Try it on, and we'll alter it to fit you. I have a hat here that matches it. You can wear this for a traveling dress."

"Oh, ma'am, 'tis one of your favorites!"

"But it will look superb on you. We need to get a few things for you to wear, because as I said, we're going as friends. Also, I've decided not to wear mourning the day after tomorrow. No one on the train will know me, and I feel it's a deception to act as if I'm in mourning when I'm not."

"I agree with that decision." Maggie said. "I'm excited too, and I would never mourn monsieur!"

The two women packed long into the night.

CHAPTER XIX

Thou hast turned for me my mourning into dancing:
thou hast put off my sackcloth,
and girded me with gladness;

PSALM 30:11

MAGGIE COULD SCARCELY BELIEVE SHE WAS on her way to California. It was late evening. They'd enjoyed a lovely dinner of roast beef stuffed with onion and green peppers that had been dusted with spices. The rice smothered in a delectable gravy had been perfect. The meals, prepared in the dining car, were elegant and delicious.

Now, they had only one more day on the train. All in all it would take six days to cross from Boston to Sacramento. When their train had rolled into Chicago, they'd had to transfer all their belongings to the Union Pacific for the rest of their journey. Mr. Humphries had arranged with the porter on the first train to oversee the transfer, and it had gone without a hitch.

Maggie wondered what the man who was supposed to meet them would be like. She looked over at Liberty, who sat with eyes closed, her head leaning back against the Pullman car seat opposite her.

She is gorgeous. I wish I was as sweet tempered. She keeps much to herself, but then so do I. I've never shared with another soul all that has happened to me, except Mrs. Jamison. Wonder what's going to happen when we get to California? I'll bet the house we're supposed to move into isn't nearly as nice as the Bouvier manse, and yet, as Liberty said, she's finally free…free from that evil husband and free from her wretched father. Wonder if Monsieur Corlay can find her and make her go back. I hope not. I like being free, too—free from being a servant.

Liberty opened her eyes, and seeing Maggie's gaze upon her, she smiled. "I was just praying. I'm concerned about our arrival tomorrow into Sacramento. The man who is supposed to meet us is called Matthew Bannister. My understanding is that he's worked for Armand and staked out a piece of property and even built on it."

"Then why are you concerned?"

"Armand never paid him, or if he did, it was a pittance, and Mr. Bannister doesn't have any idea that we have an enormous amount of paraphernalia…trunks and trunks, besides the drums of kerosene. I don't know, Maggie. I think he's not going to be a happy man when he sees us."

"My goodness! I didn't know monsieur never paid him! Mr. Bannister will likely leave us and our luggage on the platform! I wouldn't blame him either. We have a tremendous amount of luggage."

"I know, Maggie. I know. At least we have that money Mr. Humphries gave us before we left. It seemed an incredible amount at the time, but honestly, I know nothing about money. I've never had to use it. Everything has been paid or put onto the Bouvier account. Do you think you could teach me?"

"No, I can't teach you, because I don't either. I don't know anything about money."

The two women stared at each other, abashed by their confession. Maggie began to giggle, and Liberty joined in. Soon, both whooped with laughter.

"We are ignorant, but blissfully so," Maggie said.

They laughed again.

Maggie lay in her lower Pullman car bed that night and thought of how wonderful it was to be treated as a friend by Liberty. *She's never condescending, or anything close to it. I am grateful to have such a friend. In all my life I haven't had a close friend, except Clodagh and Mrs. Jamison. I don't know if I'll ever share about Elmer or what happened to me. Wonder how Mrs. Jamison is doing? She thought God helped her. How she arrived at that conclusion after losing her baby and having her husband hang himself…I declare I'll never know. I can't understand why an intelligent woman like Liberty would believe in God either. Her husband was the most wretched of men, and her father is just as bad. Why would a loving God allow her to be basically sold by her father to monsieur? I think I'd have run away if I had a husband like him. So evil. Scared me to death that night I met him in the hall. He had one of his girlfriends with him…ugh. He deserved to die. Wonder if it was one of those women he dumped after using them. A man after Elmer's own heart, no doubt. I'll bet that was Elmer's plan too. That was certainly a shock, to read that letter from his loving wife. No, I don't think there's a God. If there is, He's certainly never done a thing for me.*

Matthew Bannister's deep-set blue eyes sparked with anger. He tried to tamp it down, but as he read the telegram again, his blood boiled over.

Stomping into the enormous open kitchen of his Rancho, he waved a telegram in the air. Yanking a chair out from the huge kitchen table, he swung it around and straddled it, pouring his woes out to his cook and all-around help, Conchita Rodriguez.

"I can't believe this! I staked out that claim for Monsieur Bouvier, put in a well, and knocked up that shack. I did it so anyone nosing around from the government would see improvements had been made. I don't know if you realize, Conchita, but because it's a government grant, you can lose the property if there's no improvements. Bouvier hasn't paid me a fourth of what it cost me to do it, and now I get this!" He waved the telegram again. "The gall of that man!"

"What ees thees you ees talking about?" Conchita asked, her accent heavy. She took a cup off the shelf and filled it with the coffee that was always available on their large cooking stove, which had just arrived the month before. Filling the cup to the brim, she sat it on the round table in front of her boss.

"Bouvier had his lawyer send me a telegram to tell me his wife is on her way here, and she plans to stay for a bit and look over the property." Matthew threw the scrap of paper on the table and fumed some more. "She's bringing a maid with her. What a mess! What am I supposed to do? Tell her she has a louse for a husband? I know we have plenty of room here for her, but it means more work for you, Conchita. She's most likely used to ordering many servants to do her bidding. She'll probably stick her nose in the air like a Boston snob."

"You doan know what she ees acting like, Meester Bannister. Maybe you geeve her a chance before you judge her. We weel know better when she comed here."

"Yes, you're right, Conchita. We shouldn't judge someone before we know. I reckon Jess has put blinders on me that any woman can be truly good, except you, Conchita. You are the best!"

"Who is the best?" Kirk, Matthew's younger brother, strolled into the kitchen, heading straight for the coffeepot. He poured a cup while Matthew answered him.

"Conchita is the best."

"Oh, that goes without saying. What's that, a telegram?"

"Unfortunately, yes. We're going to have a couple guests within the week. Don't reckon they'll stay long once they see the condition of Bouvier's shack. I have a feeling from the telegram, they think it's a real house or something."

"Well, it'll be nice to have a couple females around."

"Uh huh, you would say that. You've become a real womanizer, Kirk. You'd better watch your step with Consuelo. She'll have you wrapped up, and in no time, you'll find yourself with a tight gold ring around your finger."

Conchita spoke before Kirk could vent a reply. "She be my niece, but I am knowing she no good. She not a good woman for you, Meester Kirk, an' she not be the marrying kind."

Kirk's head jerked up from his cup of coffee. Conchita was always plain speaking, but she usually stayed out of one's private affairs.

"Reckon I'll be making my own opinions about the women in my life, thanks just the same." He gulped down the rest of his coffee and went to the sink, dropping his cup into a large tin pan full of soapy water. "And now I have work to do." He stalked out of the kitchen.

"He no thinking weeth hees brain." Conchita knew her niece and the sorrow she had caused her sister. Conchita had several sisters. The one she was closest to lived in San Francisco, but Consuelo's mother, Evita, lived nearby in Napa.

"That is an understatement." Matthew stood and stretched. "Thanks for the coffee. Reckon tomorrow I'd better head down to Sacramento. At any rate, it should be interesting. With the snow the way it is in the Sierras, there's no telling how long it'll take for that train to arrive. If it was summer, it'd be pulling in tomorrow for sure. I just don't know, but if not tomorrow, it'll arrive in the next few days. What a mess. I've so much work I need to get done, and instead I'll be babysitting a couple women from Boston. Guess I'll go out and help Diego with that fence." He gave Conchita a quick kiss on the cheek and left, whistling, "Home on the Range."

The two women had become bored with the little compartment and the restrictions of being on the train. Excitement bubbled within them at the thought that this was their last night traveling. After dinner, they took a long walk, going from car to car to stretch their legs.

"I've learned much from this journey, Libby, but I never dreamed the world was so beautiful!" she exclaimed,

"I'm glad you're calling me Libby. It's what my mother called me. And yes, the world is awe inspiring, isn't it? God made it, you know. His ways are unsearchable and His love so powerful. I came to know Him while I was at boarding school, when I felt so unloved. I've never felt alone since. God helps me in so many ways. Oh, Maggie, I wish you knew Him as I do. I could never have survived living with Armand without the strength of God leading me day by day. I would've been crushed by Armand's treatment of me. I know I'd never have developed into the woman I am. I give God all the praise for it, and now I'm free!"

"You're a beautiful woman. I've seen your beauty, inside and out. I have so much wanted to be as you are," Maggie said. "The other day, when that woman with the skimpy dress tripped me, I was incredibly angry with you for going up to her and apologizing for us, and yet I knew deep down it was the right thing to do. I think part of the laughter was embarrassment at seeing so much skin. It was the lowest-cut bodice I've ever seen!"

"It wasn't right that we laughed at her the first night we were on the train. I think most of that laughter was a letting down, or relief that we escaped from Boston before my father found out about it. I'd never have apologized to her if Jesus hadn't spoken to my heart and told me it was the right thing to do. So often people do things because they feel like it, or they don't do things because they don't feel like it. I've learned that it is not about how I feel—it's about what God's Word says to me and me wanting to please my Savior. If I went on my feelings, I'd do very little the right way. I look at Jesus as my King. Maggie, my King. I'm a servant, and I do the bidding of my Master, just as you served me so faithfully and did everything I asked you to do." Liberty gave Maggie a big hug. "I wish you'd ask Jesus into your heart. It's really living."

"I'll think about it—I truly will. It's a big step, and I have never given much credence to religion. God hasn't been particularly nice to me, in my estimation. I used to think your religion was a crutch for you to be able to escape Monsieur Bouvier's attentions."

"Oh, Maggie, it is a crutch. I lean on it because I can never walk the way I was intended. I know that I need that crutch the same way I need air!" She laughed, giving Maggie's arm a squeeze. "I think we should go back to our compartment and close out those journals. What say you?"

"Good idea, but I think yours is much more interesting than mine."

"Why do you say that?"

"Well, growing up with a father like yours, and then having him marry you off to a man just as evil…yes, yours is much more interesting." Maggie didn't say she was leaving much out of hers. She never wanted anyone to read about some of her past.

The two women wrote in their journals, but Liberty's writing morphed into a prayer. She was worried about the kind of reception they would receive, especially when Mr. Bannister saw the number of trunks and paraphernalia. She hoped he would see them to the house he'd built on the property. It was an intrusion on his time, and she was sure he was a busy man. Elijah Humphries had told her he'd sent a telegram to Mr. Bannister, and she could only pray he'd received it.

When the train pulled into the Sacramento station, both women were ready to get off. The friendly porter, whom they had spoken with earlier, had promised to find them help to offload their luggage. The train slowed. Libby and Maggie stood next to the exit, with their satchels and a basket, chattering excitedly.

As they stepped from the train, they realized the weather, although cool, was totally different from what they'd experienced in Boston and on the journey. The sun shone brightly with some warmth. Fluffy clouds scudded their way across the heavens, and the two women felt their spirits lift.

Matthew Bannister had come to Sacramento early so as not to miss the women's arrival, but he hadn't planned to be there so early that he had to waste two days waiting for the train. A body never knew when it would arrive, because of the snow pack and various other problems that could occur.

When the train finally pulled in, he leaned against the wall, arms crossed in front of him. *Maybe they aren't on this train.* He reckoned he'd just wait. He knew he was on edge. Usually he was pretty long on patience, but after two days of waiting, he was on a short fuse. He looked around the platform—the place was crawling with people. He waited as the bustle died down a bit, but the crush of people blocked any view he might have of two women searching for him.

Why would a man send his wife all the way across the country to check on a property? Why now? It's been three years since I staked it out. And why extensive luggage unless they plan to stay? Why did the lawyer send the message instead of Bouvier? Were the Bouviers planning to move west? Matthew had many questions, and none of his own answers added up. He'd been asking them ever since the telegram arrived a few days ago at his place up in the Napa Valley.

Matthew saw no sign of the women. He surveyed the platform again. As his gaze reached the back of the train, he saw two women standing together where they were offloading. He ambled down the cobbles toward them, but he swallowed a big lump in his throat as he took in the pile of luggage, seeming to grow larger with every step he took. He swallowed again, trying to control his temper, but he seethed under the skin.

He tipped his hat. "Name's Bannister," he said. "Matthew Bannister."

Both women stared at him in surprise, but the taller one recovered first. "I'm Madam Bouvier," she said, proffering her hand.

He took it in a firm grip.

"And I am Margaret O'Neill—Maggie," said the other as she almost dipped a curtsey.

Maggie felt off balance. This man wasn't what she'd expected. He was tall, lean, and quite good looking—clean shaven with a small cleft in his chin and deep-set blue eyes. He had a gun strapped to his hip and was dressed in denim trousers, something no one in the East ever wore. He had on a checked shirt with a bright scarf tied around his neck. A black vest and cowboy hat, covering dark-brown hair, completed his outfit.

"Which luggage here belongs to you? We need to get it sorted out, because the train for Vallejo will be here soon. From Vallejo we'll head north up to Napa, by wagon."

His voice was clipped, and Maggie's eyes rounded. She was too scared to answer.

"It's all ours," Liberty said firmly, looking steadily at him. "All of it." Her green eyes sparked as she said it.

Maggie said soothingly, "We didn't plan to bring so much, sir. It just turned out that way." She tried smiling at him winningly, but he didn't return the smile.

He spun around and yelled, "Jed...hey, Jed! Can you help us over here?"

Jed was an icon in the railroad business in Sacramento and the outlying areas. He rode the train round trip every day between Sacramento and Vallejo.

"Be happy to help you, Bannister. Just a minute and I'll get another pair of hands."

Matthew, with a withering glance at the two women, pivoted on his heel and bit out the words, "Wait here!" He strode down the platform, going into the station to wire his brother to bring several more wagons to Vallejo.

Mr. Bannister returned, and Maggie thought he didn't look quite as angry. The train for Vallejo was in, and the men were loading their things.

The man named Jed asked, "What's in these drums, Bannister?"

Matthew looked at the drums in surprise. "I've no idea, Jed."

Maggie and Liberty were both standing at the edge of the platform, out of the way.

"It's kerosene. The drums are full of kerosene," Liberty said.

Matthew looked at her with a bit more respect than he'd shown thus far. Kerosene was not easy to come by. It wasn't that expensive, but shipping it was costly. It was a coveted item for folks living in the country. He looked inquiringly at Madam Bouvier.

She could clearly see the questions in his eyes, but she said nothing.

What's going on here? Matthew wondered. *Why all the trunks and even kerosene? They must be moving west.*

CHAPTER XX

God setteth the solitary in families

PSALM 68:6a

THE TWO WOMEN WATCHED AS THEIR possessions were loaded, with a speed and efficiency that pleased them, onto the train bound for Vallejo.

Matt ordered the two women. "Go buy three tickets to Vallejo while we're loading your stuff."

The women walked down the platform, and Maggie said, "He's rather short on manners, isn't he?"

Liberty didn't reply. "I'm getting the distinct impression Mr. Bannister doesn't know Armand is dead. I think I want to keep it that way, at least until I'm acquainted with the situation here. No slip-ups Maggie. Armand's still alive as far as Mr. Bannister's concerned. It's a lucky thing I'm not dressed in mourning. Before I trust him, he's got to earn it."

Liberty stepped up to the window and said to the stationmaster, "Three tickets to Vallejo please."

"One way or round trip?" the stationmaster asked.

"One way, please." She handed him a wad of money, and he handed her over half of it back. "You could ride to Timbuktu with that amount, lady." He smiled at her.

"Sorry. Thank you." She stuffed the tickets and returned the money to her reticule. They went back out the door, and as they headed down the station platform, a man stepped into Liberty's path.

"Excuse me," Liberty said, looking up at him.

The man leered. "Hel-lo, little lady. How'd you like to go an' have a drink with me, honey-girl?"

"No, thank you." Liberty started to step around him.

He grabbed her arm. "Aw, don't go bein' so uppity, little girl."

Liberty tried to wrench her arm away, saying firmly, "Mister, kindly remove your hand from my arm, now!"

"Leave her alone!" Maggie hissed at the man.

He responded by grabbing Maggie's arm with his left hand. "An' now I got me a little spitfire. You're some redhead! I like a woman with a little spirit and spunk."

Maggie pulled back with her right arm and slugged the guy on the tip of the chin. He let go of Liberty and grabbed Maggie with both hands, raising a hand to slap her. When Liberty saw that the man was going after Maggie, she dropped her satchel, and kicked the man's kneecap as hard as she could. She thought she'd broken her toe.

Matthew Bannister came running up, spun the man around, and with one smart clip to the chin, the man dropped like a ton of bricks.

"Sorry about that, ladies." He stepped over the man, picked up Liberty's satchel, and handed it to her. "We need to be going, or our train will be leaving without us. It's getting ready to pull out in just a few minutes."

Maggie gasped as she saw another man coming out of the station door behind them. Liberty looked at her questioningly, but didn't say anything, as she saw Maggie's already pale complexion go pasty. Her eyes had widened in shock, and Liberty wondered at it. Abruptly, Maggie turned her back to the station and became engrossed in looking at the train.

Maggie glanced quickly at the man who passed them hurriedly and boarded the train they were to ride. *Will he recognize me? Oh my stars, I thought never to see that bogus minister Brooks again! I suppose I look very little like the twelve-year-old girl he saw at that sham wedding. I hope I don't have to look at him on the train. Wonder if he lives out here somewhere. Oh…this has certainly brought up ugly memories. I thought I had them all buried.*

Maggie's discomfort brought a gentle squeeze from Liberty. The sudden sympathy Maggie felt emanating from her employer-turned-friend brought tears to Maggie's eyes and was nearly her undoing. She took a deep breath, hoping to stay the tears. Swallowing down her fear, she gave Liberty a wavery smile.

"Sorry. I suppose I'm now beginning to feel overwhelmed by our new circumstances."

Liberty nodded but detected the falseness of Maggie's statement.

Matthew strode ahead of them, and as he reached the steps of the passenger car, he reached out to hand each woman up and jumped up himself as the train tooted out its intent and began to roll slowly down the track.

Maggie glanced quickly around when she reached the top step.

"You'll meet all types of men here in the West," Matthew said, his demeanor calm. "For the most part, women are well respected, but every once in a while you'll meet a character like that one." He jerked his thumb backward, where the assailant still lay on the platform.

It amazed Maggie that no one was paying him any attention.

Matthew Bannister led the way to leather seats that faced each other. He seated them facing forward and then sat across from the pair.

Maggie drew a sigh of relief and slumped back against the seat. She was so tired she felt she could drop. She'd spotted Mr. Brooks seated at the back of the car, and stifled a tremor that threatened to run through her body. *How can a man murder like he did and get away with it? I suppose I can be glad no one ever questioned me. I never thought how I could be accused.* The tremor she'd tried to suppress ran through her.

"Well, ladies, just exactly what are your plans?"

Maggie was glad Liberty was in charge. She doubted she could think clearly right now, let alone give a coherent answer.

"Plans, Mr. Bannister?" Liberty looked the man straight in the eyes. She tried her best to hold her gaze steady. "Miss O'Neill and I are planning to live in Napa for a while. I'm here to see the property and make sure improvements are made. I must apologize to you for my husband's neglect in paying you. It must have slipped his mind. Please write a receipt for the amounts you have paid out for supplies, and include what you think decent for labor. We," she glanced at Maggie, "we wouldn't think of cheating you, Mr. Bannister. I will certainly pay you whenever you're ready with those receipts."

Matthew Bannister looked shocked at the possibility of the money and tried to hide it.

"The improvements I made on the property were just the essentials, such as a well and a shack," he said to them. "I don't believe it's habitable. I'm quite sure it's not for you women. I don't live there. My property abuts yours. The shack might leak, and it sure isn't big enough to hold all your stuff. I did the minimum because your husband didn't send out any money. I didn't want him to lose the property I'd staked out for him."

"How many acres is it?" Liberty asked.

"Well, it's one hundred sixty. That was the maximum the government would allow, so that's what I staked out for your husband. As I said, it abuts my property. I own another one hundred sixty acres myself. I staked it all out three years ago. I've been building a house on mine ever since."

The women looked totally done in. He supposed they'd be guests at his Rancho until something could be done with the shack on their property. "I reckon you'll be my guests till we get something fixed up for you. I'd no idea you planned to stay there. Reckon I figured you'd be visiting your property and then be going back east." He looked at them quizzically.

"Are you saying the house you made is uninhabitable?"

"What I'm saying is, yes, essentially it's nothing but a one-room shack. I stayed in it when I was staking out the property, but it's not meant to live in. I knocked it up to prove that an improvement had been made on the property if anyone came looking. I'm sure it must be full of mice right now. It's very small," he replied.

Maggie, who'd been fairly silent until she heard the word mice, piped up. "Thank you, Mr. Bannister. Madam Bouvier and I would be very happy to accept your invitation. We're both exhausted and need a place to lay our heads."

"Well, you're more than welcome to stay at my Rancho for as long as you need. I've plenty of room." Matthew Bannister, too, was surprised. He had thought Mistress O'Neill to simply be the madam's maid, but evidently she wasn't just a maid. Two beautiful women sat across from him, looking out the window. He sat back, deciding he'd talked enough. Scooting himself over into the corner, Matthew slid down the seat a bit and tipped his hat down over his eyes.

The train pulled its weight across the undulating landscape, the scenery completely transformed from the winter panorama Maggie and Liberty had been seeing for the past week.

They soon arrived in Vallejo. Matthew, looking out the window, felt relieved seeing a string of wagons with Kirk and Diego, his foreman, heading up a crew of men.

The journey by wagon seemed to take hours. By the time the wagons pulled into the long lane of Matthew Bannister's Rancho Bonito, it was pitch black and difficult to see. Maggie was sitting in a wagon with Kirk and looked around with curiosity. She was beyond exhaustion and thinking back to disembarking from the train in Vallejo. She'd felt Mr. Brook's eyes on her back. She shivered, trying not to think about it. Her attention swung back to her surroundings.

The drive was lined with some kind of shrubbery, but it was too dark, and she couldn't see much farther. The smooth lane swept around in front of a beautiful one-story house, the roof a rounded red tile. Huge dark beams made a beautiful contrast to the creamy stucco front. There were arches evenly spaced across the front, painted a pale orange on their underside. A flagstone walk led from the drive to the flat veranda that stretched itself across the front. Maggie thought it lovely with pruned orange trees, heavy with fruit, growing on either side of the front door. The entire place blazed with light, as if a party were taking place.

Kirk helped Maggie down. "You've had a long day. I imagine you must be exhausted."

"That's an understatement, Mr. Bannister."

"Kirk, please just call me Kirk. My brother is Mr. Bannister." He grinned and took her arm after she'd collected the satchel she'd need for the night. Walking her up the walk, they entered right after Matthew and Liberty.

The house was beautiful, but before they could even look around, a plump woman entered the room and took over.

"I yam Conchita Rodriguez, Diego's wife. Meester Bannister, he own thees casa"—she waved her hand expansively—"an' me, I run eet." She laughed, and strong white teeth were startling in her swarthy face. She was a beautiful woman with long, black shining hair hanging in a braid down her back. Her black eyes sparkled with delight at the two women.

"You hungry? You wanna eat now?"

Liberty looked over at Maggie. Both shook their heads. They were too tired to eat.

"I haf the room ready for you. I know you tired. Come…you come."

The short woman led them down a wide hall of flagstone to bedrooms lined on either side. The first she showed to Maggie. "And your name ees?"

"Maggie, my name is Maggie O'Neill. Oh my goodness! This is a gorgeous room."

The bedroom was done in different shades of apricot. White organdy-lined silk curtains hung in the two windows, and all the trim was stark white. There was a white mantel over the fireplace, which looked as if it hadn't been used much. A large picture graced the wall above the mantel, a painting of a terrace with delicate chairs and a lacy tablecloth and an ocean in the background. Maggie was delighted. A little room had been built between the two bedrooms, and Conchita led them both into it.

"Thees Meester Bannister's idea," she said. "He haf the leetle room for all guest." The room contained a large tub for bathing and a large commode containing two chamber pots, behind two different doors. A high window and a floor-to-ceiling cupboard for towels, soaps, and candles filled one wall. There was another door leading into the second bedroom.

"Thees room, eet ees for you. What ees your name?"

"I'm Liberty Bouvier, but you may call me Libby. Thank you for being so thoughtful, Conchita. We're both very tired. You've made our arrival here special by being ready for us. Again, thank you."

"I thank you, too, Conchita. We are exhausted, and you have already made us feel at home."

Maggie followed the two women into the connecting bedroom.

The room was painted an airy yellow, making the entire room look sunny. French doors—all glass—led to the outside. A curtain on the door was pulled to one side, with matching curtains at the large windows. It was fresh and warm. The four-poster bed looked inviting. There was a fireplace in this room too, but the mantel above it was a dark mahogany. Above the mantel was a picture of a field of daisies.

Maggie saw tears spring to Libby's eyes.

Conchita took Libby into her generous arms and patted her back, murmuring, "Oh, niña bonita, es bueno. Oh, pretty girl, it's good. You one tired girl." She glanced over at Maggie, thinking her the maid Matthew had spoken of. "Mees Maggie, I put her to the bed. You go now to the bed too. You tired."

"Thank you, Conchita," Maggie murmured gratefully. "I need my night things out of the satchel."

"There ees fresh nightdress on bed, Mees Maggie. Eet ees nice name you haf." She smiled a wide smile.

Maggie smiled tiredly back. "Thank you, and good night." She closed the door quietly behind her. She used the "leetle room," smiling to herself about having such a nice bedroom. Hurriedly undressing, she picked up the soft cotton nightdress, donned it, and turned the lamp wick down. It flickered softly, then went out. Maggie closed her eyes and knew no more.

The sun was shining brightly when Maggie awoke and stretched. She lay looking around the beautiful room. The different shades of apricot with the white trim were striking and lovely. Her room at the Bouvier manse had been adequate, serving her basic needs, but this was gorgeous. She stretched again in delight and thought about her change in circumstances. *People seem to look at you and treat you differently when you aren't dressed as a maid.* She thought back to the day before. She'd been scared of the man who'd accosted them, but angry too.

I guess I have little real experience of men, even though I spent the most wretched night of my life with one. I loved my da, and both Otto and Sigmund were good men, but to judge whether a man is trustworthy or not...I don't know. I don't think I can trust my judgment. Kirk Bannister seems a nice sort, but with my past, I don't suppose any man would love me.

She sighed and swung her legs over the side of the bed. Stretching again, she padded into the little room between hers and Liberty's. Opening the connecting door, she peeked in to see Libby still in a deep sleep, one arm flung over her head, her coppery curls spilling out over the pillow. Maggie closed the door silently. Dressing in the same outfit she'd been wearing all week, she felt in dire need of a real bath. She looked longingly at the tub. *Later,* she promised herself. *Later. Filling up the tub now will probably wake Liberty.*

Maggie stepped into the wide hall and admired the color combinations. A stark-white wainscoting covered the lower walls of the hall. The wall above it was a mint green with white trim at the top of the wainscot, and the floor trim board was white. Pictures of what must be family members or friends lined the hall on both sides. The pictures were different sizes, but all were framed in white. The contrasts were beautiful and eye pleasing.

She entered the living room, wondering if there was a parlor or dining room. This room was of natural woods and leather. To Maggie, it was homey and beautiful at the same time. The floor was a smooth red-brown tile with a braided rug. One wall was all windows, two walls were in some kind of beautiful wood, and the fourth wall was short, dividing the entry from the room, painted a rusty red. There were end tables, a large square coffee table made of varying shades of wood, and deep leather chairs.

Conchita, with an armload of laundry, entered from the hall. "*Buenos dias,* Mees Maggie. You haf comfortable bed? You sleep good, no?"

"Yes, thank you. I slept wonderfully well. The bed was comfortable, and the room is lovely. I feel good as new today."

Conchita responded with a wide smile and asked, "Mees Libbee, she awake?"

"No. I just looked in on her, and she was still sound asleep."

Conchita nodded toward the kitchen. "You come eat. Ees good breakfast." With her arms still laden with clothes, she headed toward the kitchen, with Maggie trailing behind.

The kitchen was gigantic, at least twice the size of the Bouviers' kitchen. It smelled of freshly baked bread and bacon. Gleaming copper pots hung from a large rack over a wooden island, serving as a counter and cutting board. Dominating one entire side of the kitchen were windows, with a round scrubbed-oak table that could seat fourteen easily. It overlooked a courtyard. Another wall held large glassed French doors, which stood open to the courtyard that extended past the end of the house. It was open, sunny, and cheerful.

Two young women were working in the kitchen, and Conchita introduced them.

"Thees ees my nieces, Guadalupe and Lucinda, but we call them Lupe an' Luce."

Maggie greeted them warmly. "I'm happy to meet you. Your breakfast smells wonderful!"

"Een the mornings, we haf everyone helping themselves to the buffet breakfast. Eet be cooked early," Conchita said. "Sometimes, Meester Bannister, he call an early meeting. He call eet the powwow breakfast."

Maggie simply nodded.

Conchita showed her the silverware, plates, and mugs for coffee, telling Maggie to help herself. She also said Maggie could eat at the scrubbed-oak table or go through the French doors and into the courtyard that let in the sunshine but blocked any wind. Maggie chose to sit outside and think about her new surroundings.

CHAPTER XXI

Give unto the LORD, O ye kindreds of the people,
give unto the LORD glory and strength.

PSALM 96:7

MATTHEW AND KIRK CAME INTO THE kitchen to get coffee, taking a break from working in the vineyard. They filled their cups and went into the courtyard to join Maggie. Both were dusty from working out in the fields.

Maggie looked surprised they would join her.

Matthew grinned. "Good morning, Miss O'Neill. I hope you slept well. Tell me, why did Madam Bouvier come instead of Monsieur Bouvier?" he queried. "For that matter, why'd you come?"

"I came because it was a chance to look at this great country of ours. I was Madam Bouvier's chaperone."

"Miss Maggie, you forgot one," he said softly. "Why'd she come instead of the monsieur?"

Maggie took a swallow of her coffee, giving herself time to form an answer. *Liberty doesn't want this man to know monsieur is dead.*

"Monsieur Bouvier's been quite indisposed, and I, in truth, don't know their personal affairs. I think Liberty wanted to see the property. I think it's to see if something can be done to make it a business concern, or perhaps they are going to move here. Do you know," Maggie asked, changing the subject to throw him off his line of questioning, "that Madam Bouvier has a discerning palate?"

"A what?" Matthew asked.

"A discerning palate," Maggie replied. "She's able to tell you, just by tasting, any wine grown in France and what region it comes from. The German wines are a little more difficult, she said, but she can tell a Chardonnay from a Merlot or a blend of the two. Quite a talent, wouldn't you say?"

Matthew's deep-blue eyes had gotten a little rounder, and his eyebrows raised up.

"Are you serious? Can she really do that? I've heard of people who can tell by taste the wine and region, but I've never met one. I can tell the difference between wines, but not their place of origin. That really is something." He pushed his hat back off his brow and stared at Maggie.

"Yes, I'm serious, and yes, she really can."

"Well, I'll be darned," Kirk said. "That's an unusual talent." He grinned at Maggie.

"How are you feeling this morning? Are you sore from your ride in the wagon?"

"No," Maggie replied with an answering grin. "I feel fine and have enjoyed a wonderful breakfast and delicious coffee. This"—she waved her hand to include the courtyard and the house—"is magnificent. Who designed this house? It feels homey and is comfortable, and yet it's beautiful."

"Matthew designed the entire house and layout of the vineyard while I was away at school. I didn't begin college until I was twenty-five, about nine years later than I should have. Matthew lost hope that I'd ever go. He paid my way, and I finished up last year. This is nice, isn't it?"

Elijah Humphries had visited Inspector George Baxter as soon as he had loaded the women onto the train. He found out the details of Liberty's husband's murder from him. Both men were astute and figured Jacques Corlay, Liberty's father, had something to do with it.

With permission from Liberty, when Baxter had finished interviewing Bouvier staff, he'd made a thorough search of Bouvier's desk. In it, he'd found a secret compartment with all kinds of information pertinent to Bouvier and Corlay's dealings. He shared everything with Elijah.

Later, before the reading of the will, Elijah had found a second secret drawer in the desk. It was a gold mine of paperwork showing Bouvier and Corlay's perfidy—as well as detailed accounts of all the men they had cheated. It also contained a letter from a man living in England. The letter was as old as Liberty.

The letter made clear that Liberty was not Jacques Corlay's daughter.

Elijah had given George Baxter the paperwork he'd found, but not the letter. He wrote a couple letters to England to see if he could track down Liberty's true father.

George Baxter had taken his best detective, Cabot Jones, with him to the residence of Corlay's hired accomplice, Hans Holbein, and found the incriminating evidence of murder.

Liberty didn't know it, but the man she thought her father, Jacques Corlay, was arrested for the murder of his son-in-law, her husband, Armand Francois Bouvier.

And if Jacques was convicted, and he unable to manage the estate, the will contained a codicil stating that all Armand's properties and wealth would revert to Liberty.

And upon Jacques' conviction, the manse and all Armand's wealth would revert to Liberty.

Matthew had gone out to work on some wire fencing, expecting Kirk to join him, but Kirk was enamored with Miss O'Neill.

"Would you care to see the grounds and get your bearings, so to speak?" Kirk asked Maggie.

"Yes, I would." Maggie blushed as Conchita showed her where to put her dirty dishes.

"You take my shawl, Mees O'Neill. It steel be not so warm." Conchita glanced at Kirk, knowing Matthew would not be happy if he spent time flirting rather than helping with the new fencing.

Liberty awoke and lay drowsily for a while before realizing where she was. A feeling of peace suffused her being, yet she was utterly exhausted. She opened her eyes as the day before came flooding into her mind.

"Oh Lord," she whispered, "what are Your plans for me?" She lay deep in thought and prayed for a while. "Thank You, Father God, for safety and protection throughout the long journey. I pray for guidance." She prayed for Elijah and her staff in Boston. She prayed for Maggie most of all. "Father, Maggie is such a wonderful friend. Help her to find You as her Savior. Lord, I thank you that we've become friends. I know, after yesterday, that something is bothering her. I pray You will help her to trust You...to know Your plans for her are right and just."

The peaceful feeling gave way to one of needing to get on with the day. She was excited at the thought of being a landowner.

Liberty padded barefoot into the little room. She was surprised by the steam that enveloped her upon opening the door. *That Conchita is one wonderful woman.* Conchita had filled the tub with hot water. Liberty dipped her fingers into it to see how warm it was. *It's perfect.* She couldn't wait to soak in it. Going back to her room, she rummaged through the large satchel, and came up with a clean chemise but no corset, as well as the muslin dress she'd packed. It was wrinkled, but she didn't care. Stripping off the soft cotton nightdress, she threw it on the bed and entered the bathing room, sinking down into the tub. There was a bucket of water nearby for rinsing her hair. Fragrant soaps and shampoo lay on a table next to the tub, along with two towels on the second shelf of the table. Libby sighed, enjoying the relaxing heat.

Conchita was in Maggie's room and heard Liberty bathing. She went into Liberty's room and collected her dirty clothes and stripped off the pillowcases so they would be fresh for tonight. She was wondering what would be a good dinner to welcome these women. She talked aloud to herself as she worked.

"Mees Maggie, she catched Meester Kirk's eye. He always going out with different womens. He the flirt, that ees sure."

Kirk had left a string of brokenhearted women in his wake.

"I hope he no break thees Mees Maggie's heart. I doan know what thees redhead ees like. Perhaps she a siren, or maybe she a sweet girl. She look young." Conchita thought about it a bit. "I surprise I feel some kind of closeness to Mees Liberty. When I first set eyes on her, I know here ees a good heart. When I show them the rooms, Mees Liberty, she seem so grateful to me. That politeness weens my heart. I weel help her all I can." She crossed herself as if it were a vow. Conchita had watched as Kirk took Maggie out to show her the grapevines. She muttered to herself about Kirk needing to go out and help Meester Bannister.

Conchita heard Liberty step out of the tub, and she bustled back to the kitchen to make sure everything was ready for that sweet lady to have a bite to tide her over until lunch, which was nearly ready.

Liberty was glad to be clean. Straightening up her mess in the bathroom, she'd hung her wet towel on a hook. Combing her curls out had been work. Usually Maggie did it, but Maggie was a friend now, no longer Liberty's maid. *I'm glad we're friends. I'd rather have Maggie for a friend than a servant. I've come to love her.* She smiled as she thought, *Maggie won't be doing my hair anymore. It is nice to have her button me up...but now I button her up too.* Liberty grinned at her reflection.

Her hair was thick, and instead of putting it up, she left it down. In this climate, it wouldn't take long to dry. It was something she wouldn't have dreamed of doing in her own home. *Already I am experiencing that freedom Elijah Humphries said I would.* Smiling, she exited her room, impressed with the freshness of greens and white in the hall. When she went into the great room, her first thought was comfort. *This is comfortable. My home in Boston is so heavy, dark, stiff, and uncomfortable.* She walked over to the large bookshelf and was intrigued by the variety of books and authors. She loved to read, and these books didn't smell of cigars.

Maggie was enjoying her walk with Kirk.

"Here's where we turn the grapes into wine. We store this stuff in here after the harvest and crushing are finished." He led her into the tack room. "Matthew also designed this. If we have lots of guests, I sleep out here."

Kirk explained that Matthew had built the stable with an eye for comfort, knowing that sometimes Rancho Bonito would overflow with company. There were two rooms along one side of the stable. One was fairly small and seemed to collect junk, but there was a bed in it for emergencies. The tack room was much larger, roomier, and homier. The walls were knotty pine, stained and varnished. It held a fireplace and a trundle bed with a thick mattress, pushed up against one wall. A beautiful patchwork quilt Matthew's mother had made covered the bed linens. There were some pegs on the wall for clothes, a small chest of drawers with a mirror over it, and a comfortable old easy chair with a side table. The other end of the long, narrow room was where the harnesses and saddles were kept. There was a skylight built into the ceiling, but there were no windows along the side, except at the end of the long room. The tack room smelled of leather but had been made into a spare bedroom, if needed. It was clean, private, and comfortable.

"This is nice," Maggie said. "Anyone would be happy to sleep in here." She smiled up at Kirk, who returned her smile with a wide grin.

He took her arm and led her outside. He spent the entire morning showing her around. Finally, nearly lunchtime, he led Maggie back into the house.

The two entered the kitchen, with Maggie bubbling over, telling Liberty about her tour of the grounds.

"I've been exploring, with Kirk as a guide. This place is fantastic!" Before she could say more, Matthew walked in.

"Where've you been, Kirk? I needed help, and you said before the coffee break you'd be out there to hold the wires."

Kirk replied laconically, "I was showing Maggie around."

Matthew's lips thinned. He averted his face to hide his anger, but Maggie and Liberty saw it.

"I'm to blame, Mr. Bannister." Maggie spoke up quickly. "I kept asking questions. I should've known he had work to do."

"Never mind. Diego came out and helped. Is lunch ready, Conchita?"

"Sí, Meester Bannister, ees nearly ready. You tree go wash, an' eet be ready pronto."

She clapped her hands, and Lupe and Luce started setting the large oak table. They set it for four.

Matthew returned to the kitchen first and noted an apron on Liberty. He smiled as he spoke. "I didn't know I had a new cook. Welcome to Rancho Bonito."

Liberty responded to his smile. "Mr. Bannister, if I cooked for you, you'd be as skinny as a starved cat. I don't know how to cook, but I want to learn."

"Meester Bannister, I tell Mees Libby, she cannot cook here. She ees guest," Conchita said. "Then she say she want to eat weeth me. I tell her no again."

Matthew was surprised. First, because he didn't know she went by Libby. It had a friendly sound to it. And she wanted to eat with the hired help? He smiled inwardly at his mistake in thinking he would be hosting a couple of uppity Bostonians. He was glad to hear Madam Bouvier was friendly. He wondered if she wore her hair down often. It was beautiful, like gleaming copper.

Liberty took a bite. "What's this? It's delicious."

"It's tacos," Kirk said. "It's nothing special, just tacos."

"It's delicious." Liberty's green eyes shimmered as she took another bite. The sauce was making her eyes water because of its hot tang. "What's in the tomato sauce? Whew, that's hot!"

Maggie and Liberty enjoyed the wonderful lunch, but not before Maggie had thoroughly embarrassed herself.

Everyone except Maggie started laughing at Liberty's comment, but Maggie hadn't started eating yet. She stared at Liberty, wearing a muslin dress, with her hair hanging down. *She looks as if she belongs here! That's amazing! My employer…new friend…looks as if she's always lived here, as if she truly belongs. She looks very tired but happy. I've never seen that look before, not ever, in Boston.* Thinking of Liberty and all the heartache she'd had over the years, Maggie's eyes teared up.

"Eet's the *jalapeno* pepper. We call eet salsa." Conchita laughed. "Look—Mees Maggie ees crying too."

Maggie took a big bite of taco to cover the fact that she hadn't even started eating yet, but it was a mistake. The salsa was hot—very hot. She was embarrassed as she started to choke. She walked out the open French doors into the courtyard. Could she spit the whole mess out of her mouth? Conchita came up and held out the peelings bowl in front of her. She spit her food out and coughed and coughed. Her tears flowed in earnest now, and she wiped her eyes on her sleeve and started laughing—laughing at herself for making such a spectacle, laughing that they all thought initially that she'd teared up because of the salsa, laughing that she really had teared up from the salsa, laughing for the joy of seeing Liberty's look of contentment.

Conchita laughed too, with relief that this girl could laugh at herself. No fake snobbery here. She thumped Maggie's back and told her to raise both arms over her head.

Conchita wanted to plug her nose. *Whew, thees girl! She ees needing the bath.* And she laughed again. Lunch was a merry time, with jesting and good conversation.

Matthew spoke to Liberty. "Are you up to going over to take a look at your husband's property?"

My property, Libby corrected him in her head. "Yes, yes, I'd enjoy that. I've been looking forward to seeing it for quite some time." She nodded to Kirk and Maggie. "You're welcome to come too, if you wish."

"Thanks, but no thanks. I've neglected enough chores this morning." Kirk winked at Maggie.

Maggie beamed at him but addressed Liberty. "I'd love to come. We've been dreaming for some time about it, and now it's a reality."

"There's not much to look at, but it's in an excellent location, and the view is beautiful."

"What do y'mean beautiful, Matt? It's just rolling hills with scrub oak and quite a few rocks, if you'll remember. There's a few eucalyptus trees scattered here and there." Kirk looked at Liberty. "Some Australians introduced the eucalyptus and planted groves of it in the Sacramento Valley. They thought it could be used for railroad ties because it grew fast. It didn't work out though. The trees have to be really mature to not warp and twist when they're cut. Some of the trees were planted as windbreaks for orange groves. Some of them border your one hundred sixty acres on the west side. I suppose that was because sometimes the wind will pick up from the Pacific Ocean. We border your south side. Your property's due north of us, and yours and our eastern border is the Napa River. I guess you're right, Matt. It is beautiful, and I'm finished with my soliloquy." He took a long drink of water.

Everyone rose, and Liberty started to pick up the empty plates, but Conchita took charge.

"You weel go now weeth Meester Bannister."

"Can you ride?" Matthew asked.

Pleasure stood firmly in Liberty's eyes. "Yes, I'd love that."

"No, I've never ridden a horse," Maggie said. "I wouldn't mind learning though."

"Oh," Matthew said, "if you plan to be out here for any length of time, you'd be wise to start learning." He looked questioningly at the women, but they didn't respond.

"Right. Well, since you don't ride, Maggie, reckon we'll take the wagon. It'll be a few minutes. I need to go out and hitch up."

Matthew swallowed as he stood waiting for the two women who came out of the house giggling. Both were easy on the eyes—Miss O'Neill with her bright halo of red hair and Madam Bouvier with her shining coppery curls and moss-green eyes that seemed to hold secrets.

Liberty pushed Maggie to get up first. She didn't want to sit that close to Matthew Bannister.

Matthew grasped Maggie's hand to help her up and then Liberty's.

The day was fair but quite nippy. Maggie snugged her shawl closer around her shoulders. No wind stirred the leaves on the orange trees, and blue skies hugged the hills, giving them an almost hazy look.

In awe of the weather, Maggie closed her eyes and lifted her face to the sun. *All that snow in Boston, and across the country on the train, and look at this! It's gorgeous and almost Christmas.* She was content to sit and look around as Liberty, who'd mentioned starting her own vineyard, plied Matthew with questions.

"Mr. Bannister," Liberty asked, "have you planted in every direction? Are you planting more rootstock? Do you have enough workers?"

"Yes." He grinned at her. "I've planted almost my entire property. When you give me the money your husband owes me, I'll be able to buy more rootstock. I've been buying from a man down south. His vineyard grows a grape that makes a wonderful Merlot. He also has another type of rootstock that he's made into a very light Chardonnay. I've just started buying the stalk for Chardonnay from him. Last year was the first year of production for Rancho Bonito. We kept very busy, and selling is slow. But once it catches on, more people will buy. It was a decent Merlot, but I've tasted better. I've found that a south-hill planting yields a much better grape. More sunshine, I suppose. I've been reading everything I can get my hands on about growing grapes. And yes, I have enough workers. There are migrants who come north just to work as they are needed, and after the season is over, they go back south."

CHAPTER XXII

The LORD is the portion of mine inheritance and of my cup:
thou maintainest my lot.
The lines are fallen unto me in pleasant places;
yea, I have a goodly heritage.

PSALM 16: 5–6

THE WAGON WENT OVER A RISE. The sky was cobalt, so blue it looked like a painting. Not one puff of cloud marred its perfection. A faint wind blew softly. It was beautiful. Maggie and Liberty, used to the bustle of the city, reveled in the stillness and beauty of their surroundings. A hawk spiraled lazily overhead.

"You see those stakes there? That's the end of my property and the beginning of yours."

They could tell the difference without the stakes. Mr. Bannister's property had all been tilled at one time or another. The demarcation was quite evident. Matthew stopped the wagon, and the three gazed into the distance.

"What kind of trees are those, way over there?" Maggie pointed up at the surrounding hillside. The trees lined the top of a hill, as if sentinels to keep watch over the valley.

"Those are the eucalyptus trees Kirk was talking about. They have a very distinct shape and smell. They also drop bark, leaves, and branches all the time."

Leaving Matthew's land, the wagon bumped over ground that was rough, uneven, and strewn with rocks. It, too, was rolling hills like Matthew's, though Liberty's was untouched, and grasses dotted with wildflowers waved in the slight breeze.

Maggie spotted the tiny shack. "Is that the house we were thinking to move into?"

"Yes," Matthew replied. "As I mentioned, I only built a shack so anyone coming around would see an improvement on the land. It's not habitable."

Liberty swallowed her disappointment and knew with a sinking feeling that she and Maggie would be Mr. Bannister's guests for quite some time. *Well, at least I'm a landowner.*

"Thank you, Mr. Bannister, for bringing us out here," she said. "Do you think you can bear the two of us as guests until we can get a house built here? Miss O'Neill and I'd be happy to help with whatever jobs you'd like, and I could pay you some money for room and board." She, in truth, had no idea how much anything would cost. It was ridiculous that she had rarely handled money. Mr. Humphries hadn't known that when he handed her a wad of bills. Here she was twenty-nine years of age, and she hadn't a clue how much she had or what it was worth. She was going to have to swallow some of her pride, and her reserve, and have a real talk with Mr. Bannister.

"You're welcome to stay as long as it takes. If we need the barns, we'll knock something up to keep your trunks dry. For now, I guess you'll just be family. I'd like both of you to call me Matt or Matthew." He smiled at them but still wondered why Madam Liberty Bouvier would move out here.

Liberty looked at him with a smile in her green eyes. "I suppose it isn't proper, but I'd like you to call me Liberty or Libby, and I'm sure Miss O'Neill would prefer Maggie." She was relieved that they wouldn't be booted out and was thankful for his hospitality.

"Mr. Bann—ah, Matthew." She held out her hand to shake his. "Thank you very much for being so generous. Maggie and I are both grateful and indebted to you. We'll do our best to not be a nuisance. Maggie will have to promise not to keep Kirk from his chores." She smiled most winningly.

"You're welcome…and both of you can stay for as long as you need."

Maggie chattered the whole way back to the Rancho. Matthew, listening with half an ear, responded only if necessary.

Why are they moving to Napa? Why isn't Monsieur Bouvier with them? Is he ill?

Liberty was lost in her own thoughts. *Do I even have enough money to pay Matthew what is owed already? How will I be able to build when I know nothing about my finances? I hate to have to tell him I know nothing about money. Is that pride?* She sighed, not having heard a thing Maggie had been jabbering about.

They pulled up in front of the Rancho, and Matthew lifted them both down. As they entered the front door, Conchita handed Libby an unopened telegram. Liberty thanked her, knowing it must be from Elijah, but she didn't intend to open it in front of the others.

"It smells wonderful in here. Is it your *enchiladas?*"

"*Sí*, Mees Liberty." Conchita smiled widely. "We make the salsa and the guacamole and many good things we eet weeth eet. You weel like what your mouth tells you."

"It does smell good." Maggie's nose twitched. "I want to enjoy it, so I think I'll have a bath first. Where would I draw water for heating?"

"Luce, she feel the tub for you weeth hot water, Mees Maggie."

"That's wonderful! How thoughtful of you! Thank you for having it ready." Maggie left hurriedly to take advantage of the hot water.

"I believe I'll lie down for a few minutes. I'm still quite tired. Thank you, Matthew, for taking us to see the property." She smiled a bit wanly at Matthew and walked down the hall, knowing two pairs of eyes followed her exit.

Once in her room, she tore open the telegram.

HOPE ALL IS WELL STOP
UNLIMITED FUNDS AVAILABLE STOP ELIJAH

Liberty began to cry. *Oh Lord, sometimes it seems we wait forever for Your answer. I've prayed and prayed that my father could be a man I understand, a man I could love and who would love me. Father, you know that I prayed that even before I came back from boarding school, and yet he's so evil. I prayed for Armand to be a man I could love, and yet he hardened his heart against me, never loving me. Now, I have prayed about a need of how to proceed here, and look at this. I asked for help not more than half the hour past, and already my answer is here. How did Elijah get the funds, Lord? Not from my father, I'll wager. Thank You for answering my prayer so quickly.*

She slipped the message into the flyleaf of her Bible and wiped away her tears. Taking off her shoes, she undressed. She'd foregone her corset and had only her chemise to deal with after taking off the muslin dress. She slid between cool sheets. Hearing Maggie splashing in the tub, she heard her singing, but the sounds faded as she slipped into sleep.

Maggie sang softly to herself, enjoying the bath. She thought about Libby and wondered what was in the telegram. *My, this bath is wonderful. Life is certainly different not being a maid. In all my life no one has ever drawn my bath, except my mother when I was young.* She hummed to herself. *This is the life. I hope Liberty never wants to go back to Boston.*

Maggie looked forward to seeing Kirk. *He's quite good looking and so easy to talk to.* She leaned back to soak a few minutes and closed her eyes. *I need to be careful, though. I don't know the ways of men, and I certainly don't want to be a nuisance or think there's more to this than just being friends.*

By the time Maggie was finished and dressed, Liberty was awake and dressed also.

She tapped on Maggie's door.

"Come on in, Libby."

Liberty entered, sitting down on a comfortable chair upholstered in a deep-apricot color. Maggie was combing out her beautiful red hair. Liberty saw the bloom in her cheeks. *What a beautiful woman Maggie's become.*

"I'm curious, Libby. Who sent you the telegram—or is it private?"

Liberty blushed. "I don't quite understand it myself. It's from Elijah. I guess I have enough money to build or do whatever I want. It was pretty cryptic. Maggie, I have to tell you, after looking at that shack, I felt very depressed. I didn't know what I was going to do. I've never handled money. I don't know how much things cost, and I didn't even know if I had enough to pay Matthew for all his help in the past. I don't suppose what he invested was all that much, but I'm certain having someone come in to dig a well wasn't cheap. He also had to file for the property and pay for someone to survey what he had staked off. Also, he did use lumber and his own labor to build the shack. Oh, Maggie, when I thought of all that, I felt we were going to be in a heap of trouble. I don't even know how much money I have, or even if we had enough to pay for tickets back to Boston."

"Back to Boston! Why in the world would we want to do that? We just got here!"

"I know. I know. I'm simply making the point that we could have been helpless. While we were riding back from the property, I prayed that God would make His will known to me. It wasn't one half hour later that my prayer was answered, in the form of that telegram. I praise God that He knew I needed some real help before I did."

"That's just a coincidence, Liberty."

"No, Maggie, it's not." Liberty spoke firmly. "I don't believe in coincidences. I know that God watches over me. And the more dependent I am upon Him, the more I see His help and care over me." With that statement, she started toward Maggie's door to the hall.

"I love you, Maggie." She pulled the door shut after her.

Maggie stood there, brush in hand, thinking about what Liberty had said. *Is it possible God is that intimate? I've always thought of Him as way out there, a stern God who just waited for you to do something wrong and then He'd get you good. Could it really be true that He loves each person as much as Liberty keeps telling me?*

George Baxter and his right-hand man, Cabot Jones, were discussing Corlay's capture, arrest, and the upcoming trial. Tabitha, Baxter's maid, knocked on his library door.

"Enter," George said.

"Mr. Humphries here to see you, sir."

"Bring him in, Tabitha, bring him in."

Elijah entered and saw Cabot already there. He cleared his throat as he strode across the deep carpet. He stretched out his hand to greet the other two men.

"Welcome, Elijah."

"Well, George, I've had news from England. Abigail and I will be setting sail in just three days' time. We're going to hunt down Liberty Bouvier's true father and see if the man even knows he has a daughter. If he is happily married, Abby and I will leave well enough alone. If he's single or childless, we're going to tell him about Liberty, his daughter."

George looked surprised. "You don't say. You, in truth, know where the man is? How'd you find out?"

"You're not the only one who can do a bit of investigating," Elijah said with a grin. "Alexander Liberty is, according to the vicar in Reading, Berkshire, an oblate of a monastery in Florence, Italy."

"Interesting…however did you find him?"

Elijah proceeded to tell George how he'd written a couple letters and the outcome.

"But it's not the only reason I came by." Elijah leaned forward. "I've been going over Bouvier's papers. He had so many concerns going that it's taken me this long to find there's a definite problem with one of the companies."

George and Cabot both perked up. They knew something was coming that would concern them.

"There are seventeen companies owned by Bouvier," Elijah said heavily. "I think sixteen of them are on the up and up." He sat a moment and drank some of his cider. "I am quite sure one of the companies is just a front, George, a front for an unbelievably filthy business."

"What is it, man? Out with it!" George exclaimed.

Elijah said, "I'm quite certain one of the companies, the one in San Francisco, is dealing in white female slavery." He glanced from George to Cabot. "Bouvier was receiving money quarterly from the company, a lot of money. It's a salmon canning company, but the monies going in are enormous. There are shipments of women going to Hong Kong and Chile."

Both George and Cabot looked shocked. George recovered first.

"We'd like to go over those papers with a fine-toothed comb. I hope you'll give them to us, Elijah."

"Of course." He smiled. "It's why I came by." He pulled a sheaf of papers out of his satchel. "Here are all seventeen businesses. The bottom one is the salmon canning company in which I think you'll be most interested. I think I'm giving you another job."

"I'm glad that you came by today, Elijah. Cabot and I were just going to have a bite to eat before going to Corlay's trial. It's set for one thirty this afternoon. Would you care to join us?"

Elijah pondered the question for a minute. He still had much to do this day. "Yes, yes, I think I would."

All three men ate the delicious luncheon Mrs. Roos, George's cook, had made. They talked about Corlay, Holbein, and of course, Bouvier getting what he deserved. Cabot spoke about what he'd heard about white slavery—that entire ships were coming from Scandinavia with women who were drugged and sold to the highest bidder. It was a despicable business, to be sure. The three men finished eating and made their way into the city proper to the courthouse.

Corlay was found guilty of fraudulent business dealings and of hiring an assassin to murder Armand Bouvier. He was sentenced to three life imprisonments.

Elijah and his companions grinned at each other, and George held his thumb up.

Liberty is free, Elijah rejoiced. *She is finally free.*

Jacques Corlay sat impassively, showing no reaction to the verdict of guilty. He had a backup plan. Rufus was his point of contact and had been in the back of the courtroom. Corlay had laid out his plans earlier, telling Rufus to grease a palm. There was always a guard willing to look the other way for greenbacks. Jacques' main plan was to escape and find Liberty. He blamed her for all his misfortune. She had his money. She was the real thief, and he was going to make her pay and get his money back if it was the last thing he ever did.

Maggie and Liberty had been at the Rancho over a month. When they'd arrived it'd been almost Christmas. Liberty had produced gifts for everyone from her trunks. Maggie had nothing to give anyone. She had saved a bit, over the years, but had no way of buying any presents.

She thoroughly enjoyed being a guest instead of a servant and tried to make herself useful and not a burden. Kirk asked her out several times, but it was usually to go to Consuelo's house. Maggie didn't like Consuelo at all.

Standing in the smelly chicken coop thinking about her change in circumstances, Maggie was collecting eggs into a basket. As she walked back to the house, she again wondered where Mr. Ethan Brooks lived. She shuddered whenever he came to mind. His snapping Elmer's neck was a vision she would never get out of her head.

"Here are the eggs, Conchita." She sat the basket on the table.

"Thank you, Mees Maggie. I no like to get eggs. I never like the pecking birds. No, not me." She was plucking one out while talking. Maggie didn't mind getting the eggs at all, but she didn't even like looking at someone plucking chickens.

"I don't mind gathering eggs, but that!" She pointed to the dead chicken. "That's not anything I ever want to do!"

"You muss learn thees one, Mees Maggie. Ees good to know."

"I'll just watch, thank you. It's nasty, and putting your hand in that thing and pulling out the entrails…ugh!"

Liberty walked into the kitchen and started expertly plucking the second chicken.

Matthew had just come into the house and leaned against the doorway to the kitchen, watching the three women, unobserved.

Maggie looked at Liberty in total surprise. "Where in the world did you learn to do that?"

"Right here, a couple weeks ago. I'm going to learn everything I can about cooking. I may have to be the chief cook and bottle washer when we live in our own home. Conchita's been graciously teaching me how to cook. I don't want to be only proficient—I want to be good!" She grinned at the astonished Maggie. She added, "You know, Maggie, there're many things in life we don't like to do. I don't imagine Luce enjoys emptying chamber pots or that Conchita really likes plucking chickens, but they do it because it needs to be done. There's a verse in the Bible that says, 'Work heartily as unto the Lord.' It means that in all we work to do, we do everything as if we are doing it for God. That's truly the best way, because then if it's not recognized by anyone here, our feelings aren't hurt. We've done it for God, who truly appreciates us. Our reward is in heaven."

Conchita nodded her head sagely and murmured, "Por Dios."

"That's right, Conchita, for God." Liberty added, "I love it here! I'm enjoying learning to cook, and I love not wearing a corset. I feel free. No one makes fun of me if I have an opinion, and here, I'm allowed to voice it. I have never in my entire life been so happy. I plan to never go back to Boston. Never!"

Matthew slipped back out of the kitchen doorway and went outside. *So that was interesting. Is she leaving her husband? Is he planning to join her here?* Matthew was no closer to any answers than he'd been when he first laid eyes on the pair of them. *Conchita said Liberty cried that first night she was here. Did her husband kick her out? Had Bouvier left her for another woman? It's been known to happen.* He couldn't see why anyone would leave someone who had so much personality, seemed so nice, and was gorgeous to boot. Matthew was frustrated not having any answers.

CHAPTER XXIII

*But my God shall supply all your need
according to his riches in glory by Christ Jesus*

PHILIPPIANS 4:19

ELIJAH AND ABIGAIL'S TRIP TO EUROPE had been successful.
They'd not only found Liberty's true father, but her grandmother as well.
It had been an exciting adventure and a blessing. Alexander Liberty and
his mother, Phoebe, made plans to move to California, wanting to be
close to Liberty, and would soon arrive into Boston.

Elijah had ridden in his carriage to George Baxter's and was being
ushered into the library.

"Hello, my friend!" George came around his desk to greet him. He
shook Elijah's hand and clapped him on the back. "I'm glad you came to
see me, as I would have been knocking on your door as soon as I heard
you were home."

"Yes, yes, it's good to see you too, George," Elijah responded.

The two men walked over to the chairs before the fire to sit comfortably.

"Have you heard Holbein was hanged?" George asked.

"No, no, I didn't." Elijah looked down at the carpet. An unconscious
part of his mind took in the rich colors and thought, *How beautiful.* His

conscious mind thought about the waste of such potential and how God must hate it when people ruined their lives.

"Elijah, I've some very bad news besides Holbein."

Elijah looked at him questioningly, feeling in his gut a reluctance to hear what George was going to tell him.

"Jacques Corlay escaped. He's on the loose."

Elijah, upset, stood abruptly and paced. *I'll need to wire both Mr. Bannister and Liberty when I leave here. The sooner, the better.*

"That is, indeed, very bad news. I'm quite certain he'll try to get at Liberty somehow. He's a reprehensible man. Do you know exactly when he escaped?"

"He was being transported…ah, let me see." George couldn't exactly remember. "Yes, I remember—he escaped the day you left for Europe."

"Five weeks ago! He's been on the loose now for five weeks?" Elijah stopped pacing and sat down as if the air had been knocked out of him. *If he hasn't been caught by now, he won't be. Oh Lord, please protect Liberty. Hedge her in behind and before with Thine angels.*

"There's another matter I have news about." George spoke softly, knowing Elijah was upset. "The company you reported to Cabot and myself is definitely a front for white female slavery, just as you thought. It's operating under the cover of a valid salmon cannery. The company, located in San Francisco, has shipped girls out to high bidders, mostly to Hong Kong, but some to Chile."

Elijah took a deep breath. "That is also bad news. It's not often I hope I am wrong, but in this instance, I hoped I was."

"How long a break did you take from your office?" George asked.

"I took four months. We were planning to do a lot of sightseeing in Europe, but Abby decided she was through and wanted to come home, so I've only used five and a half weeks, but we're planning to accompany Alexander and Phoebe out to California. Why…why do you ask?"

"How'd you like to go to California—I mean, for me?" George asked. "I need someone I can trust to be a go-between for the San Francisco police and me. I am sending Cabot Jones out to go undercover in the salmon company. He is leaving today."

Elijah watched George with incredulous eyes as George continued to talk.

"Right now, my understanding is the companies are under your jurisdiction, isn't that correct?"

"Well…yes, yes, I suppose it is since I am handling the estate," Elijah said. "But it's a nasty business, and I don't like the idea that a company like that is under my authority."

"I understand that, Elijah, but you must see that this nasty business, as you put it, must be exposed, but first we must find who all is involved. If we don't and we only rescue the girls, whoever is heading this up will just start doing this in another place. Your going to California is a godsend. My, God does work in mysterious ways, doesn't He?"

"Yes, yes He does. I know Abby'd like to go tomorrow. She's tired of this cold, and she wants to meet Madam Bouvier. She has some idea of opening a mission there."

"A mission? For what purpose?"

"Oh my! Oh Lord! Oh my goodness! There's the answer I've been searching for. Oh my, George, sometimes when the Almighty opens your blinders, you feel as if you've been hit over the head with an answer you should've seen coming!"

"What are you talking about, Elijah?"

"The mission! I had a dream the night Abigail was miraculously healed from her illness. I'd wondered if it was just a dream, or was it a direction from the Lord? Now I know, George. Abigail and I are supposed to open a mission for battered women! Battered or abused or homeless or whatever. I feel it in my spirit, George. I know Abby will feel the same way. We're to go to California and will help those women who have been kidnapped by that female slavery ring in San Francisco."

George looked at him in astonishment. "I'm thankful you're willing to go. I didn't know who I could send there to coordinate with the office here. We will, of course, pay for your passage and Abigail's, I should think."

Elijah was a bit dazed from the rapid change in his immediate future. He thought back a few weeks to Florence and how his words had changed the entire future of Alexander Liberty and his mother. *What will*

Abby would think of it all? I'll need to inform Sigmund as well as distribute my clientele among the remaining lawyers. So much to do!

He rallied quickly. "When would you like me out there, George?"

"In about three weeks' time or so, I think. It gives Cabot time to establish himself in the company and find out what is going on. It will give you two weeks here to get your affairs straightened out. Will that be all right with you?"

"Yes, yes, I believe it would, my friend."

Maggie stretched. She loved mornings. A new day to live and laugh and learn. She stretched again and thought about the night before. *That Kirk sure is a flirt.* He'd held her hand and made eyes at her out in the courtyard. *Then along came a spider.* She remembered that rhyme from her nursery book. *That's what that slinky Consuelo is, a spider. Black widow, most likely. She'll suck the blood right out of Kirk, and nothing will be left but a husk of a man.* She giggled at the thought. She liked Kirk, but she didn't love him. They had long talks, and she was quite sure he liked her. *But look at what he did last night. Consuelo and Kirk left together when he'd said he'd spend the evening with me. And anyway, I'm what they call damaged goods. I'm glad we're living here. If we lived in San Francisco, I'd be afraid of running into Ethan Brooks. I'm almost positive that man would not be living in some small town. No, he'll be living in the big city where he can have as many contacts as possible for his evil schemes.*

Maggie thoughts swung to Liberty. *The longer she waits, the harder it's going to be to tell Matthew she's a widow. She isn't lying, is she?* Maggie liked things straightforward. She was not at all devious by nature—at least, she didn't think she was. She knew she had a temper, and she couldn't abide that Consuelo. *Who'd she think she was anyway? She'd even made eyes at Matthew, but he'd laughed at her and told her to grow up.*

Maggie sat up and pushed her hair out of her face. She slipped on a pair of mules and opened her curtains. Leaning on the sill she gazed out at the vineyard that stretched itself over the hillside. Her thoughts swung to Jessica Bannister. She'd shown up at the front door a few days before.

What a shock that was to see that woman with the revealing dresses who'd tripped me on the train. I tried to get to her hair...I was going to pull it out if I could, but Liberty wouldn't let me. She shoved me forward and then went back and apologized to that woman. Now she's shown up here sicker than anything. I didn't even know Matthew was married. I suppose that was a real shock for him. He'd told Liberty he thought she was dead three years ago. She'd run off with another man, taking all his hard-earned money with her. He'd received a telegram saying Jessica was dead. Matthew now thinks she must have sent it herself so he'd stop looking for her.

She's dying, and Dr. John said it's only a matter of days. I feel sorry for her, but I can't abide the smell. I don't know how Libby can sit with her like she does. She's such a wonderful woman. I wish I could be like her.

"Oh, it's gorgeous outside!" she whispered. "It won't be long before work will begin on Libby's house. I'm glad Matthew's helped Libby to lay in supplies and tools for beginning the construction. Ordering all that wood and stuff means as soon as the mud dries, work will start." She saw a bird sitting on the fence and watched as it warbled its song to her.

Think I'll take a sponge bath. When she finished dressing, she made her way to the kitchen, where Conchita was singing a song in Spanish.

"Good morning, Conchita. Isn't it a lovely day?"

"*Buenos dias,* Mees Maggie. Sí eet ees a wonnerful day."

Maggie laid a corn tortilla on her plate, dished up scrambled eggs, beans, tomatoes, and onions, expertly wrapping it up. She picked up a dish of salsa and a cup of coffee and set her breakfast on the scrubbed wooden table.

"Oh my, Conchita," she said, talking with her mouth nearly full, "this is deeelicious!"

Liberty walked into the kitchen as Maggie was speaking.

"*Buenos dias,* Mees Libbee," Conchita said. "An' these comed yesterday when you at your property. I almost forget." She pulled a letter off a shelf, handing it to Liberty.

Liberty took the letter with dread, fearing it was from her father. She breathed a sigh of relief when she saw that it was from Elijah. Before she even read the letter, she poured herself a cup of coffee and sat next to Maggie.

"Conchita, would you please sit down here with Maggie and me for just a few minutes? I need to talk with you," she said.

Maggie eyed Liberty with surprise and then relief. *Libby is going to tell Conchita the truth about Armand.*

Conchita looked serious. She poured herself a cup of coffee and sat down.

Liberty took a sip of hers and, reaching across the table, took Conchita's hand in her own.

"Conchita, I didn't know what to expect when Maggie and I came out here. Maggie and I are now close friends. In Boston, Maggie was my personal maid. We've shared many things together for the past four years. When she came to work for me, I was twenty-five and Maggie just fourteen. Even though she's been my servant, she's been a constant comfort to me. I have been all alone since my mother died twelve years ago."

Conchita interrupted. "But your husband, he be weeth you!"

"Yes, and many other women as well, Conchita. Armand brought some of them home at night. I was never enough, not even the first week of our marriage. I was young, just turned sixteen. It's a long story, but the short version is Armand was an evil man. He ruined many people's lives and caused some men's deaths. His will left everything we owned to my father, who is just as evil. They were business partners. I was only given the property here in California. Armand was murdered five days before I boarded the train for California."

Conchita gasped. "Murdered!"

"Yes, Conchita, and I cannot mourn him—to do so would be a travesty. I tried to love him, and I tried to respect him, but I failed. When I left Boston, I believed I would receive twenty dollars per month for necessities. The telegram I received, my first day here, told me without any explanation that I have unlimited funds. I don't really know what it all means. I do know that I've been praying I'd not be bitter, not be distrustful. The only good man I've ever known, besides servants, I only knew for little more than two days. He was my husband's lawyer and is a trustworthy person. That last telegram was from him to tell me that Jacques, my father, has escaped jail. He's supposed to go to prison for fraud and for hiring the man who killed Armand. So, the property

Matthew staked out for Armand is all I own. Now that I'm here, I'm finding it the home I've never known."

Conchita stood up and hugged Liberty. "I love you, Mees Liberty, and weel not tell your story, no, not eef you say no."

"I don't know why I kept it secret. I suppose it's because I didn't know what kind of man Matthew was. I've not trusted men so easily in the last few years. If you wish to tell it, then tell it. Elijah sent a wire to Matthew as well as me about my father escaping. It probably made no sense to him, since he thinks I'm a married woman."

I'm glad Liberty told Conchita about Monsieur Bouvier, but her comment about trusting men…I feel the same way. I don't trust them so easily either. Elmer and Mr. Brooks were evil. I don't think I'll ever forget seeing Mr. Brooks murder Elmer right in front of my eyes. And now, look at Kirk, asking me to go to that barn dance with him. But afterward, he wouldn't listen to me when I said I didn't want to go to Consuelo's house. And after we get there, he had the gall to go off somewhere with her and leave me with only her mother to talk to. No, I don't trust men either.

It was quiet in the kitchen that was usually so full of laughter. Conchita started cleaning up the breakfast clutter while Maggie sipped coffee.

Liberty opened the letter. It was dated a few days before she received the telegram telling her of Jacques' escape.

My dearest Liberty Alexandra,

I want you to know that my wife, Abigail, and I pray for you every day. We trust you are well and enjoying California. It would be helpful if you could send a telegram and let us know how you're doing. I'm writing to inform you of certain events here in Boston.

First of all, as you well know, Monsieur Corlay was arrested during the reading of the will. We found papers your late husband kept of every transaction he and Corlay made. I suppose I should say I'm sorry, but I am not. He was sentenced to New Bedford Prison for life. Now that he's escaped, you must be very careful.

On a happier note, in the event that Corlay was unable to administer the estate, it reverted in its entirety to one Liberty Alexandra Bouvier. So congratulations. You are now a very, very wealthy woman.

After closer inspection of the companies owned by Monsieur Bouvier, we have found that one company is a cover-up for white female slavery. The girls are being shipped in from Europe and sold to the highest bidder. This company is located in San Francisco and is a valid salmon cannery. The women, once rescued, are going to need a place to stay until they go back to Europe, or even if they stay here. Abby and I want to help them. We will be opening a mission somewhere close to, or in, San Francisco. We feel called to aid these women once the investigation is over. As owner of this company, and me representing you, please advise me as to your wishes in all these affairs.

Sigmund and Matilda had a lovely wedding and send their love. They're enjoying your house.

Abigail and I arrive in Sacramento on March 15, 1883. We're bringing two people with us that you will be very happy to meet. They will need separate rooms, if that is possible. So please prepare for four of us. We are so looking forward to seeing you again, my dear.

May our Lord watch over you.

Fondly and respectfully yours,

Elijah Humphries

Liberty wiped her eyes, looking up at Maggie. "Well, Maggie... Conchita, it looks as if I inherited after all." She read the letter aloud to the two women.

Maggie jumped up, upsetting her chair, and asked as she picked it up, "You won't go back to Boston, will you, Liberty?"

Liberty looked up, surprised by her question. "No, of course not, Maggie. California is my home now. Do you think I'd want to go back where I have so many unhappy memories? No, Maggie, I may have to go back once in a while for business, but I think even that can be done out here. Perhaps I will open an office in San Francisco."

Maggie commented on the letter. "Is Mr. Humphries saying women are kidnapped and then sold? How horrible! What a despicable thing! I've never heard of dealings such as that."

"I know. Why can't they expose the whole business to the police and let them arrest everyone?"

Conchita chimed in. "I haf heard of such things en Mehico. The womans ees sold to bad men. We just property, you know. Mees Libee, they must catch all thees mens who do thees thing. Sometimes we muss wait for the good to come."

"It's horrible, and I don't want to own a company that does such ugly things." She picked up the letter and looked at it again.

"Conchita, will we have enough room for Elijah and his wife and their two guests? It means three more bedrooms."

"*Sí*...we haf the room. Sometime Kirk, he sleep ina barn. We haf the nice room there. Sí we haf two rooms ina barn. Dere ees plenty room, an' we are liking the company."

CHAPTER XXIV

*If we confess our sins, he is faithful and just
to forgive us our sins, and
to cleanse us from all unrighteousness.*

I JOHN 1:9

NIGHT FELL WITH A SUDDENNESS, DUE to heavy fog. Sounds were muted by the heavy damp, and lanterns swinging from hands held high for lighting cast an eerie halo around themselves.

"Hey, you men! Take it easy on those girls! They're not sacks of potatoes to be dropped or stacked. We don't want any unnecessary bruising. Each one of these gals will fetch a good price for all of us. Be careful now!"

A couple men guffawed at the remark and added lewd comments, touching a bit more than necessary.

Ethan Brooks, his hair greasy, his face needing a shave, stood directing his men as he oversaw the loading of girls onto wagons that would carry them to a ship heading for Hong Kong.

He spoke to the man next to him, dressed like a dandy. "What'd you do give them, extra opiates? They're out cold."

Saul Simmons looked at Brooks with a wicked smile on his face. "Yeah, they seemed ta be restless, an' I was scairt some might make a break fer it. I puts 'em all ta sleep fer th' night."

The two men appeared poles apart. One was dressed like a man of the town, the other a redheaded rumpled mess, but they were business partners. They were not friends, but in agreement in their efforts to make money selling human flesh.

"How many ya gots on this shipment, Brooks? How many goin' out?" Simmons asked.

"Twenty-five head going out on this load." Ethan yelled at a man on the second wagon. "I told you not to drop them, Smitty!"

Brooks turned toward Simmons. "Now, this is the last time I'm going to ask you. When is that bookkeeper, Jones, going to be finished with the books? Does he have any idea, besides putting ink on those pages, what we're about here? Has the man a clue as to why the books have such huge discrepancies?"

"Naw. He's jest workin' the books, an' he don't know nothin' 'bout where the extra money's comin' from. He should be wrapping 'em up afore long."

"When he does, I want you to take care of him. No loose ends. Do you hear me? No loose ends."

"Yeah, I hears ya. An' I know 'xactly what ta do." His smile didn't reach his eyes.

Neither man trusted the other.

Once the three wagons were loaded, they headed slowly across the cobbles toward the pier where a ship awaited them.

Maggie stood watching the meeting of Liberty with her father, Alexander, and grandmother, Phoebe. It wrenched her heart to see the happiness. Her thoughts traveled across the years, and she thought of how happy and content she'd been living with her da and mam.

I don't think I will ever find the love and contentment I saw between my mam and da. I see the same between Diego and Conchita. I know Kirk is a flirt, but I'm not interested in him as anything other than a friend. I doubt any man would look at me twice if they knew my past. Ah well… Maggie drew a deep sigh as tears misted her eyes. Liberty looks so happy, and her father and grandmother are drinking her in with their eyes. Anyone can see they're related—what a family resemblance! Well, they arrived just in time for Jessica's wake. Sure didn't take long for her to die. Last night Liberty slept for over twelve hours. She must have been exhausted, nursing Jessica the way she did.

"It's good to see you, Mr. Humphries, and nice to meet you, Mrs. Humphries." Maggie smiled and almost curtsied, but caught herself just in time. *I'm a lady now, not a servant.*

"We are excited to be here, and thank you for the warm welcome." Elijah smiled back at Maggie.

Matthew introduced Elijah and Abigail to Conchita and Diego.

Maggie listened as Elijah spoke to Matthew, telling him they only planned to be guests for three days.

"I have business to attend to in San Francisco, and Abigail and I plan to look for a place somewhere south of here," he explained.

"Well, welcome to Rancho Bonito, and come on in. You must be tired from your long journey. I should tell you that we are having a wake tonight. It's a long story, and once you get settled, I'll tell you about it. You need to know, neighbors will be coming for a potluck tonight."

"Thank you—and yes, we certainly are worn out. I am sure Phoebe and Abigail will both enjoy putting their feet up, so to speak. We thank you for your generosity. And I'm sorry for your loss, Mr. Bannister."

"You are welcome. We enjoy visitors here at the Rancho, and we have plenty of room. My cook loves preparing food for a crowd. And please, just call me Matthew. We're not so formal here as you are in Boston." He smiled warmly, looking forward to talking to this man Libby so respected, but feeling a bit deceptive, as he wasn't mourning Jessica.

Matthew had been to the bank in San Francisco to deposit some money and to open an account for Liberty. The banker had told him that Monsieur Bouvier had been murdered, but he didn't know anything more than that. Matthew, shocked, hadn't had a chance to talk to Libby, who certainly wasn't forthcoming. Then he'd traveled to Sacramento to pick up this group.

Maggie went to the kitchen to help Conchita while everyone was shown to their rooms.

"Oh, Conchita, Libby looks so much like her father and grandmother! I'm glad Monsieur Corlay isn't her real father. He is as bad as her husband was, evilness pouring out of his bones. Mr. Humphries told Liberty he's afraid Monsieur Corlay knows of our whereabouts from papers Mr. Humphries left on the desk before the reading of the will. Evidently, Monsieur Corlay let himself into the house without anyone knowing he was there."

"Sí. Mees Libbee, she tell me about eet. Meester Humphries, he ees thinking Monsieur Corlay weel come here to geet Mees Libbee. We weel take good care her. Meester Humphries, he a good man."

"Yes. He was a great help in getting us on the train before the reading of the will." Libby was thankful she hadn't had to suffer the humiliation of sitting there and having to hear that the entire Bouvier estate was to go to Monsieur Corlay, except this piece of property here. "Yes, Mr. Humphries is a very nice man."

Maggie wasn't much good at cooking, but she was a big help in setting out plates and getting things ready for neighbors from all over the area who started pouring in. Matthew was taken by surprise at the amount of people who'd come for the wake. It touched his heart that so many came in support of him, as most of them did not know Jessica.

After eating, Libby spent time with her grandmother and father. Maggie helped to clean up. Many of the women who'd come also helped, and it wasn't long before the kitchen was back in order.

Conchita said to Maggie in a soft voice, "I no be at the wake. I no like Jessica, no not me. Eet be a lie eef I go an' act like she special to me. She cause Meester Bannister so much heartache even before she runned away."

"It's all right. I can stay in here and talk to you. I'm not going to the wake either. I had a bad experience with that woman on the train, and like you, it'd be a lie for me to act as if I'd been her friend when I didn't like her at all."

"Sí. Mees Maggie, you weel stay an' halp me. I haf much to do. Now we make the dessert for later thees evening."

Detective Cabot Jones lay in a bed that was too short for him. His arms pillowed his head.

Friday can't come too soon as far as I am concerned. I'll be glad to meet with Mr. Humphries, and for sure I won't be returning as the cannery's bookkeeper. That Simmons is a real stinker. Wonder if Ethan Brooks is holding him back from killing me, or perhaps Brooks wants me dead too. I can feel pending disaster if I stay there much longer. I've drug out filling in those ledgers as much as I can, but Friday, please come quick!

He rolled onto his side, thinking about what he'd seen this very night.

Whoever is in charge of this operation needs to hang. All those poor girls in the warehouse. It's one thing to hear about it, but quite another to see the misery and mistreatment. I'm glad those fire escape stairs didn't squeak. How can anyone think they have the right to kidnap those girls and sell them? Wonder who Bouvier has leading the operation? It's not only Brooks. It's someone else, and I'm going to find out who the wretched man is.

Cabot lay pondering for quite some time, the thought of the cold, damp warehouse and the misery of girls being sold to the highest bidder keeping him awake far into the night.

Maggie didn't hear anyone up, but she saw the sun shining and stretched, grateful for a full night's sleep. She swung her long legs over the side of the bed and sat stretching and grinning to herself.

I do believe Liberty will begin building. The weather has turned, and I think the rainy season is behind us. Wonder how long she stayed up last night?

She dressed quickly, braiding her bright-red hair and pinning it into a bun. She slipped on her shoes and made her way to the kitchen, where Conchita was making pancakes.

"Good morning," Maggie said with a lilt in her voice. She loved breakfast. "Where is everybody? Mmm, that maple syrup smells good!"

Conchita looked mournfully at Maggie. "Someting no right, Mees Maggie. I can feel eet een my heart. I doan know where anyone ees. Diego, he always haf hees coffee before he go to the barn, an' Meester Bannister, he always up by now."

"Wonder if they went out somewhere together?"

As they were talking, they heard horses' hooves coming right up to the front door of the Rancho. Conchita and Maggie ran to the door. Conchita threw it wide open.

"Oh my goodness, Matthew! What happened?" Maggie gasped. She saw the black bruising on Liberty's chin and her left arm was definitely broken.

Conchita ran to hold the horse's reins.

Maggie saw Liberty gritting her teeth, her lips pulled back in a grimace of pain.

"Corlay got her." Matthew dismounted clumsily with Liberty in his arms and gently carried her into the house "Conchita, wake Kirk and have him ride for John."

Conchita sped down the hall toward Kirk's room.

Maggie, right behind her, threw open Liberty's door. She returned to the kitchen to put water on to heat, but Conchita had a pot already bubbling.

Maggie ran back to the bedroom to see if she could help Liberty.

Matthew had just laid her down, and she looked up at him, trying to smile, but pain etched her features, and a huge swelling was darkening her chin.

"Wh-where's Jacques?"

"Libby, he was bitten by a rattlesnake. He's dead."

Maggie gasped as Liberty closed her eyes, tears seeping through her thick lashes as they lay on her cheeks.

She said nothing as Matthew looked down at her. She turned her face to the wall, not wanting Matthew to see her tears. Matthew picked up a blanket lying on the arm of the chair and covered her with it, tucking it around her.

"Kirk's going for Dr. John," Matthew said softly.

He went out into the hall, and before tapping on Alexander's door, he asked Maggie, "Is there water heating?"

"Yes. Is Liberty all right?"

"Not really. Jacques Corlay got her at the pump by the shack. He took her up to a cave, and by my reckoning, he let her fall off her horse with her hands tied. Her wrist is broken. He must have slugged her on her chin and knocked her unconscious. She was unconscious most of the ride back, which was a good thing. Dr. John will find out if there's anything else broken. There's really nothing you can do right now. I'm going to have her father sit with her. I think he'll be of good comfort."

"I'm glad Monsieur Corlay's dead. He was so mean to Libby and evil to boot." She strode down to Liberty's room, walking softly to the bed.

Seeing that Liberty was awake, she spoke. "I'm sorry this happened, Libby." She smoothed Liberty's brow.

Liberty's eyes filled and her throat was clogged with them. "Oh, Maggie. He was so full of hate…it was horrible, and that will always be my last memory of him." She closed her eyes, and Maggie, thinking she had fallen asleep tiptoed out of the room.

Matthew tapped on Alexander's door.

"Come in." Alexander had just finished his morning ablutions and felt better for washing away the sleep. He was fully dressed.

Matthew filled him in on what had transpired that morning, and when he was finished, he went to the ice house to get some ice for Libby's chin.

Alexander went to Liberty's room. Her door was opened wide, the way Matthew had left it. Her face was hidden from him, but he could see her left hand lay at an odd angle. He picked up the chair from the desk and sat it next to the bed. He gently took her right hand on the coverlet, encasing it with his. Her fingers felt icy, and he wondered if she was in shock. She turned her head, looking at him with tears seeping from green eyes, so like her mother's.

"Jacques was incredibly evil. I don't understand how a person can grow up from an innocent child to be such a monster and not care at all for life, or love, or any of the things that make living meaningful."

"Romans eight talks about the sinful mind, how it is hostile to God and does not submit to God's law, nor can it do so," her father replied. "Those controlled by the sinful nature cannot please God. Liberty, honey, there are many people who end up trying to please only themselves, and they never can, because it's contrary to the law of God's Spirit. Many people fill themselves up with other things because our very being was created to worship, but they worship the wrong things."

Liberty looked up at her father. She wondered that he could comfort her with so few words. Her lids felt heavy, and she closed her eyes, drifting off to sleep. Alexander continued to sit quietly holding her hand.

Two days later, Elijah Humphries and Matthew left for San Francisco, Elijah a bit nervous about the coming meeting with Cabot.

Friday, late morning, Maggie was in the chicken coop gathering eggs. *Wonder why Mr. Humphries didn't take his wife with him?* Maggie thought it strange. *Why did Matthew go with him? Mr. Humphries said earlier he and his wife would most likely look for a house in San Rafael, so why did he go to San Francisco?*

She slapped at a chicken who tried to peck her. *Libby seems much better. I do hope she doesn't have any permanent damage to her arm. I'm glad Monsieur Corlay is dead. He was just as evil as Monsieur Bouvier. Both of them came to a bad end. Wonder if that's because they were so evil? No, that can't be true. Many people who are good can come to a bad end.*

Maggie carried the eggs into the kitchen. "It's amazing that we can eat so many eggs."

Conchita was making lunch, and Abigail, Elijah's wife, sat at the kitchen table with Phoebe and Liberty.

"*Sí*, we haf many eggs and many foods. Eet ees good," Conchita replied.

Maggie laughed. "It is good, and you are a wonderful cook."

"I concur," Liberty said.

"It sounds as if Meester Bannister ees back," Conchita said.

The front door opened with a bang, causing quite a commotion as Matthew and Elijah carried an injured man into the house.

"Conchita, what room is empty? And get Diego to ride for John. Tell him a man's been shot."

Maggie ran ahead and opened the door to the room Jess had occupied. "This one's ready. Lay him in here." She pulled back the covers. Everything in the room had been washed down, and the bedding had all been boiled. All was in readiness for the next guest, but it looked as if the next guest would need nursing, too.

Maggie hadn't liked Jess at all, and Jess had responded in kind, so Liberty had done all the nursing. Maggie decided she would undertake the task to nurse this man and hoped she could do it with a cheerful heart, the way Libby had.

The two men carried the man to the room. Matthew backed in holding the injured man by the shoulders, and Elijah bore his feet.

Before lying him down, Matthew asked, "Maggie could you put a flannel blanket atop the bottom sheet for protection? Cabot is still oozing blood."

"What's happened? Who is he?" Maggie questioned as she began untying the man's shoes.

"Elijah and I are going to get something to eat while we explain. We haven't eaten all day. And his name"—he nodded toward the bed—"is Detective Cabot Jones."

"Well, don't explain until I'm finished here. I want to hear your story."

As the two men walked out the door, Maggie carefully pulled a fine leather shoe off the unconscious man and let it drop to the floor.

She took scissors carefully cutting off Mr. Jones' shirt. She was sorry because it was a nice linen one. Blood had soaked through the bandage. She was aghast when she saw how much there was. Maggie covered him with a blanket. *We'll just have to wait for Dr. John.* Wanting to find out what had happened, she hurried to the kitchen. She checked to make sure Conchita had water heating on the stove, and then she sat near Libby, who was sitting between Alexander and Phoebe at the kitchen table. Kirk and Abigail also joined the circle to hear the tale.

Matthew and Elijah had begun to recount what had transpired that morning.

Elijah related how he and Matthew had arrived at the church where he was to meet Cabot Jones, a Boston detective uncover in a company Liberty owns. They'd been inside waiting for Cabot when shots rang out.

Matthew said, "When I opened the church door, Cabot Jones fell inside right at my feet, and a bullet plunked into the door next to me. I pulled him in the rest of the way. When I cracked open the door, I got shot at, so I returned fire and saw the assailant run like the dickens."

"Sure wish I'd been there," Kirk said. "I would have enjoyed shooting some varmints."

Matthew looked at him grimly. "I would have been glad for your help, Kirk. You could have chased that man down."

"That's why you've been acting so offish, Elijah," Abigail exclaimed. "You knew something could happen, didn't you?"

He looked at her sheepishly. "Yes, Abigail, but I didn't want you involved. This whole situation is dangerous, as you can see. They tried to kill Cabot because of his knowledge about one of the companies Liberty now owns. I need to get into Napa and send a more detailed wire to George once I find out from Dr. Meeks just what shape Cabot's in."

"Is this the man you were talking about, Elijah? Is this the detective from the Boston Police Department? Is he a good man?" Liberty asked.

"Yes, yes, I believe him to be an exceptional man—a very exceptional man. Cabot Jones went undercover in your salmon cannery company. I was supposed to get information from him and relate it to the chief of detectives in Boston. Cabot's the detective who caught the man who murdered Armand. That man was Hans Holbein, and he tried to murder me as well."

"Elijah! You never told me about that!" Liberty exclaimed.

"I'll tell you about it later, Liberty. Matthew and I are hungry!" He gave Liberty a smile of deep affection but looked expectantly at Conchita.

"Oh, you mens! You tell us womans theengs, an' then you wants to eat an' no feenish your stories. You mens." Conchita mumbled some more as she dished up two plates for Elijah and Matthew, who grinned at her comments.

Elijah gave thanks for their food.

Matthew was hungry, his head ached, and he felt emotionally drained, but as he reflected on the morning, his heart felt light and clean. He'd prayed in the cathedral where Elijah was to meet Cabot. He'd asked for forgiveness for his sins and asked Christ into his heart. He knew the anger he'd lived with for so long was gone. He was grateful. Very grateful.

CHAPTER XXV

For the life of the flesh is in the blood.

LEVITICUS 17:11

MAGGIE RETURNED TO MR. JONES' ROOM with a glass of water and a wet cloth.

Kirk trailed after her. He wanted to know more about the detective, but when he got to the room, he realized the man was unconscious. He watched as she bathed the detective's forehead. Cabot stirred a bit. She dipped the corner of the cloth and dribbled it on his lips, totally ignoring Kirk.

Maggie studied the man lying in the bed. He had thick brown hair and a very handsome face with a deep groove in one cheek. His brows were smooth, and his lips were full and well shaped. She wondered what color his eyes were. She took the cloth and gently washed his hands; his nails were even and clean. Turning to see Kirk staring at her, she returned his look evenly without flinching or any embarrassment. Maggie, upset with Kirk's cavalier treatment of her, went to sit in the rocking chair as she awaited the doctor's arrival. Her face was serene.

Kirk, with the sudden realization he'd lost Maggie's high regard, pivoted on his heel and left the room.

Maggie sat until Dr. John Meeks came to check the wound. He eased off the bandages, not wanting to start any new bleeding. Maggie cleaned the area around the wounds, and after Dr. John poured a little carbolic onto the cloth, soaking it, she dabbed carefully, dripping the carbolic into the wound. Cabot's eyes flew open and looked straight into Maggie's. He moaned with pain but again lost consciousness. Dr. Meeks took the cloth from Maggie and cleaned both wounds, glad to see the bleeding had stopped.

"This man's lost a tremendous amount of blood," he told Maggie as he wrapped the man's thigh with sterile strips of cloth. "Try to get liquids down him, chicken and beef broth to build up his strength, Miss O'Neill, and just plain water would be good. Also, give him this every four hours or so."

"What is it?"

"It's an elixir I mix up to help patients who are in pain. It's laudanum mixed with some herbs my grandmother taught me about when I was young. She was part Indian and knew much of folklore. This young man's going to feel it when he wakes up. The bullet went clean through his shoulder and shouldn't bother him too much, but the doctor who dug that bullet out of his thigh probed around and dug deep. Who is this man anyway?"

"He's a detective from Boston, investigating a crime in San Francisco. He's a brave man to do what he did." Maggie's eyes shone as she spoke to the doctor.

"I don't know the story, but if he was shot in San Francisco and he's a detective, he's most likely being hunted down by whoever committed this crime."

After giving Maggie a few more directions, he left the room.

Maggie sat again, rocking back and forth, beginning to worry about what Dr. John had just said. *Well, I can't do anything except keep an eye on Mr. Jones. If someone is hunting him down, Matthew and Kirk will have to take care of it. Her thoughts shifted to her patient. His eyes are brown, dark-chocolate brown. It was almost frightening when he opened his eyes! The look he gave startled me. It seemed like a silent cry for help. Well, that's what I'm going to do. I'm going to help this man get well!*

There was a light tap on the doorjamb, and Maggie looked over to see Mr. Humphries step into the bedroom.

"Why, hello, Mr. Humphries."

He sat down on a leather chair facing Maggie, who continued to push with her foot to rock.

Elijah looked around with interest. Most of the guest rooms were almost feminine in decor, but this one was more suited to a man's taste. The walls were two shades of brown, light on the top, chocolate on the bottom, with a wide trim of light sage green dividing the colors. The wall with the fireplace was a solid sage green, as was the mantel, door, and window trim. The effect was very different, yet fresh and peaceful. The curtains and bedspread were a blend of those colors with splashes of cream mixed in, bringing all the colors into an eye-pleasing coordinate. A huge painting of a frigate running before a storm, sails billowing in the wind, hung over the mantel opposite the four-poster bed. *It's a comfortable room*, Elijah thought. *Cabot will have a nice view of the courtyard from his bed.*

Elijah and Maggie talked quietly together while Cabot lay listening. He'd regained consciousness but drifted in and out of the conversation, feeling the effects of the laudanum.

Elijah noticed Maggie's abundance of beautiful, bright-red hair braided into a crown around her head. Her gray eyes sparkled. Elijah thought it was an unusual combination—gray eyes and red hair. Her mouth, perhaps a little too wide, had a warm, welcoming smile. He wondered if she was as intelligent as she was pretty, and smiled at his thoughts. *No doubt she is a good, loyal friend to Liberty.* He'd escorted Maggie from Liberty's house in Boston to the train station, but his mind had been set on all that needed to be accomplished, so he'd paid little attention to the girl.

Elijah jerked his thoughts back to the present. He asked Maggie how she came to work for Liberty.

Maggie studied Elijah's face for a few moments as her thoughts took her back to the time she'd gone into service for the Bouviers. The sparkle in her eyes faded as she spoke.

"I had turned fourteen when Mr. Jamison, my previous employer, committed suicide. I cannot even begin to tell you the horror I felt—for I was the one to discover him hanging from a rafter in the basement. As much as I'd like to, I don't think it's a sight I will ever be able to erase from my memory. I didn't know it at the time, but Libby's husband and stepfather took Mr. Jamison's company right out from under him."

Elijah made a clucking noise of sympathy.

"I needed to find work, as the entire staff was to be let go. Mrs. Jamison and the children were to go live with her sister. The Jamisons' cook told me to go to the Bouvier manse. She'd heard they were looking for a personal maid for Madam Bouvier. I was, in truth, desired by employers because it's difficult to find a personal maid with proper English. The Bouviers' cook, Mrs. Jensen, was quite personable and asked me in for a spot of hot tea. She told me to wait, and she would get Madam Bouvier to see me. Liberty interviewed me and hired me right then and there. I can't begin to tell you how thankful I was."

"How did you come to be in service?" Elijah asked kindly.

"Well, sir, my father was a professor in Dublin but died while we were sailing to America. My mother taught English and found a job soon after we arrived in Boston. However, she contracted lung fever and died a short time later. We had no family in America who could take me in." Maggie paused to take a breath, thinking, *There's no reason to tell him about Elmer.* "The landlady where my mother and I stayed was the one who got the interview for me with the Jamisons. I was fortunate to get employment there, for I was only twelve. I could have ended up in the poorhouse."

Cabot stirred, and Maggie immediately went to his side. She felt his forehead; his temperature had climbed up again. He opened his eyes and smiled as he looked into hers.

"How are you feeling, Mr. Jones?" Maggie asked.

"Detective Cabot Jones, this is Miss Margaret—Maggie—O'Neill, recently of Boston herself."

Cabot lay there smiling at the girl like an idiot. She smiled in return. Maggie's smile was sweet, with her dimples dipping deeply into her cheeks.

She felt Cabot's forehead again, making a mental note of how warm he felt. She went to the little room Matthew had built between every pair of guest rooms. She loved the convenience of it. Before coming to the Rancho, she'd never seen such a room. Dampening a washcloth from the pitcher of water next to the sink, she took the cloth and went back to the bedside to wipe Cabot's face and hands.

Elijah sat in silence while Maggie ministered to the young detective.

"How are you feeling, Mr. Jones?" she asked again as she touched the wet cloth to his forehead. Maggie washed his face as if he were a baby. He seemed to enjoy it.

"I'm feeling a bit tired, and my brain seems foggy. I don't even remember getting shot."

She took the cloth, dampened it again, and began to wash between his fingers.

He kept smiling up at this beautiful gray-eyed angel.

Elijah asked, "Are you able to talk a little? I'd like to give George a detailed account of the situation in San Francisco."

Cabot suddenly registered the fact that it was Elijah with whom Maggie had been talking. Elijah stood and come to the bedside.

"Yes, I feel weak, but I think my brain is clearing."

Maggie slipped her arm behind Cabot's shoulders, helping him sit up to drink some water. He was sure her touch made his blood pressure rise. He tried to concentrate on Mr. Humphries.

Maggie said, "I'll leave so you can talk." She left quietly, feeling Cabot's eyes on her as she walked out the door.

Once the door was closed, she leaned against it, her hands pressed flat against the door. She drew a deep breath and wondered at her fluttering heart. She berated herself. *Margaret Regan O'Neill, do you really need to look at every stray man as if he's marriage material? You need to stop it, Maggie! First Kirk, and now this man, Mr. Jones. Just stop it and mind yourself. You are not marriageable material—you are damaged goods, and no man worth his salt is going to want you.*

With dragging steps, she walked down the hall, trying to paste a happy look on her face.

Dr. John Meeks was still at the Rancho, having been invited for dinner. He found a chair next to Liberty. He enjoyed jesting and grandstanding with the group. Everyone listened to him and laughed at his comments. He was witty, but Liberty found him a bit overbearing and was tired of him constantly dominating the conversation. She smiled, only half listening. She couldn't seem to think of much else these days except getting her house finished. She faced her father as he began to speak quietly to her from across the table. John regaled the other end of the table with a strange case he'd recently had and was so intent on his story, he didn't notice Liberty's attention was elsewhere.

Maggie sat on the other side of Dr. John and thought him great fun. She wasn't attracted to him, although he was single. She breathed a little sigh of relief. *Perhaps I'm not after every man after all. I certainly don't feel an attraction to the doctor, and Kirk has about cured my interest in him. I don't want to fall for a man who flirts with everyone who wears a skirt.*

Maggie laughed delightedly at Dr. John's jests and quirky humor.

There was a knock on the door, and Conchita went to answer it. It was a man from the other side of Napa, saying his wife was ready to have her baby, and he hoped he had tracked the doctor down.

"Sí, he ees here. I get heem for you." She relayed the message to Dr. John, who rose reluctantly, thanked Matthew for his hospitality, and bid them all goodbye. He winked at Liberty, who blushed under his perusal.

The festive air continued even after the doctor had been called away. Before eating, Maggie had made sure her patient was comfortable. He was very weak, but his fever had lessened. After dinner, she immediately took some chicken broth back to the bedroom to feed Mr. Jones, but she found him asleep, and his temperature had climbed.

She set the broth on the table and took a clean cloth out of the cupboard. An ewer of water was on the washstand, and she poured some into the large matching basin. Sponging him down with the cool water, she bathed his head, arms, and hands. She'd done the same for her mother when she'd had a raging fever before dying. Maggie drew the blanket down to his waist as well, and she sponged his chest with the cool water. She'd never been this close to a man since Elmer, and that had been one of the worst nights of her life. She was amazed at Mr. Jones' hairy chest. The hair was soft and narrowed to a vee above his navel. She carefully sponged him down, and beginning again with his head, she repeated the process.

Liberty wanted to help with cleaning up after dinner, but her grandmother shooed her out of the kitchen.

"I should probably spell Maggie for a while so she can get a few things done. She's been nursing the detective since he was brought in today."

Conchita nodded her agreement as Liberty left the kitchen.

She walked slowly down the hall, thinking about how a person's circumstances could change in an instant.

Detective Jones was supposed to meet Elijah and then return to the salmon company and work today. Instead, he ends up being nearly murdered and brought here to Napa to recover. She thought, too, about Maggie. She's become a young lady, changing from personal maid to personal and trusted friend. She looks, dresses, and acts like a lady. And look at me, Lord, how quickly my circumstances have changed in the last few months. How grateful I am for Your hand guiding me. Please let me know Your perfect will for my life. May I not go astray but stay close to You, keeping You the center of my universe. Help me to somehow touch Maggie with Your love. I pray she comes to know you.

Liberty tapped on the door, quietly entering. Cabot saw her first because Maggie's back was to the door as she bent over him, sponging down his arms.

"I wanted to thank you, Mr. Jones, for your service and sacrifice. You're the man who caught my husband's murderer, are you not?"

Cabot paused before answering. He hadn't known who she was when she'd entered the room. He'd heard much about her though, through Elijah.

"Yes, ma'am," he replied, "but if he hadn't attacked Mr. Humphries, I don't know if we'd have ever caught him. Supposedly, Hans Holbein was a banker. If Mr. Humphries hadn't sensed Holbein behind him and turned, he'd not be with us today. Holbein was not only a murderer, madam, but he was also a key player in helping your deceased husband

and Jacques Corlay steal companies from honest, hardworking businessmen."

"Mr. Jones, I'm so, so sorry for the damage done you. This would never have happened if Armand hadn't been involved in such nefarious schemes."

"Thank you, madam, but it's my job. It's what I do."

"Yes, and you do it quite well." She spoke to Maggie. "Do you need a rest? I came in to spell you if you need a break." Liberty smiled as she asked, her eyes closely observing Maggie's face.

Maggie glanced at Liberty with a smile on her lips. "No, no I'm fine. I just had a long break for dinner."

Cabot breathed a little sigh of relief. *I have no doubt Madam Bouvier would be a fine caregiver, but I've become smitten with this beautiful redhead! Wonder what Maggie's last name is. Elijah had said earlier, but I can't recall it.*

"What's your surname, miss?" he asked. "I can't go calling you Maggie. It isn't proper." He wished he could, but it just wasn't done on such short acquaintance.

"My name's Margaret Regan O'Neill," she replied. "Here in the West, people are a lot less formal than Boston. You may certainly call me Maggie."

Liberty's eyebrows lifted imperceptibly, and she excused herself. "I need to go talk to Elijah." She left, thinking, *Au revoir, Kirk.*

Ethan Brooks met Saul Simmons late in the evening at a saloon. The two needed to talk without fear of anyone overhearing what they said.

Brooks, president of the company the Bouviers owned, looked unkempt, his hair greasy, his face needing a shave, and his coat rumpled.

He always looks like a person who mucks out stables, thought Simmons, who was impeccably turned-out. He felt pure distain for his boss. He wondered if he should do away with him and take control of the company himself. He would have to think on the idea.

Ethan Brooks looked at Saul, distrust written all over his face. He was upset with Simmons. "Since you bungled it with Jones, we're going to have to move those girls. We can't keep them there much longer. How badly do you think Jones was hit anyway?"

"The man I hired said he wuz hit bad 'nough to keep 'im out of commission for a while, maybe even die. I'm thinkin' the man Jones wuz working alone. He don't know 'bout the girls anyhows. He wuz only doing the bookkeepin'. I had 'im watched, an' he never did talk to nobody."

"Anybody," Ethan corrected. "How do you know? Are you positive he never talked to anyone?"

"Yeah, yeah, I'm sure, he went to that thar church three times a week, reglar as clockwork. Musta bin a religious man, I reckon. I had 'im followed, an' I buried the man who shot 'im. We don't want no witnesses in this here business. I'm thinkin' we should get rid of the guards and get a new set of 'em if we're gonna be a movin' the girls."

"And just how do you propose to do it?" Brooks sneered.

Simmons gave Brooks a look of loathing. "We jest take the girls an' tell the men ta wait cuz we're gonna be bringin' in another whole shipment. None of 'em knows where our office is, an' they'll be a sittin' thar waitin' fer another load, onlys we won't be bringin' 'em any."

"Hmmm, that just might work. Then we wouldn't have to pay any of them anything. I'll need to think about it. You better see to it those men don't touch the girls. They won't be worth anything if they're damaged goods."

He laughed wickedly, and Simmons joined in.

CHAPTER XXVI

But I would strengthen you with my mouth,
and the moving of my lips should asswage your grief.

JOB 16:5

CABOT HAD FALLEN IN LOVE. He didn't know how it had happened, but there was no mistaking it. He was head over heels in love, and yet he wondered where it would lead. He was Bostonian, born and bred. He had a sister, brother, and parents in Boston. His job, which he valued, was in Boston. He'd heard Maggie say, a couple times, how thankful she was Liberty did not wish to go back east. His beautiful redhead loved it here, and he knew she hoped never to go back to Boston. That was the crux of a massive dilemma for Cabot. He didn't want to make any advances in his relationship with Maggie if it was simply to end in heartbreak for both of them. What was he to do?

Still weak from losing blood, he'd not been permitted up yet, but he felt stronger every day. He was feeling so much better. Today he was getting up, doctor's orders or not. Being in bed for over a week, he was done with it. He pushed up the pillows behind him as he heard a tap on the door.

Maggie entered with a breakfast tray. "Good morning, Mr. Cabot Jones! Isn't it a glorious day?" Her dimples dipped into her cheeks; her gray eyes sparkled with life and good humor. Swept up into a knot on top of her head, tendrils of bright-red hair fell around her ears. Setting the tray down, she walked over to pull back the curtains. As she did, she asked, "What's your middle name?" Light poured into the room, letting in the beauty of the day.

Cabot smiled at her. "Good morning yourself, Mistress Margaret Regan O'Neill, and I don't have a middle name." He could see puffy clouds dotting a deep-blue sky. "Yes, now that I can see out the window, it is a beautiful day. It also looks to be a beautiful day in here." He smiled warmly at Maggie, who blushed becomingly. He wondered if Maggie was naturally a morning person or one by necessity. A smile curved his lips, good humor glinting from his dark-brown eyes.

Maggie stood still a moment, smiling back. She pulled a little table next to the bed to eat breakfast. She had opted to eat with him, and it was a comfortable time.

The first time they'd eaten together, Cabot had thought it would be stilted, but it wasn't. It was as if they'd done it many times before. The ease with which they had settled into the little routine together had surprised him.

They ate a breakfast of corn tortillas filled with eggs, chopped bacon, cheese, and the tomato salsa Maggie had told him about. She'd laughed when she told him the story of choking on the first mouthful she'd ever eaten.

They sat, chatting about the fact that today, Dr. Meeks would bring a cane for Cabot to use. As they drank their coffee, a rap sounded on the doorjamb of the open door.

Before Maggie could respond, Cabot said, "Come on in, Conchita."

She came in saying, "Eet ees telegram for you, Meester Jones. Eet comed just now." She looked at the two of them. "You like the food, Meester Jones? How your leg be doing? You theenk Mees Maggie, she the good nurse, eh?" She laughed and without waiting for an answer to any of her questions, left the bedroom, chuckling.

The telegram was from George Baxter.

The days were passing swiftly. Cabot struggled with the fact that George Baxter had wired him to get himself to San Francisco as soon as he was able and notify the chief of detectives about the entire situation. His shoulder was a little stiff and sore, but it was close to being back to normal. His leg was another matter. It pained him a great deal. Dr. Meeks told him that was to be expected, since the tissue had been so damaged where the bullet had been.

"That San Francisco doctor," Dr. Meeks had said, "went right through your thigh muscle, instead of pulling the muscle to the side a little to see if the bullet was underneath, which I'm sure it was. He evidently has never heard of that technique, but it causes a lot less damage than cutting through the muscle to dig for the bullet."

Dr. John Meeks was pleasant enough, but grated on Cabot's nerves. He always seemed to smile, even when relating bad news.

Cabot knew he was short on patience. Tired of being bedridden, he'd begun walking around the bedroom with the cane Dr. John had brought with him. It was painful, but he could endure it, though the stabbing pain was intense and made him wonder if he'd ever walk properly again.

Maggie stood under his good arm, helping him walk a little each day. He liked the feel of her there. It comforted as well as distracted him. He refused to take the laudanum for pain. He felt it clogged his brain and made him feel even more incapacitated. He was glad to be out of bed.

Cabot talked often to Maggie about the work he loved. He didn't boast about it, but it had taken much training, hard work, and dedication to get where he was in the department. He had family in Boston and told Maggie he didn't think he could live anywhere else. He knew his heart was firmly planted there. He didn't talk about his family much. What was there to talk about? He talked about his nanny more than anyone except George Baxter. Cabot was dedicated to his chief. Not only was George Baxter a sagacious boss, he was a father figure to him as well. Maggie's desire to stay in the West made Cabot feel off balance. He wasn't comfortable with uncertainty, usually knowing what he wanted and going after it. He wondered if she would even consider going back to Boston.

They walked the length of the room, back and forth, several times. Maggie steadied him.

Cabot grimaced. "I guess that's enough for now. I feel I need to be moving more, but I reckon I'm as weak as a newborn kitten."

"All right, sit here a minute, and then perhaps you'll feel like walking to the great room."

Cabot sat down heavily on a chair at a little table in his room. He drummed his fingers on the table, looking at Maggie.

"I really need to get to San Francisco. My boss, George Baxter, wants me to inform the agency there about the salmon company. I'll tell you, more than once I thought I would be murdered when I was a clerk doing the books. Simmons didn't scare me half as much as Ethan Brooks."

"Who? Who did you say?" Maggie had blanched, her face becoming a pasty white.

"Saul Simmons and Ethan Brooks."

Maggie could not control herself. She began to cry. She hid her head in the crook of her arm on the table and sobbed, and gulping shudders enveloped her.

Cabot got up, having no idea what was wrong. He slid his chair over next to hers, and took Maggie into his arms.

"What is it, Maggie? What's wrong?"

"Ethan Brooks is a murderer! Six years ago I saw him murder a man!"

Cabot's arms tightened as he digested this information. His eyebrows rose in surprise that Maggie would even know such a degenerate at Ethan Brooks.

Maggie, beside herself and throwing all caution to the wind, told Cabot everything. She left nothing out. She even told him about Mrs. Jamison and how Maggie had planned to give her baby to her.

Cabot, still holding Maggie in his arms, was aghast at what had happened to her as a twelve-year-old girl. His arms tightened even more, as if by holding this woman close he could bear some of her pain.

"Oh, Maggie. I am so sorry for the things you've gone through. We will make Ethan Brooks pay. I promise you—he will be caught and hung for his crimes."

Maggie, knowing her chances with Cabot were over, sat back and wiped her eyes. She took a deep breath, wiped her nose, and said, "He is an evil man, Cabot. You are fortunate to be alive." She wiped at her eyes again, barely able to look him in the eye. Shame filled her heart with grief and remorse.

Cabot released her but still held her hand. "What I saw through those dirty windows under the eaves of that warehouse made me want to hang Brooks myself. Maggie, again I say, I'm sorry for what happened to you. The man is even more evil than I thought. He was in cahoots with Bouvier and Corlay."

Maggie was surprised that he would know. "All of them evil—beyond belief. They've ruined lives for a few greenbacks." She wiped her eyes and smiled tremulously.

"Let's walk down the hall to the great room. Then I'll be able to change your bedclothes while you enjoy a change of scenery." Maggie stood up, taking another deep breath. The door was open, and standing under his arm, they traversed the hall. Cabot hadn't been out of the bedroom since he'd been carried in. It did make him feel better to be out of its confines.

He eased himself into a deep leather chair, and Maggie pulled up the ottoman, placing both his feet on it. He felt his body relax from the effort of walking and smiled a bit wanly.

"Would you like a drink?"

"Yes, a cup of tea would hit the spot, but I don't want to be a nuisance."

"Never a nuisance, and I'm sorry I burdened you about my past. Liberty doesn't even know about it. What you must think of me!"

Maggie went off to the kitchen before he could reply.

She called back over her shoulder, "I'll just be a minute."

He could hear her talking to Conchita, and then she was back.

"Conchita will bring it in as soon as it's ready. I'm going to change the bedclothes now." She walked down the hall toward his room, her shoulders sagging with remorse.

Liberty, Maggie, and Phoebe were having their first lesson firing a gun. The three women chattered together, as they walked out to the area behind the barns where Matthew sat on a stump waiting for them. Maggie carried the two guns Liberty had bought at the mercantile store in Boston. Liberty carried the box of bullets because her arm was still splinted. Both Phoebe and Maggie were dressed in casual muslin dresses, but Liberty had on her long leather boots, split skirt, and wide-brimmed hat. Liberty, taking one of the guns from Maggie, proudly showed it to Matthew. She had a beautiful pair of Smith & Wesson New Model Number Three revolvers.

Matthew was duly impressed with the gun. He took it from her and liked the feel of it in his hand. "It's a mighty nice gun, Liberty," he said. "I like the feel, and it has good balance. Most lawmen use these—they're a good handgun." Giving it back to her, he said, "All right, ladies, the first thing you need to know is whether a gun is loaded or not, it's never pointed at anyone unless you intend to shoot them. When you load a gun or handle it, you point it downward, especially if anyone else is around. That's crucial to keeping us all alive!" He grinned. *This is going to be interesting.*

The women were standing with rounded eyes, hanging on to every word, and he could tell they were nervous.

Maggie said, "Libby and I wished we had been able to make that man dance on the train station platform when we arrived in Sacramento. Remember what you said, Libby? You said if you had a gun, you'd have made that man do a real dance right then and there."

They laughed, and Matthew and Phoebe joined in, which helped to ease the tension.

Matthew pulled his own gun out of his holster, showing them how to load it. He unloaded it and then reloaded it. Looking at each woman, he saw no one had a question mark in her eyes. He quickly unloaded it again and handed it to Phoebe. Liberty and Maggie each had one of the new Smith & Wessons.

"Now you do it," Matthew said.

Phoebe loaded first. "I think I have it," she said.

Matthew was amazed she did it so fast. "Are you sure you've never loaded a gun before?"

"No, I never have. I daresay I've not seen one loaded before today either." She smiled, a feeling of pleasure coming over her that she had done so well. Carefully keeping her gun pointing downward, she thought how wonderful that even at her age she could learn to shoot.

Maggie loaded hers next. Liberty needed help because of her left arm. It was too cumbersome, the gun too heavy for her splinted arm.

Matthew loaded her gun slowly so she'd know how to do it.

He spoke, nodding his head to Phoebe and Maggie. "Now I want you to empty all the chambers in the cylinder—not you, Libby. You can do it when your arm is better."

Maggie finished this task first, and Matthew praised her.

"Now reload your guns. We're going to shoot at those pieces of wood I have nailed to the posts." He pointed at the fence line where pieces of wood were sticking up.

"Maggie, you go first. Hold the gun straight out as if it were an extension of your arm. Look down the barrel." He tapped the end of the gun. "This is called the sight. You look down the barrel through the sight and aim at the wood. You fire by squeezing the trigger. Don't jerk it. Just a gentle squeeze." He shot at one of the sticks, and wood chips flew…the noise earsplitting. "Now, you try."

Maggie carefully aimed, the end of the barrel wobbling.

"Wait." Matthew took the gun from Maggie, adding, "If you take too long, the gun will become too heavy and begin to waver. Maggie, take the gun, and when you're ready, lift it, aim, and fire."

Maggie lifted the barrel, aimed, and squeezed the trigger. The noise deafened her ears, but she didn't hit anything. She wondered if she had unknowingly closed her eyes.

"Did I close my eyes?" she asked.

Liberty looked at her, humor sparkling from her green eyes. "Do you think I'm going to stand in front of you and look?"

The two grinned at each other.

"I didn't realize the gun would feel so heavy. It's not too bad when it's snuggled up next to you, but to hold it straight out...I'm lucky I didn't shoot at the ground."

"Perhaps you did. You certainly didn't hit any sticks." Phoebe laughed.

Alexander was up in the loft watching the women with Matthew. *Matthew certainly looks as if he's enjoying himself. He's a good instructor. He's patient and thorough.* Alexander sat reflecting upon the scene unfolding below him. *I believe Matthew is very attracted to Liberty, but I don't believe she even recognizes admiration from anyone. Her dead husband must have been the lowest of cads.*

Matthew said to Phoebe. "All right, now it's your turn." He got behind her, wrapping his arms around her to show her how to aim. Stepping back, he said, "Now, remember, look down the barrel through the sights...shoot!"

Phoebe fired the gun and began to laugh, "My ears are stopped up! Those things are quite thunderous!" Matthew enjoyed hearing her English accent. He grinned at her.

"All right, now you, Libby." He stood behind her, wrapping his arms around her, thinking, *This feels so right.* He had difficulty talking.

"You aim like this, Libby." He stepped back to let her fire.

Liberty lifted her arm, aimed through the gunsight, squeezed, and wood chips flew in all directions.

"Whoa, we have an Annie Oakley here! Shoot again, Libby."

Liberty raised her arm, aimed, and fired. The stick on the fence splintered and flew apart. She spun toward Matthew and pointed her gun to the ground.

Matthew pushed his hat back a little and looked Liberty in the eyes. "All right, where did you learn to shoot, Libby?"

"What did you say?" Liberty's ears were ringing.

Matthew spoke louder. "I asked, where'd you learn to shoot?"

"I've never shot a gun before today."

"Come on, Libby. Stop your jesting. Where did you learn to shoot?"

Liberty looked at him blankly. "But I've never shot a gun before, Matthew Bannister, and I am not jesting, nor do I lie."

Matthew looked stunned. "You're not jesting...I don't believe it, I mean, I do believe it, but it's pretty incredible. It's very rare a person can shoot like that without a lot of practice. You're a really good shot, Liberty, a natural. I can't begin to tell you how much practice it took me before I could hit something as narrow as those sticks." He grinned at her. This beautiful, petite woman was a sharpshooter.

Liberty spoke softly to Maggie. "Reckon I missed an opportunity back there in Sacramento. I really could have made that man dance!" Liberty grinned, and Maggie chuckled, their eyes sparkling with laughter.

Matthew joined in. "That would have been something to see!"

Maggie laughed, waving her gun at an imaginary man. "Dance, mister, *bang*, dance. I said, *bang, bang*...higher...*bang, bang, bang*." All three women whooped with laughter, and Matthew had to laugh too.

CHAPTER XXVII

The bloodthirsty hate a person of integrity
and seek to kill the upright.

PROVERBS 29:10

"**HAVE YOU FOUND ANOTHER PLACE YET?**" Ethan Brooks questioned his partner.

"Nah, it's hard findin' the right place fer hidin' so many girls," Saul Simmons responded. "There's too many of 'em. Mebe we could dump a few of 'em inta the bay." He chuckled.

"Let's not jest—each of those sows is worth a pretty penny, and I'm not willing to part with the money," Brooks said grimly. "You need to look harder, Simmons. If Jones survived the attack, he might tell what he knows about the books, and we can't afford any close scrutiny at this point. I don't want anyone snooping around getting wind of our business."

"I looked them books over, an' I kin tell you nobody's gonna be findin' nothin' wrong with them thar books," Simmons stated. "Why, I'd stake my reputation on it." He laughed again, knowing his reputation wasn't worth anything at all. "Thar's one thing that pansy-faced Jones did well. It shore took 'em long enough. Those books is fine, jest fine. I'll be keepin' my eyes open, an' iffen I find a place, I'll let you know. Bouvier's gonna be wantin' his cut again, an' ya knows we hafta keep him happy, or we don't have no company fer a cover fer this here operation."

"All right, all right, but I'm starting to get a gut feeing it's time to cut our losses and run. Perhaps this will be my last shipment. I'm beginning to smell disaster written all over this. I don't care to end up strung up for some lousy women. The fact that you don't know whether Jones is alive or dead really has me on edge. I have men out looking for him. One of my men reported he was taken from the church to a doctor's office. The doctor didn't know where they were taking him. He'd been closed mouthed about the wounded man, only saying he probably died, but what if he didn't?"

"Aw, it'll be all right. I think Jones is dead. Once we gets those wimmin' moved, we'll be safe enough. We can jest relocate 'em, and start up again. It's good money, an' I don't aim ta be a givin' it up so easily. The reason it's tooken so long fer me ta try ta find a place, is tryin' ta find the owners of the warehouses close ta where the girls is now. I ain't aimin' ta move 'em a long ways."

Brooks decided they should go to the warehouse. He needed women who looked halfway decent when he sold them. He'd sent one shipment of twenty-five girls the week before to Hong Kong.

Simmons' oily smile grated on Brooks. He wondered how much to trust this smooth-dressing illiterate. *Maybe I should shut him up permanently. His ilk can be bought anywhere. He's certainly not indispensable, and he knows too much. Maybe I better talk to Sawyers.* Although Simmons didn't know anyone else was involved in the organization, Sawyers was the true brains behind it all. Sawyers had orchestrated every step they'd taken. *He'd sure been angry when he found out Simmons wasn't certain the bookkeeper, Jones, was dead. "No loose ends," he'd said. He said it a lot.*

Cabot sat in one of the deep leather chairs in the great room at the Rancho, thinking about priorities. He knew he was in love with Maggie. She was the kind of girl he'd been looking for all his adult life. Being from Boston and loving his job was the real rub. *What should, perhaps, come first is my family, but I'm not from one that's close knit. I'm closer to Sofie than Robbie, or anyone else, for that matter. Maybe it's because we're the closest in age. She's been a good sister, although we don't see each other all that much. Robbie's so much younger, I've never felt very close to him. Then there's my parents, always traveling, junketing*

here and there, never home much. In all honesty, I've been raised by my nanny and then sent off to boarding school. If truth be told, I don't know my parents—it's sad but true. I love my nanny, Chloe, more than anyone in the family. I'm glad I continued visiting her long after I'd finished school. We both look forward to those visits. It's strange she's the only one I told about coming west on this assignment. I think she'll really take a shine to Maggie. Family is family, but it's not necessarily blood that makes it.

Cabot's job had become his biggest priority. He asked himself what was the most important thing in life. Was it a job, or was it someone whom he loved? A man worked and worked to provide for his family. *What if I let this redhead go? I have a feeling she will be a handful. Will her past ruin her for a normal relationship between a man and a woman? I reckon I don't really care. I have a lot of patience, and I will care for her and try to help her forget her past. Will life ever have quite the zest it has right now if I let her go? I love this girl. I can admit it to myself. Do I want to settle for second best sometime in the future?*

Cabot had never settled for second best in his life, and he wasn't about to start now. So now it was yes, he would go all out for this woman, and it would be an "until death do us part" kind of love. He thrilled to the knowledge he would be willing to grow grapes if it made this woman happy. *I wonder…does she love me? Would she be willing to give up everything for me? I reckon it doesn't matter. I love her…most ardently.* He let the feelings wash over him. He, Cabot, loved Maggie, and that was the way it would be—forevermore!

The days raced by, and Cabot, although still limping heavily, was healed up enough to carry on with his assignment. Lunch was over, and he sat across the table from Matthew at Rancho Bonito. The two men were discussing the telegram that had arrived from George Baxter.

The telegram stated that Cabot was to get himself to San Francisco and notify the head of police there about the warehouse.

Matthew said, "I'm going with you, Cabot. I don't think you should go alone. Whoever shot you is most likely still looking for you." Matthew thought it too early for Cabot to be out and about, but there was no persuading him otherwise. Cabot had made up his mind. Matthew hitched up the buckboard, as a horse took thigh muscles to control.

"Thanks, Matthew. I appreciate your help, more than you know."

Matthew and Cabot had begun to forge a lasting friendship. Matthew planned to stick closely to Cabot. He wore his uniform of checked shirt, black leather vest, denims, and a gun strapped to his hip, his hat pulled low on his brow.

They set off, and because of intense conversation, they were at the Sausalito ferry before they knew it. The ferry had pulled in a few minutes before they arrived, and they were the last ones to board. Because of the wind and noise, they made the journey without talking, each man alone with his thoughts.

When they arrived at the police station, they walked up to the front desk, Cabot limping heavily and using the cane Dr. Meeks had given him.

He said to the front desk clerk, "I'd like to speak to the chief of detectives, please."

"Do you have an appointment with him?" the clerk asked.

"No, I don't. Do I need to have one?"

The clerk telephoned upstairs to see if the chief was free. Cabot and Matthew both marveled at the instrument, and the clerk showed them how it worked. Bell Telephone was installing these in the West now, he said proudly. He was a friendly young man.

"Name's Billy," he said. "The chief is just now free. Please follow me." He led them over to the steps. The stairs were wide, and as Matthew and Cabot started to follow him up, Cabot glanced at two men coming down from the top. He froze for a second, and then keeping his head well down and sideways, he proceeded to follow Billy up the stairs. He went slowly, one step at a time, trying not to put pressure on his bad thigh. Matthew kept the slower pace, at the same time blocking the two men from seeing Cabot.

He'd seen the startled look on Cabot's face, so he casually, but thoroughly, perused the two men coming down the stairs. Deep in conversation, the two descended slowly, ignoring the men coming up. One was a tall, elegant-looking man with a thin mustache; the other man looked as if he'd just rolled out of bed. Greasy red hair, a frock coat that had seen better days, and a face badly in need of a shave was in distinct contrast to the other man.

They passed by each other, and when at the top of the stairs, Cabot hurriedly glanced down at them. Walking a little way down the hall, he quietly asked the clerk if he knew the two men who'd gone down the stairs.

"Sure I do," Billy replied, proudly. "The tall man is Mr. Brandt, and the other is Mr. Brooks. Mr. Brandt is curator of the museum, and Mr. Brooks, well, he's president of a very lucrative company selling canned salmon. He's the best of friends with our chief. Well, here we are."

He knocked on the door before Cabot could stop him. The Boston detective did some fast thinking as Billy ushered them into the room and then left.

"Yes, what can I do for you boys?" Chief Detective Harold Sawyers continued to sit as they entered the office. He was a portly man with slicked-back dark-red hair, his mustache a rusty red. His eyes, set wide apart, were small. He narrowed them still further, staring at the two men through a haze of cigar smoke curling up in front of his face.

Cabot said, "Yes, well, this here's James Jacobs, and I'm Stanley Jonas. James here and I, well, we'd like ta train ta be detectives. We decided ta ask you what we need ta do ta join up."

Sawyers looked the two men up and down and said, "You work your way up around here. What's wrong with your leg?"

Cabot replied, "I broke it tamin' a horse. It's healin' up nicely... thanks fer askin'."

"Well, we don't hire cripples for police work. Here you start out as a street policeman. If you do well, then you work your way up. You need to talk to someone downstairs." He stood up and pointed them to the door. "Good luck getting hired."

"Thank you," they said in unison. They went out the door and down the stairs, after Cabot, perusing the lower floor, made sure Ethan Brooks was nowhere to be found. The two men headed out the front doors and across the street to the buckboard.

"I think I understand those men coming down the stairs are bad business. Correct?" Matthew inquired.

"Yes, one of them anyway," Cabot answered. "That sleazy character is Ethan Brooks, who heads up Madam Bouvier's canned salmon business. It's the company being used as a front, selling girls from abroad into white slavery. You heard Billy. Mr. Sawyers, head of the detective branch, is best friends with Ethan Brooks. I think we need to telegraph Chief Baxter, and I don't want to do it here in San Francisco. Do you think we could ride up to San Rafael? I think it'd be better to inform Elijah of this. I can feel in my gut that Sawyers is a rat."

"Why are we wasting time?" Matthew said with a grin. "Let's go!"

Cabot returned his grin, clapping his new friend on the shoulder. *I really like this man,* he thought. Strangely, the back of his neck prickled. Looking up quickly, he saw Chief Detective Sawyers staring at the two of them from his second-floor office window. Cabot let his eyes slowly travel the distance of the building as if he were admiring its facade. *It's not a comfortable feeling...knowing the chief detective of a large city wants me dead.*

Matthew, oblivious of the stare, helped Cabot up onto the buckboard, and going around, climbed up himself. He'd noticed his new friend's limp was even more pronounced. Cabot didn't complain, but Matthew knew he was in a lot of pain.

Clucking to the horses, they headed north to San Rafael.

The Sausalito Land and Ferry Company made five round trips a day, and the two men didn't have long to wait before boarding the ferry. It had turned into a beautiful day. The skies were blue with scattered wisps of white. The sun shone brightly, but the air freshened as it blew across the strait, feeling as if spring had not yet arrived. As they crossed to Sausalito, the ferry pitched with the waves, the wind pushing at their faces. They yelled to each other above the noise and clamor around them. Matthew spotted a whale and pointed it out to Cabot, who said it was a humpback. They both adjusted to the movement of the boat beneath their feet. Cabot leaned heavily on the railing to ease the weight on his bad leg.

They climbed onto the buckboard as they neared the northern shore. The horses, familiar with the ferry, were not at all skittish to debark.

Making good time, they drew into San Rafael little more than an hour later. Cabot was glad, as his thigh burned with pain. It felt like a hot poker had scorched its way through it. *This day is a bit too much after my idleness. I wish this'd heal quickly. There's too much to be done, and it needs to be done quickly. Those poor girls. I have no doubt Sawyers' men will be moving them soon.*

They pulled up in front of an imposing yellow house. Matthew jumped down, tying the reins to a hitching post while Cabot eased himself down, reaching for his cane as soon as he had alighted on one foot. They didn't plan to be long, both wanting to get back to the Rancho.

George chewed mint leaves to relieve his indigestion. He was worried. *I certainly hope Cabot doesn't go back to San Francisco.* After receiving Cabot's telegram, he'd gone straight down and bought tickets to Oakland, California. Next, he'd wired Elijah and Cabot and then had gone home to pack for the trip to the bay area city.

Nearly ten years earlier, Oakland, located across the bay from San Francisco, had become a thriving, deep-channel port city.

Samuel Xavier Kerns, chief of the Oakland Detective Branch, had gone to school with George. He was a good man, and George looked forward to seeing him again. To personally know the head of Oakland's chief of detectives would be a great boon in straightening out the problem in San Francisco.

He boarded the train west the next morning. After two days on the train, George lost some of his patience. It angered him mightily that a man in such a sensitive position as Chief Sawyers would misuse his power and involve himself in the sordid business of trafficking in human flesh. *How did a man rise to such a position and not be exposed for the man he is? I have no doubt the San Francisco department is riddled with graft. A man can't head up a clean organization when he himself is evil.* George chewed more mint leaves to settle his stomach.

CHAPTER XXVIII

You are altogether beautiful, my darling;
there is no flaw in you.

SONG OF SONGS 4:7

EVERYONE AT THE RANCHO HEARD THE NEWS about Cabot almost running into the man who'd either shot him or had him shot.

They were eating supper together in the courtyard. Two round tables had been pushed together and were covered with red-and-white checkered tablecloths. Kirk, Maggie, Cabot, and Matthew sat across from Alexander, Liberty, and Phoebe. Alexander offered up a prayer of thanksgiving to God before anyone began to eat. Conchita had made delicious chicken fajitas, and the conversation was interspersed with outbursts of laughter.

Maggie was amazed at how easy life seemed to be at the Rancho. The memory of Boston was fading. It seemed more like a bad dream to Maggie, who tried to keep thoughts of Ethan Brooks pushed to the back of her mind. She glanced at Cabot and hoped he'd be safe. He and Matthew and Elijah would be going back to San Francisco to help George Baxter capture the chief of detectives and all his henchmen involved in the kidnapping and selling of human flesh.

It'd be a worse fate than I suffered at the hands of Ethan Brooks and Elmer. I can't imagine being sold to a man. It surprises me that I told Cabot everything about me. I've never done that to a single soul except Mrs. Jamison. I'm sure he won't be interested in me as someone he could marry, but he still seems friendly enough. She took a big sigh and a bite of her *fajita*.

Turning to Maggie, Kirk asked quietly, "Maggie, would you care to go for a walk down to the river with me after dinner?"

Maggie looked at him sweetly, lowering her lashes. "No thank you, Kirk." She gave him neither excuses nor any reason for declining. *I have no intention of spending any more time with Kirk. He made it very clear he is fickle, and he also doesn't care about my wishes. When we went to Napa several weeks ago, I asked him to bring me back to the Rancho before going to Consuelo's, but he ignored my request. I spent a very boring but introspective evening sitting and waiting for them to come back from a walk. It was the end of me wondering if I had any future with Kirk. I like him for a friend, but that is all.*

Cabot watching the exchange between Maggie and Kirk, heaved an inward sigh of relief, glad that Maggie didn't seem to care for Kirk. Looking at Kirk, Cabot saw a nice-looking man whose brow was wrinkled. He looked disappointed and confused.

Good! thought Cabot. *I will not be cutting in on another man's claim.*

Kirk finished eating without saying another word. When he finished, he walked out of the courtyard, heading for Consuelo's.

In the kitchen, Conchita watched him go with a sad shake of her head.

At the table, Cabot whispered into Maggie's ear, "I'd ask you to walk with *me* to the river, but you'd probably have to carry me back."

Maggie smiled at him, her deep-gray eyes glowing, and she whispered back, "Why, Mr. Jones, what makes you think I would walk to the river with you in the first place?"

Cabot's chocolate eyes shined with feeling. "Because I am quite sure I love you—the till death do us part kind of love."

Maggie almost choked on her salsa. Her eyes teared, and she swallowed twice, looking at him smiling innocently at her. She swallowed again, opened her mouth to make a comment, but nothing came out. She closed it again.

He grinned, commenting lazily, "I fear this will be the last time I will ever see you speechless, Miss Margaret Regan O'Neill."

The attention in the courtyard had suddenly shifted from Kirk stalking out to Cabot and Maggie. Cabot smiled at the rest of them and looked back at Maggie, who was desperately trying to regain her composure.

"Would you care for a stroll around the courtyard Miss Margaret?" Cabot asked her.

"Y-yes," she replied, "yes, I-I'd like that very much." She swallowed, becoming aware of all the eyes focused on her. Glancing around at the faces, she pushed back from the table and stood. Cabot, slower to stand, offered Maggie an arm on his good side and grabbed for his cane on the other. Slowly, they walked around the courtyard.

Cabot's arm tightened its grip on Maggie's hand, squeezing it to his side. "Maggie, I didn't mean to spring it on you so suddenly. I have fallen head over heels for you." They were now on the opposite side of the courtyard, screened a bit by the fountain and flora in the middle. "I don't even care who's watching." He faced her, getting down on one knee, which was no small feat, his thigh stretching painfully.

"Miss Margaret Regan O'Neill, I, Cabot Jones, love you. I love you with all my heart. Will you do me the honor and make me the happiest man alive. Will you marry me?"

"Oh, Cabot." She put a hand to her heart. "Yes…yes, I gladly will! I don't care if we live in Antarctica as long as I can be your wife. I think I fell in love with you the day they carried you into the house! Oh, Cabot, you've made me the happiest woman alive! I never thought anyone would ever want to marry me." Maggie, overcome by emotion, felt tears slide down her cheeks.

Cabot, leaning heavily on the cane to get himself back up, declared, "I love you, Maggie." He stopped talking as he took Maggie into his arms. He took her chin with his thumb and forefinger and lifted her head to face him. Looking into her luminous gray eyes, he said, "I have a feeling you have no idea of your worth. You are precious, more precious to me than anything."

His mouth came down on hers, gently at first, and then eagerly with more passion, his arms drawing her to him. Her arms slipped unconsciously behind his back, feeling the deep beat of his heart. She kissed him with all the love she had stored within her. He broke off the embrace reluctantly, holding her away from him.

"Fireworks!" he said, laughing.

Maggie smiled tremulously, still wondering how Cabot was able to love her.

Cabot took her arm, and they proceeded to walk around the courtyard. He loved this woman!

The days passed, but they couldn't pass fast enough for Cabot, who was chomping at the bit to have George Baxter arrive. He wanted to get the crooks rounded up and those girls out of the warehouse.

The day was gorgeous with fluffy clouds scudding their way across a sea of blue. The sun shone down with real warmth in it. Spring was on its way to becoming summer.

Maggie and Cabot were taking a walk. They'd been walking together every day, increasing the distance to help strengthen his leg. It was much better, and although he limped, the cane was gone. It stilled pained him a bit but was a minor distraction.

He couldn't rid his mind of the girls he'd seen crying in that dark warehouse. Cabot told Maggie how he'd climbed the fire escape ladder, peeking through the scummed-over glass window into the warehouse where the girls were being held.

"There were women all over the huge floor. Several were just sitting there crying. It was a horrible sight. I decided right then and there I want those men to hang for what they've done."

"It scares me, Cabot. I know how evil Ethan Brooks is, and I know what he can do. He's a strong man. He snapped Elmer's neck like it was a thin stick." She shivered, and Cabot put his arm around her shoulders.

"I won't be alone. I don't know what George has planned, but he doesn't do anything half-cocked. He's astute and knows what's what. He'd never put any of his men in a dangerous situation that he wouldn't be in himself. I have the greatest confidence in him."

As they entered the house, Conchita met them at the door. "Meester Cawbot, you haf telegram here." She handed him the envelope and walked with Maggie back to the kitchen. Conchita had skewered a large cut of beef, which roasted over the open fire. She chopped vegetables for a salad.

Sitting down in the great room, Cabot rested his leg on an ottoman. He read the telegram from George, who was on his way. He'd wired from Chicago. Cabot rose to inform Maggie.

"It looks like my boss, George Baxter, will be in Oakland the day after the morrow," Cabot said as he entered the kitchen. "I'll need to be there to meet him. I sure hope he has a plan. This whole business is a situation that's going to take kid gloves to handle. With the head of a large detective agency being involved in the crime, I would imagine Mr. Baxter is at his wits end to know exactly how to proceed."

Maggie looked at Cabot with shining eyes. Being in love suited her. She glowed in the aura of Cabot's love. Her dimples deepened. "Perhaps he has come up with a plan already," she said. "He sounds like a man who doesn't waste time—at least, Liberty and I got that impression from his handling of Monsieur Bouvier's murder. He may already know what he's going to do."

"Well, he's not going to be able to do it on his own, that's for sure."

"Not do what on his own?" Matthew asked, entering the kitchen.

"I'm talking about my boss, George Baxter. He should be arriving the day after the morrow, into Oakland. He's not going to be able to round up the men and charge the chief of detectives of San Francisco with anything unless he has some hard evidence and some people helping him."

"Well, I'll throw my two cents in, for what it's worth. I like you, Cabot Jones, and I am in this with you, through thick or thin. I'll go with you to Oakland and find out what the plan is. If you need more men, I know I can rustle up a few around these parts."

Cabot looked at Matthew, whose gun always rode his hip. "I appreciate it—you're a real comfort to have around, Matthew Bannister." He stuck out his hand to shake Matthew's.

Liberty, sitting at the kitchen table across from Kirk, asked, "How long did Matthew say he'd be in Oakland?" She smiled at the younger man, more than a little sorry he was so involved with Consuelo.

Kirk was not a happy man. No contentment or peace flowed within him. Liberty prayed daily for his soul, that he'd follow Matthew's example and allow Jesus to control his life rather than the emotions she sensed were at war within him. Maggie was now spoken for, and Kirk seemed out of sorts by it. He liked women, and Maggie had not returned the favor. Liberty sighed. Consuelo was not the woman for him either. She hoped he'd find it out for himself, and soon.

Kirk, feeling guilty he hadn't gone with Matthew and Cabot, replied, "He never said. He just wanted to tag along with Cabot." Looking at Liberty, he thought, *I have never, in my entire life, seen someone so well put together. She's a gorgeous woman with those coppery curls and green eyes. A body could lose himself in those eyes.* Her mouth smiled at him, full lipped and desirable. He blinked, mesmerized by her beauty. Her figure was perfect. A man's hands could span her tiny waist. *Consuelo is going to be heavy. Right now, she has that dusky, full-blown figure, but it isn't real beauty, and it certainly isn't going to last.* Kirk sighed, looking at Liberty. *Many women who are heavy are very beautiful, but Consuelo's beauty is only skin deep. True beauty, I'm beginning to think, comes from within. Wonder why we men seldom look beyond the exterior?*

Liberty felt uncomfortable when Kirk kept staring at her.

"Conchita, are you saving dinner for Cabot and Matthew?" Liberty stood, glad to remove herself from the stare. She wondered if she were going to be uncomfortable around men for the rest of her life. She felt at home around Matthew, but if he moved too close, she could hardly breathe. *I think about him all the time. What's wrong with me?*

Conchita rinsed off the dishes before Luce and Lupe washed them. She didn't like greasy plates. "Mees Libbee, I no save Meester Bannister's deener. I sure he be the whole night gone, and Meester Cabot too."

"Did they tell you that, Conchita? For some reason, I thought they'd be back tonight."

Entering the kitchen, Maggie had overheard the conversation. "Cabot didn't think they'd be back tonight. First they were going to Oakland, but he hoped they'd end up in San Francisco."

Kirk spoke to Maggie. "So I'm going to miss out on all the fun, aren't I?"

I am almost sorry for him, except he makes his own decisions. He spends a considerable amount of time with that slinky Consuelo. "I thought you said you were too busy to go today," she replied. "I think you made your own choice not to go." Maggie's attitude changed abruptly, and with hands on her hips, she stared at Kirk a little disdainfully. Irritated by his lack of maturity, she had the fleeting thought that, perhaps, some people never did grow up.

Kirk was tired of defending his actions. Indeed, he was tired of himself, and he was very tired of Consuelo. He knew he was moody. Seeing the change in his brother only served to make him more irritable. Getting up abruptly, he said as he left the kitchen, "By the way, Maggie, I really did have work to do today."

He walked outside and saw Elijah and Abigail Humphries had just driven up.

"Hello there, Kirk! Good to see you." Elijah shook hands with Kirk, who looked a bit out of sorts, a frown marring his good looks. Pulling the younger man to himself, Elijah gave him a manly hug, which caught Kirk by surprise and warmed his heart.

Kirk smiled, and it lit up his face. He liked Elijah. "Here, let me take care of your rig there. I'm supposing you're spending the night?" He walked around and easily lifted Abby down.

"Yes, we're spending the night here. We happen to know Matthew has an empty bed for tonight and came to relate that news to the family. Thank you, young man, for helping an old lady." Abigail grinned. "Yes, I know I am an old lady, but it's certainly all right by me. If one doesn't get older, one dies." She laughed up at him, her blue eyes sparkling with good humor. Abigail reached out and patted his arm. "I like you, young man, and thank you for your warm welcome. Elijah is tired. He'll certainly be happy for you to take care of the horses."

"You know you're both welcome here anytime," Kirk replied. "You are like family, and Abby, you're not old yet."

"Thank you, Kirk. It does my old heart good to hear you say so." She turned, hearing footsteps behind her. It was Diego. "*Buenas noches,* Diego."

Diego responded with smile. It wasn't often he heard his native language spoken by a gringo.

"Buenas noches, señora. You ees a welcome sight. Good evening, Meester Humphries."

Elijah came around the wagon and shook Diego's hand. "It's good to see you, Diego. Thanks for your welcome. Think I'll head on in. I'm pretty well bushed, and I plan to call it an early night."

Elijah walked to the door while Abigail spoke with Kirk and Diego. *I feel unbearably tired. I can't wait to go to bed. I suppose I'll have to sit up and talk for a while. Ah, well,* he reflected, *it won't hurt me to be sociable. My body will simply have to wait.*

Maggie heard him at the door and let him in with a surprised look on her face.

"Welcome, Mr. Humphries! Come on in. What a nice surprise." She stepped back as Liberty came flying into his arms.

"Oh Elijah! I'm glad you're here! Is Abigail with you? What a delightful surprise!"

Alexander and Phoebe stood ready to greet Elijah, who went into the great room.

While they continued to talk, Maggie went to the kitchen to help Conchita. They made coffee, and Conchita cut large slices of a chocolate cake that she had made earlier.

CHAPTER XXIX

CONCHITA CARRIED THE TRAY INTO THE great room herself. She sat down to join in the fellowship, which was rare. She liked Abigail very much, knowing Abigail was wise in her knowledge of God's Word. They chatted for some time before Conchita went to go change the linens on Matthew's bed.

Maggie rose to help her. "Before I go back to help Conchita, I wanted to ask you, Elijah. How is Cabot?"

"He's fine, just fine. Everyone was fine when I left, but then, nothing had happened yet." He smiled up at Maggie. "Best wishes, young lady. Have you set a date yet?"

"No." Maggie dimpled up. "But we will quite soon. So…he told you we're getting married."

"Yes, yes, he did." His blue eyes twinkled. "Do you know why we say *best wishes* to the bride to be?"

"N-no, I don't." Maggie had no idea what Elijah was going to say.

"We say *best wishes* with a desire that the bride to be will have smooth sailing and a happy marriage. We say *congratulations* to the groom-to-be that he was so fortunate to be able to catch such a lovely woman."

Her face glowed with pleasure. "Thank you. I hope Cabot feels the same way! Now, I need to excuse myself and go help Conchita, but thank you for the information." She went down the hall humming a little ditty to herself. She hummed a lot lately.

Elijah went on to relate to the rest of them exactly what had transpired since meeting the train in Oakland. "Samuel Kerns is head of the Oakland police department. He went to school with George Baxter, and he thinks within the next three or four days, something will break open with the warehouse of girls, and the matter will be taken care of. Matthew asked me to tell you not to expect him for a few days. Cabot thinks it won't be later than tomorrow before something happens. He believes they're going to move the girls either tonight or tomorrow at the latest."

Alexander asked, "You think the detective from Oakland will have any proof that the man running the agency in San Francisco is tied up in all this? Cabot was quite concerned they wouldn't be able to connect San Francisco's chief with the corruption going on."

"Yes," Elijah replied, "it seems to be a huge worry. The major concern, of course, is getting those girls rescued. We'll have to pray all those concerned with the ugly affair will be rounded up. Otherwise, they'll change their location but persist in their wretched business elsewhere."

Liberty scrutinized Elijah's face and said, "Let's not keep you up, Elijah. You've been going strong since early this morning, I would assume. You must be very tired." She saw lines of weariness creasing his face.

Abigail didn't want to go to bed just yet. "Yes, Elijah, do go on ahead to bed. My day was easy, and I'd like to stay up for a bit and visit."

Elijah, glad for the respite, said his good nights and made his way down to Matthew's bedroom at the end of the long hall.

The next morning during a tasty breakfast, Abigail and Elijah broached a question to the women of the house. Elijah asked Liberty, Maggie, and Conchita if they'd be willing to help at the mission. Alexander sat quietly, listening to the exchange.

"It'll only be until things settle down and we know how many people we need to hire. Just a few days, I would imagine." Abigail was excited about the girls from the warehouse coming to the mission. Her dream was finally coming true.

"I'd like to come help too, if I'm needed," Phoebe said.

"I would be delighted to have you come," Abigail said. "I think there will be much to do, and you know the saying, 'Many hands make light work.'" She smiled at Phoebe, who had become a friend. "I suggest we get ready to go."

They left for San Rafael midmorning. Everyone was excited to see Abigail and Elijah's house as well as the work that had been done to the mission.

Liberty rode Pookie, one of Matthew's horses, and Elijah drove the wagon with Abigail, Maggie, Conchita, and Phoebe. The trip seemed like no time at all to Maggie, who enjoyed conversing with the other women.

Maggie had been thinking a lot about the people in her life. She grew quiet while conversation whirled around her.

She thought about how kind her parents were. *Wonder why my mam told me God loved me as she was dying? Did she know God? I never saw either of my parents acknowledge Him the way these people here in the wagon do. I look back at the people in my life, and yes, some of them were kind and not believers, but the ones who are believers seem to have a peace about them I've never seen in anyone else. I don't want to live a life all wrapped up about only me. I keep thinking about what Liberty said about God being her refuge, how she could even put up with monsieur's evilness because God helped her to get through each day. What was it she said? Oh yes. "God gives me grace daily. When the grace is gone, I'll leave Armand." She must have had an abundance of it. I don't know how to love people who are wicked, but Liberty said we are all made in God's image. I don't understand so much of it. If we're made in God's image, how do we dare to be wicked?* Maggie took a deep breath. *I am beginning to think Liberty has it right. I think I'll talk about this with Cabot. Oh, I do hope he'll be all right!*

Ethan Brooks received a telephone call from Sawyers, who wanted to meet with him. Since all phone calls went through the operator, Sawyers didn't divulge what it was he wanted, because many times an operator would listen in on the call. However, Brooks knew from the clipped words that Sawyers was hopping mad. Meeting him the evening before in the Mission district had been an eye opener. He hadn't known some of the mistakes Saul Simmons had made. He sat in his office drumming his fingers on the desk, thinking about the conversation with Chief Sawyers. The more he thought about it, the madder he became at the blundering efforts of Simmons. Sawyers wanted Simmons out of the picture. Too many mistakes, he'd said. Simmons knew too much, and Sawyers felt he was a noose around their necks because of his bungling with Jones. *Wonder if he's really dead like Simmons said. I somehow doubt it.*

Going downstairs, he barked out, "Simmons, I want to see you in my office—now!"

A secretary glanced up, but seeing Mr. Brooks glaring at him, he looked down and began writing again.

Saul Simmons looked at Ethan Brooks and thought about how awful the man looked. He was unshaved, disheveled, his clothes looking as if he'd worn them for a month.

Saul sauntered over to him and asked, "What'd' ya want?"

"I said, my office!" Ethan roared, angry Simmons would think to question him.

"All right, all right." Simmons started up the staircase after his partner. He entered the office still trailing after Ethan Brooks, who kicked the door shut with his shoe.

Letting all his anger and pent-up frustration with Simmons and Sawyers get the better of him, he started screaming at Simmons. Next, he hissed.

"I have been paying you to take care of the warehouse!"

"I've bin takin' care of them thar girls! After the first few problems, ever thang's bin jest fine!"

"What do you mean by problems, Saul?"

"Aw, nothing'. It's all tookin' care of now."

"No, no it's not! One of the girls escaped!"

Saul's eyes narrowed at the impact of Ethan's words.

"A girl escaped?"

"Yes, and it's your mistake! She's been caught and put in that small cubical in the warehouse, but now that place is compromised. You bungled with Jones, and now you've bungled in a big way! I need you to go down there with me now! We need to make sure everything's in order. We're going to have to move those girls…tonight!"

"We cain't be movin' 'em tonight," Simmons whined. "I ain't got no place to put 'em!"

"You took too long. It's just one more thing you've mishandled. You're incompetent, Simmons, and I'm sick to death of it. I found a place, and we need to move them after dark. Come on. Let's go."

The cobblestone streets were shining, wet with rain, as they headed to the wharf. The two men rode in a hansom cab. The rain stopped soon after it had drenched everything. Puddles splashed as the coach made its way to the Embarcadero. Ethan told the cabby to drop them off, only he named a street two blocks south of the warehouse. Brooks paid the driver, who drove off muttering about how cheap the man was.

"What'd we get out so soon fer, anyways?" Simmons whined. "We ain't needin' ta walk so far."

Brooks looked over at Simmons with a sneer on his lips. "We don't want anyone to know where we're going, not even a cabby. Now come on. Walk faster!" Brooks walked quickly down the street.

Simmons was much shorter and had to nearly run to keep up.

Ethan continued to talk. "We need to go around the back way, down this alley, and then behind the buildings on this block."

"Why'd we do a dumb thang like that fer?" Simmons wasn't happy.

"For one thing, because I said so, and for another, if the building's been compromised, we don't want to be seen heading for it, that's why!"

As they neared the end of the building, Ethan Brooks pulled out a gun and shot Saul Simmons. He shot him again, just to make sure and, turning on his heel, headed back to the main street.

"Jones, did you hear that? That was a revolver! There it goes again!" exclaimed Dan Mapes, an Oakland police officer. He ran swiftly but quietly, bent low, across the roof of the warehouse, with Cabot on his heels. Matthew Bannister was already there. The three men crouched. They could see a man about two blocks away coming out of an alleyway. The man looked furtively around as he stuffed a gun into his trousers. He headed quickly toward the warehouse.

"He went into that alley not even a minute ago with another man! I watched them get out of a hansom cab together," Matthew said

The three men were on the roof of the warehouse to make sure that if the girls were moved to a different location, they'd know where they'd been taken. The rest of Oakland's posse, along with George Baxter, were trying to get some sleep in a nearby hotel.

"I'm going for Chief Kerns now," Dan Mapes said, "and your"—he nodded at Cabot—"Chief Baxter. We're going to need help, and pronto!"

He climbed down the ladder and mounted his horse, setting off at a gallop. Cabot was right behind him on the ladder, but he headed toward the back of the building.

He still limped, though most of the pain in his thigh was gone. He dashed to the far side and ascertained there were no other doors to the warehouse except the ones in the front. All the windows were covered. He retraced his steps, climbing back up the ladder.

"There aren't any other doors except these front ones. We'd probably be better off to sit tight down below and see what comes next."

Matthew and Cabot heard the front doors slam open against the building and ran to the front of the roof. They saw a most amazing spectacle. Women were being herded, like cattle, two by two, guarded by men on both sides.

Without saying a word, the two men ran for the ladder. It was deep dusk, nearly dark, and shapes at any distance were becoming difficult to see. They both clambered down, standing in the deep shadows close to the side of the building, watching. Finally, the last girl was herded out, and Cabot and Matthew ran toward the front doors of the building just in time to see a man entering the warehouse.

Ethan Brooks stood watching as the girls were herded to another warehouse close by. When they were all out, Brooks entered the warehouse, thinking to get rid of the girl who'd escaped and now knew San Francisco's chief of police was head of the ring of white female slavery.

"Halt, or we'll shoot!" Matthew ran into the building, thinking Cabot was right behind him.

Startled, Ethan Brooks paused in opening the door, but his hesitation was his downfall. He stared at Matthew, quickly grabbing for his gun. As he jerked it out, Matthew whipped his gun out and took a shot. He caught Brooks on the left shoulder. Brooks, giving no quarter, shot back, but his bullet went wild. Matthew shot him, again, this time in the chest. Brooks collapsed to the cold, cement floor, dropping his gun as he fell. Matthew Bannister, keeping his gun aimed at the man on the floor, walked toward him. Kicking his gun away, he looked down at him, knelt, and felt for a heartbeat. Brooks was dead. It was the same man who'd likely murdered the man they'd found in the alley. Matthew stood up, looking down at the dead man, and wondered if he'd needed to shoot him in the chest, but it was shoot or be shot, a quick reflex. He turned and finished opening the door to a small room to see a blond-haired woman sitting on a mattress. She stared at him, wide-eyed, but said nothing. The room smelled putrid.

"Are you all right?" Matthew asked hesitantly.

"Yes, at least I think I am…certainly better than I was a few hours ago. My name is Janne Nyegaard. I'm from Norway."

Matthew listened to her. Her diction was perfect, but he heard a distinct accent. She pronounced her name as "Yannie."

"I think I was drugged, but I'm feeling much better now."

Matthew's nose wrinkled with the smell of vomit. *It's not as big as my tack room.*

"Are you with the detectives?" Janne asked.

"Yes, I am."

Shock filled her eyes, and she looked at him, fear dilating her pupils.

"No. No! I'm not with the San Francisco detectives. I'm from Napa, but right now, I'm with the Oakland detectives who have come to rescue the girls being held here. Are you sure you're all right?"

"Yes, I've been very sick. Mr. Sawyers drugged me and had two of his men bring me back here. You see, I had escaped and—"

"You know Chief Sawyers?" Matthew Bannister interrupted, looking incredulous.

Janne stood up, rather shakily, and Matthew went to her side, giving her his arm for support.

"I don't know him personally, but I escaped from this place and went to the police department. I must have walked for miles. I was directed to his office, and he told me he was Chief Sawyers. I told him about this place, and he gave me some tea. I know now the tea was drugged. Two men came into the office and put a blanket over me, but I don't remember anything else after that. I woke up here, groggy and sick."

"Well, you're safe with me. I think the rest of the girls are being rescued as we speak." Matthew would have liked to have gone and helped, but he decided keeping this girl safe was a priority.

The wagon pulled up in front of the mission, and Elijah, with an expansive wave of his hand, said, "Here it is. Welcome to the San Rafael mission."

Abigail took his hand as she said, "I have a distinct feeling we need to be prepared. C'mon in, ladies. We'll have things ready in no time." She looked up at Liberty and asked, "Would you mind riding down to the end of this street?" She pointed in the right direction. "Please let my cook know she needs to come down and help us. Oh, never mind. Elijah can ride down in the wagon and pick her up. That way she'll get here much quicker." She turned to him with a question in her eyes.

"Yes, yes, I'll go right now and get her."

"See if Nelda can be spared from the Hancocks' too, please. I will put Liberty and these other ladies to work."

Elijah climbed back onto the wagon, a little disappointed, as he'd wanted to show the women around the mission. It had been his first building project. He'd learned a lot but was glad he didn't have to do manual labor for a living. It was definitely not his cup of tea.

Abigail turned and led the way into the house, calling back over her shoulder, "Liberty, you can take Pookie around to the back. We have a very nice, clean stable where she can rest. Oh, I do hope Elijah remembers to get Pippi to come take care of the horses. We hired him on to help with the wagons and horses and to keep the stables clean."

She led the way up the walk, while Maggie helped Phoebe with her satchels.

CHAPTER XXX

Yet man is born unto trouble,
as the sparks fly upward.

JOB 5:7

ONCHITA'S EYES FILLED WITH PLEASURE as she looked at the mission. It reminded her of a huge hacienda. The integrity of the building had been kept when the exterior had been remodeled. Curved, pedimented gables spanned themselves across the bright white front. Red tiles lined themselves in regimental rows across the great expanse of roof.

"Eet ees beautiful, Mees Abigail. Your mission, she ees beautiful!"

"Thank you, Conchita."

They entered the massive front entry where they saw an oaken pew flanked on one side by a large plant and on the other by a large round end table where a vase of freshly cut flowers resided beside a framed quote with beautifully scripted writing. The floor was a dark-gray slate, and the walls stark white. The mission exuded charm and modern comfort blended with antiquity and culture.

Maggie picked up the frame and read, "Do all the good you can. By all the means you can. In all the ways you can. In all the places you can. At all the times you can. To all the people you can. As long as ever you can. Signed, John Wesley." She didn't know who he was, but she thought, *I'll bet that man is a Christian. I really need to talk to Cabot. I keep feeling a real tug on my heart, and I have no doubt it's God wanting me to acknowledge Him.*

Abigail led the way into the enormous kitchen and sat down at one of the many tables. "I'd like Liberty, Phoebe, and Conchita to help in the kitchen. Bessie and I have gone over and over this, and she knows exactly what needs done better than I do. Maggie and I will go up and begin making beds."

Abigail added, "Bessie will be here shortly, and Maggie and I need to get started. I don't know why I have this feeling of urgency, but for some reason, I think those girls will be here by tomorrow night." With Abby and Maggie working steadily, with no breaks, the rooms were finished by evening. All the rooms could sleep six, but five would be less crowded. Abigail felt once the girls were assigned rooms, things would become a bit more manageable.

"I've made lists for all kinds of things," Abby said. "The girls will do everything in shifts. I hope a few of them have relatives or places to go. We're just not able to accommodate a large number of girls for any length of time."

Maggie looked at the last room with satisfaction. "I'm impressed. Look at this room. It's beautiful, and you've done every single one with a different theme. Are you calling them by the colors? Is this the lilac room?"

"Indeed, it is the lilac room." Abby laughed, and Maggie joined in. "We had workmen do the painting, but thank you for the compliment. They do look lovely, don't they? Daphne and I chose the colors schemes. Daphne is the wife of one of Elijah's colleagues."

The room they were in had been painted a pale lilac with trims done in palest yellow. Lilac-flowered prints with hints of pale yellow and bits of green could be seen in the pillows, curtains, and bedding.

The two women lingered in the rooms, Maggie exclaiming over their comfort and beauty, Abby being pleased at what had been accomplished.

Before leaving Oakland, Chief Samuel Kerns had alerted the California governor, George Stoneman Jr., of his intention to arrest San Francisco's chief of police. Governor Stoneman, a graduate of West Point and roommate of Stonewall Jackson, had served in the Civil War. He'd been elected governor in 1880 and was a personal friend of Sam Kerns.

Hiding in the warehouse with the girls, Samuel Kerns and George Baxter heard a large number of horses riding up to the building.

The horses halted on the cobbles, and they clearly heard the man in charge.

"All right, men, we don't know which warehou—"

Samuel Kerns threw open the door and stepped out as at least twenty guns were drawn and trained onto him.

"Hello, Jake, what brings you this way?" Sam Kerns was so happy he could dance. He could use the help.

"Well, hel-lo, Sammy Kerns, you son of a gun. We were sent by the governor to help out with a little party we heard was going on over here. Never did care much for Sawyers. Do you need some help?" Jake Daniels was head of the US Marshals for the state of California.

His men holstered their guns.

The other door was thrown open by George, and some of Sam's men came out of the warehouse as Sam and Jake conversed.

"Jake, this is George Baxter, chief detective of the Boston department," Sam said. "He's the one who broke this whole thing open."

"Howdy, Baxter. Welcome to California. We have a crime-free state here. Yes siree, a crime-free state…well, at least some people here don't pay for their crimes!" He laughed at his joke.

George and Sam both laughed.

"In answer to your question, yes, I do need your help." Sam pulled out his watch, looking at it and then up at Jake. "We've been busy. We've arrested one crew of men, two of them now dead. We put the others in a lockup in another warehouse, and I've posted two guards. In about twenty minutes the next crew should arrive. You can't see, but behind me is a warehouse full of women who've been kidnapped from European ports. All, save two, speak no English." Sam nodded toward the warehouse behind him. "I've never been so happy to see your ugly face, Jake!"

Several of Jake's men laughed.

The two chief detectives and Jake decided it was time to go to pay a visit to another chief. George asked that Cabot Jones and Matthew Bannister to go with him. Sam wanted Dan Mapes to accompany them.

The six men mounted their horses and headed out. Samuel Kerns had been to Sawyers' house for a state dinner a few months before. Governor Stoneman and his entourage had been present. Sawyers wasn't married, as his wife had divorced him; it was unheard of but sometimes happened. Jake, too, had been to the dinner.

They rode to Pacific Heights, which wasn't far. Harold Sawyers lived in a large two-storied house. All six men dismounted. Dan Mapes, Cabot, and Matthew went to the back of the house. They were going to wait there until the all clear or until they were called. Samuel Kerns, with George and Jake, walked up the front steps. It was after ten, but lights blazed throughout the house. There were numerous rigs with horses tied to the hitching post around the sweep of driveway that fronted the residence.

Sam used the heavy door knocker, and a pretty little maid answered the door.

"Yes, are you here for the celebration?"

"Yes, we are," Sam said, "but I didn't read the entire invitation. It's for Harold's birthday, isn't it?"

"No, it's his engagement party."

"That's right." Sam smacked his forehead.

Jake stepped up and said, "How could you forget Harold's getting married?"

George put on his best smile and asked the maid, "Can we come in?"

"Oh yes, yes. Of course." Opening the door wider, she stood aside it, ushering them in. Beautiful music wafted its way down the stairs as she pointed the way. "Chief Sawyers is straight up those stairs."

The three men ascended the double-wide stairway and saw many people present. It was, in truth, a celebration. Musicians were sitting at one end of the grand ballroom, playing Strauss, and people were waltzing around on the highly polished marble floor. Others were gathered in little groups, chatting. Women were dressed in elegant evening gowns, and the men were in fancy dress frock coats. *Yes indeedy,* George thought, *it's a grand ole party.* Samuel and Jake took the lead, as they knew Sawyers and what he looked like.

Sawyers nearly dropped his cigar when he saw them. Brushing some ashes off his frock coat, he tipped his head back, arrogantly squinting at the two men through eyes veiled by his short red lashes. Cigar smoke streamed from both nostrils.

"Well, well, well, what can I do for you boys?" As he spoke, George looked around and saw several of the dancers stopping to stare. *They must be in on this.* He circled around behind Sawyers.

Jake stepped forward and spoke with deep authority in his voice. "You are under arrest, Harold Sawyers, by the authority of the State of California and the power vested in me as a United States marshal."

Several people gasped. Sawyers turned to run, but George was there, ready. He grasped a wrist and did a hammerlock so quickly, Sawyers was totally caught off guard. He was spun back around to face Sam and Jake again. Sam looked at George in appreciation for his quick dexterity and forethought.

"You are going to be sorry!" Sawyers hissed. "I've done nothing, nothing, I tell you! You've no right to come barging into my home. I'll get you. I'll get you both!"

Jake spun around and made an announcement. "Ladies and gentlemen, the party is over. Get your wraps and clear out!"

Several men looked as if they were going to head toward Sawyers, perhaps to help him. George had a whistle, and he blew it sharply. It was a prearranged signal for Matthew, Cabot, and Dan to come inside. The men entered the back door and came running through the house, leaping up the stairs two at a time. When the whistle blew sharply again, several women screamed and ran to get their wraps. Most of the people queued up, descending the stairs quickly, but there were still a few men who looked as if they wanted to help Sawyers.

"If you want to be arrested, stay and join the party!" Samuel bit out the words.

Sawyers' men assessed the situation, looked at each other and over at the three men who'd come up the stairs. They filed past Matthew, Cabot, and Dan Mapes, starting down the stairs. One man brushed hard against Dan to throw him off balance. Dan spun as the man's foot touched the top stair, and grabbing his wrist, he did a hammerlock on the man.

"You're under arrest for assaulting an officer," Dan said.

"Arrest yourself!" the man bit out. "I am an officer of the San Francisco Police Department!" He tried to wriggle out of the hold, but Mapes held him firmly.

"Well, now, are you? That's not a good thing to be right now!" Cabot said to the man.

The other men who'd lingered quickly descended the stairs.

Sawyers started yelling after listening to the altercation by the stairs. Calling Sam and Jake foul names, he swore revenge on all the men present.

Cabot strolled over, putting his face close to Sawyers'. Looking him straight in the eye, he enunciated each word in a staccato-like voice. "Brooks and Simmons are dead, and I'd be very happy for you to join them! You can shut your trap, mister, because I've seen those girls and their misery. I worked for Brooks and Simmons and cooked the cannery's books myself! You're never going to be free, because if the law doesn't string you up, I will!" He spun around, stalking over to Matthew.

Sawyers stopped yelling, and the man held by Dan Mapes cowered.

Matthew and Cabot, happy no bloodshed had taken place, left to saddle up horses for Sawyers and the other policeman.

"He's got some beautiful horseflesh here," Matthew said to Cabot. They led the horses to the front of the house. They joined the other men where the rest of the horses were tied. Jake, Sam, and George came out with Sawyers and the policeman whose wrists were tied together. George helped Harold Sawyers onto his horse.

Jake took the reins, leading Sawyers' ride, while Sam took the reins of the policeman's horse. Riding silently down to the Embarcadero, Harold Sawyers was taciturn, not saying a word or trying to bluster his way out of the situation. The policeman hadn't said a word since Dan Mapes had hammerlocked him. Jake and Sam put both men into the box with the rest of the men being held there. They were miserable. It was hot with all those bodies in the tiny room, and there was no room for all of them to sit. It would be a long night for them. It was nearly midnight when the six men rode back to the hotel.

Cabot struggled to sleep. His thoughts kept returning to those poor girls who had spent night after night on a cold cement floor. *What misery.*

Abigail linked Maggie's arm in hers. "Shall we go down and eat? We certainly have earned our keep!"

Maggie stepped back from Abby. She sensed in Abigail a deep spiritual dedication. "Abigail, may I ask you something?"

"Of course."

"How do you know God is real?"

"That's a good question, Maggie. I cannot see Him. I cannot touch Him. It's something I know deep within me. I am fortunate because I was dying when we lived in Boston, and an angel came to me, and I was healed—"

"An angel? A real honest-to-goodness angel?" Maggie exclaimed.

"Yes, both Elijah and I saw it, and the angel told me to rise up and get out of my bed. I felt the hand of the Lord upon me. As far as knowing before that, I believed because I had faith. It's really a conundrum when one pauses to think about it. God gives us the faith. Honestly, I don't have all the answers, but what it boils down to is faith. Do we know George Washington really existed? We believe he did because of the writings and witness of other people. We learn to know about God the same way, from the writings and witness of many people. Hebrews, a book in the New Testament of the Bible, says in chapter 11 verse 1, 'Now faith is the substance of things hoped for, the evidence of things not seen.' As I said earlier, I cannot touch God, but I have placed my hope in Him. I know, Maggie, that God is more real than my sweet Elijah."

Maggie's eyebrows rose. *How could God be more real than your husband?*

"Thank you for your answer. I am wavering between becoming a believer and just going along the way I always have. I'm going to have a good talk with Cabot. Lately, I've felt confused."

"If you can find it in your heart to pray, I'm sure God, in His infinite mercy, will answer you."

"That's one of the parts I struggle with, Abby. I've had some really bad things happen to me, and I feel God doesn't give a hoot about me. Why would a loving God allow some of the things I've endured?"

"No one, Maggie, has suffered as much as God's son has, and God allowed it to happen. His ways are higher than our ways, and His thoughts are higher than our thoughts. We have no idea why bad things have to happen to us. I do know if I hadn't been so close to death, I would never appreciate each day as much as I do. I don't have all the answers, but I do know I have a living Savior, and there is nothing that can separate me from the love of Christ Jesus."

Maggie nodded, still not totally convinced.

CHAPTER XXXI

Know therefore that the LORD thy God, he is God, the faithful God,
which keepeth covenant and mercy with them that love him
and keep his commandments to a thousand generations.

DEUTERONOMY 7:9

THERE WERE TWO GROUPS OF GIRLS WHO arrived at the mission the next day. Abby, thankful she'd felt compelled to get everything ready, was prepared for them. The first group arrived, accompanied by Matthew.

Maggie found him talking to Liberty, who looked a bit discombobulated. Her cheeks were rosy, and Maggie sensed Matthew must have kissed her.

"Where is Cabot? Is he all right?"

"Yes, and if he wasn't engaged to you, he'd be in hog heaven with all those girls he's bringing up here. He can't think straight for thoughts of you keeping him distracted."

Maggie's eyes lit up with Matthew's comments, and her dimples dipped into her cheeks.

"Will he be here soon?"

"Yes. There wasn't room on the ferry, so we tossed a coin to see who would come first, and I won. It's a good thing, too, or you'd feel swamped here. There are over a hundred girls in all."

Maggie's eyebrows rose, and Liberty drew in a big breath, putting her hand to her mouth in surprise.

"We had no idea there were so many! I'll go tell Abigail. In truth, it looks to me as if you two would like to be alone." There was a lilt in Maggie's voice, and the blood sprang into Liberty's cheeks, staining them an even deeper red.

Maggie hummed as she left the two of them, heading for the kitchen where she knew she'd find Abigail. The first group had eaten and been assigned rooms.

Cabot arrived with the second group. He helped them out of the wagons and led them inside the mission, where he found Maggie at the top of the stairs.

Decorum flew out the window when Maggie spied him. She picked up her skirts, running all the way down the steps. Cabot had seen her face light up like a candle when she saw him. He strode over, and they met at the bottom of the stairs. He pulled her into his arms and swung her full circle. He didn't care who saw them as his mouth came down onto hers. Her hands crept up and around his neck. She molded herself into his arms, feeling the steady beat of his heart. She kissed him back in front of Abigail, who simply smiled and headed for the kitchen.

"I missed you," Maggie whispered as she drew back, looking into his chocolate-brown eyes.

"Umm, I missed you too."

"We didn't know if you'd be back today or not, but I've been so worried about you. I knew what you were doing was dangerous, and a couple of those men could identify you."

He spoke in a low voice. "Those men are no longer with us, Maggie, and most of all, you need to know Ethan Brooks is dead."

She looked at him with shocked eyes. "Tell me what happened!"

"Later. I'll tell you the whole story later." He held her face in his hands. "I love you, Margaret Regan O'Neill! No matter where we end up living, we need to set a wedding date. The sooner, the better." They walked slowly toward the courtyard, deep in conversation.

"Cabot, I need to talk to you about something Abigail shared with me today."

She told Cabot about how she'd been feeling. "I keep wondering if it's a tug on my heart from the Almighty Himself."

Cabot turned her to face him. "I've been wondering the same thing! I look at my family and know I don't care to be like them. George Baxter, my boss, is the most honest, upright man I know. He is a Christian, and I want to be just like him. I believe we should take this step, Maggie. We need to ask Jesus Christ into our lives, into our hearts. I have come to believe that if we both love God with all our hearts and be obedient to Him, we will love each other more, the way I believe we were created to do."

Maggie's luminous gray eyes shone with love at this man she'd promised to marry. "Cabot, I am so glad you feel the same as me—I don't know what I'd have done if you hadn't. Let's find Elijah and see if he will pray with us—no! Let's go talk to Liberty and Matthew. Liberty has been a huge example to me the way Mr. Baxter has been for you. You do know Matthew recently gave his heart to Christ."

The two retraced their steps to find Matthew and Liberty still talking at the base of the stairs.

Cabot spoke to them. "Would you both be willing to pray with Maggie and me? We'd like to become followers of Christ and—"

"Would we ever!" Matthew exclaimed. "It'll be the best decision you've ever made, Cabot Jones and Mrs. Jones-to-be," he said with a smile.

"Oh, Maggie, I am thrilled! Thank you for asking us to be a part of this. Come on. There's a little chapel right down this hall. We'll pray there."

Liberty led the way down the hall, and the four of them entered the beautiful little chapel Elijah and Abigail had incorporated into the mission.

There were kneeling pads at the altar rail, and Matthew knelt, with Cabot next to him. Maggie came next, and Liberty was on the other side.

Liberty slipped her arm through Maggie's and said, "I'll pray. Father, how precious we are in Your sight. Your word says Your thoughts of us outnumber the grains of sand. It's humbling, Father, to know that You sent Your only son to die for our sins so that we may have a right relationship with You. We thank You. Father, Cabot and Maggie wish to begin their married life together with You at the center of their marriage.

I pray You will guide them and give them the peace that passes all understanding and that You will guard their hearts and minds in Christ Jesus."

Cabot said, "I want to pray now. Father, please hear my prayer. I ask for forgiveness for all my sins. I have killed men in the line of duty, and I know that's not a sin, but I pray You'll help me not to feel so bad about it. It weighs me down. I pray You will help me to love others, and most of all Maggie. Again, please forgive my sins. I repent, and I ask You to come into my life. Please take over. Amen."

Liberty turned to Maggie and said, "Could you pray, Maggie, and ask for forgiveness of your sins? Tell God you repent of them, and ask for Him to come into your heart."

Maggie nodded and swallowed. "Dear God, I am sorry for all the anger and hatred I've had in my heart. I blamed You when my da died, and then when You allowed my mam to die, I think I believed you didn't exist. I'm sorry for that. I hated Elmer, the man I thought was my husband for one night. I'm sorry, God, that I was happy when Ethan Brooks, who was hired by Monsieur Bouvier, murdered Elmer, but I guess you know all about that."

Maggie heard Liberty gasp, but continued with her prayer. "I pray for forgiveness, and I repent of all my evil deeds. I know with Your help I'll be a better person. I have seen Liberty and her life with You as her Savior. I want that kind of peace in my heart. Help me not to get so angry like I did with Jessica on the train. I want to be free of being scared, angry, and hateful. Thank You, God, for hearing my prayer. Amen."

Liberty turned and drew Maggie into her arms.

"I am so sorry for the things that have happened to you, Maggie, but glad you've taken this step. God will watch over you and give your heart direction. Listen for His voice, Maggie."

Cabot said, "I feel years younger! As if a heavy load has been lifted off me!"

"I don't feel any different," Maggie said. "Maybe it didn't work for me."

"No," Matthew said. "We all react differently. Some people have a real emotional experience, but some people don't feel any different at all.

We are saved by grace, the grace of God and His mercy. Whether we are emotional or not doesn't matter one whit! We have faith that God will do what He said He'd do. You both are now Christians, redeemed by the blood of the Lamb!"

"I've waited a long time for this day," Liberty said. "It's the day of Maggie's redemption!"

"Yes," Cabot said. He stood and helped Maggie to her feet. He pulled her to him as she lifted her face for a kiss. "I love you, Maggie. I will love you until the day I die." He took her face in his hands and kissed her tenderly.

"Yes," he said, "I am redeemed, and this day is Maggie's redemption."

Books can be purchased on Amazon

Website: mary ann kerr .com (delete the spaces) (signed copy)

Inklings Bookshop, Yakima, WA

Songs of Praise in Yakima, WA

Or by writing me at:

Mary Ann Kerr

10502 Estes Road

Yakima, WA

(I will sign the book, and charge a flat 8% tax. So each book is 16.20 with tax; the cost of shipping priority mail is $6.49) (Media rate is ($3.49)

My public e-mail is: hello @ maryann kerr .com (delete spaces) if you care to order a book.

You may message me on Facebook page: Mary Ann Kerr (comments are welcome!)

When readers take the time to write or e-mail me their experience reading my stories, I sometimes put their comments on my blog if they don't mind.

Liberty's Inheritance	(sale price. . . . .$14.99)
Liberty's Land	(sale price. . . . .$14.99)
Liberty's Heritage	(sale price. . . . .$14.99)
Caitlin's Fire	(sale price. . . . .$14.99)
Tory's Father	(full price. . . . . $14.99)
Eden's Portion	(full price. . . . . $14.99)
Cady's Legacy	(full price. . . . . $14.99)
Anne's Wedding Bargain	(full price. . . . . $14.99)

If you enjoy the story, please make a comment on Amazon!

Books by Peter A. Kerr (my author son)

Adam Meets Eve (nonfiction)—$10.00 + 5.65 shipping and handling

The Ark of Time (science fiction)—$12.00 + $5.65 shipping and handling

Book by Andrew Kerr (my author son and my cover and design guy)

Ants on Pirate Pond (children's black-and-white chapter book with darling illustrations)—12.95 + $5.65 shipping and handling

RAPHAELA'S ???

PROLOGUE

Lo, this is the man that made not God his strength;
but trusted in the abundance of his riches,
and strengthened himself in his wickedness.

PSALM 52:7

HUGE FLAKES OF SNOW OBSCURED HIS VISION. The
drifts, some looking like ghosts, mounded over a couple feet deep. The
wind had picked up, causing the already cold temperatures to drop
even more. It was late November 1882, and Boston was in the throes of
a hard winter.

Good thing I live in the city, Jackson Diebel thought as he snugged his
scarf tighter. *A body could get lost in this without the aid of streetlamps.* He had
chosen to drive himself into the city, knowing he would be coming home
late. Snow swirled around his head and wetted his face. His gloved hands
felt frozen on the reins. Driving carefully, he thought about the past week.

Sure am glad I listened to Bouvier's wife at that dinner party a couple weeks ago.
I'd have lost my company just like Ben Murdoch did last week. What a philanderer
Monsieur Bouvier is! Trying to cozy up to my Dianne the way he did. Despicable
wretch of a man! Thinks he's a cut above the rest with his French ways. I'm glad I
told Dianne to stay away from him. I feel sorry for his wife. She's a beautiful woman,
but more, brave to warn me. She sure opened my eyes. It was as if I was lulled to
sleep, letting that man flirt with Dianne the way he did.

Jackson slowed, nearing the driveway to his house. The snow continued to blow sideways and made it difficult to see where he should turn in. It was icy, and he eased his carriage into the lamplit driveway, heading around to the back.

Reginald, his groom, came out of the stable, walking carefully on the slick cobbles. It was late, and he'd been waiting a long time for the master to come home.

"Evening, Mr. Diebel. Quite nasty, isn't it?"

"That it is, Reggie. That it is." He alighted from the carriage, and Reggie took the reins.

"Funny thing happened this evening, sir."

Jackson paused, for some reason feeling a deep sense of foreboding. "Yes. What happened?"

"Man drove up 'bout an hour past. I didn't help him, as he had a cabby waiting for him. Wasn't here ten minutes, but I reckon Boomer was already abed. I think the missus answered the door."

"I've been at my club, and I know the hour is late, but an hour ago was still past midnight! Who the dickens would come visit at that hour?"

"Don't know, sir. Couldn't be the doctor. He wasn't here long enough to treat anyone. This man had his top hat pulled low, and a scarf covered his mouth. I stood here within the confines of the stable, watching and waiting till he left, but it was too dark to see who it was."

"Thanks, Reggie. I'm sure I'll find out who it was from Mrs. Diebel. Boomer will be mightily upset he wasn't awakened to answer the door. Ah well, sorry to keep you up, my good man. I got into a good card game, and the time flew. I had no idea it was so late. One of my friends pulled out his fob watch, and I was chagrined at how late it was." Jackson pulled a couple greenbacks out of his pocket. "Just a little thank-you for being such a faithful groom. Part of my winnings tonight." Jackson grinned and added, "I appreciate all you do around here, Reggie. You know I've told you that you don't need to stay up past eleven. I can take care of the horse if I'm so late."

"Thank you, sir. I know you've said that, but I don't sleep easy anyway until I know you're home safe. Again I thank you."

Jackson headed toward the backdoor. The ground floor was level with the cobblestone driveway. *That was interesting. Who in the world would come visiting this time of night? Wonder if a friend is ill or something?* He removed his top hat, shaking the snow from it and setting it on a shelf. He hung his heavy wool coat on a peg in the back entry. He used a boot pull to remove his boots, and with stockinged feet, entered an area that was an extra pantry. It contained the back stairs and swinging doors to the kitchen. He went upstairs and headed to his quarters, passing Dianne's suite of rooms. As an afterthought, he tiptoed back and quietly opened her door. Her sitting room was empty, and he crossed to her bedchamber door. Opening it on well-oiled hinges, he was glad a sconce was lit. From its meager glow, he saw her bed hadn't been slept in. He strode across the wide room, his feet sinking into the Aubusson carpet. Her commode room door was shut, and he gently tapped on it.

"Dianne, Dianne, are you in there?" Hearing no answer, he pushed the door open, but she wasn't there either.

Jackson ran back through the bedchamber and sitting room to the hall, but it was dark as pitch. *There was nary a lamp on downstairs when I drove up. If there was, I certainly didn't see it. Perhaps she fell asleep in her downstairs sitting room.* He turned quickly back to Dianne's room, and grabbing the lit sconce, he shielded the flame from any draft and made his way down the stairs. *If Dianne left the house, I should think Reggie would have known about it.*

Once he reached the bottom step, he held the sconce high. His pupils dilated in shock. He dropped the sconce as he saw his wife lying in a pool of blood by the front door.

www.ingramcontent.com/pod-product-compliance
Lightning Source LLC
Chambersburg PA
CBHW060400260626
47160CB00006B/2387